By the same author

Praise for *Tessa Goes Down*

"Jason Bovberg knows how to write a go-for-broke crime novel! *Tessa Goes Down* is brutal, breathless, and black as night. Doomed lovers on the run, racing headlong from the bleached white Texas heat to the dark alley of true noir. Grungy as a truck stop bathroom and darker than midnight."
—Eric Beetner, author of *All the Way Down*

"In *Tessa Goes Down*, Jason Bovberg builds on the breakout triumph of *Loser Baby* with the lyrical voice of an alt-country singer and the leathery wisdom of a longtime street hustler. This book is a double-barreled barnstormer of sun-blasted darkness up and down the back highways of forgotten America. It's got the gleeful nihilism, grindhouse heart, and narcotic poetry of a 1970s drive-in-movie classic."
—Jim Thomsen, crime fiction author and reviewer

"Jason Bovberg is a fresh new voice in noir."
—Wallace Stroby, author of the Crissa Stone series

Praise for *Loser Baby*

"Jason Bovberg's *Loser Baby* is a beautiful noir novel for the 21st century! It's a wild, frantic ride through shady Southern California, a desperate drug-fueled search for a girl who only wants to escape a sordid life."
—Scott Phillips, author of *The Ice Harvest* and *That Left Turn at Albuquerque*

"*Loser Baby* is the real deal for hardcore crime fiction fans. A gritty and often emotional story of life on the other side of the tracks, this one grinds with the engine over the red line all the way. Hang on tight!"
—Eric Beetner, author of *All the Way Down*

"Jason Bovberg's *Loser Baby* is a high-octane thriller that moves like greased lightning! The beauty of this book is its motley collection of despicable characters whom you come to love by the end. *Loser Baby* is Bovberg's greatest book and one of the best of the year."
—Gary Phillips, author of *Blood and Asphalt* and *Birds of Fire*

"*Loser Baby* is one cool book! Bovberg writes characters who get into your head and under your skin. You won't shake this one easily: It'll stay with you long after you read it!"
—Terrill Lee Lankford, author of *Shooters* and *Angry Moon*.

Praise for the *Blood* trilogy

"An epic addition to the genre, *Blood Red* delivers a nonstop, real-time experience of the End Times—replete with visceral terror, buckets of gore, and, ultimately, a redemptive humanity."
—Alden Bell, author of *The Reapers Are the Angels* and *Exit Kingdom*

"Jason Bovberg proves he's got the goods with a whole new kind of horror novel."
—Tom Piccirilli, author of *The Last Whisper in the Dark* and *The Last Kind Words*

"With *Blood Red*, Jason Bovberg infuses a post-apocalyptic tale with a sustained sense of genuine mystery; of having no idea what's happening to the world and the people around you, or why."
—Brian Hodge, author of *Whom the Gods Would Destroy* and *Dark Advent*

"Guaranteed to creep you out!"
—Robert Devereaux, author of *Deadweight*

"Jason Bovberg's *Blood Red* is unlike anything I've ever experienced. It starts as a slow-burn freak-out and culminates in a series of horror-show set pieces that will forever be etched in my mind. This book made my skin crawl."
—Grant Jerkins, author of *A Very Simple Crime* and *The Ninth Step*

"*Blood Red* is a tour de f***ed-up!"
—Peter Stenson, author of *Fiend*

"*Draw Blood* is a real nail-biter of a zombie novel that will delight die-hard fans and draw legions of new ones to the genre!"
—Jonathan Maberry, New York Times bestselling author of *Rot & Ruin* and *Code Zero*

DARK HIGHWAY
FEAR THE ROAD'S END

FOLLOW ME!

facebook.com/jasonbovberg.author

twitter.com/jasonbovberg

REVIEW ME!

www.amazon.com/Jason-Bovberg/e/B00JJ36NNW

Wherever you buy my books, they can be reviewed!

LEARN ALL ABOUT ME!

www.jasonbovberg.com

TESSA
GOES
DOWN

A crime novel by
JASON BOVBERG

Author of *Loser Baby* and *The Naked Dame*

A DARK HIGHWAY PRESS book
published by arrangement with the author

ISBN (trade paperback): 979-8-9862158-0-8
ISBN (ebook): 979-8-9862158-1-5

Tessa Goes Down copyright ©2022
by Jason Bovberg
All Rights Reserved

Cover art, design, and layout by Kirk Whitham

For Kirk Whitham,
partner in crime,
the only person in the world
with whom I can share certain jokes

Thought of you as my mountain top.
Thought of you as my peak.
Thought of you as everything I've had but couldn't keep.
—Lou Reed

Only those who can leave behind everything they've ever
believed in can hope to escape.
—William S. Burroughs

So you've had a little trouble in town.
Now you're keeping some demons down.
—Tom Petty

ONE
FLOYD TILLMAN WEATHERS

Floyd Weathers killed a man with a baseball bat when he was twenty-seven years old and foolin' around with this hot mess of a girl in way-west Texas, town by the name of Malvado, one of those dusty wasteland settlements a stone's throw from the Rio Grande that hadn't known even a dull gleam in decades. Potholed streets lined with crumbling pale brick and peeled paint and boarded-up shattered windows. Grim faces watching you pass. It was a place no one paid any attention to. *No one.* You felt so removed from civilization that the earth was rug-flat and you were underneath it, in the deep dark with the grime and the smokybrown roaches.

Just the way Floyd liked it.

The girl shimmied into his sights from out of nowhere, and later he'd understand that she was just what he needed to regain that spark, yeah, to find life worth living again. She'd do this tight little dance that could distract him from *everything*, even the devil, and then he could give a shit that he was holed up in ol' Henry's failing motel off the grey asphalt edge of Route 67, with all that money taped up in the false backing he'd added to the motel bedroom's nightstand. All that money that wasn't even his, all that cash that he couldn't even touch.

But, see, now his head was stuck on the gal again. That scrumptious thing, that sweet split-cherry bottom, that twisty smile. The way she could turn an innocent gesture into a naughty come-on, like she wasn't even trying.

Tessa was her name.

Tessa Rae Jayne.

That's the way she spelled it for him one morning in the deep dark, her voice hesitating through the last name like she was full of crap. Tessa Jayne, one of those deals where you don't appreciate a thing till it's done its whole number on you. Till much later when you're snugged up against her milk-chocolate self in her little twin bed, in the room where she grew up, and you're whispering in her ear about the roads you're gonna travel together.

But he was getting ahead of himself.

Floyd first spotted her in a cramped convenience hut attached to a two-pump gas station, place always smelled like sweet armpit. She'd stopped for a few gallons of 87 octane and a Coke and some sugar candy. Pleated jet-black hair wild and frizzy from the hot wind, her yellow convertible Beetle at the one working pump, the pumping done with. A station wagon trembled impatiently behind her VW, driver starting to fume, she didn't care. She was jawing with Irene, the dead-eyed broad inside at the clanky register. Irene with the withered tattoos of inscrutable significance and the expression that communicated years of deadened misery. Irene was a fixture in Floyd's life, for sure. At least, for the past three months.

"How far's the border?"

The gal he'd soon know as Tessa Rae was paying for her stuff with quarters fished out of her jeans pocket, and Irene was gritting her grody teeth. Her look said she'd rather be back in her double-wide watching WWF with her man on a flowery couch.

"Bout an hour."

"Shit, sign back there said twenty-some miles."

"Guess you know how far it is, then."

Wounded shrug. "Just passin' the time, sheesh."

"You wanna clear that pump now?" Handing her some pennies in change.

"Uh huh, sure." She sucked on her Coke, swallowed the sweetness down. "That border easy to cross?"

"Depends what color you are," Floyd put in, walking up with his stuff. Tessa turned her fetching head his way, eyed him. "And which way you're going. You got your papers, right?"

She kept eyeing him.

"Personally, I'd say you got the color *going on*, but you're probably gonna raise some hackles coming back across the line."

And then *there* was the smile Floyd would come to know, the dangerous smile.

"That right?" she said.

It was his first good look at her, and he felt a tug somewhere. A pair of round, red-lensed sunglasses hid her deep brown eyes, but her sharp brows were sarcastic and jumpy. A big-ass necklace pendant lay gleaming and ostentatious above generous cleavage, and a full expressive mouth got her personality across right quick. She was the kind of gal a fella wanted to dabble with, whether any small talk led to anything or not. He was a sucker for a mouth like hers, and despite all his instincts to shut up and fade into the background like he'd been told, he stepped closer to her. It wasn't often that a woman like Tessa Rae Jayne passed through town.

Floyd had wandered over from the motel for some Winstons and PBR, some canned dinner for the hot plate. It's not like he'd *tried* to lay down a pattern or anything, but yeah, he went to that store pretty regular. As if there was much choice. He'd probably worn a path in the old asphalt with his boots.

"Seriously," he said, "the problem isn't *going* to Mexico, the problem is coming *back*."

She nodded, shrugged. "Not a problem then."

He stored that for later.

"Where you coming from?" he asked her, enjoying the view.

"Same as you, probably—no place in particular."

"Nice place," he said, amiably. "Used to be, anyway."

He felt Irene rolling her eyes.

Tessa gave him a long appraising look. "Yeah, well . . . not anymore."

She left it at that and skedaddled, didn't even look back, and Floyd set his shit on the counter and watched her go. A clanky bell announced her departure, and then the woodslap of the door. Through the grimy window festooned with dusty neon beer signs, he saw the hop in her step and was convinced he'd never see her again. A glimpse of something that coulda been but wasn't meant to be, something maybe he'd reflect on down the line, a missed opportunity but also perhaps a bullet dodged.

"Five ninety-two, hun," Irene said after grabbing the Winstons from the shelf behind her without him asking.

He paid her with six singles, let her keep the change, and she even managed a cracked smile.

"Big tipper," she mumbled. "How you holdin' up today?"

They were alone now in the little shop.

Floyd moseyed over to the grimy window and watched the rear of the VW as it moved to the edge of the lot. Girl already had her eye on the road. When she pulled onto Route 67 headed south, her frizzed hair whipped about in the dry wind of her departure.

He got to thinking about paths not taken. He'd read a poem about that once, back when poetry meant something to him. Back when he was a Longhorn. The hefty weight of everything he'd done, everything that had brought him to right here, right now—he felt the burden of it once again, sharply, as the car vanished from his sight, beyond the crumbling corner of an abandoned storefront.

He turned back to Irene.

"What day is it?" he said.

She murmured a smoky laugh. "Thursday."

"Well, I'm still breathing," he said, and that was enough of an answer for her.

Outside in the searing heat, hands full of junk food and coffin nails, Floyd paused beneath the tattered awning and took a long look around. He was careful every time, no hurry. A scrawny straw-colored canine runt was ambling north across the highway, hunting for something, anything. Up that way were the sheds and motorhomes where most of the town lived, everything fenced off as if it were a theme—barbed wire, rusty tin, cinder blocks, brown-dry Mexican needle grass threading through all of it. There was a little cemetery that way, also overgrown with weeds, also hemmed in with broken fencing. One of these days that dog was gonna catch one of the chickens that scurried around the cemetery. Floyd was rooting for the little bastard. Every morning at the crack of hell, some rooster crowed.

To the south sprawled the ramshackle structures that made up the business district of Malvado. An old water tower stood like a gangly sentry at the south end, solid and still functional. A certain yellow Beetle was probably passing it at this moment. Then there was the closed-up bank, with the inscrutable H. G. Blevins signage aging in place above interlaced brick and two of four surviving dormer windows. (Some old-timer around here surely knew the history of the building, it was the most impressive in town, but that person was a long way from here.) Locally owned mercantile storefronts followed in a loose line, only one of them still in business—a thrift shop that specialized in "antiques" better characterized as "dusty junk." There was a second decrepit motel down the way, maybe had once been competition for ol' Henry. It was on a broad windy corner, but it was closed up and merging back with the unforgiving earth, its big awning crooked and leaning and dangerous, and it even had a drained pool out front with something long dead in its murky brown drain sewage.

Across the street, diagonally from where Floyd stood, was a bar called, imaginatively, Bar. There was a decaying pool table in there that Floyd had played many solo games on. A dart board and a boxy TV. And a long dimly lit bar that was always mostly barren. Floyd tended to settle into one of the booths in there couple times a week. The proprietor was an all right fella named George, minded his own business, never asked him a god-damn thing, only talked when Floyd wanted to talk, no need for more.

Maybe Floyd would spend a few bucks over there tonight.

Just as he started walking back toward his room, he caught a glimpse of yellow and his stomach did a little *ping*.

"Well, fuck me."

The Beetle was drifting back up Route 67. It finally came to a juddery stop in front of the bar. Floyd heard the engine stall with a hiccup, as if the gal had let the clutch slip. There was no movement for a while, and then she got out and bounced her way up the couple concrete steps to George's front door.

Floyd attempted to calculate the odds that he'd not only bumped into this woman in the convenience store but that he'd just now caught this *second* glimpse—that fate had dealt him one more card. It was the kind of bet you had to put down on.

He hustled back to his flytrap, dumped the shit and put on a clean shirt, and made his way back to the sidewalk. There was a big dusty gap in traffic, so he crossed to the bar, where the Beetle was still parked all alone on the edge of the highway. He opened the bar door and paused, let his eyes adjust.

The place was empty.

Floyd walked over to the bar, sat at one of the stools. Waited.

"Huh."

It was so quiet, he could hear the toilet flush. Water rushing at the grimy sink in there. Footsteps, then swing of the hollow laminate door.

She came out of the restroom with her glasses still on, and she saw him straight away. She paused with a distinct uncertainty, removed the glasses, put 'em up in her hair, and twisted her generous mouth into a smirk. She came closer, and now he got a look at those deep brown expressive eyes, and he was hooked.

"You remind me of my uncle," was what she said. "Same eyebrows."

"Your uncle a swell guy?"

"One I'm thinkin' about? Far from it."

She took a quick detour to pick up her drink from one of the booths, and she brought it to the bar, sat two stools away from him but swiveled his way. The drink looked like a whiskey and soda.

"You live here?" she said. "Like, in this town?" As if to say, *You're kiddin' me, right?*

He shrugged. "For the time being."

George came out of the back, did a little double-take, as if his joint was suddenly rip-roaring busy. He had a bald head, like completely bald, and a big ol' compensating walrus mustache. His steely eyes let you know he took zero shit, and his beefy chest backed up that notion. Gray amateur tattoos up and down his arms, probably from prison at some point. Not something the two of them had ever talked about.

"Gimme one of those," Floyd said, gesturing toward the girl's glass.

"That's Southern Comfort and 7-Up."

"What?" Floyd laughed. "Never mind. How 'bout some of that cheap bourbon over ice?"

"Sure."

George went about his business, giving Floyd an encouraging glance now and then.

"Top shelf," the girl commented.

When George set the drink down in front of him, Floyd took its measure and then a sip. He set it back and gave the girl a good look. She was staring right back at him.

"All right, first things first." He was genuinely curious. "Why'd you turn back? Why on earth come *back* into this town after you've gotten past it? I gotta know."

She took her own sip, her eyes never leaving his face. "When you gotta go, you gotta go."

"You coulda let loose at the gas station. Makes more sense. They keep a surprisingly clean commode over there."

"You always this charming?"

"You're the one talkin' piss."

"Here's to piss." She raised her glass, and he met with his—clink.

"So you're headed for the border," he said.

"Guess so."

"You running from something?"

"You get right to it, huh?"

"It's a common question around these parts."

"That so?" She took another sip, her legs bouncing as if to music, but George didn't have any music playing. "You sayin' I'm a cliché?"

"Maybe."

"Are *you* running from something?" she countered. "Or should I say, *hiding* from something?"

"I guess we're figuring each other out."

She raised a shoulder. "What's your name?"

"Floyd."

"*Floyd?*"

"What of it?"

"How *old* are you?"

"You don't get to choose your folks, unfortunately. Mine happened to love the country music."

"I'm gonna order another drink while you explain that non-sequitur."

She flagged down George, who was reading a paperback mystery down at the end of the bar. Floyd noticed that Tessa's fingers were festooned with cheap rings.

"Believe it or not, that was a sequitur." He frowned while she asked George for another sugar drink, waited for her to turn back to him. "Floyd Tillman? Honky tonk? Nothin'? He was big dog down here in the lone star state. Houston, San Antone . . . ."

"Yeah, well, I don't know jack shit about Texas."

"Or music."

"I know about *good* music."

"Do you now?"

She didn't say any more on the subject.

"I'll tell you one thing about Texas," he said. "It's a big place."

"You don't have to tell me that. I think I've been driving across it for a week."

"So how about *your* name?"

"Tessa."

"Tessa?"

"Tessa Rae." She laughed. "Origin unknown."

"Fair enough."

George placed Tessa's second drink in front of her almost daintily, went back to his perch. Floyd nursed his own and glanced outside as a huge ugly big rig rushed past, musta been doing fifty or sixty down the business route. He assumed long ago those long-haulers must have an agreement with the local law. The window vibrated, and glasses tinkled. Then nothing again, just the quiet seethe of the desert. He felt a warmth in his belly that wasn't entirely due to the bourbon.

Last time he'd spoken a word to a pretty girl was probably a year earlier when he was in Little Rock, some joint famous for its cheese dip. She was a sweet little flirty college girl behind the counter. Christ, he couldn't even remember her name anymore, and he knew it had been emblazoned on a tag over her left tit. For weeks, Floyd had been *certain* something was on the edge of happening, but nah, she was only engaging with him for the tips. Those wait girls, they knew how to string you along. Last time he'd been *involved* with a gal had been waaay too long ago. That had been Shirley from Oklahoma, the one who'd gone slowly batshit. He'd had to take the cowardly way out. Left without a word in the middle of the night, gone.

"Can't believe anyone would wanna, like, *exist* in a place like this," Tessa said, crunching an ice cube.

"Sometimes it ain't by choice."

"Oh, you're here against your will?"

"Let's just say circumstances can force a person's hand." He took a deep swallow of bourbon, and his own ice clinked against his front teeth.

"If it was me, I'd do *everything in my goddamn power* to get out. That's all I'm saying."

"Power's relative."

"Power's what you make it."

"Maybe that's easy for someone like you to say."

"Someone like me?"

"Uh huh."

"What's *that* supposed to mean? You don't know the first thing about me."

"What I mean is—you've got some charms. You're on the deep end of the gene pool. Power comes with that."

She frowned at him and if not understanding him. "I see what you're trying to do, but that kinda shit doesn't work on me."

"I'm looking at your clothes and your funky hair and your car, and I'm not exactly seeing a difficult life." He kept his tone light, teasing her. "And, like I said, you know, you're gorgeous."

"Oh, *whew*, for a second there, I thought you might be a fucking prick."

"No, you're right, I am that."

"Just as I was warming to you, too."

Floyd finished up his drink, decided on another. He watched George fix him up.

"Anyway, I'm only here for a while," he said. "Till I decide I need to move on."

Tessa spun a half turn on her stool, put her back to the bar, draped her elbows on the hard wood. She seemed to be gazing with dull interest toward the framed historical photos on the opposite wall. Floyd had wandered over there a few weeks ago to check them out. They showed Malvado in its heyday, or what passed for a heyday in west Texas. The town had boomed in the early nineteen-oughts for about three seconds, thanks to a trio of enterprising mercury miners, before the amateur mine flooded and fell into ruin, along with mineral prices. The photos documented meager settlements with promising young well-dressed chaps all proud against a background of yellow dust, those misguided young Americans with their parched dreams, lost now to eternity, and the town now standing as a puttered-out testament to wrong-headedness.

"You dodged my question," Floyd said, feeling the booze at his forehead. "You *are* making a run for the border."

She turned her head to study him. "Guess so."

"All righty then." Then, emboldened, he said, "What are you doing that for?"

Yeah, the bourbon was starting to loosen him up. He watched her expression twitch. It was subtle, but he generally caught these things. She had something going on, something buried just under the surface.

"I'm sorry, do I *know* you?" she said. "Are we, like, sharing secrets now?"

Floyd put up his hands in surrender. "Just hate to see you go, is all."

She half-turned, took a swallow of her sweet drink. "Well, that's all I want, man—to get the fuck outta here. Outta this godforsaken country."

"Seems to me the states could use more gals like you."

"Like I said, *Floyd*, you don't know me."

"Maybe I'd *like* to." He tried turning on the charm. He knew his best attributes were his whiskery smile and his eyes. That was just honesty, not bragging or nothing. He felt by sheer effort he could make his baby greens sparkle. "Maybe that's why I'm sitting here."

Sometimes the eyes and the smile worked, and sometimes they didn't. His instinct told him at that moment his best features were failing him. All Tessa did was turn back to the bar and begin the process of finishing off her drink. In between swallows, she messed with her little turquoise purse, fresh and bright as if she'd just picked it up a couple days earlier in Santa Fe. Another instinct was shouting at him, something along the lines of *this is wrong, you shouldn't be encouraging this gal, you shouldn't be getting involved with anyone, like Philip told you, just lay fuckin' low and wait it out.*

Tessa slapped down a couple bills and nodded at George, who didn't notice until she announced, "I'm taking care of both of us."

George nodded.

Then Tessa gave Floyd a look that was different from the looks she'd given him before.

"Where's your place?"

TWO
TESSA RAE JAYNE

Tessa Jayne had always found it pretty easy to compartmentalize.

She pondered her almost supernatural capability while she lay next to this man named Floyd in his narrow bed, in his little sun-bleached clapboard rental, in this decimated nothing town in southwest Texas. Turned out, Floyd snored a bit, just a tiny bit, like a dog almost, and the sound reminded her of Terrell before everything happened, like when he'd sleep on the floor of her room after a nightmare. She was about as far away from her brother as she could possibly get, short of venturing into literal foreign lands, the great unknown, and she felt now as if Terrell were waaaaaaay behind her, part of another existence altogether.

It was early morning, and she was naked beneath a thin warm sheet, and she'd just awakened with zero recollection of drifting toward sleep. She did remember a lot of half-drunken careless fucking, straight from the bar, here in this flattened sweaty bed. Typically Tessa was noisy and boisterous in the saddle, had always been that way, at least since she was sixteen, but last night her lovemaking had been slow and easy and slippy-slidy, eyes closed as she'd felt exhaustion creeping up on her. And then her only memory of unconsciousness was a long, rumbling dream of endless road coming at her, and her running right in the middle along the broken yellow lines, out of breath.

Compartmentalization.

She likened it to that open road slipping beneath the Beetle's tires and then disappearing behind her like the sand in an Etch A Sketch. What was ahead of her consumed her, and what was behind her no longer mattered. She'd faced a crossroads, no doubt about it. Was *still* facing it. She'd been pondering that crossroads for nearly two full days now, and for all her deep thinking on the subject, the truth was . . . the decision was already made. It wasn't as if she could turn back.

There was blood in her wake.

Tessa extricated herself from the bed and made her way out to the front room, her toes navigating threadbare pile. She found her phone plugged in next to an ancient scuzzy coffee pot. She powered the phone on and swiped through her shit for about seven minutes. She recognized the names in her call history, every one of them, but she didn't listen to any messages or read through any texts.

She scanned the Decatur news for mentions of herself or the address of the fire, and there were two—the original paragraph from early yesterday morning, and then a follow-up that identified the old woman who'd been in the house when it went up. Evangeline Eastman.

Shit.

That made it real, didn't it? A name made it real.

On the roads out of Illinois, away from Decatur, she'd wept openly at first, wind whipping her hair as she listened to the initial reports on the AM dial, but at some point flying down the 55 through Arkansas the music had come on, blues-jumpy Motown from her phone, and she'd found herself singing out loud. That's the compartmentalization she kept thinking about. Every once in a while she'd sensed the curvy meander of the Mississippi to her left, and it had felt like miserable freedom.

She'd gotten all the way to sweaty Texarkana with the gasoline cans still in the rear of the VW. These new-fangled Beetles had their engines up front where they should be. She'd found some dumpsters in the middle of the night and gotten rid of the canisters.

The long southwestward sweep through Texas had been hot and monotone and endless. Christ, what a dreary stretch of land! But she still had it in her to make the trip in one haul, day and night, paying for fuel and food with the cash from Uncle Johnny. Sticking to the speed limit, everything on the level, she'd estimated twenty hours. Actually took twenty-three, thanks to a nap at a rest stop near Dallas.

She didn't know how to be a criminal. That *had* to be in her favor.

She knew there were lots of things in her favor, and that was one reason she could bust out in song while barreling away from everything that had gone down.

She hadn't *meant* for anyone to die. That was the thing, really.

Like she could explain that to the Decatur police. Or Harlan.

When she'd merged onto Route 67 south, far away from home, things got lonely and dry and gritty-clear. The border loomed before her, an hour or two, and she realized she'd come all this way on defense, and

... okay ... she hadn't really thought everything through. Twelve hundred miles of asphalt behind her before she'd thought about her passport. When the dude at the gas station would ask her about her papers, she'd lie and smile her way out of it, but the truth was, Tessa Jayne could no more legally cross the border than return home to justice.

So it was in this little dusty nothing town, Malvado, where Tessa finally caught her breath. Pulled back from the brink and took a moment to think about what was on the horizon. Full tank, a little over six hundred dollars left from what Johnny'd given her, and adrenaline to spare. She'd envisioned passing into Mexico at a small border crossing with zero trouble, just zipping through, and then her future was wide open. She'd disappear into the ether. There was no one left to care about.

She *could* still do that, passport or not, but it was a one-way ticket. Wasn't it a one-way ticket anyway?

A new life on a Mexico beach, white sands, a little hut.

The stuff of fantasy? Was it like Johnny told her all the time, that she lived her life according to silly movies and TV shows on Netflix? *Goddammit, girl, the world ain't like the Shawshank Redemption,* he'd said on the phone an hour after she'd launched herself away from Decatur.

She owed it to herself to give her immediate future some thought, now that she was fifteen hundred miles from home and twenty from the border.

When she caught a glimpse of the unlikely OPEN sign in the window of the bar—the bar called Bar that looked invitingly empty and seemed to call to her—she drove on another half-mile before pulling the U. She'd figured she'd earned the overdue respite from the road, here at the end. And then, when the flirty guy from the mini mart appeared in front of her inside the hooch joint, it was like some kind of magic wish-fulfilment trick, because it was at the precise moment she was flashing on him anyway, wondering what might have been. And then it was like it was meant to be, and she'd *known* they'd hook up. Foregone. The ol' sweet genital grind, man, it could be like a drug, and at that point she'd been in withdrawal for weeks.

She didn't even care if Floyd ended up being trouble. That kind of thinking used to be dangerous. Who knew if she'd been followed, or even tracked? Neither was likely, but now, since Decatur, the possibility would haunt her. Nothing she could do about that anymore. Besides, when did troublesome men ever give her pause? She liked dudes who exuded trouble like a vibe, like sweat. An aura. Floyd was the kind of man she was drawn to—like, since way back. Hard, rugged, sarcastic, even kinda mean, but a sweetheart down deep where it counted. She could see it.

I've got a frickin' weak spot, all right?

"How 'bout some breakfast?" came Floyd's voice from behind her, speak of the devil.

She jumped a little, cocked a smile, glanced over her shoulder at him. "You're a stealthy one."

"Well, I'm still kickin'."

Floyd was leaning against the bedroom doorjamb enjoying the view. She set her phone down and twisted a bit to give her ass a slap.

"Whattaya have in mind?"

"More of *that* later, for damn sure."

"You're SOL, cowboy, I gotta get back on the road after some grub."

He looked disappointed. "You're really doin' it. You're hoppin' the border."

"That's the plan."

A nod, then, "You headed through Ojinaga? Straight south? Then, what, Chihuahua?"

"Chihuahua, yeah."

He gave her the slant eye. "Not the safest part of Mexico, gotta say, 'specially for a young gal on her own—no offense to any MeToo sensibilities. You sure you want to go that route?"

"No, but I'm doin' it anyway."

Floyd's gaze made her face burn. He was locked on her eyes now, like trying to figure her out, get in tune with the rhythm of her synapses.

"Got time for breakfast, though," she said. "Buy you a cup of coffee before I never see you again?"

"How 'bout my treat, but you go get it, bring it back here?"

Tessa faced him fully, leaned back against ugly Formica. Equal footing. She let him get a good look at her tits while she took his measure. Dude was something to look at, in a rough-and-tumble kind of way, and frankly she knew she had it goin' on, too. But apart from all that, she watched his eyes. It was her first inkling that something else was going on there, that Floyd Weathers was hiding something from her—as surely as *she* was hiding something from *him*. Why else would he want her to fetch the coffee?

"Sure." *Hmmmm.* "I don't know my way around, though."

"There's a diner around the corner that's been barely hangin' on for decades."

"Sounds delicious."

"Might want to put somethin' on. I mean, the streets are close to empty, but you'd be givin' ol' Henry a show."

"Maybe I *want* to give ol' Henry a show." She pushed away from the counter and squeezed past Floyd into the bedroom. "Who's Henry?"

"Henry owns this place." Behind her, Floyd was drawing some wrinkled dollar bills from the pockets of his jeans, which were draped across a busted beige couch. "Cranky as a pissed-off snapping turtle, you'll like him."

Outside, the day was already heating up toward misery. Tessa had thrown on her white stretch pants and equally white, equally figure-flattering halter, which she'd imagined wearing while crossing over into Mexico. You know, that virginal thing. First time and all.

She was already envisioning herself back on the road, the final stretch into Mexico. At the same time, making that crossing was a completely alien idea, and she was terrified about it, no matter what reassurances Uncle Johnny had kept rehashing over the phone. It *wasn't* going to be a cinch, she knew it. Far from it. Well, crossing the border might be a cinch, but *then* what? Johnny had given her a big wad of pesos from his time there a decade earlier, and he'd given her some names and places— all shouted, all in a rush—and thinking about all that was like slipping her heart into an icebox. She recalled the mess of tattered bank notes, the purple and orange fifties and hundreds looking like ragged remnants of an old foreign land, and she shivered.

It was no wonder she'd flipped the U yesterday toward the bar and ended up diving straight into Floyd's pants. A freefall into the familiar, throwing caution to the wind. Hell, she'd ripped across hundreds of miles of hot asphalt, a constant eye on the rearview, at least a dozen winding detours to discourage any followers—and absolutely no sighting of anyone on her tail. All of Johnny's words of caution like alphabet soup sloshing inside her skull. She'd seen nothing but repetitive road, anonymous traffic, and nobody gave a good goddamn about her.

Still, she crept into the daylight with an abundance of caution, wearing Floyd's Rangers ballcap low, hair tucked up inside, hiding her face, subtly altering the sway of her walk. She saw no faces, only heard the occasional drone of a motor as sparse vehicles rushed through the dusty downtown.

Clear of the motel—no sign of ol' Henry—she walked the long sidewalk in the concrete shade, passing a number of boarded-up storefronts. One of the spaces had been a bookshop, according to its faded door signage—SECONDHAND READS. She paused to peek through the boards and saw empty shelves, some dusty placards littering the floor, cheap unused plastic bags. Not a single book to be seen. She'd brought a couple horror novels that she'd grabbed off Terrell's bedroom shelf, but what about after that? In Mexico, would it be hard to find books in English, or were all the paperbacks there in Spanish? What else was she supposed to do with her free time, laying around the beach?

She kept walking, suddenly gripped by existential panic—thanks to a boarded-up bookstore window.

Well, a lot more than that, she realized. Probably it was last night, too, that final desperate grab at a hunk of good ol' USA in the form of this mysterious Texan.

Floyd Weathers.

Somethin' about that man, what was it? Was it worth learning? If only for a short while?

In the middle of the night, she'd awakened with the urge to pee. She'd sat up on the edge of the lumpy bed, palm to forehead, listening to him snore lightly behind her. Idly, she'd pulled open the drawer of the nightstand to find a large midnight-black pistol staring back at her. It was on top of some loose papers and a Ray Slater western paperback. The matte finish of the weapon looked nothing but sinister to her; it was a workmanlike piece of brutal efficiency. *Oh shit*, she breathed, quietly sliding the drawer closed again. Out in Floyd's front room, she knew, there was a weathered baseball bat leaning in an unfurnished corner, and she also remembered being flummoxed by the placement of a rusty crowbar next to the stove. If she hadn't been so drunk last night, perhaps these observations might have given her pause. The pistol was a whole new thing, though.

Floyd Weathers had a story. Question was—was it a story that she wanted to know, or was it a story that she wanted no part of?

Even at the thought, Uncle Johnny's voice was shouting in her inner ear. *No distractions! Get the hell over the border, and we'll talk when it's done! Christ, girl, you are the queen of distractions! You don't do this right, you're gonna wreck everything. Can you focus, please, for the love of—*

She turned the corner and glimpsed the DINER sign up the street to the right. Malvado's main thoroughfare, the three-block business stretch for Route 67, was called 1st Street, and the diner was called—*oh man*—1st Street Diner. She judged that it was the only place of business on the stretch of road that was open for customers. The diagonal parking spots in front of it were populated by exactly three vehicles, all of them coated with the identical texture and thickness of gray-brown dust. The rest of the street was tumbleweed territory. She could just see George's bar on the far corner from where she strode, but it probably didn't open till the afternoon.

A smile took hold of her mouth, and it felt good.

She recognized a bounce in her step, and she decided that she dug ol' Floyd. It was more than his delightful tongue, and it was despite the implications of the drawerful of pistol and the baseball bat and the crowbar. Or maybe it was *because* of all those things. She liked his face, and she liked his strong, lean chest and the way he talked to her.

Uncle Johnny was shouting in her head again. Yeah, well, maybe she'd fled far enough. Maybe it was time to tell Uncle Johnny to calm the fuck down. She shook his specter away.

Tessa opened the door of the diner and made her way inside.

Country music was drawling out of bad speakers somewhere, and there was the clatter of dishes in the back, and a couple of conversations stopped cold. All eyes were on her.

Two tables were occupied, and there was one old fellow at the counter. One of the tables was inhabited by three middle-aged women, and they appeared to be an odd mishmash of hillbilly and native people—slightly dark, weathered skin, long gray-red-brown hair, and severe features. A fat husband and wife, probably retired, sat at the other table, also weathered. And the old guy had a cowboy hat on, above a Santa beard and a skinny-chested purple shirt and jeans. All of them turned away, then, silent, sipping their coffees, and Tessa shrugged and went to the counter. A flat-gazed, cream-uniformed woman came out of the back, eyeing her warily. Her hair was coiffed as if from another era, and her nametag read SHEILA.

"Help ya?"

"Hey, can I get a couple coffees to go?" She caught sight of a meager selection of pastries in a dim case. "And a couple of those—whatever those are. What's in those?"

"Green chili."

"No shit?"

"No shit." If such a thing was possible, the woman's eyes looked grimy.

"All right then. Two of those."

"That it?"

"Uh huh."

"All righty, two coffees, two pastries, that's seven bucks, hun."

"Here's ten, you keep the rest."

The woman named Sheila nodded her thanks, plopped the pastries in a paper bag, and began filling up tall cups of coffee. Tessa turned her back on the counter, propped her elbows on it, and surveyed the room. The Malvado residents were sneaking looks at her, and she faced them head-on, smiling.

These people had lived here a long time, she knew it, and she was trying to wrap her head around that. What was it made a person settle in a town like this? Had they just given up on everything?

"Here ya go," the woman behind her said.

Tessa turned to take the coffees, which Sheila had nestled into a cardboard carrier.

"Thanks!"

Tessa gathered everything and stepped toward the door, still feeling all eyes upon her. They'd be talking about her after she left. Uncle Johnny would say it was no goddamn good, calling attention to herself like that, but that advice didn't amount to a hill of shit in a nothing town like this. Tessa Rae was as good as a ghost this far from home. Absolutely nobody would find her here.

The thought sliced cleanly away, and she came to a stuttering stop at the sweaty glass door. Four parking spots south, a familiar Ford truck was pulling in. Tessa stepped backward as if yanked by a string.

She couldn't move for a long moment, enough time for Ossie Perkins himself to open the truck's door and step down to the asphalt and adjust himself. She swallowed hard in stunned disbelief, backing away from the door as calmly as she could manage.

"You know what?" she said over her shoulder to Sheila. "Uh . . . you got a bathroom?"

THREE
FLOYD TILLMAN WEATHERS

Floyd ogled Tessa Rae's sweet butt as she sashayed away, down the cracked and crumbling sidewalk. She didn't glance back once. He liked that; it spoke of confidence. She knew he was watching her, and she fed off it, played with it. He estimated she was on the young side of her twenties, hallelujah, and the damn girl had a spark that made him feel all warm inside. He hadn't felt that kind of thing in too long.

He'd been a tucked-away week-to-week resident of the motel for three months, awaiting word from Philip back in Little Rock. Floyd carried the burner phone in his left front pocket at all times like a hand grenade, set to vibrate like a motherfucker when the man finally called and gave him the A-OK. Floyd had never worked this big a job for Philip before. He was still a little bewildered by everything Philip had put in place—the safe car before the switch, the double-blind handover, and of course Floyd's lack of any personal connection to the assignment. Now here he was with the entire stash in this little podunk room.

Floyd figured he could easily disappear into the Mexican ether with the cash, but then what would happen to his family? Philip had met all of them, had dined with them. Had laughed with them. It had all seemed harmless at the time, but the next day Floyd had gotten it. It was never a thing that had to be spoken, but—shit, man, it wasn't rocket science.

While he waited for Tessa to fetch coffee and breakfast, he took a quick shower under meager water pressure, washing off the sex and sweat. The odors brought back the slow sweetness of the night, the slippery fumblings and the intense couplings and the lewd laughter. Tessa had felt good—soft but also drumtight in all the right places. He hated the idea of the girl taking off for destinations unknown, and not only for reasons of the flesh. He didn't think she was remotely prepared for what lay ahead of her.

Back in the front room, he peeked outside through the thin curtains. Tessa's banana-yellow bug was parked in the shadows to the far left, on the other side of his Camaro. He knew there was a reason she'd nestled the vehicle in there, out of view from the street. Last night they'd skirted around that reason, all flirty smiles and naughty laughter, but she hadn't wanted to budge. Floyd imagined that given another day or two, he'd pull the reason out of her.

Alas.

Tessa was fixin' to do something stupid. The more he thought about her, the more he suspected that was the truth. He didn't know much about Tessa Rae beyond what he'd gained from the flirting, but he knew enough to begin to feel protective. Funny what a single night of sweaty fun could do, 'specially when it involved such an enthusiastic participant—

The front door erupted with a clamor of pounding fists, and Floyd's heart was abruptly in his throat. He staggered back toward the bedroom, toward his Beretta M9, which lay loaded and ready in the nightstand. But then there was Tessa's voice, and it was urgently pitched.

"Floyd? *Floyd?* Can you open up please?"

Floyd went for the Beretta anyway, securing it in his palm.

"You okay?" he shouted.

"Yeah, can you let me in please?"

"You alone?"

"What? Of course I'm alone."

"You sure?"

A pause. "Ten more seconds, and maybe I won't be."

"Shit, girl."

He went for the door, against all instinct. He straight-armed the pistol, peeking out the small window to the left. Centered himself at the jamb, avoided framing himself in the center of the cheap paneled wood. He saw little glimpses of her, caught quick movements. Her eyes looked nervous beneath his downturned baseball cap. No one else was out there.

Floyd opened the door quick, yanked her in, shut the door. He stayed there at the window, watching, searching the sidewalk, the lot, the street. Turned briefly to face her, hiding the pistol at his thigh.

"What's wrong?"

Tessa was a bundle of nervous energy—completely the reverse of everything she'd been so far. Her confidence and humor were gone. In their place were fear and doubt.

"Okay, so what if I told you I did something bad back home, and it turns out I've been followed?"

"What?"

"There's, like, a lot of shit that I never intended to tell anyone, and that includes you, no offense, 'cause I didn't think I'd *need* to, but all of a sudden, yeah, I probably need to tell you."

Floyd stared hard at her for a moment, then turned back to the small window, pulling the threadbare curtain aside.

"Wait!" Tessa said, grabbing for his bicep.

Too late.

A large angry man with a red face and a receding hairline came into view, striding quickly across the parking lot. The dude meant business, Floyd could tell—that leaning-forward gait, the darting eyes, the fists. He didn't appear to be armed, but Floyd would've been shocked if he weren't carrying something on his person. For now, though, the man's hands were empty and balled into fists. He was a sloppy cube of a man, his body a contradiction of angular muscle and globular fat. The hairline came to a sharp, sweaty vampire point, thin and combed mercilessly, and the eyebrows below it mimicked it. Dude was wearing tight slacks and a flowery Hawaiian shirt with stained armpits.

He got to the center of the parking lot and did a jerky 360, staring wildly about, and his gaze landed on Floyd's window.

Floyd let the curtain fall.

"Well, shitballs," he murmured.

He wasn't about to have a goddamn firefight here if he could help it. He engaged the safety on the pistol and secured the weapon at the small of his back.

"How'd he follow you?"

"He's there?" Tessa said.

"Pretty sure that's your man, yeah."

"I don't know! Did he see you?"

"Uh huh. Probably your silly yellow car, too."

"Oh Jesus."

Floyd backed into the center of the room, keeping Tessa behind him. "What exactly does he want?"

"Uh . . . me?"

"*Why?*"

"Can we get into that later?"

"Fine. What do I need to know right now?"

"He's mad."

A barrage of heavy blows came crashing against the door.

"*Is she in there?*" the man's voice boomed. "*Is that dirty cunt in there? Tessa! I see your fucking car over there, you retard. Get your ass out here. I mean it. Right now. Enough is enough!*"

Floyd leaped to the left and grabbed the Louisville Slugger, balanced it in his grip, got the feel of it in his fists.

"Just tell me one thing," he said to Tessa.

"What?"

"He's the bad guy in this scenario, right? I mean, tell me, he's the bad guy. I'm not gonna find out that he's justified trying to break in here, and calling you a dirty cunt and all?"

"*Dude!*" she said.

"I mean it."

"*Come on!*" the voice outside erupted again, and then there was another fusillade of fistfalls on the door.

"I swear on my daddy's life," Tessa said, solemnly, into Floyd's ear.

He glanced into Tessa's wide eyes. "Do you like your daddy?"

"He's dead."

He choked up on the bat. "Good enough for me."

"What are you gonna do?" Tessa whispered hotly.

Floyd shooed her back toward the bedroom and faced the door.

"What the fuck do you want, man?" he shouted to the man outside, giving his voice an angry drawl. "I was asleep."

"*Open the door.*"

"What do you want? There's no one in here."

"*Open the door, you fuckin' liar.*" Pound pound pound. "*Open it!*"

"Well, lemme throw some clothes on," Floyd tossed out, voice heavy and slow. "Jesus!"

He turned toward Tessa, who fidgeted in the shadows beyond the open bedroom door. She was chewing on a nail and watching him. Her shoulders lifted into a small shrug.

"So," Floyd told her, "there's a possibility that man knows you're in here."

"I think he saw me going out the back of the diner."

"You think so?"

"Uh huh."

"You're not very good at this, are you?"

She stomped her foot on the frayed carpet. "How on Earth did he find me? I mean, how could he have followed me? I was fucking *careful*. I took *detours*, man, I *back*tracked . . . there's just no fucking way."

"Hey!" came the booming voice from outside the door. *"Tessa! I swear, you've got thirty seconds, and then I'm coming in there."*

"Who *is* this fucker?" Floyd asked. "He's *very* unpleasant."

"His name is Perkins," she said with a snarl. "He's—"

"You gotta face the music, honey," the now quieter, muffled voice went on, suddenly verbose and contemplative, "you gotta face everything that's waitin' for you back home. Ronnie sent me to get you, and that's what I intend to do, even if I have to drag you back to Decatur, I swear to G—"

"I'm not going back there!" Tessa screamed. *"Harlan tried to kill my fucking brother!"*

Floyd closed his eyes, gritted his teeth, flared a look at her over his shoulder.

What? she shrugged.

"Gotcha," the man outside said, just loud enough for Floyd to hear.

Six feet from the door, Floyd watched it rattle in its frame. Then it stopped, and the man seemed to settle down. He'd found his prey. Definitively. Floyd understood the satisfaction in that. The man's large shadow paced in front of the door and window.

"Come on, now, girl," the voice said. "I'm serious here. You should be glad it's me out here instead of the cops, right? Let's make this easy, huh? For the both of us."

"Go away!" Tessa cried.

As Floyd winced and sighed, he considered the situation. Obtaining a little unexpected tail on an otherwise lonely Thursday night was one thing, especially when that tail belonged to someone as delicious as Tessa Rae Jayne, but this was something else entirely. That wiggly bootie wasn't worth the retroactive price of admission, wasn't worth this Illinois jagoff pounding on his door when Floyd was under strict instructions to lay fucking low. He could practically see Philip's clenching jaw hundreds of miles away in Little Rock. The tightening of his gloved fists.

His mind flashed on the bundles of cash taped up inside the nightstand, back in the bedroom. This overfed asshat was oblivious to it, clearly was here only for the girl, but—still—he was creating a scene. There were scant few people around to *notice* the scene, sure, but it was a scene just the same. Floyd imagined ol' Henry getting an eyeful of the drama from the office window.

It was that thought more than anything else that pushed him to act. He needed to defuse the situation, stop the yelling. Hell, even get these two together and send them on their way. Floyd knew next to zero about Tessa's situation, and he wanted to keep it that way.

He stepped forward, reached for the door—and stopped.

Holy shit, he thought, frozen in mid-stride.

As the pounding continued monotonously, Floyd turned back to Tessa, stared at her wordlessly for a time. Her expression said *What?*

"Tell me you're not here for me," he spat. "Tell me this isn't some ruse, and that asshole out there is really here for me."

Tessa's look of shock turned mystified, blindsided—and immediately Floyd knew he was wrong. He could read a face, even a pretty one. But he had to follow it through.

"I don't need this, okay? I got my own problems." He reared back from the wounded look she was laying on him. "Look, paranoia is vital to my survival, you understand? Don't take it personal. It's not cool to bring this to my door, is all I'm saying. Not cool at all."

Tessa stood tall.

"This isn't *about* you, Floyd. Look, I'm sorry I brought my shit here, but I didn't mean to. I *promise*." She paused as they stared at each other. "You must think a whole lot of me, to get into it like last night, everything we did, all the fun we had, and for that to be—"

"Fine."

"—for that to be fucking *fake!*"

"Okay!"

"I mean—"

Perkins pounded on the door some more. *"Come on!"*

"All right, I get it." Floyd eased up, softened his gaze.

Tessa smirked at him. "I knew there was somethin' about you, though. We're gonna talk later about *that*, cowboy."

Floyd flicked his gaze from her to the door and back again. Then he stepped forward and kissed her hard, eliciting a surprised gasp. With one free hand, he reached around and squeezed her ass, pulling her toward him, and their teeth clicked together. When he drew back, Tessa bounced on her toes a little.

At that moment, the door rattled in its frame as Perkins laid a boot into it. One more kick, and the door was going to splinter wide.

"Hey, what's your problem, man?" Floyd slow-drawled loudly for Perkins, then, over his shoulder, "Get ready."

The door gave way, and Perkins was suddenly there, sweaty and huge and fragrant—and armed. Floyd caught the glint of steel immediately, some kind of fat snub-nose wheel gun, a Ruger perhaps, and the man was flailing it in all directions. And the man was squinting. Perkins couldn't see a goddamn thing in the comparatively dark room.

"Where is she?"

Floyd took aim and swung the bat savagely, calling on all his years in Arkansas Little League and high school ball. The business end of the slugger made contact with Perkins' right hand with sickening percussion, and the revolver went flying across the room, knocking hard against the far wall and falling to the carpet. Perkins let out a girlish wail, spinning, grabbing his disfigured hand. Three fingers were splayed out in garish impossible angles, and blood was abruptly welling and dripping from several spots. Perkins cradled the hand against his stomach, screaming.

"Shut up!" Floyd snapped.

Perkins didn't shut up—at least, right away. His wailing became an unintelligible string of would-be curses, and then that stream of throaty rage turned into a strangled gagging noise, and his bulging eyes were flitting from Floyd to Tessa and back again as if begging for help. The big man gasped, fell to one knee, and slowly collapsed onto his back like a flipped tortoise.

"Oh, take it easy, *take it easy!*" Floyd yelled. "Fingers can be fixed."

In his peripheral vision, Tessa was bouncing up and down, one hand firmly affixed to her mouth. She was making little *eww eww eww* sounds.

The man named Perkins, purple-faced, mouth stretched into a downturned scarecrow grin, was holding his wounded hand straight up into the air when he expired in the space of one brutal death grunt. Floyd remained poised to take another swing as he watched the stiffening arm gradually ratchet to the floor like a crippled railway gate. The mangled hand dripped a straight dark line of blood as it fell.

"Hey!" Floyd barked at Perkins. "Get up!"

"He's dead!" Tessa cried.

"No he's not," said Floyd, because he *couldn't* be dead.

Goddammit, he can't be fucking dead because that wouldn't make any fucking sense, and I do NOT need this right now, no way in hell.

Floyd let the bat slip down through his curled fingers, and he poked the large man in his prodigious gut with its business end. Perkins wasn't moving. Floyd watched the thick neck for signs of a pulse—nothing there.

"What *happened?*" Tessa said, voice pitched toward hysteria.

"Your man have a heart problem?"

"Hell if I know! You think I've had, like, deep *conversations* with this guy?"

Floyd stepped back and assessed the situation. Finally, he jumped over the corpse and shut the door to a crack, peered outside through the window. He leaned the bat softly against the wall, kept watching.

"What is it?" Tessa said, still antsy.

"Was that guy *with* anybody?"

"No."

"For *sure*, no, or you *think* no?"

"For sure. He was the only one that got out of the truck."

"And the truck is parked in front of the diner?"

"Uh huh."

Floyd swallowed, tried to corral his zig-zagging thoughts. The morning had turned to shit, and it had started so damned promising, too. What the fuck was wrong with him? He now regretted every decision the day before—hell, even leaving this apartment to pick up food at the gas station. If he'd stayed here five minutes longer, he never would've run into the girl, and by extension this fat dead fuck, and he'd still be quietly biding his time, awaiting his modest share of the Little Rock haul.

You had one job! he imagined Philip barking in his ear. *Easiest job in the fucking world. Sit in a goddamn room at the edge of nowhere and fucking wait, man. Sit and fucking wait! But no, you let Little Floyd enter into the equation, didn't you?*

"All right, let's fix this," Floyd muttered.

His veins felt as if they were filled with liquid nitrogen.

FOUR
TESSA RAE JAYNE

When Tessa'd set fire to the house in Forsyth, dead north of Decatur, she'd done so behind a mask—one of those ubiquitous pandemic masks that had become as much a fashion statement as a political firebrand. Back then, everyone was busy arguing over their efficacy, but there were a few people who considered them a boon for other reasons. She was one of them. If not for the mask, Tessa was *positive* that she wouldn't have had the nerve to go through with it—despite everything, despite the weeks of Terrell's writhing agony.

She felt as if she'd be seeing discarded masks for decades. Over the past few months, in the wake of the vaccines, she'd find them in alleyways back home, in gutters, one time stuffed behind a public toilet as if in disgusting victory. Even as she'd raced toward this godforsaken Texas berg, she'd occasionally caught glimpses of the cloth or blue-synthetic rectangles on the side of the road, fluttering and filthy. They were still out there, millions of them, and it was almost as if humanity—as a collective—wanted the nasty things to stay where they were, mashed down into the dirt, a reminder not that they'd once been a necessity but that they'd finally been vanquished. Finally—after all the politicized bullshit, and all the resulting contagious inanity.

Jesus, what a time that had been. Still seemed unreal that it had all gone down.

But apparently the mask had merely given Tessa a *false* sense of security. Perkins—Harlan's rotund monkey man—had been on her tail the *entire time*, and it was impossible, *impossible*, and all she could do was stand there in the crappy vestibule to Floyd's bedroom, staring at the big man's equally impossible corpse.

She knew it could easily be *her* dead on that floor right now.

When Uncle Johnny had ushered her into his house, and her stinkin' of gasoline, that wild look in her eyes, he'd already known that it was really her who'd done it. (Apparently *everybody* did.) She'd denied it, and he'd only stared at her with a kind of sadness. He'd taken her by the shoulders and tried to put the fear of a dark lord into her. She'd taken his words mostly to heart—how could she not, considering the fire in his eyes? She'd felt tears bubbling up, she'd felt the burn inside her chest, and it had gotten her moving like she'd never moved in her life. She'd gone and gathered her essentials, her cash and her valuables, and she'd hit the road. And after five hundred miles—somewhere around the Oklahoma border, churning RPMs toward Tulsa—she'd eased up on the gas, took some more detours, found some hiding places in off-the-beaten-path rest stops . . . and finally took a breath.

Five hundred miles.

It wasn't until that moment that she considered the possibility her Uncle Johnny was full of shit. He was her dad's younger brother, after all, so there was a lot of *that* in him. He was the uncle that was a little off, you know? The one who was susceptible to conspiracy theories and stupid populism. He was *that* one in the family—the one with the sense of confident foolishness. But that was only his politics. She loved him for the *other* aspects of him. He was the one who'd always looked after her, especially after her daddy died. In the stuff that mattered most—like survival—she trusted him.

They were after her. It was real. It was a thing.

She was in danger.

Floyd was digging in Perkins' pockets, grunting as he shoved the body left and right to reach the man's wallet and his keys. To her horror, something deep inside Perkins' body gurgled loudly, and then it loose with a long, flabby fart.

"He's still alive?" she said, so embarrassed that her voice came out as a squeak.

Floyd had a grimace on his face as he turned to her. "Just gasses releasing," he said, although he kept watching the body warily.

"Oh Jesus that's so unpleasant," she said.

Finally, he backed off, stood up, Perkins' bundle of keys in his hand. He took a few nervous paces across the small room. He kept throwing irritated glances at her.

"What?" she said, hearing her own petulance.

"What have you gotten me into?" he whispered so low that she could barely hear him.

"Uh, it's not like I *invited* him here."

"Nevertheless, he's here. And he's dead. He's a big ol' mountain of dead."

"Well—"

"You told me his name, but who *is* he?"

Tessa took in a huge shaky gulp of air, then forced herself to breathe in long, measured breaths. One at a time. Like Terrell used to say, with his sleepy toothy grin, *Calm blue ocean . . . calm blue ocean.* Maybe it was those words that had subconsciously propelled her toward Mexico, where she might find some abandoned pristine beach where no one would ever find her again . . . .

She was flashing on the last time she'd laid eyes on this man, this dead man. Perkins. It had been at Wayne's, of course. Couple nights before the fire. That was just last week, back when she had a *job* at Wayne's! Back before she'd grabbed her last cash on her way out of town, Sara watching her go, open-mouthed, having fuck-all to say to her.

That night, Perkins had been very much alive and very much reprehensible. He'd been sitting with that pierced freak Harlan at one of the high tables, nursing a pitcher of Bud and watching Tessa behind the bar. Only reason he and Harlan were there was because Terrell was *also* there that night, flirting with Sara in the corner, poking at her feather earrings or whatever.

Tessa's little brother was shameless and confident—a dangerous combination. He knew Perkins and Harlan were sitting there at that table watching him, and he didn't care. Terrell had always been fearless that way, and dumb, too, almost a little slow, and as he'd grown older those traits had morphed into a kind of peevishness. And look where it'd gotten him. Who knew when he'd wake up?

She still loved the big goof.

Obviously.

It was the reason she was here in this crappy motel room at the edge of nowhere in the first place.

"Yeah, he followed me, okay?" she answered Floyd. "It doesn't make any fucking sense, but he followed me. I did something back home, something bad, and he wanted to take me back. He wanted me to face the music, like he said."

"Face *what* music?"

She looked at him squarely. "It doesn't really matter right now, does it?"

"Look," Floyd said, sighing, wiping his lips with shaking fingers, "I'm gonna help you with this, Tess, but then . . . we're either gonna be real straight with each other, or we're gonna have to say goodbye. Okay?"

The room was utterly silent for a moment, in spite of the deafening sight of Perkins sprawled like a pile of inconvenient garbage between them. They were both staring at the corpse, couldn't seem to look away from it. Like it was yelling at them. Then it was as if her ears popped.

"Well," she said, "it's not like I envisioned hanging around."

"Okay . . . ."

"As enticing as this place is."

Tessa heard the singing of the keys before she grasped that he'd tossed them at her, an underhanded lob. She caught them awkwardly.

"Go get that truck, and park it right out front, willya?" Floyd said. "Do it real casual-like, got it? But if you see anything unusual, anyone else you know, or some kind of crowd, a cop, whatever, just stroll on back."

She swallowed, nodded, didn't move. She felt a burning in her throat and knew it was because of what Floyd had said about saying goodbye.

Tessa liked to think of herself as tough. She'd carefully cultivated a persona of wise-cracking freewheeler on the outside, hard-as-nails bitch under the surface. It was partly how she justified burning up the rock house in Forsyth—first dreaming about it, and then planning it, and then fucking carrying through with it, all by her damn self. But despite all that, there were moments when that infuriating softness got the better of her. Crying for what felt like a hundred miles after speeding away from Decatur, for example.

She'd known Floyd for all of fifteen hours, but his words, and the pissed-off look on his face, brought on another of those moments, and this one was even worse, for some reason. Made her feel small. Young. Like she'd never make a worthwhile friend again in her life. She felt all these things on the inside, but no way was she gonna show them on the outside.

But the door was shut, and everything was quiet except for the distant sound of occasional vehicles, and there was a line of stagnant drool hanging from Perkins' open mouth, and his skin had gone all flat and yellow, and Tessa's world had tumbled upside-down. Before, she'd felt only an illusory fear, the flight south from invisible terrors. And then an easing up, and a jolt of adrenaline happiness at the bar, a heady hour of frisky delirium in the bed behind her. Then a good nine hours of sleep, the road coming at her relentlessly in her dreams. A jouncy trip to the breakfast joint, *craving* coffee and then *losing* coffee—and fucking *wham*, shit was real.

She still couldn't move.

Abruptly, Floyd was in her face.

"Look, it's all right," he breathed. "I'm sorry." She felt his hand at the small of her back, felt his warm breath on her cheek. "Tess, it's gonna be okay. We'll take care of this together. Now I need you to take a breath and get yourself back in order, you hear me?"

"Yeah."

"You sure?"

"Yeah, man, of course." She pulled away, frowned at him. "I'll go get the truck."

She went straight to the door, reached for the handle, began to turn it.

"Hold up," Floyd said.

He moved to the door, and she could smell his scent, and she swallowed involuntarily, not sure what was going on inside her. He eased the door open, snuck a look around. Peered left and right through the narrow gap.

"All right."

Floyd opened the door, and she slipped out into the great wide open, and she heard the door close behind her. She turned back to face the room and found herself staring at peeled blue paint, which revealed weathered wood underneath. Her heart was beating like an oar slapping sludgy water, and her eyes burned. And then just as she felt this weakness, she experienced an involuntary growl rise up inside her. She turned back to face the parking lot, and although it was bone-empty, she thrust her chest out defiantly and started back up the sidewalk toward the diner.

Around the corner, the business route was empty, though she could see the ass end of a slanted pickup south of town, and there was a lazy cloud of dust rising from the east. Malvado was so close to a literal ghost town that it freaked her out. The place felt like the end of the fucking world; it was like the nightmare endgame of a pandemic—a much worse one.

She felt herself nearly running down the empty sidewalk and had to force herself to slow down and act casual. Not that it mattered. There was *no one* around. Then again, that was what she'd thought while driving south from Decatur.

As she approached the diner, she cast surreptitious glances in every direction. Perkins' truck was nosed into the same spot, crooked and hulking, and there was an old gray Chevy parked two spots away from it. She thought she recognized it as one of the vehicles from earlier.

She paused, pretending to study the hollow, dusty shell of a former antique store. She considered the scene in her peripheral vision. Still no movement that she could see. She bent down, fiddled with her shoe. She stared at a scraggly, barely alive patch of quackgrass struggling between two slabs of old cement, planning her next move, gathering courage.

She decided to go for it.

She stood up and strode toward the truck, holding herself straight and confident. Rounding the Ford's rear end, she had the key ready but she didn't even need it for the door, which was already unlocked and in fact only half-latched. She swung it open, and that's when she heard a man's gravelly, twangy voice.

"Hey little lady."

A fat lump of adrenaline thudded through her veins.

"Heya," she said.

The man appeared to be the cook from the diner, dressed in filthy whites and a cap, but he had the comportment of an owner, too. He had a smoker's lined face, a pitted nose, and thinning salt-and-pepper hair. He was wringing a gray towel in his hands and watching her with an expression that was caught between mirth and suspicion.

"What was all *that* about?"

She had a flimsy story ready. "Huh? Oh, that! That was my dad, ha! We had a little disagreement, but we're good now."

"That was your dad," the man said, flat-voiced.

"Long story."

He was nodding. "Uh huh."

His gaze moved from her to the truck, and then back again. Beyond him, Tessa could see Sheila the waitress at the window, hands on hips.

She dangled Perkins' keys from her finger, let them jangle. "He just wanted me to grab his truck. He told me to apologize, he started drinkin' early. So . . . yeah."

"You made quite a mess in my kitchen."

"Oh my gosh, I'm *so sorry,*" she said, playing up the persona, even trying to inject a little southern twang without mocking him. She did recall bumping into at least two counters and spilling her coffees. "Can I pay for that?"

He paused but then waved his towel as if in surrender. "We took care of it. Mopped it up. Just be careful out there, young lady, all right?" He was already turning back toward the diner, shaking his head.

"Take care!" she called, and in response he raised the towel again, flapping it like a little white flag. "Sorry again!"

Tessa scooted up into the truck and immediately smelled Perkins' Marlboro sweat. She scrunched her nose in distaste. In the humid cab, she glanced around at the items strewn across the bench seat and on the passenger floor. The first thing she noticed was a large Samsung phone, dark and grimy in the center console. It was plugged into an AUX port. An impromptu ash container was strapped to the scratched plastic there, and it was filled with butts. Eight or nine squashed-up fast food bags littered the floorboards, and there was a 2-liter Mountain Dew bottle half-filled with either soda or urine. Looked a little too yellow for Dew.

"Fucking degenerate," she snarl-whispered.

A leather satchel occupied the passenger seat, and she wanted to root through it, but she knew she had to get off this street first. Feeling the eyes of the diner staff, Tessa started up the truck, fluidly, assertively. She maneuvered out of the space and cruised carefully along the business route, took the immediate right to double back to the motel. She followed an empty alley to a side street, then cut around a dilapidated used car lot onto a cracked, weed-choked path that took her into the motel's parking lot. She could see the manager's office at the far end, hundred yards away, but the windows there were shiny with reflected morning sunlight. No telling whether ol' Henry was watching her, and even if she did see a figure behind all the glare, she had no idea what ol' Henry looked like. Could just as easily be Henry's mongoloid brother Delmar or something.

She actually found it inside herself to laugh, although it came out a bit too loud and hysterical.

She parked right in front of Floyd's room and shut off the engine, had a look around. Besides Floyd's black Camaro and her Beetle, there was only one other vehicle in the lot—a beaten-down Camry—and it looked as if it hadn't moved from its spot in years. In the rearview, occasional trucks whisked by, north and south, on their way back and forth to nowhere.

She knew the feeling.

For the first time in her memory, she felt lost. There was a sore bruise in the center of her, and she couldn't breathe deeply enough to reach it. She wasn't entirely sure what was ahead of her, and she didn't *want* to know what lay behind her. If Perkins' relentless chase was a taste of the hornet's nest she'd left behind in Decatur, then she had no home to go back to. Like, ever. And now Floyd had made it clear that she had no place with *him*.

Well, she'd left home alone, and that's how she'd see it through.

Mexico it is.

She could do it.

Tessa bounced down to the already warm asphalt.

FIVE
FLOYD TILLMAN WEATHERS

For the second time that morning, Floyd watched Tessa's ass as she walked south along the crumbling sidewalk toward the diner. Except this time, his head was in an entirely different place. Lord help him, hers was a fine ebony ass, sculpted and smooth, but he felt a new sheen of sweat all over him and his breathing was jagged as hell, and *fuck her* for bringing this suddenly extinct goon into his life. He had to take care of this situation—like *now*—and every instinct was also telling him that once he cleaned it all up, he needed to get as far away from that fine ass as he possibly could. Tessa Rae Jayne was the devil in disguise—this temptress could easily be the end of him.

When she was out of sight, Floyd made a beeline for the bathroom and yanked down the still-wet plastic shower curtain. He wanted to get Perkins wrapped up before the fool leaked any more DNA into the fucking carpet. The damage was already done, he knew that, but encasing the body in plastic would at least protect Floyd's car, if that's how he decided to get rid of him. Or maybe Floyd just didn't want to look at the fat bastard anymore.

What *was* he gonna do with him? Hell, this shouldn't even be his *problem!*

"Goddammit!" he hissed into the empty room.

He'd dealt with body disposal exactly once in his life, and that had been against his will—a trial, of sorts, early on. The flat heavy-lidded eyes, the slimy gray skin, the stink—maneuvering the corpse over asphalt and into the hole. The stain of that night was still on him, would never be wiped away. As in, whatever awaited him beyond this life, he'd have to answer for that night, and the judgment wasn't going to go in his favor. When he thought of that starless evening, of one-eyed George dumping the broken body of the would-be backstabber at his feet and telling him to deal with it, he still got the palm sweats.

Even now, as he dragged the curtain back to the front room, his mind was running through cartwheels of possibilities. As successful as his first and only body disposal had been, that methodology was out of the question. It wasn't as if he was going to find a construction site in this armpit of a town. The panic solutions—dismembering the body and spreading it far and wide, dissolving it in acid, burning it, finding a body of water and submerging it with stones, smuggling it somewhere and burying it where no one save badgers and coyotes and foxes would find it for years—flew out of his brain as soon as they occurred to him. Most of these methods were impractical or too damn messy and time-consuming. Besides, he'd argue—even if confronted by one of the sad-sack local cops around here—that he'd had very little to do with this slob's death. In any *other* situation, that's the route Floyd would take: Go straight to the law, and tell them exactly what had gone down.

Wasn't gonna happen this time, was it?

What he needed was time. He didn't need to dispose of the body, really. He needed to put it somewhere where no one would connect it to him—at least for a while, at least long enough for him to get out of town and get out of the town's memory.

Abruptly, he had a simple plan.

He laid out the shower curtain next to Perkins' corpse, carefully stuffing a slippery edge under the mangled hand. Then he stepped over the body, knelt next to it, and heaved it over into the plastic. He felt like Sisyphus with his fucking rock. Dude on the floor probably weighed two ninety, and it was mostly flabby fat around the middle, along with some residual muscle around the barrel chest, as if the fucker had once played football or wrestled. Jesus, but he stank. Like he'd been in his truck with no A/C for days following a week of field work in Missouri.

After the body flopped over onto its stomach, Floyd began wrapping it tightly in the curtain, shoving it over again and again—*whump! whump!* Four tight revolutions. By the end, Floyd was on his knees gasping. He considered the crimson stain on the carpet as he caught his breath. That blood would have to come completely out of the fibers, same with the minor dots of residual spray that fanned out toward the bedroom. An impossible task, probably, but they had to do their best.

He'd get Tess on that chore while he checked out the truck. He understood the girl's peril, to a certain extent, but he had to stay on top of this situation. He'd call the shots.

He stood up and went to the kitchen, rummaged around under the sink to find a box of granular soap. He dumped about a quarter cup into his bucket, then at the sink let loose a torrent of water into it. While that filled up, he gathered some rags. Finally he hauled the bucket out of the sink and took it to the body.

At that moment, he heard the rumble of a large vehicle outside in the parking lot. He dropped the rags and hurried to the window. It was Tess, pulling in. He watched her shut off the engine and sit there for a moment while the motor ticked, glancing around the desolate lot.

Christ, she was beautiful. All he could do was stare at her. Goddamn, if it hadn't been for the asshole wrapped up in the shower curtain behind him, Floyd would say she was easily the best thing to happen to him since Little Rock—and that was, what, three months ago? And it wasn't just the sex, although that was *rockin'*. It was something else, something ephemeral. It wasn't every day you clicked with someone on so many levels. As if they'd been destined to meet.

He shook his head at himself. It was a dangerous way to feel. He was stronger than that, letting his frickin' balls do his thinking for him. Because look at the shit she'd *already* dumped into his quiet little corner of Texas.

She stepped down from the truck and swung the big door shut. She looked good, casual, as if nothing at all had gone down. Tess from Illinois was either a fantastic actor or, you know, sociopathic. Floyd opened the door for her as she approached. She whisked in, and he closed it behind her, keeping his eye on the window. No movement.

"That go okay?"

"Guy at the diner asked me what was what."

"Shit."

"It's okay, it's fine."

"No it's not." Floyd scratched as his stubble. *"Shit!"*

"I took care of it."

"No you didn't. Was it a customer, someone that works there . . . ?"

"I think it was the cook."

"Sal? Oh Christ."

"I'm telling you, it's fine. All right? He walked away like he didn't care. He's probably back at his fucking flat top, slinging hash for his *one customer.*"

Floyd chewed at the insides of his cheeks, thinking. Chances were low that any employee of the diner had followed Tess and connected her to him—it was always a skeleton crew over there—but Floyd couldn't say the same about any customers whose curiosity might've been piqued. He watched the parking lot for a full minute, scanning.

"What's your deal, man?" Tess said behind him. "Why are you so paranoid?"

He turned to her. "What are you goin' on about? This asshole just descended from the fucking moon and attacked you."

"He's dead!" She gestured toward the floor, and her gaze seemed to stick there.

Perkins' shoes were poking out the bottom of the shower curtain, and his mangled hand was stuffed tightly by his side, a large red spot smearing the plastic. Tess appeared to be fixated on the sticky blood droplets on the dingy carpet, as well as the pool of it where the devastated hand had ended up.

"You think this is the end of it?" Floyd said. "You think everything's free and clear now?"

"*No,*" she drawled, petulant.

"You have to assume *everyone* knows where you are now."

"But how would they—?"

"The 'how' doesn't matter. It's just what you have to assume."

She shrugged.

"Well, what do we do now?" she said.

"I'm gonna check out that truck, and you're gonna get scrubbin'."

"*What?* You're the one who—"

"You brought him here."

"Are you *blaming* me for this?" All attitude.

"Tess, seriously, I'm just trying to get all the information I can."

She stood there, straight-backed, facing him.

"You ever do any hardcore cleaning?" he asked her, nonplussed.

She was shaking her head, becoming resigned to her immediate future. "I mean, I worked at a hotel in Chicago once, and we had some pretty gnarly—"

"Good, gimme those keys."

Sighing, Tess snagged the keys out of her pocket and tossed them over. Floyd checked the window again, lingering, said, "Get to work, start with the little droplets, don't make anything worse, and don't get any blood on yourself," and then he slipped out, leaving her alone with the corpse.

Watching his periphery, Floyd strode to the truck and opened up the door, climbed inside. He stuck the keys in the ignition and eased the windows down. He saw a leather bag on the passenger seat and grabbed it, pulling it into his lap. It yawned open as if it had been waiting for him. There was a fingerprint-encrusted black laptop and some assorted messy papers, charging cables, receipts. He closed the satchel and set it back on the seat. Spotting the phone in the console, he took it up and powered it on. A logon screen stared up at him, mocking him. He put the phone back in its cradle and harrumphed.

Floyd would bet his left nut that Perkins had some kind of GPS tracking app on that phone, and it was probably plugged in for that reason. GPS tracking sucked power like an Arkansas whore.

Question was—where was the tracker device itself? He glanced across the parking lot at Tess's Beetle, whose rear end was peeking out past his Camaro's front end. That's where it was, he was 99 percent sure, it was somewhere in or on that Beetle—either attached magnetically to a wheel well, or taped to the undercarriage, or secreted inside some inner compartment. He could do a reasonably thorough search in about twenty minutes—and he would.

He checked the visor above him, opened the glove box, felt behind the seats—to diminishing returns. He did find three Snickers wrappers, and two empty Big Gulp containers. There was a half-full jug of Mountain Dew to his right, and it filled him with revulsion. He knew exactly what ol' Perkins had used *that* for.

Floyd unplugged the phone, stuffed it into the satchel, and hauled the bag out of the truck, walked back to the weathered door of his room. There was no one outside in any direction, and that made him breathe a little easier. For now.

He slipped into the room to find Tessa on her knees scrubbing, the string of her purple thong panties visible above her denim waistband. She was doing a good job with the blood, by all appearances, even though she took a half-second to cast an irritated glance at him as he passed her.

He went straight to his little kitchen table and laid out the bag and phone. He started first with the phone, powering it back up.

"Is there *anything* you know about this Perkins character?"

"Just that he was an asshole."

"Think that might figure into his PIN?"

She kept scrubbing, gave him another brief eyeball.

"You don't happen to know his birthday," he said, "or his kids' birthdays, when he graduated, any anniversaries, whatever . . . ?"

"*Pssssh*, no. That dude coulda been gay-married to a midget, for all I know."

Floyd tried the obvious passwords—*1234, 1111, 0000, 1212,* and so on—to no avail. At length, the lock screen prevented further attempts. He stared at the blank screen for a while. His buddy Craig the Egg back in Little Rock had the tools and the talent to hack his way into a device like this, but fat lot of good that did Floyd now. No time for it. He set the phone aside. It might still help him, like if someone were to call, or if a text appeared over the lock screen.

He took a pensive moment to watch Tessa scrub. That ass on her, that bewitching figure.

"Betcha didn't expect to be taking care of a corpse this morning."

She blew hair out of her face. "It was way down on my list."

Floyd nodded thoughtfully, then moved to the laptop. He flipped the lid open to find the screen grossly smeared as if with curdled mayonnaise. He gag-frowned and stood up, headed to the kitchen. He gathered some paper towels and a bottle that he'd filled with his personal mix of water, vinegar, peppermint oil, and vodka. Ever since the goddamn virus, Floyd carried the disinfectant with him wherever he went. He spritzed a few of the towels and gave the computer a thorough cleaning, then put everything away and washed his hands.

He powered up the laptop, and sure enough—password screen.

"Fuck."

"What?"

"Locked out."

He slapped the laptop shut and cracked his knuckles, watching Tess on the floor. She was still scrubbing the largest crimson stain with distaste writ large on her pretty features.

"All right, so let's walk through this."

"Walk through what?"

"Whatever happened to you back in Chicago—"

"Decatur."

"Whatever happened to you in Decatur—"

"Look, man," she said, suddenly rearing back, defensive, "I still hardly know you, okay? I mean, you're practically a stranger to me, and it would just feel fucking weird to just lay out everything to you like you're some kind of preacher man, you know? All you gotta know is some shit went down, and I got the hell outta there, but, man—somehow, I don't know how, but one of 'em found me, all right? Isn't that enough?"

She stopped looking at him, returned to scrubbing.

"What I was gonna say," he said, "was that, whatever it was, it was bad enough to get this Perkins asshole on your tail immediately and relentlessly. He almost certainly tracked you, but it's possible he was just a really good tail."

She paused again. "There's just no fucking way."

"Why?"

"He was *retarded*, man, he was dysfunctional, just a . . . just a fucking *galumph*."

"All right, so he was tracking you. What are the odds he was chasing you alone? By himself. I mean, can you be absolutely sure it was just him, not only alone in his truck but the *only* person after you? Or did he have a crew, or a boss, that might've been—"

She stopped scrubbing and glared at him. "I don't know a goddamn thing about any of them."

"Any of *them*? So it's a crew?"

"*Oh my fuck*," Tessa breathed, rhythmically rubbing a wad of paper towels at the stain. "Well, yeah, I guess you could call it that. There's Harlan, Harlan Eckhart, he's the main guy, piercings all over his punk face, but he's got the snake eyes, you know? He watches you, like, ruthless. And there's Perkins. Well, there *was* Perkins, the stupid fatass, he was in the desert war, at least he always liked to brag about that, for some reason. And Leo and Dank, about the loserest losers you ever met." She paused to think. "Couple others that hung around. Guy named Eric. Another two or three. Those are the ones I always saw at Wayne's, the ones my brother worked with up at the house—"

She stopped.

"What house?"

"You're good."

"What do you mean?"

"Just get me talkin'." She bent into the scrubbing a little more vigorously, turning the towels for a clean side.

Floyd took a breath. "Tess, at some point you're gonna have to trust me, at least a little bit."

She dropped the towels and faced him, and Floyd was surprised to see her reddened eyes rimmed with moisture. "How do I know I can trust you? Huh? How do I really know that?"

"How 'bout the fact that I'm here right now, helping you take care of this m—?"

"I mean, it's not like I've been able to trust anyone in my entire fucking life, except for my brother, and now I can't even trust *him*." She wiped savagely at her eyes with her forearm. "Why should you be any different?"

"Because I'm fixin' to save both our asses. I told you I've got my own crap to deal with, but here I am, making you a priority. So you can zip that shit up, I can't do anything about your tears right now."

"*Fine!*"

Beyond her, Floyd spotted a tiny dot of blood on the old wallpaper next to the window, and he understood what a fruitless endeavor this was, wiping up gore with under-the-counter cleansers and a wad of Bounty towels. Especially that crimson flood in the carpet, there was no way they had any chance of wiping it away completely, no way it would stand up to any kind of investigation, were that to happen. Resigned, he stood up anyway, walked to the wall, wetted a finger with his tongue, and wiped the dot away, scanning for others.

Tessa blew more hair from her forehead as he went over to her. Staring at the red smear, she put voice to his thoughts, "This shit is never gonna come up."

"I know." Floyd touched her shoulder as if to apologize.

"Well, then, why am I—?"

"We're gonna have to tear the carpet completely away, make it look like, I don't know, like I scraped a hunk of furniture across it too hard."

It was at that moment that someone rapped sharply at the door.

SIX
TESSA RAE JAYNE

Tessa froze in place, watching the shadow of a man's baseball-capped head move across the window curtains.

"Floyd, man, you okay in there?" The man's voice had an easy Texas twang, but it was underlaid with concern.

She watched the muscles of Floyd's jaw tense before he answered.

"That you, Henry?"

"Not sure who *else* it would be." Henry let loose with a dwindling chortle.

"Oh, sure man!" Floyd called, his voice easy. "I just got my ol' friend here, down from Dallas. Surprise visit." He shrugged in Tessa's direction. "I'll introduce you a little later, if you like. We're just catching up right now."

There was a pause. Then:

"Who was that fella makin' all the noise?"

Floyd's eyes closed. "Fella?"

"Big fella, the one pounding on your door."

Tessa watched Floyd wince. "Oh, *that* guy," he called. "Yeah, Tess here had a little trouble with him at the diner . . . Hey, hold on a sec, I'll be right there."

But Floyd seemed incapable of movement. Plastic-wrapped Perkins lay directly at his feet, and he was staring at the dead man, poised, like he was ready to do something, *anything*, but couldn't commit. And suddenly the weight of the moment collided with Tessa, too. She felt it like a full-body slam, the same way she'd felt just days ago when Uncle Johnny told her they were after her, that they knew exactly what the fuck she'd done. That same adrenaline bomb, that live-wire kick to the belly.

She fell to her buttcheek for a moment, then sprang awkwardly to her feet. She calculated the vantage Henry would have if she were to open the door.

"*I got this,*" she whispered, hot. "*Can you pull him closer to the couch?*"

Floyd swallowed audibly and did what she said, hauling the bulky corpse along the carpet until it was farther out of sight.

When it came to it, Tessa knew how to use her body. She wasn't above taking advantage of her assets. Even before she'd hit her teens back in Decatur, she'd learned she could catch a boy's eye by simply walking a certain way. She could dominate a boy's attention by cocking her hip in the right clothes. Yeah, she understood the power she could wield, had in fact honed it over the years. She'd made mistakes early on, had let them fuck her too soon, had relinquished that power at times— and she'd come to regret those episodes. But she always learned from them. Got smarter. Understood how to take aim and not waver.

She flung off Floyd's ballcap, let it fly into the bedroom. Then she whisked off her halter in a fluid motion, leaving her in the stretch pants and her sheer white bra, the no-wire plunger that already had a long track record of driving 'em crazy. Hell, the only reason she'd bought it in the first place was to give a boy the bug eyes, that was Pete at the movie theater, and it had been on a bet. Pete had a long-term girlfriend, since high school, and Angela had wagered that Tessa couldn't break them up. Mission accomplished in one fucking night.

Tessa adjusted her tits carefully and wiped her face of perspiration, put on the right expression. Glanced at Floyd, who was glaring at her in both confusion and appreciation.

"What are you doin'?"

She looked away before he could say anything back.

Opened the door, all smiles.

Henry was a crevice-faced codger, probably in his sixties but looked like seventies, dust-lined and ravaged by the desert, inside and out. His gnarled hands dangled out of the cuffs of a starched white shirt, and his knuckles were bulbously arthritic and dry, the nails gray. His baby-blues were the only moist thing about him, and they opened in surprise when he saw her. He stepped back a bit, nearly to the asphalt. His denim hat had a large, faded U.S. flag stitched on it.

"Hey there, you must be Henry!"

A stunned pause.

"We-ell—!" Henry stuttered.

"I'm Tessa," she said, fake-bright.

"I . . . I . . . well, hello, little lady!"

"Floyd told me this is your place!"

"I sure didn't mean to interrupt anything."

She gave him a big dismissive gesture, emphasizing boob jostle.

"Listen, I'm sorry about all the noise. That awful man who was making all that racket? He gave me a pinch down at the diner, and I just won't stand for that, so I gave him a piece of my mind. He followed me here and let off some steam, but he's gone now."

Henry shook his head, laughed dryly. "Boys will be boys." He swiveled his eyes up and down her. "But ain't you a sight for sore eyes!"

"Oh gosh, this?" Tessa glanced down at her outfit, twisted herself, faux embarrassed. "This is nothing."

"You'll turn heads around here, I can tell ya that." He made a clucking sound with his dry tongue. "Only pretty ladies we see around here are passin' through."

"Oh, I'm doin' that, for sure, but I had to stop and say hello to Floyd."

"He's a lucky man."

"Now you're making me embarrassed," she said, strategically covering herself so that she wasn't really covering herself but in fact showing off.

Beneath his arid exterior, Henry was blushing—and he knew she knew it. She had him in her fist as surely as any boy whose balls she'd squeezed through high school. She'd taken away any swagger he might've had when he knocked on this door. Henry cleared his throat, a dry rasp, and looked down at his feet, seemed to shake himself from a reverie.

"You tell Floyd I'm sure sorry I disturbed you two." He began to turn away.

"Hey Henry?" she said, leaning against the door and cocking her head forward in a near-whisper.

"Uh huh?"

"You think I could come by for some extra towels after a while? We're fixin' to get ourselves wet in here."

He got even redder. "Hell, I could bring some over."

"That's all right, I need to get a little sun anyway. I'll be around in a few minutes."

"You got it, little lady."

Henry ambled off, down the crooked sidewalk, toward the office. He raised a hand over his head in a backward wave.

Tessa closed the door.

Floyd was still kneeling next to Perkins' corpse. He brought both hands to his face and rubbed his eyes vigorously.

"Boy, you're somethin'."

Tessa nodded. "I know it."

She found she was breathing in a heavy rhythm, as if her body had unconsciously shifted into panic mode beneath her surface. Her hands were trembling, and she clenched them to hide it. Now that the door was closed and she was slumped against it, the fear tumbled through her. She consciously took over and kept breathing evenly through her nose, forced her muscles to stop shivering. She'd been in dicey situations before; she knew how to deal with them. It was a matter of sheer will.

"You're good," Floyd said. "I gotta hand it to you. Thought we were done for."

"Get me cup of water?" she said.

"Sure."

Floyd hopped up, went for the kitchenette. She felt his eyes on her the whole way.

"You all right?" he asked. His voice sounded far away.

She nodded.

Tessa felt control coming back. Her pulse calmed, and the cold sweat at her scalp became less prickly. She took a deep breath, her eyes wandering from the corpse to Floyd at the sink to a couple of blood droplets that she hadn't wiped up yet. Even as confidence returned, she felt a new understanding of the gravity of the situation.

"Hey, uh, listen," she said. "I'm sorry, okay? I'm sorry."

Her words were met with silence while the sink faucet ran. She could hear pipes groaning somewhere behind the walls. Finally, Floyd shut off the water and came back to her. She accepted the white cup with a steady hand and took a long, slow drink.

"Sorry for what?" Floyd said.

"Bringing this—" She jutted her chin contemptuously toward Perkins. "—this pile of trash into your life."

Floyd went to the window and peered out. He let the curtain fall, then went to the ratty sofa and perched on the arm.

"Wasn't your fault."

"Of course it was!" She pushed away from the door, better now. She placed the cup on the window ledge and shook her hands out, ridding herself of residual nerves. "In any other, whatever, potential timeline of my life, any other trajectory, I'm on the Gulf somewhere right now sipping rum on a beach, and Perkins is being tortured by the fuckin' narcos down there for being the stupid fat American that he is."

Floyd was already shaking his head. "No, in every other alternate timeline, he catches up to you in Mexico and quietly takes you out, Tess, and you know it. That, or he drags you back."

"You think I'd let that happen?" Staring him down.

"You think you'd have a choice?"

Tessa didn't answer him. She bit at her thumbnail, staring unfocused in the direction of Perkins' corpse. She'd always looked upon the sweaty man as a fool, a fucking Costello blundering into any situation, and now she had to come to terms with the fact that he had actually been here to kill her, to *murder* her, if it had come to that. He had been dead serious, obviously on someone's orders, and that someone had to be Harlan— who else? Behind his tattoos and his piercings, Harlan Eckhart had a gaze that could slice right through her, it was true, but before she'd burned his house she'd considered that gaze essentially harmless—just another primitive boy stare.

"Are you even armed?" Floyd said.

"No."

"Listen, Tess, forget about it, okay? Shit happens, right? We've got a handle on it."

"This isn't your problem," she said, shaking her head.

"Hey, I'm gonna help you. Okay?" He shoved at her a little. "I've got a knack for seeing the good in people, and in your case it ain't just the booty. Get over it."

She gnawed on her lower lip. "I just want you to know . . . I never expected to get all tangled up with you and then have this . . . this fat bastard die in your room."

"I know that."

"I didn't *orchestrate* this or anything."

Floyd was smiling at her.

"What?" she said.

"You're hot when you're embarrassed."

"I'm not *embarrassed*."

"Your face is all red."

"Fuck you." She smiled at him but felt unbidden tears coming.

"Let's get this guy taken care of. I have an idea—as long as you don't mind flirtin' with ol' Henry some more."

"What is it?"

While he explained what he had in mind, she covertly wiped the moisture from her eyes. And when he was done, she jumped toward him, abruptly took him in her arms. Startled, he was stiff-backed for a moment, then he returned the embrace, and soon they were kissing, and it didn't even feel weird, getting hot and bothered directly above Perkins' cooling corpse. In fact, it felt the opposite. Even back home, she didn't really have anyone on her side anymore—besides Uncle Johnny, anyway. It seemed as if all her friends had dropped away over the years, like they were never really friends at all. When the shit began hitting the fan with Terrell, there'd been *no one* to turn to. They'd all wanted no part of it, and Tessa had kicked herself for ever thinking they'd be there for her.

She wiped her lips when she pulled away from Floyd. She retrieved her halter and slipped back into it, conscious of her nipples standing up like stingers.

He was still watching her closely, and there were questions in his eyes. He seemed on the edge of giving voice to them, then stopped.

"You ready?" he said instead.

She slow-nodded. "Fuck yeah." She grabbed hold of Floyd's crotch with an eager hand.

Outside, the skies were cobalt and the morning humidity was giving way to an unrelenting heat—a heat that had followed her southwest throughout the massive, empty geography of Texas. Most of the state had felt abandoned as she'd sped through it, and Malvado was the inevitable endpoint of that emptiness. The town was so quiet that it felt part of another world. Just as that thought wisped through her, she heard yet another big rig rumbling down the highway, and then it was fading away like thunder.

Henry's office was at the south end of the L-shaped property, and it had a big picture window that looked out on all dozen-or-so units. She felt him watching her already, so she put a little bounce in her step, pushed her tits out. She tried on a mischievous smile as she came to the entrance.

"Knock knock!" she called through the screen door.

"Come on in, little lady!"

She entered the small, dim room and let her eyes adjust to the shadows. The whole room smelled like Henry's sweaty baseball cap mixed with a weirdly earthy mint scent. A rotating fan was groaning and blowing fetid air across loose papers. And then she saw the source of the mint—an open wintergreen Skoal disc sitting half-empty on top of a ratty phone book that looked about thirty years old. Henry had heaved himself out of a '70s-era cracked-vinyl office chair and was stepping around an equally ancient metal desk. He was all smiles, revealing the fresh chew, and his eyes were locked on her breasts. Tessa put on a big goofy smile.

"Aren't you a sweetie!" she gushed.

"Floyd's a lucky man," he said again. He put his hands on his hips, and his lips twisted like rubber around the tobacco.

"We have fun."

"Appears so!"

"Oh, go on." All bashful.

"So you need some towels?"

"If you've got any to spare."

"I think we can round up a few." He about-faced and went for the peeling wood-panel door behind the desk, pushed it half open. "You just hang tight, and I'll—"

"Is that where you *live?*"

Henry cast a glance back at her and cocked a grin. "It ain't nothin' fancy."

"Ooooh, can I have a peek?"

He paused, gave her a curious glance, and she knew she'd gone too far.

"You'd find it awfully disappointing," he said.

"I doubt that." Flapping a hand at him. "I'm sorry, I'm just naturally curious. It's gotten me in trouble more than a few times. My daddy always said curiosity killed the cat, and he said I was lucky cats had nine lives. Anyway, don't mind me, I'll wait here."

There was a moment when ol' Henry's eyes flickered—an acknowledgment that the situation might be turning into something far different from what he'd expected at first. A tremor went through his eyebrows, and he straightened up. Tessa stood there, hip cocked, waiting for him, watching his rheumy eyes register the low-voltage shock, and then he shrugged like it was no big deal.

"Ain't no problem, little lady, come on back!"

"Really?"

"Well, sure. You can meet Betsy."

"Betsy?" Tess blurted, not sure if she was going to be able to handle keeping *two* people away from the window. "Is Betsy your wife?"

"Oh heck no, I lost my wife almost two decades ago. She never knew Betsy."

Tessa squeezed behind the desk and through the narrow door into a small vestibule, following Henry, who trailed that heavy mint scent along with an undercurrent of musty sweat. Inside a small room between the office and the living quarters was an array of tin shelves holding towels and tiny bathroom bottles and plastic cups and extra pillows and ash trays and coffee cups and all manner of cleaning supplies. On impulse, with Henry's back to her, she grabbed a handful of tiny soaps as she passed through.

And then she was in a cramped two-room hovel—a narrow kitchen that appeared to lead into a bedroom-slash-living-area. Immediately Tessa smelled dog, and it was clear who Betsy was. At the thought, she heard a low, lazy, ululating *wooooof.*

"Betsy's my hound."

As Tessa's eyes adjusted to the dimness, she discerned a lumbering shape approaching her from the next room. It reached her and nudged her knee with slobbery jowls. She petted its greasy head. The dog must've been ten years old and reaching its end.

"What a cutie!" she cried, repulsed.

"Well, she was once, at that."

"So this is your little place." She snuck a peripheral look to make sure the office window was out of view. "Cozy!"

"One word for it."

In the shadowed distance, a lumpy queen bed was unmade—in fact, hadn't appeared to have been made since before Tessa was a mass of cells in her mama's belly. The bed was a bare mattress with a ratty sheet and handmade quilt over it. It was pushed over into a corner, leaving space for a plain dresser, two drawers open and spilling. And there were old cardboard boxes all over the damn place, droopy and splayed open. Either ol' Henry was a hoarder or he was just dirt-poor, living out of boxes—despite owning a business. She'd always imagined that business owners must be inherently wealthy, even when they owned crappy motels that hardly anyone stayed at, but, shit, in a forgotten town like Malvado?

Christ, he's a dead man walking.

She was about to turn back to Henry, maybe ask for a soda or a deeper tour of the man's home—anything to give Floyd a few more minutes—when she caught sight of a small assemblage of framed photos on a little table to her right. A woman's face snagged her attention. It was a young woman that looked like Tessa in one startling way.

The woman was the same color.

"Who's this?" Tessa asked, gesturing.

"That's my Athena."

"You are *shittin'* me."

Tessa bent down to the photo in the front, a portrait of Athena, old-school, faded with age and humidity. The woman was about Tessa's age, fixed in amber, and although Tessa couldn't discern any other personal similarities other than skin tone, the photo had stopped her in her tracks. A big ol' laugh was turning Athena's mouth into a wide, toothy O—perfect white teeth!—and her hair was grown out into a well-tended afro. She had wayfarer shades on in this front photo, but in the others Tessa could see the coffee brown eyes, full of mirth and confidence.

"I took that picture on a bridge in Austin when we spent our honeymoon there," said ol' Henry behind her.

"You were married to a black woman?"

"That I was." He took off his hat and used its edge to scratch his forehead. "My chocolate bonbon. But the honeymoon was too short."

Tessa stood up straight. Her entire conception of Henry—admittedly a first impression—had done an about-face.

"What happened?"

"Breast cancer, yep."

"Oh, Henry, I'm so sorry."

"You know, that was all so long ago that it feels like a different life."

His eyes were lingering on the dusty clutch of photos as if he hadn't laid eyes on them in years. "She was somethin'."

"How on earth did you two meet?"

"Malvado used to be a *town*, young lady, can you believe it?" He picked up the picture frame, dusted it with a polyester-sleeved forearm. His voice was a slow, soothing drawl. "Used to be honest-to-god people living here. They'd put on dances down at the barn, before it fell into ruin. Athena showed up there, one miracle of an evening. She was passin' through, on her way to who knows where. We hit it off over some coconut pie, as I recall." Henry's old baby-blues glistened with nostalgia. "She was co-owner of this here motel, for a short while. That was much later, a' course."

Tessa stared at Henry wordlessly for a long moment.

"Did you ever . . . I don't know, did you ever meet her folks?"

"Didn't have any. At least, none that she acknowledged anymore."

"Did she ever meet yours?"

"We were alike that way, little lady."

"You don't have any family?"

"End of the line."

He didn't appear sad about that, but the way he chopped off the end of the sentence, the cold finality of it, brought a little lump to Tessa's throat. All she could do was nod and touch Henry's arm with her fingers.

SEVEN
FLOYD TILLMAN WEATHERS

"You ready?"

Tessa nodded. "Fuck yeah."

Floyd watched her fling the door open and go about her task. He shut the door behind her, keeping an eye on her ass for the *third* time that morning. She cast one frisky look back his way—she knew he was watching, oh yeah—and then she was approaching Henry's office. The old man responded to her verbal *knock knock*, and she disappeared inside, and Floyd was in business.

Predictably, Perkins weighed a metric ton. Floyd's past months of early-morning prison-style pushups and dumbbells every evening would apparently pay off. He dragged the wrapped body to the door, grimacing at the feel of the big flabby arms as the corpse twisted along the floor. He got to the open door, gave a quick look outside, both ways, and then hauled Perkins out onto the sidewalk.

Floyd knew the third unit from the end—number 9—had a wonky door lock. Henry had complained about it a few times since Floyd had taken up residence, in that dismissive way he had, throwing his gnarled hands in the air, but it didn't bother the man enough to get off his ass and repair it. The motel averaged about three residents a week, and Henry never had a reason to rent out that room, so he just let it sit. It sat there gathering dust and occasionally supplies or broken furniture. It was little more than a storage room.

Floyd dragged Perkins straight to it, jimmied the door open the way he'd seen Henry do it, and pulled Perkins in. He shut the door and panted, feeling his muscles burn. The room looked exactly like his—the heavy orange curtains, the throwback kitchenette that reminded him of old-school Vegas for some reason. He took a moment to recover, then got back to it, yanking Perkins toward the closet in a series of grunting heaves.

"Jesus Christ, ya fat fuck!" he yelled into the musty confines of the humid room.

After taking a moment to catch his breath, he grasped the edge of the shower curtain and began rolling Perkins out of it. After a gasping eternity, the large man flopped out onto the carpet, on his back, his flat dead gaze aimed in Floyd's direction, almost accusingly.

"Yeah, same to you, you dick."

Floyd stood straight and brushed himself off, and as he caught his breath he flipped on the overhead light and gathered up the shower curtain. He would need to dispose of it the right way. It was covered with his prints. He hurried to the bathroom and, without touching anything else, carefully removed the pristine shower curtain from its pole. He'd attach this fresh one to his own shower, and no one would be the wiser.

He strode back through the silent room, delivered a final swift kick to Perkins' midsection, and used his shirt to polish the doorknob of any prints. He let himself back out onto the sidewalk. After a quick glance around and particularly toward the office, which appeared still empty, he set the door back into place. He quickly wiped the outer door handle, then walked casually back toward his room carrying two shower curtains, one of them folded carefully to contain any blood.

Floyd slipped quickly into his room and dropped the curtains into his tub. Then he went back out to the sidewalk, closed his door, and went straight to Perkins' pickup. He climbed aboard, stared at Henry's office window for a few seconds, and then cranked the ignition. He pulled out of the space and swung around to the north of the building, ultimately settling against a curb fronting a vacant lot a block away. He locked up the cab and hustled back to the motel, firing up a cigarette along the way.

When he got back to his room, he stopped short of the door, turned, and sat down on the curb, stretching out his legs.

"Shit," he murmured, breathing heavily.

Obviously, it was time to leave this place.

He judged it could be days if not weeks before Henry found the body in room 9, probably because of the stench, and even then it could be a while before they connected the body to Floyd—if ever. The important thing was that it would buy him time. Enough time to get the fuck out of this hellhole and set up somewhere else for a while. Shit, maybe there was *some way* to take Tess down into Mexico after all. Do it right. Do it carefully.

At some point, Philip was gonna call him on the burner and tell him everything was clear, and at that point if Floyd wasn't back in Little Rock with the money within a day or two, he'd be in about the same boat Tess was in right now: They'd come after him, and it wouldn't be because they were worried about him. They'd come after him, and they'd come after his family—his dad probably ensconced his lounger watching a game, his mom folding laundry or putting together one of her nature puzzles, still sequestered in the little home where he grew up, yeah they'd still be holed up in there, long after the vaccines, long after the stupid plague was in the past.

Jesus, the plague.

It had all felt like a reckoning from on high—God himself spiting his world and watching his creation react like the petty turds they'd already proven themselves to be. Floyd imagined God up there in the clouds, chuckling as he popped tequila shooters and watched the disasters unfold.

And sanity *still* had not been restored. Not completely.

There was no denying that *that* was one of the reasons Floyd had taken the opportunity and roared screaming to the border, the very bottom of the nation he once loved. To squat there and wait everything out. Hoping everything turned out okay, though he'd kinda doubted it. He'd been loitering here on the edge of nowhere as much for the country to calm the fuck down as he was for Philip's call.

Floyd blew out a nicotine sigh.

A block over, he spotted a familiar truck moseying north along the business route. It was Eduardo in his spray-painted pickup. He was the owner of the corner grocery at the far end of 1st Street, the one with the United States flag whipping proudly next to the Mexican one. Shelves stocked with candy bars and religious doodads and sugar skulls. Dude was always blaring mariachi shit out of his radio, and Floyd loved him for it. The faded bandana Eduardo wore around his neck, the wet eyes, the neatly combed thinning hair. He was always laughing, that deep belly laugh, like *ahhh-hyeh-hyeh-HYEHHHH!*

Shit, man, he was gonna miss that guy. It wasn't as if Floyd had made himself any kind of fixture in town. Quite the opposite. But a man couldn't help but immerse himself in the environment.

The truck disappeared beyond the old post office, into the mostly abandoned neighborhood there. Eduardo was probably on his way to his home to attend to one of his many children who sometimes pitched in at the grocery, outside school hours.

As deadened as Malvado was, there was still a semblance of life here. It was desperate and tenuous, sure, but it also showcased the best of the country—patriotic, free, diverse, and always with a stark understanding of the significance of those things. The contrast lay blatant on the other side of a fence, mere miles away.

Just as Floyd finished up his cigarette and let it fly onto the ancient asphalt, he heard voices to his right, and there were Tess and Henry exiting the office. Tess had a couple of neatly folded threadbare towels in her arms, and Henry closed the office door behind him, watching Tess's ass as he followed behind her. Floyd didn't blame him.

And here came the gal that was gonna detonate everything.

Floyd hadn't seen *that* coming, despite the impression she'd made on him the night before. He'd fully acknowledged that the silly girl would briefly rock his world, but the way he'd envisioned the morning was a fresh exchange of fluids and an appreciative wave goodbye, thanks for dropping briefly into my life—*so long!* And then dreaming about her into an uncertain future, wondering whatever became of Tessa Rae Jayne, that fetching filly who thrilled him one night—and one morning—down in the underbelly of the U.S.A.

It wasn't gonna work out that way. No, in the immortal words of Lou Reed, Floyd was fixin' to take a walk on the wild side.

As Tessa drew closer, he could see that she had a determined look on her face that recognized the same thing. Sometimes the gal was inscrutable, and he liked that about her. He appreciated a woman with some mystery to her. There was an ugly death in their immediate past, and here they were smirkin' at each other. Hell, that was enough for him to drive her all day in any direction she wanted.

There was a little quote he'd written on a postcard he'd picked up in Dallas on the way down here, off a wobbly rack at a gas station. It was from an old samurai text. The saying went, *There's surely nothing other than the single purpose of the present moment. A man's whole life is a succession of moment after moment. If one fully understands the present moment, there's nothing else to do and nothing else to pursue.*

The postcard had been pinned to the wall at his bedside for weeks, next to some of his favorite Bukowski, and he didn't think he'd really understood it until this moment.

But at some point—some point soon—he was gonna need a few more answers.

"You didn't tell me Henry here was so interestin'."

Floyd nodded at Henry. "Hell, he never told *me* that."

Behind Tess, under the partial shade of the overhang, Henry was smiling in a way that Floyd had never seen him do. His whole damn face was lit up as if Tess had just helped him get his rocks off.

"You oughtta actually talk to him some time."

"Aw, Henry and I talk all the time, ain't that right, Henry?"

Henry nodded. "That's so."

"We've had an agreement in place for weeks."

"And what's that?" Tess said.

"Well, that's between me and Henry."

"Sheesh, that's just like men, ain't it?"

Tess sat next to Floyd on the curb, towels neatly pressed between breasts and bare thighs. She let her body fall against him, and she kissed his stubbly cheek.

Behind them, Henry registered the disappearance of the truck. "Hey . . . did that fella come back?"

Floyd paused.

"Oh, yeah," going for casual, "he took off, tail between his legs."

"Good riddance to bad rubbish, then," the old man said.

"Hope he stays away for good," Tessa said. "Henry, I'm so sorry that asshole followed me here."

"I'll tell you what, sweetheart," Henry said, removing his sweaty ball-cap and slapping in against his leg, as if to smack the dust off it, "men are no damn good."

"Present company excepted," she said.

Floyd stood up. "Henry, looks like Tessa here wants to go on a hike somewhere. We're gonna pack up some food from the diner and go see the sights."

"Ya can't beat this place for its tourist spots." Henry had suddenly gone all snarky.

"She wants to check out the border fence, and then we might head down to Big Bend. My girl loves a good sunset, so we'll probably end up camping out there a night or two."

"I remember taking Athena out there one time," Henry said, mostly to Tessa.

Floyd had no idea what (or who) the fuck Henry was talking about. Catching sight of the bizarrely affectionate glance that flitted between the old man and Tessa, Floyd pondered the choices he'd made inside his own peculiar circumstances, and the opportunities he'd never explored, the connections he'd never forged here. He knew that life threw curveballs at you every second of a life. The way you forged your path in the face of that onslaught was as unique as a fingerprint. Sometimes it was a nice clean etching, with crystal clear edges, and sometimes it was an impatient smear. Often, you weren't even aware of the marks you were making.

As the sun reached its peak and then began its descent toward the evening, after they'd packed up, Floyd made a special point to leave an envelope for Henry on the kitchen counter full of c-notes. A packet full of thank-yous, or at least some hope that the old man he never really be-friended might see his way to misdirect any would-be pursuers.

Floyd would never be back here.

It was late afternoon when Floyd situated his black Camaro at the end of a sad street lined with abandoned sheds, facing the border fence. He cut the growling motor and heard Tessa pulling in behind him. Her own engine sliced away into silence, and in his rearview he watched her climb out, towing her bag with her. Girl had a glow to her, that was for sure. If nothing else, Floyd was looking forward to some exquisite nights.

Tess already knew this was the end of the line for the flashy Beetle. Turned out, the loss wasn't a big deal to her, even though the used car had apparently been a recent and shocking surprise from her brother— or so she said.

Floyd had spent fifteen minutes going over the VW, searching obvi-ous locations for tracking devices—to no avail. They didn't need two cars, anyway. Floyd figured the vehicle would make a fine decoy sitting here all by its lonesome at the border's razor edge. By all appearances, Tessa Rae Jayne would appear to have slipped out of the country in the dead of night, never to be seen again.

As she approached him, Floyd took another moment to acknowledge the precipice he was standing on. This was *so* far removed from Philip's instructions that were his boss to learn of it, Floyd would probably earn an immediate and horrific reprisal. His family? Gone. His own prospects anywhere in Arkansas, or the notion of continuing his climb within the network? Gone. And what bewildered Floyd was the swiftness with which he was abandoning principles that he'd clutched to himself just the day before—hell, even as he'd been buying his shit from Irene at the gas station mart.

Tess was swaying those hips, and that impish smile was on her lips, and there was nothing else he could do. They were together now. Was it an old weakness reinforcing itself, or was it a new strength taking hold?

"Hey good-lookin'," she said as she came up to him. "Wanna get cookin'?"

If there was any kind of warning in Tessa's tone, any kind of personal foreboding, it was lost on Floyd. His mind was lingering on a poem he'd read once—something about finding nirvanas of all shades and hues.

The particular grimy cul-de-sac in which he stood belied any lofty description, as did any number of desolate streets in Malvado. But once you took a higher-level view of a place, despite your reason for being there, and despite your state of mind and solitude . . . it started to get romanticized. After all these weeks, he felt as if the town had given him safe harbor, and he owed it for that.

He nodded. "Let's get out of here."

"Where we goin'?"

"I don't know." He glanced around, then gestured. "That way."

Pointing west.

EIGHT
TESSA RAE JAYNE

Nestled in Floyd's black Camaro, shotgun, Tessa gazed out the window and saw a scrawny gray horse nosing through wheat grass next to a rusty mailbox, and then a series of leaning sheds and ugly old motor homes and fucking fences *everywhere*—constant metaphors surrounding nearly every abandoned home, chainlink and chicken wire and picket, wrought iron, even a hideous barrier constructed out of PVC pipe, didn't matter as long as everything was contained to its borders. Every border delineated and protected.

A chicken fluttered in front of the car, but Floyd paid it no mind as he rumbled toward Malvado's limits. Tessa winced and cringed, looked back through the rear window, and as if on the wings of a miracle, the frenzied chicken emerged beyond the muffler intact and perturbed, a whirling dervish.

"Been down to Laredo?" Tessa said, breaking the silence since they'd left the Beetle.

"Yeah."

"When I was first thinkin' about it, you know, back in Illinois, I thought I'd cross the border there."

"Why there?"

She shrugged. "Liked the sound of it. Think I read a book about it once."

"I went down there one time, spent the better part of a day." Floyd fiddled with the radio dial, zeroing in on some honky-tonk amid the banda music and ballads. "Saw a couple of guys making a break for it across the Rio."

"No shit?"

"They were pretending to fish for a while, and when they saw their chance, they dove straight into the current. That's a hundred yards, darlin'. They made it, too, quarter mile downriver—at least, the two of them I saw crawl up onto the shore, all soaked and exhausted. And then straightaway taken into custody. That shit happens all the time."

"Guess they're pretty desperate."

"A lot of 'em get away with it."

"I'm sure."

Next to her, Floyd seemed to get wistful. "Ate some fucking great tacos down there. Place called Jaunita's. Jesus H. Christ."

"I could use some tacos."

"Well, way we're headed, we're more likely to find fish and fruit than tacos and tortas."

Tessa liked the way this man pronounced things. They joked some more about food—particularly Malvado's delicacies (or lack thereof)—until the conversation petered out. After that, she fidgeted in her seat, feeling Floyd's occasional glances.

The Camaro felt like a sparking tinderbox, full of rumbling and startling potential but also uncertainty. Her path had seemed so clear just yesterday, when she'd imagined herself streaking across a foreign land, no real *specifics* but definitely throwing herself into that atmosphere. And now with the double body-slams of Floyd and Perkins barricading that path, everything had changed.

They roared along the searing yellow road in silence for a long while, leaving Malvado in their dust. It felt like leaving behind an archeological relic, with nothing on the immediate horizon except further ruins. It would probably be hours before they found honest-to-god civilization again.

There was a ghostly part of her that was in Mexico right now, in some kind of alternate universe. She was in her Beetle, high-tailin' it toward Baja California or Los Mochis or Mazatlán along the endless winding roads that Uncle Johnny had told her about—the copper canyons of the Sierra Madre ("puts the Grand Canyon to shame") and the downtown Spanish colonial structures of Chihuahua, the laughing kids and colorful women that he spoke of with contagious nostalgia. The way her uncle's gravelly voice spoke of central Mexico's treasures was enough for her to imagine basking in them. A new life, a rebirth into something more primal, earthy, and real. In moments of clarity during her screaming jag southwest from Decatur, those secondhand images of Mexico had burst in her brain like the toy kaleidoscopes of her sheltered youth.

She watched Floyd in the driver's seat. He seemed to be lost in thought himself. She thought she could detect a little nervous movement in his fingers as he ran his big hands over the stubble on his chin. She supposed that had something to do with the mysterious duffel bag he'd placed carefully behind the rear seats. The man apparently had his own secrets. Didn't everybody?

But what was it, really, that she was feeling? It was more than his or her secrets, and it was more than last night's slippery sex, the memory of which was bringing occasional small smiles to her lips. No, what she was feeling was all tied up in who she was and what she'd thought she could be.

Truth was, her entire *existence* up to this point had been dominated by boys and men. Was it cliché to admit that? Sometimes it felt like the world was a great wall made up of gross men, lined up and leering at her. The moments when she felt the most strength in her young life—as a human, as a young woman—were when she managed to burst through that wall, either by lurching past the generational sexism of her late father, or taking out a lowlife at a bar, or saying "fuck you" to everything and setting fire to the world and raging south toward Mexico. Her hair flying in the wind, her voice screaming itself hoarse as she sang to some grrrl-power anthem on her USB stick. What did it say about her that just when she'd found the gumption to make the leap across the border, it was another man who'd not only caught her eye but pulled her back from the brink? This man, right here next to her in his bucket seat, lean-muscled and grizzled and contemplative.

Not to mention the arrival of one of the same old men from her past, huge and gross, literally standing in her path, raging with spittle and spite. Dead now, forever out of her life, but still looming large.

I mean, how typical.

But she was no murderer. Was she? Even with two corpses in her wake?

That predawn ride into Forsyth, she'd been half-drunk on cheap wine and yeah maybe a Vicodin swiped from her mom's bathroom cabinet. She'd felt warm and fucking *righteous*—and still did in the *memory* of it, of cruising toward the decrepit house her brother had pointed out to her a week earlier. *That's the one.* The look on his face, the morbid humiliation and shivery fear, like *was he gonna die a fucking snitch?* Crying and everything. Her little brother, large-boned center on the JV football squad, this wall of brown muscle reduced to tears as he inched down the Beetle's passenger seat a block away from the falling-apart tenement on the crummy side of godforsaken Forsyth, Illinois. At the time, she'd merely registered embarrassment for Terrell, no plan or anything, but she'd stored the location at the back of her head. Then came the morning she'd found her brother laid out in the front yard, unresponsive, jerking and trembling from the cold, eyes straining back into his skull, like a seizure . . . arms rigid in the air and legs folded, almost fetal.

Ahh, god.

Right then, as if predestined, the rest of her life had rolled out ahead of her, off into the unknown distance, off into Mexico (or not).

The dead grandma was never part of that destiny.

She blinked out of the turmoil in her brain. Everything was coming to the surface.

She realized Floyd was talking.

"—out west?"

"Huh?"

He glanced over at her curiously. "I said, do you know anyone out west?"

She shook her head, but then she remembered her Aunt Gloria, her dad's sister, whom Tessa hadn't seen since she was little. The woman lived in a bland neighborhood near Disneyland with yet another male asshole—a *big* enough asshole that Tessa's mom wanted nothing to do with her despite the occasional cards and $5 bills that came from Gloria during the holidays. Like, what use was a woman who let herself become attached to a man like that?

"No," she said, and he shut up.

The road came at them endlessly, relentlessly, and it was already fucking *hot.*

"What, you don't believe in AC?" she said.

"Hell, baby, that broke down years ago."

"Great." She fluttered her hand out the window. "I mean, that's great."

"You strike me as someone who can take the heat."

She started poking at the old-school radio in the dash. Tessa couldn't abide country twang for more than twenty seconds, when it would start digging needles into her ear canal. She plopped through an astonishing number of Spanish-language channels before landing on a grainy pop station and reluctantly left it there on some Beyoncé. She guessed she couldn't count on any Migos or even Wu Tang broadcasting on any frequencies in these parts. She noted that Floyd's radio deck had no USB input, and neither did it have a CD slot.

Whatever. She sighed and fell back into her seat.

"Sorry," she said, "I get cranky."

"You're allowed. But what the hell did you just put on my radio?"

She went aghast. "That's Queen B, man, that's Beya. That's 'Single Ladies'!"

"I have no idea what you're saying to me right now."

"Dude. Beyoncé!"

He took a moment to listen.

"So *this* is Beyoncé," he said.

She stared at him.

"Maybe we should've talked about this shit before I got in the car," she said.

"No doubt."

The edge of Tessa's mouth curled up, but she knew they were only avoiding the conversation he wanted to have. The conversation about the fat corpse at the motel, and every goddamn thing that had led to it. The whole story. *Her* story. She couldn't find her way into it, though. Or she wasn't ready for it. She felt it coming, though. He was gonna yank it out of her. Somehow. He'd ease into it, make it seem natural.

She decided to head him off.

"So what's in the bag?" Glancing at the back seat.

Floyd gave her a look, returned his eyes to the road, then gave her another look. Then he did the same thing again. The highway rolled beneath them as if they were speed-hovering over sandpaper.

"Four hundred and seventy thousand in cash."

She tried but failed to contain her shock.

"You're lying."

"Strike me down."

"Fuck you."

"Okay."

"There's almost *half a million dollars* back there?"

"Uh huh."

"Shit, man, we *should* be crossing the border. Or at least *you* should. Set up on the beach somewhere, kick back in a little shack. Live off the interest."

"It's not mine."

"Who cares?"

"I do."

She glanced back again, as if her gaze could penetrate the seats and see the old blue vinyl duffel she'd watched him shove back there.

"You stole that?"

"No."

"Where'd it come from?"

He looked at her again, like he was on the verge of telling her, and then he gave her the faintest of shrugs, like *Okay, you asked for it.*

"It's from a bank job in Little Rock, but I didn't have any part in the actual robbery. I'm the third and final link in a handoff chain to throw off the law." There was the faintest of catches in Floyd's throat, but she caught it. It was a tell. She knew *he* knew he shouldn't be telling her this. "The money stays with anonymous ol' me while the cops eventually find themselves at a dead end back home. Might take six months, a year, for things to calm down, and I just lay low, keep it safe, see? When I get the call, I bring the loot back real quiet-like. And for my trouble I get seven percent of it."

Tessa cleared her throat after she registered his words. "I knew you had a secret or two, but *daaaamn.*"

Floyd stretched his ropy-muscled arm out the window, his fingers buffeting the hot rush of air.

"It's a living," he said expansively. "A modest living, but a living."

Beyoncé on the radio had given way to warble-yodeling Christina Aguilera, and Tessa reached over and stabbed it off. She watched the flat landscape drift past. The Camaro was dashing along Route 90, doing seventy last she'd glanced at the analog speedometer, just a hair over the posted limit. *Keeping it cool,* Floyd had said.

Blond dirt and low, sloping, beaten-down hills fanned out into the infinite horizon to the east, punctuated by stunted scrub growth. To Tessa, the contours of the terrain sometimes looked like naked female curves, shifting as they passed—a sultry hip rising with the movement of a suntanned thigh. But then the scrub growth became more prominent, like scars. Narrow dirt roads meandered off to who-knew-where, up into the foothills, like stretchmarks across skin. And then the whole landscape distorted in her eyes, becoming pockmarked and old, stabbed with road signs and chicken-wire fences, gouged with gray roads. Maybe once it had been beautiful.

Civilization here was limited to the fringe—occasional single-pump gas stations dotting the open acres, and flat weathered homes right at the edge of the highway, tractors here and there, at the ends of half-plowed paths, doing nothing but rusting. From what Tessa had seen of this gargantuan state, this landscape was pretty typical, but there was a further desperation to it here, a wrung-out quality that spoke of dull tension, simmering resentment. She could glance to her left and see Mexico, kind of glorious, actually—its distant mountain ranges, colorful vistas beyond her reach, and in that moment everything around her seemed all one land, sensual again, if not for the demarcations she might see on a map. If not for, you know, mankind.

Her thoughts returned to the duffel bag full of cash behind the rear seats.

"It's still *stolen*," she said.

"Not by me."

"But you'll get part of it." She let her hand wander out her window, too, played with the wind. "You'll get some of the stolen money."

"After I earn it."

"That's some twisted logic, man." She watched her undulating hand. "Not exactly above board, is it?"

A smirk manifested itself above his blunt stubbled chin. "I'd hoped we were gonna start being honest with each other here."

"I didn't steal any money," she said.

"Neither did I."

The sizzling miles whisked by, and her mind wrestled with Floyd's story. She knew she was still in avoidance mode, so that in itself did some heavy synapse-navigating for her, but she did have a helpless curiosity about Floyd Weathers. If only because he was a magnificent distraction.

They traveled a half mile in silence before Tessa spoke again.

"So, Little Rock, huh? What is that, Arkansas?"

"Little Rock is in Arkansas, yes. In fact, it's the capital."

"That's where you're from?"

"Born in Texas, as I believe I mentioned last night, but yeah, Little Rock starting around middle school."

Tessa drew her hand away from the window and started playing with the fringe of her red blouse above the hem of her denim shorts she'd changed into. She felt herself growing more and more jumpy, didn't like how the occasional silences between them had started to hum with tension.

"What was it like?" she said, and the words felt stupid in her mouth. She winced privately.

"What was what like?"

She shrugged. "Little Rock."

He took a few moments to gear up, several expressions crossing his face. She couldn't read them. He poked the cigarette lighter and fished around in his pocket for his smokes, shook one out onto his lip.

"Lost my cherry under the bleachers at Central High School. To this day it's the best sex I ever had—and I mean no offense by that."

"You think when I asked about Little Rock, that *that's* the kind of thing I expected you to say?"

"Jennifer Kincaid, baby. Dirty Catholic girl." He laughed around the dangling cigarette, then shrugged. "That's the first thing that comes to mind about Little Rock."

"Must be a hell of a place."

"I don't know. The city itself? It's fucking hot and humid, like you walk out of the shade and it falls on you like a truck."

"I know what that's like."

"It's nothing like this here. Just miserable. We'd always end up at the river, we had a special spot on the Arky where we could hang out, skinny-dip at night, drink cheap beer, smoke cheap weed, anything for an escape, you know? We had a good crew there for a while. But it was a completely dead town, everyone wanted out. And they got out, too, like one at a time, disappeared into the ether, never heard from them again. There was this one guy, Pete McReady, he was on the varsity squad with me at Central, he was this big movie guy, and he found a way to copy DVDs, even the copy-protected ones, he was like this computer savant, and they were perfect copies. He taught himself to do the labels and cases and all that, right there in Central's fucking AV room!" Floyd let loose with some deep laughter. "And he made a business off pirating the things, made a fortune, right there in high school, never got in a whiff of trouble. He turned that into a legit business later, video processing or whatever, he's a millionaire now . . . ."

As he spoke, Floyd lit his cigarette and kept talking, opening himself up to her in a way she hadn't expected. Any other day in her life, she might have laughed at the discovery that a man like Floyd could suddenly become what Uncle Johnny used to call a raconteur, bloviating like he did, but Tessa found herself relaxing more deeply into her seat. She couldn't even say precisely why.

It was something about the honesty flowing from him, like liquid, like smoke—the ease with which it escaped him, so effortlessly after what had happened. It scared her, maybe because the notion of reciprocity was built into it.

She let him talk and talk about his old haunting grounds, until he was done.

And then it was just a matter of counting the seconds.

The first real question came about two hours into their journey— "*So . . . you ever gonna want to talk about what happened back there?*"—and by that time Tessa had already been through a regimen of nervous tics and stomach turns. She'd worked herself up to the question for a couple hours, and by the time it left his mouth, all she felt was tired. An almost tired relief. But that didn't mean she wanted to address it. Not at all.

She chewed her gum, watched him for a bit, returned her gaze to the endless lonesome road.

"How much farther to El Paso?"

"Another hour, I'd say."

Tessa shifted in her seat a few times, tried the radio again. She was just about to punch it off in frustration when she found an exuberant mariachi song at the end of the dial. She couldn't help but get caught up in it. It made her smile.

After a while, she undid her seatbelt, tossed her gum into the wind, and turned in her seat, facing him. Leaned over toward him. She kissed Floyd briefly, deeply, and began undoing his button fly. When she pulled away from his mouth, Floyd let go with a little grunt of surprise.

"What are you up to, Tessa Rae?"

"Just passin' the time."

She bent down toward his lap.

"Get fucked, Jennifer Kincaid," she said, devouring him.

He lasted about fourteen miles, according to the odometer.

NINE
FLOYD TILLMAN WEATHERS

Floyd couldn't exactly say why he'd blathered out his history to Tessa as if she were some kind of shrink, hypnotizing him and coaxing his life story out of him, but it probably had something to do with how much he needed to hear *her* story. He had to admit, though—talking had felt like the release of some rusted-shut water main. He felt as if he hadn't said a word to anyone in months.

It had mostly been innocuous stuff from back home that he'd gone on and on about. Yeah, he'd also come clean about the cash, despite the fact that Philip had told him that was verboten—like, in any situation—but the fact was, given the events that had transpired at the motel, he figured he could count on Tessa Rae Jayne now. She was a vault. They had an implicit understanding, see? He knew it, and she knew it, despite the fact they hadn't brought it up in words.

As they drew close to El Paso, the twisty exuberant road head was at least forty-five minutes in his past, and goddamn if the naughty episode hadn't altered his mood. There was a danger in that, the way Tess could wield her talents, both psychological and physical. He'd come to terms with the fact that she'd used her talented mouth to ward off any clumsy questions he might have, but that realization had occurred a full thirty minutes after his release.

I see what you did there.

El Paso appeared in fits and bursts—increased traffic, maintained roads, shouting billboards—and then it seemed they were enveloped by concrete, overpasses swirling and snaking above them like a bow-tied American dream of endless roads and revving motorcycles. Suddenly the Camaro was surrounded by fast food joints and stripmalls and motels and banks and car dealerships, and Floyd felt more anonymous here than in Malvado. He'd never been to El Paso before, and yet he'd set foot in this kind of town a hundred times across the country. Sometimes it was as if America was a fucking illusion.

"So this is El Paso," Tess murmured next to him.

They'd passed beneath another massive array of overpasses, and the downtown district had materialized on their left—a motley assemblage of earthy sandstone buildings hunkered down as if baking under the heat. Stately rows of streets made a beeline from the downtown area toward the sedimentary foothills beyond the center of commerce.

Tessa was all eyes, checking out the views as if she were entering a foreign land.

"In all its glory," he said.

He watched her watch the city, and he found himself cocking an eyebrow. For all Tessa's attempts at worldliness and confidence, there were times—like this one—when she was like a little kid. He realized he knew the outward Tessa a lot more than he knew the inner Tessa. Maybe that was a good thing, but damned if he wasn't gonna get inside there anyway.

"Is that a baseball stadium over there?"

"Oh yeah, that's new, I heard about that. George was talking about that at the bar."

"Who plays there?"

"The Chihuahuas."

"Ha!" She smiled, then looked over at him seriously. "You're kidding me."

"I'm not, that's the Padres' triple-A team—you know, minor league."

Tessa was getting restless again.

"Hey, man, get off this fucking highway, let's go look around."

A little kid.

Nevertheless, he couldn't see a *huge* downside to her idea. His ass was ready for a break, and his limbs could use a stretch.

And for much of the past three hours, he'd been thinking about how Perkins could have tracked Tess so *accurately*. He kept going back to the Beetle. Even though he'd checked out the vehicle's obvious places for a device and had come up empty, it had to be there somewhere. It *had* to. Floyd had taken extra time to go through all of Tess's things back at Henry's motel—much to her bickering dismay—and those had come up blank, too. It wasn't like they could just keep driving forever. They simply had to stay on guard. And *that* he could do.

Ten minutes later, Floyd was creeping the Camaro along a crumby boulevard of old brick buildings that appeared abandoned and in disrepair. For all the driving they'd done, they were still a stone's throw from

Mexico, and the edge of the nation seemed tattered here, still unsettled. If what George had told him was true, Pancho Villa himself wandered these streets and surrendered here. This area was like Ellis Island for Mexican immigrants, apparently. Politicians wanted to wipe away that history and make way for some kind of entertainment complex. Nobody cared anymore—or at least too few people for it to matter. Floyd found himself narrating these thoughts to Tess as she took in the crumbling edifices and leaning fences, but she didn't seem to be hearing him.

He parked the car in a relatively heavy-trafficked area in front of a funky little joint called the Jalisco Cafe. The restaurant stood out colorfully at the end of a row of outdoor-mall sameness, like a piece of ornately painted folk pottery, and he realized he was fucking starving. Making sure he'd be able to watch the Camaro from the restaurant's wrought-iron-barred windows, he heaved himself out of the car and stretched. Tucked his shirt back in. Gave a thought to the Beretta in the glove box, left it there.

Over enchiladas and tacos, they talked about ol' Henry and the body that lay in store for him.

"That wasn't nice of us," Tess said, mouth full of fried tortilla.

"He'll get over it."

"That dude's been getting over shit for decades."

"Yeah, some of us dwell, and some of us move on."

"You mean, like the people who want to bulldoze those old buildings out there?" She smiled around her food.

"Yeah, touché, smartass." He took a big bite of his enchilada.

"I'm just sayin'," she said, swallowing, "he didn't deserve that."

"You talked to the guy for all of ten minutes, and you think you have the measure of him. It doesn't work that way." He wiped his mouth. "People are more than the . . . the tragedies or the mistakes of their life that can be summed up over coffee or whatever. What matters is how they deal with it, how they come out on the other side."

"The way you talk, it's like those things don't matter."

"Of course they matter." He took a swallow of iced tea. "They're just not *all* the matters."

She took another bite of taco and watched him. It was like she was studying him. Taking his measure. Her eyes were so brown and deep that he could easily get lost in them—in fact, probably already *was* lost in them—but increasingly Floyd saw something else in there. Some kinda deep smarts. She was a contradiction, maybe. On the surface, a young fun-loving blonde-like black girl, but underneath, a whipsmart and clever would-be player. Was she playing him? Even a little? That delicious move in the car had been something of a tactic, for sure.

Her gaze relented. "Well, I feed bad."

"Perkins wasn't your fault."

"Oh yeah he was."

A pretty but harried Hispanic waitress came to fill up their waters and check on them. Tessa put on a big smile and chatted with her for a minute, complimenting the food and the décor. As soon as the now-smiling woman turned heel, Tessa went back to serious mode.

"I mean, what are you talking about? The only reason Perkins was in that motel room was me."

"Damn, girl, you can really turn it on and off."

"What?" Hands into fists on either side of her plate.

"Like you say, I'm just sayin'."

"Pffff." She shook her head in frustration, lowered her voice to a hot whisper. "We shoulda taken that fat bastard out to the desert, buried him somewhere."

"We'd *still* be shoveling dirt for that fool, and there'd probably be a border copter or a drone watching us."

Tessa bent to her food and picked at it with longish nails. When she glanced up again, Floyd noticed moisture in her eyes.

"It's gotta stop," she said. "Somehow."

"What's gotta stop?"

"What I started."

He nodded. "You wanna talk about it now?"

"Not here I don't." She sniffed, shook out her hands, then ate some more taco.

She was volatile, she was. She wanted to be tough, but she had this soft, vulnerable underbelly that she was letting him get a peek at every once in a while. He finished eating before she did, and as she chewed and watched the traffic drift by outside the window, he sat back and considered her. The girl was a unique beauty, and he generally liked the way she comported herself. He got the strong notion that she was a standup person. Young, sure, that was all too clear sometimes. But she wasn't irrevocably damaged, like a lot of the women who'd passed through his life. Shit had befallen her, a lot more than just what'd happened at Henry's place, but she was—at least so far—staying above it. Give her some more time, and she'd probably slip under, like the rest, but so far, she was hanging tough.

Plus, obviously there was something about her that had dragged his ass out of his exile—and that was no mean feat.

Floyd paid for the early dinner with one of the bills he'd peeled off a brick in the duffel. He'd already dropped two of them to placate ol' Henry, and he was sure that wasn't the last of the money he'd be poaching. Thinking about that gave Floyd a queasy feeling. Or maybe it was just the enchilada. But skimming advances like that was goddamn dangerous, and irresponsible, and stupid, and it was something else Philip had strenuously warned him about, and he knew it all too well, and yet here he was.

For a girl.

A girl he didn't really know at all.

Back on the interstate, Floyd was tight-lipped as he motored the Camaro west. To compensate for his relative silence, Tess got silly, drumming the cracked-vinyl dash and singing along to some of the horrendous techno-pop she'd found in the center of the El Paso FM dial. Floyd watched the twitching muscles of her thighs with an odd mixture of annoyance and desire. The contradiction *itself* irritated him. It was a battle between logic and lust, and the understanding that he was helpless against the engorgement of his baser urges—to the detriment of his own safety, potentially his own *existence*—left him feeling edgy and stupid.

For months, he'd had the seared-retina image of a glaring Philip Crouch burned into his brain, and now that image was being crowded out by the day-old memory of Tessa's cinnamon labia flared and trembling before his hungry mouth. And it was more than the sex, of course— it was her vitality that thrummed up something in his veins. He'd promised the Little Rock crew that he was strong and steadfast in his duty, he'd convinced them with his bearing and his confidence. And then the one time he was faced with temptation, he'd failed. The woman had him by the dick.

Or did she?

It was true that he'd fallen for this girl, he could admit that, sure. He'd fallen quick, and he'd fallen hard. Did that mean he had suddenly betrayed his entire task? Had he automatically gone rogue?

Maybe he was rationalizing, but he didn't think so. He was still very much in control of his destiny. It was his strong intention to finish the task that had been assigned to him and—when he was inevitably called home—return with the cash triumphant and protect his family. The prodigal son. Returning to a family who had no clue about the precipice they'd skirted. But he'd get it done. Philip had never said Floyd had to go the whole thing *alone*. Floyd wasn't some miserable ascetic monk confined to lonely contemplation of his navel and the Bukowski poems he'd tacked on the wall. It was perfectly reasonable for him to live a (quiet) life.

"So where you takin' me?" Tessa asked when the music started to crackle with static. She poked the radio off.

Floyd took a breath, shook himself out of his thoughts.

"Figured we'd just drive till there's no more road."

"Sounds far."

"Probably won't be far enough."

"From what?"

"Whoever's after you."

He felt her gaze on the side of his face, and even without looking at her he could sense the attitude behind her eyes. She wasn't acknowledging the severity of the danger she was in. Whether because of youth, or denial, or plain stupidity (Floyd knew it couldn't be that), she had let the whole dead-Perkins affair slough off her back with a shrug. It made him wonder what *else* she was dismissing as trivial.

"Ain't no one after me no more," she said, for some reason emphasizing her blackness.

"I'm telling you—you're wrong."

"And even if they *are* still after me, just look at how fuckin' incompetent they are."

"The next one might not be so incompetent."

"Ha! Or they might be *more* incompetent."

"You can't be counting on that."

"You don't know these people."

"Well, I know *people*," he said, "and the truth is, for every three or four idiot blowhards like Perkins back at the motel, there's one bastard that knows just enough to sting your ass. Whether it's a week or a month or a year, they're gonna catch up to you."

"Then this crew is a fucking *anomaly*, man." She turned away and watched the lack of scenery go by. "Retards up and down the line."

That seemed about all she wanted to say on the subject, and Floyd wasn't going to press the issue. Tess would open up to him in time. She'd already shown a willingness in the café earlier. It was just a matter of patience. And in the meantime, he could reflect on his own failings.

They drove for several miles in silence, until Tess broke the spell.

"Shit, man, I really liked that car."

"Yeah?"

"My brother helped me buy it."

He had to tread cautiously. "This is the same brother who . . . ?"

"Uh huh, Terrell, he's my only sibling."

"Older or younger?"

"Little bro."

"What, did he cosign for you, or what?"

"We didn't go through no bank, man." She gave him a look, like *What planet are you from?* "He was doing some work for these people, *different* people, and he was saving up cash on the side, never told me it was for the car. See, it was Lori who was selling it, she was going off to Pittsburgh for college. She was Pete's sister. Pete was on Terrell's football crew from high school. I needed a couple grand on top of what I'd saved up, and I was whining all the time about it, and he'd get all up in my shit about it, like *stop cryin' about it, ya fuckin' whiner*, but what he was *really* doing—"

Her voice clipped off.

"Aw, man, you got me talkin'." She pulled her sunglasses down from the top of her head, fixed 'em on the bridge of her nose.

"Sounds like a standup guy," Floyd said.

"I'm not gonna see that car again, am I?"

He bit at his cheek for a bit. "It's possible. I mean, anything's possible."

"Yeah, right."

"You'd be surprised how seldom shit happens in a place like Malvado." A piece of gravel pinged off the windshield as he passed a tanker labeled FLAMMABLE. "It's like all the oxygen in the place is taken up by what-ever's going on at the border. Could be, your car is safer where it is than it's ever been."

That didn't seem to placate Tessa.

"Well," she said vaguely.

And that was it for a long while.

Floyd pushed the Camaro out into the great wide open, and the hori-zon—straight ahead—faded into brilliant, simmering fire. New Mexico was a monotonous straight line cut through throbbing desert, the road knifing across the contours of the land itself, while above them the stars began to sear through the firmament. Floyd realized that it had been months, even years, since he'd felt this measure of freedom, as if he'd con-sciously taken an increasingly narrow path toward self-seclusion. He sup-posed he needed an actual psychologist to get at the core of that.

For now, he considered the road, and the sky, and the lovely burnt-sienna creature sprawled out next to him in her torn denim shorts and her crimson top. She'd pushed the seat back to relax, arms crossed be-hind her fetching head, but her eyes were open and watching him. She gave him an enigmatic smile, and at that moment he knew he could live a life like this. On the road with Tessa Rae Jayne, three or four steps ahead of their mutual pasts, existing on the edge. There was a fragile purity to the notion, and he knew it could easily break apart in his grasp.

But he would savor it for now.

And would tonight.

TEN
TESSA RAE JAYNE

Tessa snapped awake from a fractured doze and glanced around, disoriented. For a split second there, she thought she'd gone back in time, had drifted asleep while tearing down I-20 in her Beetle—two wheels off the blacktop spraying rocks and sand, hell-for-leather toward Mexico.

"I'm done driving for the day," Floyd announced, bringing her back to the moment.

Tessa made a sound in her throat. "Where are we?"

"Just shy of the Arizona border."

"How long was I asleep?"

"Half hour?"

She yawned. "I've never been to Arizona."

"Well, I wouldn't say we're gonna be seeing many of the state's most beautiful parts."

An I-10 business route appeared up ahead, and Floyd eased onto it. In moments, the Camaro was cruising through more of a ghost town than a business district. The place was called Lordsburg, according to the signposts. The main road was lined with anonymously square, lifeless buildings and weathered parking lots. Tessa caught glimpses of hardscrabble residential lanes off the business route, old mobile homes among '60s-era shotgun shacks and weedy lots. Most of the homes were fiercely surrounded by patchwork chainlink. American-made vehicles jutted out of driveways, and American flags slumped as if desperate or defeated.

"Man, you ain't kiddin'."

Couple miles up the main road, Floyd turned onto one of the streets and curled around until they were facing a low-lying joint called the Holiday Motel. It was a quiet, anonymous place—and she could see a tiny red Vacant sign in the office window. Floyd pulled over and looked at it for a while. He seemed to work something over in his head.

"What?" said Tess, glancing around. "What are you looking for?"

"Just being cautious."

"More like paranoid."

"Maybe." His eyes flitted about with cold precision. "Maybe not."

About ten minutes later, Floyd rumbled the Camaro to the far side of the little office and got out and paid for the room. Tess helped him unload the car of their meager belongings. He stashed the money up high in the narrow closet, just in case, but he said there was no way he was leaving this room once they settled in. He had Tess park the car back in the spot where he'd performed his little surveillance, where they could still see it sitting there next to a dark fence.

"Why'd I just do that?" Tessa said when she got back to the room.

"My new rule is: Everything is bugged."

He locked the door behind her, turned out the light, and watched the parking lot through a tiny gap in the curtains. From what Tessa could see, the area was deserted, and the only thing she could hear was the drone of big-rig traffic moving along I-10 in the distance. She liked to give Floyd shit for his caution, but the truth was that she found it sexy as hell, the way he was already protecting her. She watched him stand there like some scruffy Prometheus, and she realized she wanted him badly. And it wasn't as if he was a hulking badass or something. He wasn't *obvious*. He had an understated strength to him, combined with that steely gaze, and she had to admit it got her lubricated and antsy. She'd never felt so attracted to a white man.

Later, Tessa took her first shower in two days, washing her body of Texas grime. She let the lukewarm water envelop her, and at one point— surprising herself—she added some tears to the flow. Sometimes, her preternatural ability to compartmentalize failed her.

She'd let her thoughts skip back like a thrown stone to Terrell and the way he'd looked in his bed before she raged off toward the meth house. A ghost of the young lineman he'd been, emaciated, trembling, scared of what was happening inside him. And the worst of it was that it hadn't been sudden. It wasn't like she'd been shocked one day by his sudden transformation. She'd watched the progression of it, and his helplessness inside it. How often had she screamed at him about it? Outwardly, he'd ignored her, but during the worst of the withdrawal symptoms, and even in the grips of the highest highs, she'd recognized his pleas for help.

And she'd done it. It had been an almost out-of-body experience, even the days of planning it, assembling the cans one at a time from a few stores, hiding her tracks. Not telling a soul.

She could feel good about all that, even if it didn't end well for her. She'd come through for him, and for whoever else was linked to that house—shit, could be a hundred or a thousand people in a snaking line of connections leading off into who-knew-how-many neighborhoods and schools. In immodest moments, she saw herself as a vengeful heroine. Fuck yes.

But when she opened her blurred eyes under the tepid rain of shower water, she saw the old cracked tiles of the narrow stall, and the yellow stains, and the mildewed ceiling, and she thought, *Is this my life now?*

She missed her brother, goddammit, and she knew she wouldn't be going back to him any time soon. Her flight south had been triumphant—hell, man, she'd shrieked her joy at the top of her lungs, into the blistering wind!—but she hadn't foreseen what she'd feel on the other end of that journey. She was supposed to be there for Terrell, right now, to *keep* being there for him, and now she couldn't even contact him.

Is he even still alive?

That was the thought that'd done her in. Because god knew there was no one else. *No one.* She and her brother could hardly remember their father's name, let alone his gray face, and even their mom was slowly fading into a sad and distant existence, miserable from the aches of a hard life. And anyway, Kendra Jayne had long ago revealed that she was more interested in cute toddlers than talking-back teenagers. And Terrell's football buddies? Ha! Right. Fuck them. All of them.

Tessa finished up in the shower. She dried off slowly, deliberately, easing back into the present.

Compartmentalize.

Before long, Tessa felt a drowsy randiness taking hold of her. Wearing only a threadbare towel, she drifted back out to the unlighted main room to find Floyd still at his perch.

"Come on, man," she whispered, her fingers brushing at his hand.

She watched him drink her in, and she knew he was a goner. She relished that sense of control. She seemed to have *always* had that effect on the boys, but this was the first time she'd had it with a man, a stranger, and it felt good. The hunger in his eyes was new to her, and it helped her look beyond everything back in Decatur. It helped her get lost in the moment.

On the squeaky bed, Floyd's cock had a good heft in her hand when she freed it from his jeans, and then—as in the speeding Camaro earlier—it felt warm and fat in her mouth. But this time there were no distractions. In complete darkness, she engulfed him and lost herself in his musk, his presence, the guttural sounds she was earning from him. And outside there was the hum of the I-10 traffic, heavy and constant.

She lay her head on Floyd's belly and found a lazy rhythm. She felt his fingers running through her damp hair, encouraging.

She closed her eyes to see the scenery still coming at her, never-ending, and she was getting farther and farther away from home. She could sense the world receding behind her. Everything that had mattered before—it was so far back there, beyond the low black hills and the scrub desert and the faded billboards and the haze, that it seemed part of another world, a past life. And yet there was also a piece of thread trailing behind her that was attached to Illinois, and she felt like she'd never get to the end of it.

After a long while, without hardly realizing it, Tessa had rolled onto her back into the squishy mattress, and she had closed her eyes again, and they had switched places.

"*Your turn . . . .*" Floyd whispered.

Some distant part of her felt a flicker of apprehension as Floyd's mouth wandered south. For all her innate desire to stay in control, she rarely submitted to this act. She'd had precious few opportunities among the myriad boys she'd fooled around with and the few whom she'd let take her. It either didn't feel right in the moment, or the boy she was with wasn't remotely interested, whatever, and all that had built itself into a wall around her pussy, a wall that she came to guard almost unconsciously. It was too intimate, too personal.

Not tonight, not with this man.

She eased into it like a bath, like a drug trip, almost giggling a little as his lips and tongue explored her. Maybe it was because the sensations helped her with her compartmentalization. Or maybe it was simply because his nimble flickerings soon felt fucking *fantastic*—deep warm whorls of pleasure radiating out to the ends of her limbs in thick pulses. She laced her fingers around her skull and basked in it, little whimpers escaping her mouth. She felt herself inch up to the edge of a too-quick orgasm and found a way to ward it off, gyrating her hips to control the release. She rode the rim of a silky rapture over long minutes, as ol' Floyd went to *town*.

God bless him! God bless this man!

That little apprehension she'd felt as Floyd had gotten down to business—it smoothed away under the ripples of buzzing warmth, and she marveled at how quickly her private wall crumbled away. It was like satiating a need that she hadn't realized she'd harbored.

There were images streaming fluidly through her mind, and they were the predictable ones, the ones she'd experienced like vivid echoes since it all went down. The meth house's windows engorged with violent flame as she watched rage-sobbing from across the street, neighbors rushing from their homes in their nightclothes, shouting, not seeing her. The numbly erratic drive back to Decatur, but veering away from home. Aunt Georgia opening her door after Tessa had knocked for what seemed an eternity, and the kindly woman's sleepy eyes going wide with alarm at the smell of gas and what was surely a look on Tess's face that her aunt had never seen before, and then Uncle Johnny brushing the woman aside and yanking Tessa into the sweet-smelling home. The confusion and the incredulity, the acknowledgment that Tessa'd done something she could never ever take back—and would she even want to? The flight south, that heady concoction of freedom and exile, of abruptly growing up in one headlong burst, shedding the evidence of her crime even as she learned the extent of it—an old woman she'd never know, trapped in the flames, horrifically dead by Tessa's hand.

But none of the thoughts were stinging her right now, or provoking tears, and she allowed herself to savor that, in this moment, only in this moment. She could probably never forgive herself, but at least she knew the images wouldn't be the end of her. They flitted through her, unable to hurt her. For the first time, she found that she could at least weather them, and maybe, tomorrow, she'd begin to deal with them. To really take control of them. To not be helpless under them.

Her first orgasm took her by surprise, arching her back—an exquisite burgeoning of pressure reaching an almost drunken peak and then starbursting throughout her. A gasp escaped her throat, followed by a series of whispered cries as the aftershocks pummeled her.

"Oh fucking hell, man, what are you doing to me?" she whispered.

She could feel his smile against her upper leg, and his hand was pressed firmly against her mound as if to contain her bliss. Her quick breaths slowed, and he made his way back up her slippery body and entered her so smoothly that it was like he'd been there all along. She wrapped her arms around him, filled up, and somehow everything was different. The sex at Henry's motel last night had been just what she needed—down and dirty, sudden, necessary in its own way—but this was different.

Perhaps it amounted to trust. A new feeling of trust in the man slow-thrusting into her, trust in herself and in her actions. Trust in a universe that could become suddenly, unutterably cruel, but also contained moments like this one. Or maybe it was more about redefining the control that she craved over her life.

She kissed him hungrily, trying to find her own deep way into him.

And there was something else that wasn't lost on her—that she had so far left a trail of corpses behind her, and that seemed to be her new thing. Part of her wondered if Floyd would be next. Who knew what might happen tomorrow, in the light of a new day, on the road toward an unpredictable future? Until now, she hadn't been convinced that Floyd's fate made any difference to her. If something happened to him, he'd be just one more to add to her total, another name to tattoo on her ankle. But in truth, it was Floyd who'd killed for *her*—if inadvertently. Maybe that's what came next: She would become the girl who got men to kill for her.

Murder, she thought, as she urged Floyd onto his back. *Murder is what we do.*

She straddled him, grabbed hold of him, guided him back inside her. She rode him bareback, roughshod, without restraint, and probably because of his earlier release in the Camaro, he stood his ground beneath her fury. She could feel his eyes all over her, and in the end that's what sparked the beginning of her second orgasm—this one deeply rooted, more consuming. It was a sprawling, undulating boom when it found her, flattening and fluttering her, and as she collapsed against him she heard him grunting his own fruition. She rocked her hips, milking him. She delighted in his delight, breathing heavily from her exertions, smiling into his neck, and then they were both trembling in the aftermath.

"I think it's possible that I just might, you know, dig you," she whispered, breath quick and shallow.

"Yeah?" Floyd's grinning voice was a tickle at her ear.

"It's possible, is all I'm sayin'."

"Aw, that's just your vagina talking."

They shared cigarettes into the night—like a cinematic cliché—and it was if a dam had broken. Tessa Rae Jayne opened herself utterly to Floyd Tillman Weathers, this random man she'd met at the edge of everything she knew. This man who'd, yes, killed a man with a baseball bat to protect her. This man whose own secrets seemed to simmer under, and bolster, their shared westward journey. This man who could eat a goddamn pussy as if he'd been manufactured from muscle and grit for that specific purpose.

Her nethers still reeling, her voice soft and sometimes trembling, Tessa tried to tell Floyd how her life had gone from its meandering normalcy to a kind of nervous day-to-day to—in the end—a burst of violence that startled even her. She'd *been* there the night Terrell, her goofy always-laughing brother, had tried his first line of coke, had even awkwardly sniffed a tiny spoonful alongside him when they'd arrived at that party that Brett and Sandy had thrown at their new place in Chicago. Tess and her little brother had squealed laughter—that is, until they'd wildly and unpredictably parted ways in the aftermath, Tessa despising the loss of control even as her mind blitzed and blared, and Terrell totally getting off on the high, craving further blasts into the wee hours. He'd become a different person overnight, and with the craven assistance of his stupid buddy Leonard, the hulking center on the football squad, he dove full-steam into addiction, losing himself inside a new existence that was desperate for any cash he could lay his hands on—the meager stash in their mother's purse, the till at the burger joint where he worked (not for much longer), even Tessa's spangly little wallet.

After that had come the threatening calls in the middle of the night. The broken windows. Her brother tearing off in the old, banger Mustang that was once their father's, not to flee but (she learned later) to beg forgiveness, more time, leniency, his own servitude. Meth had taken hold of him by then. At home, Tessa had watched the gradual advancement of his sickness. She had her own shit going on, her own problems, but she saw him sometimes at night—when he was home. The sinking of the once-regal ebony cheeks, the yellowing of the proud teeth, the graying of the skin, echoing their long-gone father. She'd weeped for him, and he'd shoved her away.

To her eternal shame, *that's* when she'd turned away from him.

She'd let months go by. *Months.* She'd seen him hanging with that scumbag Perkins at Wayne's for weeks, yeah. Perkins had even hit on her once. But the worst of them was Harlan, the pierced monstrosity with the angular brow and the shaved head. He'd only had to sit there and you felt the menace. Perkins may have been the one that came for Tessa in Malvado, but Harlan was the one who'd catapulted him that way.

Because *they* were the ones whose meth lab Tessa had burned to the fucking ground. Terrell, shivering, had whimpered out his story, had told her precisely where to go.

And she'd *done it.*

Tessa and Terrell's mother had been a void in their shared life at the worst possible time. She hadn't been there to intervene, to guide them to any other solution. Tessa hadn't been able to fill the gap.

Until that night.

She'd filled the gas cans one eerie midnight, out on the edge of Decatur, while the city slept.

As she described it all to Floyd, the tears gushed out of her, cathartic as hell, all the fear and hate and sadness pouring forth. She pulled herself close to him again, skin slippery against skin, hanging on to him for dear life, and he let her do it. After a while, the catharsis was too much for her own skull. She simply stopped whispering. She'd given all she wanted to give. They lay there quietly, and he soothed her with his rumbling voice, and they listened to the hum of distant traffic, knowing they were safe for now, in this bed far from every other thing.

She was floating somewhere between doze and deep sleep when she realized he'd asked her a question.

"Huh?" she whispered.

"Do you regret it?" he said.

"Regret what?"

"The fire . . . the old woman."

Time seemed to stretch out into infinity.

"Of course I do."

Out of the corner of her eye, she saw that he was nodding. He propped himself up to light a cigarette, and the glow lit the room briefly. He sighed the smoke out.

"Just checkin'," he said.

Night turned to late night, and she felt herself drifting away. Whether because of the magic he'd performed on her or because of her emotional release or because of sheer exhaustion, she let sleep overtake her. She welcomed unconsciousness in his arms. Some distant part of her heard Floyd's light snores; she could feel his warm breath against her breast.

In that perfect moment, it wasn't even in the realm of possibility that everything could fall apart in a few short hours.

ELEVEN
FLOYD TILLMAN WEATHERS

"If you make a sound or move a millimeter, I'm gonna paint your pillow red."

Floyd didn't recognize the grating, weirdly reedy voice.

The barrel of a gun bore down on the back of his head. The metal felt monstrous and heavy.

He was flat on his stomach, bleary from deep sleep, staring uncomprehendingly toward the shadows of the open closet. He couldn't see anything else. The night was still deep and dark, but the yellow streetlights outside were casting ambient light.

Abruptly, he heard the sounds of struggle—urgent muffled whimpers from Tessa, as if her mouth were covered, and then halting movement across the floor. The gun barrel pressed hard into his hair, directly behind his left ear. Near-hysterical muted cries were flowing from Tessa's mouth, as if it were blocked by a large hand. An impotent rage rose up inside Floyd, buzzing uselessly through his muscles.

Staring up into the closet, he could see that his duffel full of cash had been removed, and it was as if everything in his existence had plummeted away, and he couldn't even begin to reach for it.

How? he thought, hating himself.

Straining his eyes to the right, he glimpsed the bedside clock. It read 3:43 a.m. . . .

Things kept bumping and rattling. Floyd tried to calm his freshly jangled nerves, but he was seeing red. He forced himself to absorb details—the faint shadows on the closet door indicating the number of people behind him (at least two), the odor of sweat and cologne intermixed with fresh exhaust flowing into the room from what sounded like a running vehicle. A late model V8?

"That's a good boy," came the voice again, condescending but a little rattled.

Floyd tried to place it—both in his memory and geographically by accent. It was impossible. It was almost as if it was slightly disguised.

He heard the last of Tessa's complaints as she was dragged out the door, and then Floyd was presumably alone with his assailant. The gun barrel against his head was so steady it seemed planted there in rock.

"We'll be leaving now," the voice said. "I'm gonna take this weapon away, but do yourself a favor and just stay there, all right? Because I'm gonna keep aiming this at your head. This is a Magnum Research Thunder Snub with a cartridge full of jacketed soft-nosed rounds, and just one of them would be like a grenade going off in your brain. Nod if you understand."

Floyd nodded, feeling a steady, all-consuming misery.

The pressure behind his ear eased off, and the mattress squeaked and jostled as the man rose up and away behind him. His footfalls were barely discernible.

"Don't you dare try to get up off that bed," he said. "If I see you at the door or the window, I'm gonna come back here and turn you into a human stew."

The door clicked shut, and then after a clatter the vehicle rumbled away. Floyd shoved himself off the bed naked and went straight to the window, whose curtains were closed except for the barest of gaps at the bottom. He tried to peer through the slit without disturbing the cloth. He caught a hint of rear lights, but that was it—too dark to make out even a single character on the license plate. The vehicle appeared to be American-made, black, large. Then it was turning east. Gone.

"*FUCK!*" he yelled, jerking back from the window.

He leaped over the bed to the closet and reached up high. Yep, the money was gone. And so was Tessa. *He* had let this happen. He himself.

Floyd pulled on his crumpled jeans and burst out the door into the parking lot, digging his keys out of his pocket. Repeatedly cursing himself, he sprinted barefoot toward the Camaro. As he approached, his feet slapping warm asphalt, he saw that his tires were flat. He slowed to a stop at the car, bracing his hands against the hood, his mind in turmoil.

How had he let himself sleep through that? The assailants, whoever the fuck they were, had broken into the room and found his stash, and he'd been fucking unconscious. *How?* he thought again. Had they found help? The motel's proprietor? It was possible.

But it didn't matter how. At least, for now.

Around him, the world screamed silence at him. The neighborhood beyond the Camaro was apocalyptically dark. The scattered ramshackle homes receded into darkness, parked vehicles just gray shadowed lumps. He turned and flattened himself against his car, staring out into the black distance. His eyes flitted restlessly across the barren landscape.

Floyd pushed away from the vehicle and checked the tires more closely. They didn't appear to be slashed, meaning that someone had methodically let the air out at the valves. Floyd detected no damage there, either, but all four tires were down against asphalt.

He ran back to the motel. He stopped in front of the room, examined the parking lot, which was illuminated by several old, straining streetlamps. Floyd's was the only room that had been occupied. The parking lot was empty, save for what he assumed to be the owner's decrepit Ford. He glanced at the office window, saw no movement.

Scanning the ground, he found nothing there either. Maybe the suggestion of tire treads in dust, but what would he do with that? He wasn't any kind of tracker. All he knew, from his compromised angle at the window, was that the vehicle had turned east out of the parking lot, which meant that Tessa's abductors had hauled her to the eastbound entrance of I-10, back toward El Paso and then, ostensibly, toward Illinois. Even if Floyd could magically fix his Camaro's tires in an instant, he still wouldn't be able to pick up their tail. He wasn't even sure the car was *black*, given the lighting.

He went back inside the room, closed the door, locked it.

On waves of adrenaline, he felt as if his mind were sharpening itself against a whetstone.

The room lay eerily silent, still vibrating with the violence that had just taken hold of it. He took stock of what was still in his possession. His backpack lay propped next to his bed, and a quick check told him that his own firearm was still inside. A miracle. In fact, all of his belongings remained there, including his burner phone. He checked it quickly and saw no activity. He pocketed it, then pulled on a white tee from the pack. He patted his rear pocket, finding his wallet there.

Good.

They'd taken Tessa's little red suitcase, but they'd left the garments she'd shed in the bathroom before her shower. Christ, they'd taken her naked. They'd also left her grooming products. A pink razor, some hair products, toothpaste and brush. Floyd could faintly smell her familiar scent in the shower, masked mostly by the fragrance of her special bottled soap, which stood upright in the corner of the stall.

Back in the main room, he dropped to the floor next to the bed when he caught a glimpse of a power cord. He followed the cord from its powerpack, which was plugged into a dusty outlet on the wall. Another miracle: He found Tessa's phone between the bed and the nightstand. He sat up and powered on the device. The lock screen came up, and he stared at it blankly.

He clenched his jaw, trying to think.

First, he tried the obvious numbers that he'd also tried on Perkins' laptop. Nope.

He tore off the phone's protective casing, and turned the device over in his hand. There were no markings on the rear of the phone, no clues at all. Then he checked the casing itself, and there it was. *Ah Jesus, thank you Tess.* Stuck to the inside of the casing was an old yellow Post-It that showed her name, address, and phone number, written in a teenager's hand. Immediately, he tried the address number—15452—as the lock screen's pin. No dice. Then pieces of the phone number. No. He did, however, intuit that the pin was five digits.

Next, he took out his primary phone, brought up a glacially slow browser, and typed in Tessa's name and address. Having the combination of data gave him access to more information than he'd otherwise have found if he'd only had her name, and in this case he struck gold: The second search result gave him Tessa's birthdate, January 14, 2002. He typed 11402 into her phone, and he was in.

Blessing her for being idiotic about security, he scanned her main screen, which was mainly a hub for popular social media apps— Snapchat, Instagram, Tumblr, Facebook, Twitter. A Google search bar was at the bottom of the screen, and he tinkered with that until he found her search history. In the past few days, she'd searched—in chronologically descending order—Floyd's own name (no doubt came up empty, by design), the names of several Mexican towns on the Texas border, an address in Forsyth, Illinois, Harlan Eckhart's name, Ossie Perkins' name, and two other names that were foreign to Floyd: *Leonard McQuoid* and

Ronald Dankworth. After those, the next search term was for a type of clothing, so he stopped scrolling. He stared at the two new names for a moment, trying to get a sense of them. Had she mentioned them last night? He didn't think so.

Had one of these men pressed the hand cannon to his skull, threatened his life, and stolen everything from him? Or were they innocuous? Friends or family, associates in whatever her brother had been involved with . . . ? Their proximity to Perkins' name in the search history told him they were all linked somehow. But he couldn't count on that. Could be anything. They were a start, though.

Floyd clicked each name to go directly to a Google search. Both names were somewhat unusual, so he didn't have to narrow his search geographically, but neither name brought up much pertinent information. Leonard McQuoid was attached to a house-painting business in Decatur called AAA Painting, voted Republican, and had apparently played ball in high school years back, with consistently mundane stats. Ronald Dankworth came up almost completely empty, and that gave Floyd pause. The single item he found was a crime report whose details were hidden.

He took five minutes to check Tessa's social media feeds, mostly finding that she'd been inactive over the past few days. He brought up her brother Terrell's Facebook page, which hadn't seen any activity for over a year. The last post from Tessa was on Instagram, when she'd posted a glamour shot of herself seemingly in her own bathroom, and she'd gotten a bevy of comments about her carefully constructed hairdo.

There wasn't as much on the phone as he'd hoped. He pulled the charger from the wall and wrapped the cord around the phone, tossing it into his backpack. He decided to get deeper into it later, perhaps on the road—once he could get his Camaro road-worthy. That was the trick at four in the goddamn morning. As he worked through possibilities, he packed up the room. He threw all of Tessa's remaining belongings into the plastic bag he found lining the trash can, tied it off, and crammed them into his pack. He outfitted himself, gave the room the once-over, and stepped outside.

Still dark.

The warm, ethereal pre-dawn made everything that'd happened seem like a nightmare that he was only slowly waking from. He would be stuck for eternity in this nothingness, like something out of those *Twilight Zone* episodes he used to watch with his grandpa. He'd be fruitlessly, eternally seeking an impossible way out of this godforsaken southwestern berg, when really he was trapped in some kind of alternate reality. Someone *else's* reality.

That was the crux of it. Just as Philip had warned, Floyd had let someone else into his life, and he would probably pay for the mistake with his life. He was very probably ruined.

Philip.

Couldn't worry about Philip right now.

Backpack hanging from his shoulder, Floyd clicked the motel room door shut and went straight to the darkened motel office. He banged on the door with his fist, waited. Just as he began to clobber the door again, a light came on within. The same old man who'd sold him the room appeared at the door's adjacent window, and then the door opened a crack.

"What the hell?" his voice cracked. "Do you know what time it is?"

Floyd studied the old man for a long moment—his watery eyes, his drooped-open bottom lip, the twin lines of confusion etched above his eyes—and knew the man hadn't been complicit in anything except unconsciousness.

"Gotta go," Floyd said. "Here's your key. Sorry to wake you."

Utter befuddlement on the man's face, then a *harrumph* as he snatched the key.

The door shuddered closed, and Floyd made his way to the edge of the quiet business route. Sandstone buildings surrounded him, seeming abandoned not just by virtue of the early hour but by time itself. Some of these places hadn't seen human occupancy in years. Decades. All around him, the sidewalks were crooked and cracked, strangled weeds starving for sun, for water, for life.

About a mile distant to the west, he saw a lit-up Shell station—the only life on the entire avenue. From the south came the intermittent droning and ghostly headlamps of sixteen-wheelers surging along the interstate, crisscrossing the well-trodden path between El Paso and Tucson.

Floyd fought to keep demoralization at bay as he trudged west. His imagination would probably forever be enflamed over the non-sight of

Tessa being dragged naked out of the room, away from his supposed protection, and he had to constantly, vehemently stamp the image down if not out. His brain broiled with scenarios in which she was sprawled out in the rear of a car, tied up in a trunk, unconscious—or worst, fully aware and screaming out for him, for Floyd, to find her.

Every step he took toward the gas station was a stab of existential shame.

He began to run, his pack flopping heavily against his back.

He wouldn't dwell on Tessa's immediate predicament. He couldn't afford it. It would drive him to fucking *drink*. He had to assume that whoever'd found her and taken her wanted to keep her alive—for whatever reason. He would instead focus on strategy, on one decisive step after another that would lead him to answers. He had to be smart. He had to be on his game.

There was one employee manning the station, holed up behind plexiglass reading a paperback. The gaunt middle-aged man turned toward him, startled, when he saw him jogging across the pavement toward his enclosure. Floyd came to a stop at the bulky counter, staring at him, catching his breath. The attendant had dark, suspicious eyes, greasy metallic hair, and three days of dark stubble on his cheeks. He looked as if he hadn't bathed or ironed anything in weeks. He had a nametag crooked on his periwinkle-blue polyester shirt that read BILL.

"Yes?" Bill said through a hole in the glass.

"I have an emergency."

"Uh huh."

"Look, I gotta get the fuck outta town to help a girl, but all four of my tires are flat."

Bill glanced around as if he were being pranked. Snuck a look over Floyd's shoulder.

He shook his head.

"We just sell gas here, man." Bill's book was still splayed out in front of his face, and Floyd could see that it was a well-worn critical study of UFOs.

"I know, Bill, but you're the only human being awake right now, and I need your help."

Bill glanced down at his own nametag, then carefully placed a bookmark in the UFO book and set it aside.

"I'm not sure what—"

"Look, there's two hundred bucks in it for you. I'm about a mile down the road at a motel. Help me get my tires off, get 'em here so I can pump 'em up, then hall 'em back."

"I can't—"

"Yes you can." He gestured into the small parking lot. "That your pickup there? The white Chevy? It'll take all of a half hour. Two hundred bucks."

Floyd fished the two c-notes from his wallet. He had five of the bills left from the ones he'd slipped out of the duffel in Malvado, plus some change from lunch. He slapped the two benjamins against the plexiglass, and Bill stared at them for a long moment. Floyd didn't want to use the Beretta for the purpose of convincing, but he would. Turned out, that didn't matter. Bill's eyes went from doubtful to enterprising as he considered the offer. He stood up.

"You got three of those?"

It took the two of them considerably longer than a half hour to get the job done, so Bill earned his three bills. Turned out, Bill had a pronounced limp, preventing him from throwing anything into the back of his pickup truck, let alone fifty-pound rubber-wrapped wheels. Floyd managed. Bill merely stood there looking impatient the entire time. When he dropped Floyd and his newly inflated tires back at the Camaro, Bill waited expressionlessly in his cab while Floyd unloaded, then gave a two-fingered salute before driving off.

Almost precisely two hours after Tessa Rae Jayne's kidnapping at the Holiday Motel in Lordsburg, New Mexico, Floyd Tillman Weathers was back in his Camaro on the I-10, roaring toward a new sun. He swore on his life that he would find what was his—and that included the girl.

TWELVE
TESSA RAE JAYNE

Tessa had peed about three hours earlier, having held it as long as she'd found humanly possible, and now there was nothing she could do to get away from the ammonia stink. She thought she could even detect the odor of onion in her piss, reminding her of what she'd had for late lunch yesterday. The stench had only gotten worse as the car heated up under the daylight that seared in through the cracks. She was sweaty and miserable and terrified.

She'd long abandoned the hope that Floyd would roar up in his Camaro to rescue her, horn a-blazin', that black pistol of his blasting righteous fury. Pure Hollywood fantasy, sure, but a gal had no choice but to rely on hope when she was in a situation like this one.

It all led her to believe that Floyd was either dead or incapacitated. She'd tried to be nonchalant about the idea (she'd known the dude for all of two days, and of course it was now her *thing* to leave a trail of bodies in her wake), but within minutes she was crying at the horrors that thrived in her imagination—Floyd's life pouring from a head wound onto the floor of that crappy floor in the middle of that crappy town, or Floyd strung up by the neck from the shower head, hands tied behind his back.

She'd quickly knocked that crap off, finding it pointless.

There were other, more pressing concerns.

Besides, she didn't need any goddamn *man* to rescue her.

She felt her heart skip a beat just thinking that.

Truth was, she really *could* use Floyd right now. A rescue sounded just *fine*. She really hoped nothing had happened to him. Last night had been transcendent in a way—followed by a deep sleep, holding each other, talking about vague plans for the future in their sleepy voices—until everything was slashed mercilessly apart before daybreak.

How in the name of god had they found her? That was going to weigh on her heavily, and she was sure it was doing the same to Floyd, if he was still alive. He'd practically disassembled her Beetle yesterday looking for a tracking device while she'd sat on the curb watching him, *insisting* that he was wasting his time, that the buffoons in Decatur weren't even *capable* of such a thing. Sometimes, goddammit, she hated herself. She was a fucking *child*.

She'd gotten only a cursory look at her captors, right when it happened. All she'd felt was the bottom dropping out of her stomach as she'd been yanked from the bed. One moment, her arms had been wrapped warmly around Floyd, and the next moment, a large hand was clamped over her mouth and she was being whisked out into the night, *naked*, and shoved into a trunk. As the day had heated up, she'd tried to focus on the smeared glimpses she *had* gotten of the thugs, but her concentration was for shit.

Still, she'd seen enough—and heard enough—to be pretty close to certain that it was Leo and Dank who'd snatched her.

Fuck.

She had endured three or four violent crying jags—two of them nearly uncontrollable, dissolving into hitching moans—but now she'd regressed into a fetal position, trembling. She realized she was squeezing Terrell's necklace between her slippery fingers as if to summon him—the silver rectangle pendant with the four stars signifying the Chicago state flag, the necklace he'd given her on one of those last nights before it got really bad.

Now it's your turn to save me, *little brother.*

Jesus, why did she keep reverting to damsel-in-distress mode? Was it hard-coded or something? Shit, maybe it was just hard to live up to her own standards when she'd been locked naked in a fucking trunk for three-or-four-or-eight-or-whatever hours.

Funny thing was—*if you could call it funny*—was that she'd had a feeling, deep down, that it would be these two who would try to hunt her down, if anyone were to attempt it. Them or Perkins, of course.

Tessa would see them at Wayne's pretty regularly, either in Harlan's shadowed corner or waiting outside in their nondescript black Pontiac (was that the car whose trunk she now occupied?) or smoking in the shadows when she took out the garbage, startling the shit out of her. She'd cry out, *"Jesus!"* but they'd act as if nothing had happened.

Distracting herself from her quandary, she keyed in on their details. What she knew about them.

Leo—he was the big one, the dumb one. Leo fucking McQuoid, the huge gone-to-fat bastard that Terrell had actually hung with for a couple years in school, on the football team, until Leo fell under the sway of dangerous people. Later, Terrell would joke about some of the man's locker-room hijinks, but the jokes came under a layer of fear, she could tell. Leo was an altogether different person now, according to Terrell. Somehow, he'd ascended through Harlan's ranks to become *somebody*. He was tall and thick and bald and obviously a dullard, but he had one key skill, and that was the ability to be menacing. Tessa recalled the time Terrell had bounced into the house all paranoid, peeking around the open door, knowing he'd been followed. *"It's Leo, I'm sure of it. Fuck me, it's Leo."* She knew he was only expressing his increasing paranoia, so she scoffed at him from the couch, where she'd been snacking on Pringles while watching TV. Still, she'd jumped straight up, spinning and silly, and whisked open the front curtains to immediately see the black Pontiac diagonally across the street, Leo unmistakably in the driver's seat, staring at her emotionlessly. And as she'd stared out at him, Terrell had crashed to the floor, petrified. She remembered that cognitive disconnect. It was the beginning of her understanding that Terrell was in over his head.

The vehicle jounced violently, and Tessa's head banged metal, causing her to cry out.

She heard a voice rise up there, and—yeah—it was Dank. Ronnie Dankworth.

"Fuckin' watch the road, retard!" came Dank's nasal voice.

There was no response.

Dank's voice had given her nightmares the first time she'd heard it— also at Wayne's. Half a year ago now. Next to Leo, Dank was positively verbose, although really he didn't talk much either. When she'd first encountered him, Tessa had gotten the sense that the man was a little embarrassed of his weaselly voice. He sometimes tried to disguise it, make it artificially deeper. But the truth was that there was power in its weakness. It was like nails on a chalkboard, or rather raking down the length of her spine. Pulled from her warm dreamland this morning, the voice had registered somewhere deep, not consciously, not immediately, but rather as if drawn slowly and screeching from her soul.

Leo and Dank were basically Harlan's henchmen. Sure, Leo had that thug thing going on by the sheer benefit of his bulk, but he was a friggin' lunk. It was Dank who held the real power. He was rude, callous, and cruel. He'd once flicked a cigarette butt straight into Sara's face when she'd flipped him off for being crude. The butt had knicked off her left eyeball, the lit end, and she'd had to wear a patch for, like, two weeks. Tessa remembered Sara crying behind the bar, then crying harder because her salty tears only made it worse. She remembered Dank just laughing there at his table.

And it wasn't like Tessa had been working at Wayne's for a long time, either—what, eight or nine months?—so that shit was just a taste of the vile crap Dank could get up to. Sara'd given her an earful, had warned her about the slimy asshole. Sure enough, about two weeks into her tenure at Wayne's, Dank'd come on to Tessa, and it had been predictably annoying, just like the rest of 'em, but with him it had seemed on the edge of dangerous. He'd cornered her that late night at a booth, asking her to sit for a minute, but she'd rebuffed him as politely as she could, wanting to finish wiping up so she could go home, and he'd said, *"Wasn't a request, girlie"* in that strangely adolescent, off-kilter voice. Patting the seat next to him. She'd sat obediently—prim, hating herself, hating Terrell for asking her to *be good*, hating Richard (the guy who'd hired her) for turning a blind eye. And Dank had offered to take her home and treat her right and give her what her heart desired or some such come-on nonsense, and she'd told him she was on her period, and she'd somehow struck paydirt with that because apparently Dank was outright repulsed by the very idea of uterine sloughing (his words). Tessa had laughed about that later with Sara, but behind Dank's curled lip and near-gag had lurked the potential for danger. He'd left her alone after that, mostly, but it was if he were watching her, biding his time.

She could make out Dank's voice a bit more now, but she couldn't make out the words. Sounded like he was riding shotgun. The man liked to be served, as if he was entitled to it.

She *had* to believe the car was getting low on fuel. Tessa didn't know how much time had passed. Felt like endless hours and hours, but it had probably been about four or five. A long stretch of that time, they'd pulled off the highway somewhere and shut off the engine, she had no idea why. It wasn't to sleep. Their voices had rumbled away occasionally, talking strategy or whatever. When she'd called out, Dank had told her simply to shut her fucking face hole. The car had sat there motionless for a long goddamn time. Maybe they were waiting to see if Floyd gave chase, let him roar on past. It was pointless to even consider.

Now there was genuine heat out there, but she didn't think the day had come close to reaching noon yet. She was hungry, but not *that* hungry.

What she *did* need to do was change her position. She felt surrounded by all manner of grimy shit. She'd barely had the opportunity to move any part of herself. But she had acute aches along her entire side. If she stayed in this position another minute, she'd start developing infected pustules or something.

She started with her arms, twisting them up and around her chest so that she could get some leverage. She shoved her spine against something bulky behind her and felt it move reluctantly a few inches back while emitting a faint jangling sound. She luxuriated in the newfound space for a moment, cracking her neck, feeling as if she could breathe more deeply—even though the air was still permeated with the stink of her own urine. Then she began the laborious process of turning over onto her other side, a process done in small, painful increments. Her bare ass scraped against a shard of something, coming perilously close to breaking skin, and her knee had a bad encounter with the trunk hinge, but finally, panting, she was facing the innards of the trunk, and her injured side seemed to sigh with relief.

In the tiny light coming in from the gaps in the trunk, she found she was facing two identical cardboard boxes, both labelled GLASS—FRAGILE. She tried to angle her gaze beyond the boxes but could see very little. She glimpsed some kind of blanket north of her head—a possibility for covering herself—but when she worked a hand up to grasp its edge, she found it wedged tightly there. Stuck. She also saw shadowed cables over there, no doubt jumper cables, the greasy edge of a tire jack, and a small red toolbox. With her feet, she felt a roll of something (duct tape?) and a shapeless bag containing loose spherical objects (baseballs? apples?). She gave up trying to guess.

She considered the box directly in front of her face. Squinted at it. There was no other legible text on this side, but she decided she wanted to see what was inside. She couldn't see a way to open the top or tip the box toward her, so she started digging a fingernail into the thick card-board of its side. She nearly broke the nail, but after a few minutes, she had developed a small hole and was widening it with each stab. When she managed to get a finger inside to feel around, she found that the box was filled with small cylindrical vials. She knew exactly what those were for, and it depressed her all over again: They'd surely been bound for the meth lab that she herself had torched. To the two thugs in command of this Pontiac, these vials were probably just one more reminder of what she'd done.

She kept working at the cardboard, and in time she was able to dig out one of the vials. She held it in her hand, thinking of ways to use it. Shatter its top and use it as a weapon? A piece of glass was no use against a firearm, which she knew both Leo and Dank carried.

Long moments passed as the car rumbled incessantly beneath her, and the sweat that had been prickling at the roots of her hair began to stream in rivulets down the side of her face. It was so easy to give in to powerlessness and fear. She felt herself crumbling in on herself, and she had to force herself to resist the impulse.

At length, the sounds of passing vehicles increased. There was more traffic here—wherever *here* was. Assuming the goons were taking her back to Decatur and Harlan, they could be cruising toward Albuquerque by now, or, hell, Amarillo. Or they could be taking her somewhere com-pletely new, somewhere known only to them. Phoenix? Flagstaff? She wouldn't put *anything* past these two, but she had to assume their direc-tive had come from Harlan himself. She didn't think these two were capa-ble of going rogue, but she couldn't dismiss the possibility.

Abruptly, she began twisting back around to face the rear of the car. When she'd corked herself around, she was looking straight at the hous-ing of a taillight. She glared at it until her eyes could make out three Phillips screws holding it in place. She worked her right hand up and grasped the housing, tried to shake it, but it held tight. Determined, she reached up, barking her elbow, and pulled the grimy red toolbox to her chest. She took a breath, managed to pry the gross thing open, and fished around for tools in the darkness. The first screwdriver she found was a fat flathead. Then her fingers slid through grease of some kind, and she gagged. The sensation, combined with the stench of her own piss, was too much. She withdrew her hand and wiped her fingers furiously on the blanket above her head, took a moment to collect herself, then went back to the box. Her searching fingers scuttled past a hammer and wrapped around a thinner, longer screwdriver, and this one was Phillips.

She started working on the taillight housing, using her fingertips to find the grooves of the screwheads. Her wrist began to quickly cramp.

Up front, Dank was talking again—that scraping drone. She wished she could hear the words coming out of his rat face. She was suddenly, acutely aware of time passing. If the goons were to head to a vacant rest stop, or an abandoned horse trail, no one for miles around, there was no telling what they might do to her. Whatever she was going to do, she had to get busy doing it now, when there were potential witnesses around. She felt herself getting geared up. Now was the time. She wasn't just gonna fuckin' lie here.

After long excruciating minutes, the housing flopped out of place, attached only by dusty-greasy wiring, and she shoved it aside as far as it would go. Then she pressed her eye to the opening, peering out into bright daylight. The car was cruising along a three-lane highway, and she could see a sporadic throng of other vehicles in her wake. She wanted to thrust her arm out there and start waving, but she couldn't angle her body in such a way to do it.

Tessa contorted herself back to face the box and began digging into the cardboard again. After an agonizing ten minutes, she'd destroyed and emptied the box, gathering all thirty-six vials from out of their aggravating individual grids. As she grasped each one, she gently dropped it behind her shoulder so that they were nestled between her naked back and the rear of the trunk. Then she bent to the task of breaking down the cardboard of the box, giving herself a little more room to maneuver in.

Now she very carefully rolled herself back over, mindful not to break any glass. Because that would suck.

The vials clinked and tinged as they jostled. She gathered them into a pile in front of her, all in easy reach. She realized she was breathing heavier and faster than she thought possible, and her chest was still constricted as hell—even with the extra room.

She was scared, yeah. Scared of what she was about to do. She had no earthly idea what the repercussions would be. It was probably far more possible that her actions were about to backfire horrifically than work in her favor. But even a one percent chance of altering the course of her fate was worth the effort.

She took a breath.

And then she began feeding glass vials through the taillight hole as quickly as she could, hearing them shatter on the asphalt behind the car.

THIRTEEN
FLOYD TILLMAN WEATHERS

Floyd sat in a strip mall parking lot off I-25 in Las Cruces, New Mexico, stealing a fast-food joint's Wi-Fi and trying to keep his fingers from trembling as he opened the packaging of a micro-USB cable that he'd just purchased from a Verizon store.

He was gritting his teeth so hard that he felt as if his molars might explode like stressed concrete. Even as he typed with a clumsy thumb on his phone's keyboard, performing the equivalent of a technological hail-mary pass, he knew Tess and his duffel bag full of Philip's goddamned money were moving farther and farther away from him every second, in a direction he could barely fathom. He couldn't look past this morning as anything less than an extravagant failure, and hopelessness threatened to choke him out at any moment.

Ten or fifteen miles back, he'd faced a decision. Head toward Albuquerque on the assumption that Tessa's kidnappers were hauling ass north toward Illinois, or keep on backtracking through El Paso, swing over that way toward Dallas or even back down to Malvado. For the past hour, he'd weighed each path's potential. Which way had Tess and the money gone? South would take them back to the motel, back to the Beetle, back to Perkins—and who knew whether the fat man had already been unearthed, with all the attendant chaos, the law swarming in, talking to Henry, Sal at the diner. That was all unlikely, considering the way Henry worked, but it was certainly possible. And anyway, Floyd saw little reason for Tessa's abductors to retrace those steps beyond reclaiming Perkins' corpse and Tessa's vehicle or something inside it. But Floyd had pretty thoroughly checked out the Bug and had taken everything worth taking, and he couldn't see how unearthing a dead body made sense. And he saw no real benefit to the south-swinging route through El Paso and Dallas when the north arc to Albuquerque and I-40 was more direct. They'd want the quick and dirty path, particularly with a naked girl in the trunk, and they certainly weren't gonna take to the air.

So that had decided it.

North and then northeast, on the wings of a dark prayer.

But wait.

He *had* taken everything worth taking, hadn't he?

Dashing east on I-10 toward Las Cruces, he'd brought up his phone and fumbled through his contacts to find Craig the Egg. Stabbed the name and brought the phone to his ear. The line began ringing.

"Come on . . . ." he breathed.

There'd been a click as Craig answered with his southern drawl.

"Floyd? That you? Seriously?"

"Yeah, it's me. Sorry if I woke ya up."

"Where the fuck *you* been?" A yawn. "Haven't heard from you in *months.*"

"Ah, Philip put me on a thing."

"One o' his hush-hush thangs?"

"Pretty much."

"Well it's good to hear from ya, man."

"Feelin's mutual."

"What's up?"

"I'm in a bit of a scrape and could use your expertise." He'd sensed the desert flying by.

On the other end of the line, there was the sound of Craig adjusting himself as if sitting up in bed. It was still early for Craig the Egg, whom Floyd knew was a night owl. He lived in a drafty warehouse-like joint south of downtown Little Rock, a former business front in a lazily zoned commercial district. He did up-and-up computer services for real customers who came to him through Craigslist and Facebook, but he earned his real money doing hack work for people like Philip Crouch. And big business. Oh, and occasionally the government, too. Dude was a long way from where Floyd had first met him at the cellphone shop at the mall.

Right now, Floyd was picturing Craig's pale and expansively bald head—the inspiration for his nickname, which Craig himself embraced and even celebrated.

"Hit me."

"Need help hacking into a phone."

"And I take it you're in possession of this phone, and you're many miles away from me, and you need this like now."

"Is there anything you can do long-distance, or am I S.O.L.?"

"You wanna tell me where you are?"

Floyd hesitated. "Wouldn't want that to come back to you. Plausible deniability, and all that."

"I mean, I might have a contact close to where you are. I have a lot of—"

"El Paso."

Craig laughed, a sharp report. "The border? Jesus, you must be hoarding a wad. Never mind. Long distance it is. Uhhh, well, I probably have something that can help you, but it takes some time."

"How much time?"

"Depends on the password, depends on the device. But it's gonna be a lot slower than I could do here in the office."

"Sure," Floyd said. "But are we talkin' hours, days, weeks, what?"

"Oh, well, hours."

"I'll take it."

"Do you have a laptop on you?"

"Not one I can use."

Craig grumbled. "Why not?"

"Also locked."

"All right, we can manage it phone-to-phone, but again, might take longer."

"Fuck, but okay."

As Floyd continued roaring toward Las Cruces, Craig had talked him through the information he'd need about Perkins' phone, like brand and model (and how to *determine* those things) and how the hacking process would proceed—but that he'd need a stronger connection than cellular.

"Once I get it going, can I leave Wi-Fi and go back to cellular as it does its thing?"

"Why?"

"Gotta keep movin', man."

Craig thought about that. "I don't see why not."

Then he told Floyd to call back when he found some reliable Wi-Fi, and please tell him he had a dual micro-USB cable that would work for the hack.

"I'm sure I've either got one or can get one."

"All right, do that. I'll be here, gettin' it ready on my end."

Which brought Floyd to the Verizon cellular joint, nestled in a non-descript strip mall anchored by a Wendy's.

Lurching into a parking space in front of the burger joint, he'd cursed unrepentantly inside the confines of the Camaro, despising the motionlessness of the moment. Every stop—every gas station, every break for food—was an unforgivable pause in his sprint toward Tessa. He'd turned off the engine and taken up his phone again to search for the complimentary Wendy's Wi-Fi. Then he'd reached around behind the passenger seat and grabbed Perkins' satchel, which he'd tossed the fat man's phone into back in Malvado.

It was truly a hail-mary. If Floyd could get into Perkins' phone, he could do at least two things: check out the man's communications with his handlers leading up to his confrontation with Tessa at the motel, and also find the tracker app Perkins had been using to trace her. He strongly suspected the tracker would show a solid, unmoving dot planted at the border where the Beetle currently sat abandoned. He gave that possibility a ninety percent chance. But *that* sidestepped the vital question of how the thugs had zeroed in on him and Tess so unerringly in Lordsburg. Had they been aligned with Perkins all along and simply followed Floyd and Tessa west? Maybe *they'd* been following *Perkins*.

It was also possible—Floyd gave this a five percent chance—that the tracking app was homed in on *himself*, right now, as in *this car*, and the transmitter was somewhere in Tessa's belongings, which he'd hurriedly gathered back at the Holiday Motel. He'd searched through all that shit, so the idea seemed impossible to him, but it would be nice to know if he had a fucking tag on him and was a second target for this crew.

And those last few percentage points? Hell, man, was it possible that Tessa herself had some kind of tracking chip on her body somewhere? Seemed like science fiction, but at this point he'd give anything credence.

And that's when it hit him again—the possibility that Tessa was the one who had ripped him off after all. He sat there dumbly, knowing time was slipping away from him but helpless to do anything but consider the odds.

Was she *that* good? *No fuckin' way.* Right?

Who would have sent someone like Tessa Rae Jayne after him? Would have to be someone dug in, someone at Philip's side. Septuagenarian Randall with the swiveling glass eye? Joyner with the constant cigarillos and the bum leg? Neither of them in any shape to do anything on his own, but fully capable of hiring and sending out a perfect little split-tail operative, trained young and bestowed with certain genetic gifts.

It could happen.

Put on a little acting class at the gas station in Malvado, attract attention. Lead him by the crotch and eyeballs with her perky ass and bright yellow Beetle, flirt him up at the only saloon in town, get him in bed all sexed up and blissed out. Get him to talk—effortlessly, on his own terms. Open up with her own fictional sob story, milk his dick for all it was worth. Throw a little false danger his way, make him the hero of her little manufactured drama. Maybe Perkins wasn't even supposed to die. His purpose was simply to back up her story—but he'd ended up dying for it. A glitch in the matrix, but it still worked out. And then it was just a waiting game till Tessa found a way to contact the goon squad and stage a kidnapping—but more importantly, snag the cash for which she'd obtained a precise location.

It all laid out precisely and orderly in his mind like a perfect sudoku puzzle.

"Holy shit."

That would explain why he could never find a tracking device on that fucking Beetle. It would explain how those assholes had found them so quickly this morning In Lordsburg. It would explain everything.

Floyd sat there feeling a red flush of humiliated fury spread up his trunk and down his limbs. In that moment, his heart threatened to harden. He would throw in the towel, call Philip on his burner, lay out his carelessness and stupidity, leave his fate to the Little Rock triumvirate and then let them unleash their full power toward finding Tessa Rae Jayne. Do it in their own time. Recover the money the hard way. That he *knew* could be done. Sacrifice himself for revenge and justice. These thoughts seared the edges of his brain like an acid bath—

—and then he sidelined them. He managed to tamp them down to a simmer. He let them remain, festering at the brink of his reckoning, but he refused to give them voice.

It was *too real*, what she'd told him. *She'd* been too real.

And she still was.

A belligerently noisy diesel truck pulled in next to him, casting its noxious fumes in all directions, idling for an eye-rolling amount of time before it shut off, and Floyd watched a black door yawn open. A large woman in straining, bright yellow sweats climbed down from the cab and joined her bulky man on the sidewalk. Both of them gave Floyd a quick appraisal, then they walked toward the Wendy's entrance and were gone. The normalcy of the moment—the quick snapshot of the American dream—served to bring him back to the present.

Back to urgency.

He was going to follow this thing through.

And he was going to think only the best of the girl.

Infiltrating Perkins' messaging would prove him right.

He dialed up Craig, who walked him through the process of connecting through a VPN to a partition of the Egg's bunkered server in Little Rock, and downloading an app creatively titled ThrashPash, hacking software of Craig's own design. The download process was interminable, and Floyd grew increasingly antsy as time clicked by and the process seemed stalled—and then abruptly the installation was complete. The initial stages of the hack involved a sequence of oddly synchronized button presses, and the phones began to communicate in download mode, ushering in Craig's app, which immediately began working.

"All right," Craig said, "that'll go on in the background for a while."

"How long?"

"Patience, patience. A couple hours?"

Floyd pondered that. He was about to roar north toward Albuquerque on the *somewhat* informed assumption that that's the direction Leonard McQuoid and Ron Dankworth were headed with his girl and his cash. If it was an *incorrect* assumption, Floyd could be hundreds of miles in the wrong direction by the time Perkins' phone opened up to him. Jesus, he was in the midst of several gambles. He needed a fucking payout, goddammit.

Floyd didn't voice any of this to Craig the Egg.

"Okay," was all he said.

"It doesn't really hack the phone's password, it digs in and removes the lock screen altogether. It'll take some time, but you can disconnect from Wi-Fi and go about your business."

"Thanks, pal, I owe you one."

"I accept traveler's checks."

"Promise to make good when I see you again."

"I'm taking that on faith." Craig chuckled, a smile in his voice. "Stay healthy, man. Call me back if you have any problems. I'm just gonna be chillin' here with Serena."

Serena was a voluptuous character Craig'd met at a cybersecurity conference, one of those booth babes, and she apparently had a thing for brawny eggheads. Floyd pictured her massaging that dome with her long-nailed fingers, Craig sprawled out like a baby beneath her ministrations. Floyd had met her once at a BBQ joint in west Little Rock and had gotten a kick out of her and her demonstrative adoration for her man.

"Give her my best," Floyd said.

"I'll give her *my* best." Craig was laughing as the line went dead.

Floyd placed the connected phones on the seat next to him, and pulled out of the parking lot and blasted back onto the interstate. He'd lost over an hour messing with the phones. It made him feel itchy—particularly as he passed a mile marker that read 1. Yeah, he was at mile 1, the very beginning of the I-25 interstate that reached up a thousand miles through New Mexico, Colorado, and Wyoming. A block of gray mountains loomed ahead of him, and he wished he could use their peaks to fashion a great slingshot for his Camaro and catapult himself four hours into the future.

Because that's where Tessa was right now—the future. She'd already endured a world of shit—the depth of which Floyd could barely comprehend—and every mile Floyd drove was only another minute she was immersed in it. That was the Tessa he was rushing toward, mile by mile. That was the Tessa he would save.

As the yellow landscape rushed past him, Floyd recognized the insanity of his predicament. Just two days earlier, he could have put off his visit to the corner gas station in downtown Malvado by five minutes, and none of this would've happened. He'd have dodged the hollowpoint bullet that was Tessa Rae Jayne. In a matter of hours, she'd upended everything in his existence. She'd lain waste to everything he stood for!

What *was* that?

It had to speak to something inside *him*, something he hadn't paid enough attention to.

Floyd wasn't typically a self-reflection kind of guy.

It all reminded him of the gal he used to hang with after high school, that receptionist at the remodeling company. Celeste. Long and lithe, sinewy, drowsily magnetic in the sack, she was clingy and always hiding her fetching smile, and she had this habit of getting introspective, trying to get to the center of him. *Tell me what you're feeling.* Even in the middle of sex, she overshared and wanted him to do the same. She wanted to know how he ticked, and she made no secret of it. He guessed they ended because he never opened up as much as she wanted him to, and that frustrated her. He recalled the way she'd become suddenly venomous and full-throated when he broke it off, the tendons in her neck straining beneath a rage-red face, as if her brain had thrust forth the real personality that had been creeping under her surface all that time. He remembered thinking that he'd dodged a bullet with Celeste, but later he'd come to wonder whether we all had that creeping thing beneath our surface, just waiting to erupt. Given the provocation.

At any rate, the very notion of *opening up* was foreign to him.

No doubt he'd inherited that charming personality trait from his dad.

He pictured his father back home, endlessly tinkering in the cluttered garage, his thick fingers sorting through his buttons and bolts, his metal and his wood scraps, working on his projects. His silence and his gaze, the way it could cut you all on its own. The way he could rage at you without making any noise at all. Floyd had struggled through childhood and adolescence with his jaws clenched, and when he'd achieved the mildest autonomy he'd basically checked out, spending most of his waking hours with his crew. He'd felt his mother's weakness, had seen it in her eyes when she looked at Floyd from across the heavy living room, when she watched him go off into the night with his friends. It was if he'd become something his parents hadn't expected but couldn't define.

Floyd felt no love for Thomas Weathers at all.

Which, admittedly, had made it easy to put the man's life on the line.

At that moment, he passed a large green mileage sign that told him he had 226 miles to go till he'd hit Albuquerque and hang a right. He figured he could do that distance in about three hours, barring any unexpected delays. He set the cruise control to five above the limit and settled in, occasionally glancing over at the paired smartphones.

It was two hours later, north of Socorro, New Mexico, when Perkins' phone opened its secrets to him and everything changed.

FOURTEEN
TESSA RAE JAYNE

Tessa heard the dragging whine of tires screaming on asphalt before she saw anything. She'd probably fed two dozen vials out the metal gap before the noise began. She stopped stuffing them through and angled herself to peer through the opening. A small white vehicle—a Prius?—swerved into the adjacent lane and laid into its horn.

A stream of hysterical curses flowed from her lips as she drew back and began feeding glass vials through the metal gap again.

Now there were two horns bleating, and the vehicle in which she was imprisoned jerked to the right, raking her bare skin against grimy metal. She cried out, stabilizing herself with her forearms and her shins, and then Dank started yelling up front—a stream of obscenities that echoed her own.

As the car steadied itself in its lane and the vehicles behind her continued honking, Tessa threw caution to the wind and—screaming with pain—shoved her hand into the hole, scraping her skin and drawing blood. She gritted her teeth and pushed her arm out past the elbow and began frantically waving.

The highway became a chorus of blaring horns.

Oh Jesus, it's working.

She kept waving, furiously, and then the vehicle yawed dangerously as if about to flip, and Tessa felt her trapped arm nearly snap like a fucking twig. She pulled it roughly out of the hole and held it to her chest, using her remaining limbs to brace herself as the trunk thrashed her in its grip. The car slowed, fishtailing, and jerked to a juddering stop. Horns were still blaring. Tessa placed her eye against the hole and saw a grungy black Jeep and a shiny red Honda Accord come to abrupt halts behind her, and their drivers immediately ejected themselves and began yelling. It was hard to follow their movements through Tessa's narrow metal tunnel, but she caught glimpses of them converging, and of the traffic streaming noisily by.

"What the fuck, man!" A man's enraged baritone, sounded native American.

"There's someone in your fucking *trunk!*" A woman's shrill voice. "What're you *doing?*"

The man appeared to be trying to wave down other cars, but no one else was stopping.

Tessa heard Dank and Leo open their doors, and then the shocks lifted as they stepped out of the car. She could hear Dank's feet in the gravel on the side of the road. Her heart was hammering against her ribs. She had the sense that her entire existence was poised at a precipice. She took a lungful of stale air, then pressed her face to the hole.

"*Help!*" she screamed. "*Help! Help me! Get me out of here!*"

"Jesus Christ!" the woman yelled.

"All right, calm down!" came Dank's reedy voice.

"*Open the fucking trunk, asshole!*"

"This isn't your business, *asshole.*"

"*Open that trunk, or I'll open it myself!*"

The man, dark hair pulled back in a long ponytail, had backtracked and was reaching into the back of his Jeep. He withdrew a steel rod of some kind, looked like rebar.

"You gotta be kidding me," Dank said.

"*Open it!*"

"Back off."

The energy changed.

"*Whoa, whoa,*" someone said.

"This isn't your concern," Dank's voice leveled out. "Now back the fuck off before someone gets hurt."

Tessa put her mouth back to the hole and pleaded for help with all her breath: "*Help me! I've been kidnapped!*"

"That's enough!" There was a brutal fist knock on the trunk lid. "Shut up in there!"

"*Let her out!*"

Then a prolonged pause.

Tessa peered through the metal gap and saw the long-haired man receding, one hand holding the rebar, the other raised in surrender.

Dank had pulled his weapon on the guy.

At that moment, another vehicle, something silver, pulled in behind the Jeep, and she heard Dank mutter, "*Christ.*"

"You gonna shoot all of us?" the man with the rebar called as he eased behind the open door of his Jeep. *"Open the trunk!"*

"I'm calling the police!" the woman said, beyond Tessa's tunnel-vision view.

The inside of the trunk was suddenly an unbearable piss-stinking sauna, and the prospect of getting sprung from it only made it worse. Sweat was streaming from her hair and itching all over her body. Tessa felt a tense détente building beyond her metal coffin, and she swiveled her eye at the hole, trying to see *anything*. Yet another vehicle pulled in close behind the three parked ones, a dark sedan. If ever Tess would have a chance, this was it. She felt around her whatever she could find, her fingers brushing aside some remaining glass vials, and finally they closed around the grip of the screwdriver. She held it tight to her chest for a split-second, then twisted herself to begin stabbing it at the roof of the trunk with as much leverage as she could muster.

"All right, wait!" Dank called out. *"Mother of fuck!"*

"Open it! Now!" said Jeep man.

"Fine! *Fine!* Will you shut up?"

"Ronnie!" came Leo's voice. "We can't—"

Tessa barely made out Dank's hot whisper in response: "The girl doesn't matter anymore! We have the money. Okay? Let her out."

"Are you crazy?"

"I said, let her out!"

"Harlan'll *kill* us!"

"Shut up!" Dank spat, his voice going louder. "Give me the keys and get back in the fucking car!"

Leo pushed roughly off the car, jostling it, and Tessa waited, eyes peeled in the darkness, ready for anything. She heard the jangle of keys, and then felt the weight of Leo dropping back into the driver's seat. Her view through the metal hole was blocked for a split-second, and she felt Dank right there, could almost smell him. Her lips sneered.

The trunk came open—blinding light!—and she maneuvered herself out, banging and staggering, almost falling, feeling blunt pain in her limbs. The warm breeze electrified her, enveloped her exposed skin, and she glared at Dank, screwdriver in her fist like a knife. She heard several people gasp.

"Get the fuck away from me!" she said.

Dank looked as repulsive as ever—more so, with his strung-out gray-slate eyes, greasy hair, and mouth half-open over crooked teeth, the muscles in his face shifting as he schemed. He held his weapon loosely, tilted in Tessa's general direction, and his eyes were roaming her naked flesh. She felt the gaze physically, as if his spidery hands were stroking her. Only then did she feel truly exposed, the eyes of the bystanders and the passing cars all over her. She glanced around, absorbed the shock of those closest to her.

"Somebody get her something to cover herself with!" the man with the rebar called from behind his Jeep's door.

Tessa stood there uncertainly as traffic began to slow. She could see Dank registering it, too, with something akin to fear.

"Fucking *take* her!" he called out. "Take her! But anyone that follows us is *dead!*" He waved the gun around to make his point. *"Dead!"*

The woman with the phone had retreated to her car, but she spoke up. "I've got your plates, asshole!"

Dank's mouth curled into a grin. "Good for you."

Tessa's gaze flickered toward the car, seeing that it was indeed the black Pontiac, and noticing the yellow New Mexico plates, swapped out somewhere along the way.

"Fuck you," Dank sneered at Tessa. *"Fuck you!* We ain't done with you, you know, not after what you done. Not by a long shot."

She watched the deviant skirt around the Pontiac and jump into shotgun and slam the door. The motor fired up, and the car peeled out, spraying gravel, adding insult to injury against her skin. She recoiled, wincing. When the spray settled, she collapsed onto her bare ass on the side of the road, numb. She brought the screwdriver against herself again, as if it were some kind of supernatural protector. The Pontiac fishtailed into traffic, disappearing quickly, and then the bystanders swarmed around her, shouting, the sounds of their voices buffeting her. She felt a small blanket quickly cover her, and she noted that it was crimson red patterned with garish sugar skulls, and she was vaguely conscious of a barrage of barked questions, but her mind was clouding up like oily water, and everything was crashing into her, and she felt herself rendered incapable of anything.

She realized somewhere deep that she was crying—like copiously, hacking out gaspy sobs—and she felt soothing hands on her shoulders, rubbing, encouraging. They were telling her things, like encouragements or instructions, something about waiting for the cops, but she couldn't decipher a whole lot of their words. She was shaking and crying.

And abruptly she hated herself for it.

Weakness.

"*No!*" she cried.

The stunned strangers around her broke backward in a wave as she struggled her way out of the dirt, all knees and elbows, and stood, wavering. She glanced around at all of them, gauging their faces. She was thankful for them, all of them, but she wouldn't enter anyone's care. She'd be signing her own death warrant. Even now, she could hear distant sirens, and obviously she wanted no part of that, nor the questions that would flow from it.

Without clearly understanding what she was doing, Tessa found herself running down an embankment, red blanket flapping around her as she clutched it at her chest.

"Wait!" someone yelled raggedly behind her.

But no one followed. She sensed their confusion, their *did-that-just-happen?* bewilderment. She used it to her advantage, dashing swiftly toward an empty frontage road before they could fully react. Her bare feet scuttled through a mixture of sand and gray-brown dirt, the color of the world here—and where the hell *was* she, anyway? She caught a glimpse of a sign that read Kirkland, and it didn't mean anything to her. The southwest looked the same everywhere she'd seen—flat, dry, dreary, ugly sunblasted brown, billboards and roadwork, distant hazy-gray rock formations and stunted, tangled weeds—and it all infuriated her. She was stuck in this purgatory between home and what she'd assumed would be her *promised land*, some idyllic destination south of the border where everything would finally be good in her life.

Why wasn't she there? Naked in the surf instead of naked in the middle of this desert hellscape?

She reached a horribly rutted side road and glanced back up the hill to see a few scattered people watching her curiously, some of them gesticulating helplessly.

The sirens got louder up there, so she began sprinting toward a row of structures, what appeared to be a hotel and some squat businesses. A hundred yards later, she was squeezing into an alley unnoticed, among trash bins and abandoned wood pallets and stripped-down store displays. Pausing for breath, she squinted into the sky. She estimated that it was still before lunch. Her sense of time was scrambled, though. She wouldn't have been surprised to find the sun beginning its orange descent.

Nope. It must've been only around ten or eleven in the morning.

She took a moment to fasten the flimsy red blanket around her body as modestly as it would allow, until it looked vaguely like a tube dress. She figured she appeared on the verge of presentable. But she had a feeling the police would be on the prowl here shortly, so she catapulted herself toward the hotel to her right—an aging sandstone edifice with a smattering of vehicles parked out front. She veered away from the front entrance, hurrying along a sidewalk edged with spherical boxwood shrubs and junipers, above which loomed a wall of uniformly curtained windows. When she got to the rear of the hotel, she found a service entrance hanging open and strode in with purpose. A delivery guy caught sight of her, did a lazy double-take, then returned to his task. None of his business.

She found a hallway that led to nothing useful, so she u-turned, tried another route. She nearly headed straight into a managerial type at the end of a corridor that fed into the lobby, but she quietly turned left to avoid the encounter.

Another dingy hallway led to a series of gray doors, and—*thank Christ!*—one of them was open, revealing a break room or meeting room lined with lockers. Tessa swept inside and did a quick survey of the lockers. Most were secured with padlocks of all sorts, and the unlocked ones were empty. She hummed desperately to herself as she got to the end of the row.

She looked madly about, her gaze landing on a bunch of stacked boxes, one of which was open and spilling white cloth. She darted to it. It was filled with tee shirts. She pulled one out and read the slogan that was colorfully emblazoned on its face: HAMPTON HONORS!

She dug out an extra-large shirt and pulled it on over the blanket. As she did so, she spotted a pair of tan sandals beneath a bench. She sat and pulled them on—a size too small, but close enough.

Pants, pants, pants.

At that moment, a short Hispanic woman strode into the room casually flipping her dark brown hair—and stopped short, staring at Tessa.

"Hi, I'm new," Tessa said, quickly hiding the screwdriver next to her hip. "I'm Janey." The first name to pop into her head, this loose girl she remembered from high school, the one with the pierced lip and the enviably tight little white-girl ass.

"Oh," came the clipped response.

The woman's eyes were locked on the tacky blood slathered along Tessa's left arm.

"Do you know where the laundry uniforms are?" Tessa asked, trying to distract, but the woman's gaze was now flitting over the rest of her body, no doubt finding all the grime and the nicks and whatever else.

She had a tag over her breast that read Leticia.

"What happened to you?" Suspicion in her eyes now.

Tessa felt emotion tug at her throat, but she wouldn't let it happen.

"Had a rough morning."

Leticia nodded, then strode wordlessly to a locker at the south end of the room and extended a key from her belt. She opened the narrow door and gestured, still suspicious but not enough to act on it. She appeared to be the kind of person who had her own problems.

"Can I freshen up in there?" Tessa said, gesturing to a tiny bathroom next to the lockers.

Leticia nodded. "Rick told you where to start?"

"I'm supposed to talk to him in a half hour."

Leticia watched Tessa curiously as she went to the locker and rifled through the folded stacks of uniforms.

"You don't have real shoes?" the woman asked her, looking her up and down.

"No."

A quick *tsk*, and then Leticia crossed the room to unearth a ragged box. She rummaged around for a bit and came up with a few pairs of heavily used rubber-soled shoes.

"Oh, thank you."

"I don't know your size. They're old. You need to get your own."

"I know, just for today."

And that was how Tessa ended up walking out of the Hampton Inn fully dressed—disguised, even—in shoes that were only one size too large, and in a starchy mustard-brown uniform that was also one size too large and whose right pants pocket held the only thing Tessa owned in the world: an old Phillips-head screwdriver. Her savior.

She held herself straight as she retraced her steps toward the business strip adjacent to the hotel. She fully expected a voice to call after her, to ask her to stop—perhaps the Rick who Leticia had alluded to—but no voice came. She stepped up onto a raised sidewalk and pulled open the first door she found, which belonged to a Subway sandwich shop, empty except for a single employee behind the counter, a ridiculously young teenaged boy who was smiling at her with silver-braced teeth. His nametag read MARTY.

"Hi," Tessa said.

"Hi there! Can I help you?"

"Yeah, I *do* need some help, you handsome devil."

And *that* was how Tessa ended up ravenously chowing on a complimentary footlong ham-and-cheese sandwich with a large Diet Coke, parked in a cramped booth at the edge of a window, watching a single police cruiser wander up and down the parking lot. By the time she was done with the sandwich, the cop had given up. But Tessa sat in the booth for another forty-five minutes, just in case. During that time, the lunch rush happened—about a dozen people. She felt safely anonymous.

She took the time to think about what to do next.

She had no ID, no money, no car, no connections in this town—which she'd deduced was Albuquerque, the south portion. She was obviously being targeted by Harlan back home, and he was sparing no expense to round her up. Somehow, Dank and Leo had tracked her to that motel in Bumfuck, New Mexico, a hundred miles southwest of here, and who knew whether they were still after her—*but how would they be?* She kept watching out the window for that Pontiac, paranoid perhaps, but she couldn't help it. She felt like she'd be watching for that Pontiac for the rest of her life.

Then again, Dank and Leo had taken off with little provocation on the highway. After all the effort to chase her down, after coming all that way and staging the abduction in the middle of the night, they'd given her up on the Albuquerque interstate when a few strangers confronted them. I mean, they were armed, armed heavily. Why'd they give her up?

The money. That's what Dank had spat at Leo on a hot breath.

They had Floyd's money. Nearly half a million.

All this time she'd considered the two thugs to be just that: hired goons, basement-IQ heavies who worked strictly by instruction. But by all recent accounts, they were fucking criminal masterminds. Or at least Dank was. The question now wasn't really how he'd kept up with her. It was how he'd known about the money. Had it been strictly dumb luck? A quick search of the room?

When the Subway dining area was empty again, it was 12:55 p.m., according to the analog clock by the ovens. She cleaned up her trash and moseyed over to her new friend Marty.

"When are you off, honey?" she asked him coyly.

And *that* was how Tessa Rae Jayne got a ride downtown Albuquerque, as well as a fresh $20 bill from Marty to join the screwdriver in her uniform pocket. She gave Marty a peck on his trembling cheek, promising to see him again at the sandwich shop—she worked right across the way, after all!—but she knew she'd never see the overeager flush-faced kid again.

FIFTEEN
FLOYD TILLMAN WEATHERS

Floyd was a goddamn basket case by the time he hit the outskirts of Albuquerque. The sun burned overhead like an infected sore, reflecting what his brain felt like, and the scenery smeared all around him, greasy and hot and urgent.

Couple hours earlier, immediately as he accessed the tracker app on Perkins' phone, he'd zeroed in on a stationary blue dot that appeared to be hovering a quarter mile off the highway in south Albuquerque. He'd nearly run himself off the interstate above Socorro, seeing that. The proximity of the blue dot to New Mexico's largest city—where I-25 connected with I-40—immediately gave him vivid confirmation of his assumption about the route Tessa's abductors were taking. But why was the dot steady and still? The app was connected to Google Maps, so a quick zoom-in told him she was at a Hampton Inn south of town.

What?!

As he'd raced north just over the speed limit, he'd tried and failed to come up with a reason why Tessa's abductors might have dragged her to an Albuquerque hotel in the middle of the day.

And shit, man, that little blue dot brought everything back: How in the name of tittyfuck had this even *happened*? It was pure delirious luck—on top of Craig's assist—that he'd hacked his way into this tracking app and could follow her route, but *how on earth was she being tracked? Where was the fucking device? Buried in Tessa's ass?*

True, he'd been immersed in deep sleep when the gun had squashed against his skull, and he'd been facing away from whatever was happening with Tessa, but he was pretty damn sure they hadn't taken much else besides her. And she hadn't been wearing much—if anything. He couldn't remember if she'd even slipped on panties before sleeping.

He remembered Craig musing once over top-shelf whiskey one night about how tracking devices had evolved so much over the past ten years that it wasn't even funny. There were NSA-level trackers that went *waaaay* beyond the capabilities of the clunky battery-powered—and by nature, hobbled—devices that any ol' consumer could buy off Amazon. Even to Craig, they seemed like the stuff of science fiction, but he'd even heard rumors of subcutaneous chips you could *implant* that were as reliable as anything on the market. And given the fact that Tessa was *still* being tracked, minus her car and all her belongings and even her *phone*—well, anything was possible.

There was *also* the possibility that the dot on the app was tagging someone *else*. But, really, what were the chances of that? A decoy? How far ahead of Floyd were these motherfuckers capable of thinking? The voice that had whispered in his ear had sounded pretty friggin' confident. A chess player in a world of checkers? Perhaps. But Floyd had the overriding sense that what had happened was *exactly what had happened*. He wasn't going to drown in conspiracy theories.

These fucking creeps from Decatur had taken Tessa, brutally, and—striking an unforeseen pocket of gold—had stumbled on Floyd's money in the closet, had snatched it away, clean as could be, and he couldn't even decide what was pressing more heavily against his chest: the kidnapping or the theft. They were tied in knots with each other. Had the girl been the goal, or had it been the cash all along? How had Floyd slept through the room search? He was either stupid or simply ignoring the synaptic route that would lead him toward the notion that Tessa herself had—

Fuck you!

Impossible. Floyd simply *wasn't that naïve*.

Either way, the half a million was gone, and he had to recover that as surely as he had to find Tess.

Because Philip was on the other end of a brittle psychic line that went straight to Little Rock; it was a line of trust that had been severed. Floyd would either find a way to quickly repair that line, or he'd suffer the consequences—consequences that were surely more dire than he even understood.

Crazy thing was, Floyd had never even vaguely *considered* the possibility of losing the money. He was armed, he was anonymous and alone at the edge of Texas, he was minding his own business, and no one knew him from friggin' *Adam*.

He kept flashing on the final handshake from Philip before he'd dropped into the Camaro and rumbled south. The look in the man's flinty eyes had encompassed everything—deliberately so. It had reminded him of their first meeting behind the arcade in Boyle Park, arranged by Duane the day before, all the buzzing and chirping and clanging out front while he and Philip took each other's final measure, three or four heavies on the dark periphery of the room. And the way Philip materialized those other two times, once right in front of Floyd's folks' place, out of nowhere, the night Floyd had gone to say a sort of goodbye to his mom, at least, to urge her to be careful (knowing full well the danger he was putting her in). Philip there on the street, letting Floyd know he was goddamn omniscient. It gave him the shivers now. And the other time at the funeral parlor where Floyd worked sometimes—significance obvious. Philip's stale breath as he whispered to him in that little anteroom. The man always had the suggestion of a smile on his angular face, like he knew something you didn't, but the menace, the danger, that was always underneath it, unspoken. Didn't have to be said out loud. Floyd understood the stakes. It was amazing how Philip had made the risks apparent without actually laying them out.

And Floyd had been good with it. With all of it. Confident as hell, man.

The burner phone sitting on the passenger seat was quiet, had been quiet for weeks, and it sat there coldly, full of deadly portent. He felt as if it might sear a liquid-nitrogen burn into his skin if he touched it. It would tag him somehow, just as the app on Perkins' phone had tagged Tess.

About a hundred miles earlier, after he'd passed through a sprawling yellow ramshackle town by the unlikely name of Truth or Consequences, the dot on the digital map had gotten on the move again, inching north into the center of Albuquerque, in no apparent hurry.

So the question remained—why would they have taken Tess and the money to Albuquerque? It was possible whoever was after her had established a base there, so they didn't have to drag her ass a thousand miles. Whatever they were gonna do with her, they were gonna get it over with, and then scurry away with the bonus wad of cash they'd made on the job.

He had to assume that the money hadn't been the target all along. He *had to.*

Never taking the risk of pushing the Camaro past eighty-three, he'd raged across the dry, desolate miles. The slow desert hills rose and fell across the peripheral landscape, endlessly, eternally. He'd stopped once for fuel, in Socorro, clenching his jaw at the slow dispensation of gas, and now here he was, finally, at the bottom edge of Albuquerque.

He obediently dropped his speed as he entered the city limits.

He kept checking the app, feeling his anger bulge at the seams. He was *so close*. It was like a sweaty itch in the center of his back that he couldn't quite reach—in fact, his back *was* itching against the hot vinyl of the Camaro's cracked upholstery, and he thrashed violently in his seat, issuing a ragged yell from his throat.

Floyd veered off the interstate at Central Avenue and found himself, strangely enough, on Route 66. His heart did a little flip in his chest, although he doubted it meant anything. He knew Route 66 was a historic highway that threaded gradually northeast into Illinois, but this was surely a coincidence, right? That old highway wouldn't be nearly as quick a route to Decatur as the interstate system. But it was enough to snap him to attention.

He headed toward downtown and got snagged at a traffic signal. A trio of teen boys walked animatedly across the street in front of him, laughing as they sucked on Big Gulp sodas they'd picked up from the corner 7-11. When he brought Perkins' phone to his face, the blue dot was steadfastly immobile on the screen—tantalizingly so—and he could *feel* her there, straight ahead. He took a moment to zoom in on the map. Looked to be an apartment building, quarter mile ahead, down to the left. Adrenaline began flooding his veins.

"C'mon, Tess," he breathed. "Fuckin' *be* there, okay?"

The light turned, and he bolted forward. He made the quick left onto 1st Street and found himself gliding in front of the picturesque Albuquerque Transit Station. A big Amtrak sign stared back at him as he scanned the earthy mission-like structure. A series of archways gave way to emerald doors leading to a lobby and offices. He imagined the tracks behind the structure, waiting to carry passengers to distant locales.

Jumpin' Christ, he thought.

Yet another route out of town.

He wasn't sure what he was looking for as he got within a few hundred feet of the blue dot on the GPS screen—drama of some kind, *something*, but it wasn't happening, and it *kept* not happening. It was a normal street, people going about their midday business. There were no disturbances, there was no shouting. No vehicles peeling out, no gunfire. He needed something to *happen*, goddammit, something to tell him that these hours of suspense were coming to some kind of resolution. He was practically vibrating.

He followed the tracker app to the corner of 1st and Silver, where the Silver Horizon apartments loomed before him, quietly ominous. He yanked the Camaro over to the curb and stared wide-eyed at the square four-story building, which was decorated a mawkish palette of terracotta, lavender, and cream, and bolstered by an array of white balconies. A rainbow-colored wood fence surrounded the property. Floyd spotted the stately front entrance half a block south. The dot on the screen seemed to originate right in there.

He shut off the engine and watched five minutes more of nothing happening. He got his breathing under control, slid his slippery hands around the steering wheel.

He didn't see any cars around that might've matched the kind of dark American car that he'd glimpsed early this morning—just the usual assortment of foreign SUVs and dusty Jeeps and white sedans. A young couple walked by, jabbering, on their way to lunch maybe, and then came a grandmother with a stroller, probably on babysitter duty. The old woman caught sight of him and threw several wary glances his way, and then she turned the corner behind him and was gone. There was someone in the apartment building's lobby, moving around mostly out of view. Floyd decided to throw caution to the wind.

He glanced around for prying eyes, but the street was empty now. He discreetly checked the Beretta down next to his knee—fresh magazine, safety engaged in the slide. He lifted his ass off the seat and secured the pistol in his jeans. Then he stepped out of the Camaro, checked for traffic, and made his way across the street diagonally to the apartment building's entrance, Perkins' phone in hand.

A quick glance through the paneled windows revealed the single occupant of the lobby—a wild-haired young man now seated in one of the comfy orange chairs arranged in a loose assemblage next to a wall of mailboxes. The dude caught sight of Floyd just as he was bringing a big blue mug of coffee to his lips. There was a slight pause, and then he shrugged and began perusing his phone.

Floyd went in.

The blue dot was centered right here in the lobby, and it felt as if his chest could barely contain the hammering of his heartbeat.

"Where is she?" Floyd said, loud.

The man gulped his coffee, looked around confused. "Who?"

"The girl."

"Uh . . . look, man—"

"Shut up."

Floyd stalked the large room, peering into an empty cluttered office, checking the tile corridor that led to the elevators and a wide stairwell.

"Hello!" he called.

No one else here. But there were three floors above this one, and the app didn't care a whit about elevation, so she could be on any one of those levels.

He weighed his next move, went back to the seating area.

"You see a young lady come through here? Skin like chocolate, pretty as a peach, maybe with a couple other guys?"

"I—I just got here, man, I—"

"What's your name?"

A wary pause, then, "Tom."

Floyd got closer, stared at him.

"Think hard, Tom, you didn't see a thing?"

"Take it easy. I really don't know what you're talking about."

Before going to the stairwell, Floyd scrutinized the young man. He was seated with one leg up on a low coffee table, as if he'd been interrupted without a care in the world. His unkempt sandy hair and unshaven face told Floyd he lived here, was simply taking advantage of the amenities. He seemed to be wearing pajamas—ratty gray sweatpants and a bright green stretched-out tee shirt, string bracelets, flip-flops. He was watching Floyd with a mixture of caginess and dulled focus, as if from recent sleep. Dude was useless.

Then, on the verge of turning away, Floyd caught sight of the tiniest glimmer of something familiar.

He pocketed Perkins' phone, strode directly to Tom, grabbed his stupid green shirt, and lifted him out of his chair. Coffee spilled everywhere.

"Hey, man!" Tom screeched. *"What the fuck!"*

With his free hand, Floyd took hold of the necklace around Tom's scrawny neck.

"Where'd you get this?"

"None of your fuckin' business, you asshole!"

Floyd let the necklace fall to Tom's chest, then reached behind him to the Beretta. He withdrew it and pointed it at Tom's forehead. Tom about pissed his sweats.

"Holy fucking Christ, man, I found it, okay? I found it on the floor over there, right over there, like ten minutes ago!" He gestured toward the front windows, flinching. *"Get that thing off me, Jesus fucking—"*

Floyd pushed roughly at Tom's scrawny chest, let him trip back into the chair. Tom set the sloppy mug on a side table with distaste, wiped his scalded arm on the fabric. Yeah, he was fully awake now.

"Give me that thing," Floyd said, still aiming the Beretta at Tom's forehead. "That necklace belongs to the girl I'm looking for. You didn't think that was a detail worth mentioning?"

Tom was already taking off the necklace, watching the barrel of the pistol insolently.

"Who the fuck *are* you? I didn't see any girl, okay? I found the necklace, yeah, all right? I don't know who—"

"Uh huh."

Floyd took the jewelry from Tom's shaking fingers and studied it. It was Tessa's necklace all right—the silver rectangle pendant, the four stars. He remembered Tess fingering it last night as she'd talked sleepily about her brother, how he'd given to her from his hospital bed, in tears, how she was the only one who cared about him—all that. He could hear her voice even now, whispering and vulnerable.

He knew Tommy here was telling the truth, he felt that pretty clearly, but just in case, he told him to stay put—and should he decide to leave this lobby or make any calls, Floyd would devote the rest of his life to hunting Tom down and making him regret it.

"I'm not gonna do anything, *Christ.*"

"That's right."

"Can I get more fucking coffee?" Tom spat.

"Yeah, you do that."

Floyd slipped the necklace into his pocket, then headed for the stairs and clambered up them. At each floor, he stalked the length of the single centralized corridor, shouting for Tess, keeping an eye on the app, on which the blue dot still hovered maddeningly in the center of the building. On the second and third floors, several people responded to his shouts, countering them with their own shouted requests for him to shut the fuck up or they'd call the cops. On the edge of panic, Floyd whirled this way and that, knowing that actually searching these floors and their rooms was futile. He kept bringing up the app on the phone, trying in vain to hone in on the dot.

"Where are you?" he seethed in the barren stairwell.

It wasn't until he was striding down the corridor on the top floor when he stopped dead still, and the bottom dropped out from underneath him.

He pulled the necklace from his pocket, flipped it over in his hands. He found a slim groove at the pendant's edge and managed to get a fingernail in there.

The backing popped off to reveal a microchip.

The tracker.

Floyd backed up against a blank wall, staring at nothing.

SIXTEEN
TESSA RAE JAYNE

Downtown Albuquerque throbbed as if God herself had just recently shaped the city out of sand and glass and clay, and it stood there as if fresh from a great kiln. The city was mile-high dry and desert hot, and all its greenery seemed to be surviving against its will. Couple days of neglect, and the trees and shrubs would gasp and wither and wilt. It was hardly past lunchtime, and Tessa was so sweaty and exhausted that she was commiserating with the flora.

Traffic was light but steady, flowing through the brown city, which was laid out in a big, wide grid. She made her way along 2nd Street, determined. She looked like absolute shit in her pilfered hotel outfit, but she had an immediate strategy to change that. She'd asked ol' Marty to drop her off at a downtown shopping area, and now her eyes were furtively scanning storefronts.

Head down, she kept to the shade, getting a feel for the place. It was rare that Tessa felt as if she were sticking out like a sore thumb—but she certainly felt that in downtown Albuquerque. She hadn't tolerated that sensation often in her life, south of Chicago—in fact, she actively avoided those kinds of scenarios (and places). Life was too short. But sometimes she couldn't help it, and she felt it like a coal fire in her gut. Her instinct was always to push her chest out, get bold, get defiant, refuse that shit. But she wasn't gonna do that here, not now. She wanted as little attention paid to her as possible. Any other time, she yearned to be friggin' Augusta Savage, baby—but not today.

Not today.

After winding her way around the district, searching for a cheap clothing outlet, she made do with a thrift store on 8th. She found a good pair of slim jeans and a nondescript white blouse, as well as a sports bra for underneath it. In the other respect, she'd have to go commando; she wasn't buying no secondhand panties, *fuck* no, even if that was an *option*. She also grabbed a pair of better-fitting shoes, black sneakers that looked hardly used. She wore her new clothes out of the store, after having stuffed the hotel crap into a trash can, and on impulse she added a set of wide sunglasses—seventeen bucks for the lot, leaving her three measly dollars. Not to mention an old screwdriver, freshly transferred from pocket to pocket.

Okay. Next step, now that she was presentable.

She brought out Terrell's necklace from the neck of her new shirt, gave it a kiss for luck.

For confidence.

She headed back the way she'd come, head held a little higher, until she found the Southwest Galleria.

She found a parking lot on the west side of the building, about half full of vehicles. She wandered the area for about fifteen minutes before she found her first receipt lying forgotten on the asphalt. It was fluttering slightly on a dry breeze. She picked it up, scanned it—a worthless low-value credit receipt. She kept walking and found another receipt, this one left inside a bag resting at the top rim of a trash can, and this one much more fertile. It was a cash receipt for two pricey video games and a candy bar. Within ten more minutes, she'd found the items listed on the receipt inside the electronics store that anchored one end of the mall. She carried the items to the front registers, eyeballed the friendliest clerk, and shortly thereafter pocketed a hundred fifty dollars and change. The clerk, named Sandy, was all smiles, wished her a great day. Tessa waved as she left.

Desperate times call for desperate measures, yeah, all that.

Tessa wasn't proud of these necessary steps, and she even intended to return the money once this was all over. But she needed the cash *now*. She'd learned this particular trick from Josie Walters back home. Ninth grade. It was as if Josie had been committing petty retail theft all her life, like she'd learned it from her mom growing up or something, straight outta the stroller. Tessa had been mortified watching her do it that first time, but she hadn't been able to deny the high in the aftermath of their giggling scams across three Decatur shopping malls, the sloshing liquor and the new CDs Josie blared from her car deck at the edge of the ravine—and, yeah, Tessa's first weed, purchased from that skeevy pervert, Mike-O's older brother with the missing teeth that he'd poke his tongue through, all suggestive and gross. Christ, when was the last time she'd thought of *Josie*, that wild, dark-eyed white girl? Tessa sometimes liked to think she'd grown away from her influence, but apparently not.

She was hoping for one more score after the electronics store, pad her pocket a little more. She discreetly rooted through three more trash cans—but she couldn't make it happen. Too early in the day. That was all right, for now.

She stepped out of the mall, back into the sharp heat, and she realized a plan was extending out before her. It was tenuous and open-ended, but it was forming. A bus ticket down to Las Cruces was surely in her budget. Perhaps it was naïve of her to let her plan go in that direction, but there was no doubt that it appealed to her the most. From Las Cruces, she could either find a way back to the border and beyond, or she could somehow, miraculously, get back into the groove she'd established with Floyd Weathers. Find him, and then get back to flying west together along the lonesome highway, bound for glory, whether California or Vegas or Frisco or beyond. She'd felt feisty and invincible in her short time by his side, and even though things had turned to interim shit, it wouldn't happen again. Not after the escape she'd made.

Did she dare allow herself the luxury of imagining that she would see Floyd again? To get to *that* point, she'd have to acknowledge the possibility that he was even alive. Because a big part of her kept picturing him lying dead, right now, on the floor of that crappy hotel room—dead by Dank's hand. Maybe it was better to suppose Floyd was gone. That their interlude had been merely a strange and thrilling dream, but, in the end, the stuff of fantasy. And that she would now have no choice but to rejoin the land of the living, the realm of reality, and continue her plan toward Mexico. Having eluded her pursuers, she'd finish her exit from the scene.

Goddammit, though—she *ached* for Floyd, and it was more than the vice-grip of his hands as they held her, and it was more than the feel of his cock kissing her uterus, and it was more than that whiskery smile. The two of them shared something that they'd only just begun to explore. She felt as if she was meant to find that man. No one else in Illinois came close to what she saw in Floyd Weathers. There was something missing inside him, and there was something missing inside *her*, and when they were together in just the right way, those gaps closed on each other and made something whole.

She felt like a child, thinking some of these thoughts. Even now, she couldn't contain a bright giggle, hiding it behind her fingers. But to hell with that! Sometimes it was right to be childlike. To feel innocence. That was a lesson from her mother; that's what she used to say. *You may be growin' up, girl, but don't grow up too far. Keep that kid inside you, you understand?*

She knew it would be in her best interest to get the hell off the street, to avoid the eyes that were falling all over her. Every third person she passed seemed to stare at her as if she were some kind of foreign entity—a stranger in a strange land—and Tessa began to accumulate the somehow shameful weight of that. On one hand, seeing all these people wandering their streets without any sign of the face masks that had dominated society for two goddamn years was a jarring relief. A distant part of her savored the fact that she was seeing full features again. But on the other hand, she wanted no part of it. She felt exposed and obvious, even with her newly acquired sunglasses. With every step, she tried to stick to the shade, hide her face, turn away from the people around her. And she *despised* herself for feeling that way—particularly in light of the alternate reality, still fresh in her brain, where she was right now basking under a Mexican sun, anonymous and free, a mahogany heroine with drying sea salt on her skin and not a worry in the world about the life she'd left behind.

Maybe, just maybe, she could still find her way there.

For now, though, Tessa was thirsty.

She ducked into a convenience shop, wandered the aisles, found a bottle of water. She paid for it and lingered by the front window, gazing out at the street. The window was plastered with hand-painted advertisements, and she felt safely anonymous behind it. She took long swallows of the water, satisfying the dryness in her throat. The altitude seemed to want to suck all the moisture out of her body. She couldn't imagine living up here in the desert sky. She would never be able to buy enough lotion for her parched brown skin.

She glanced over at the shopkeeper, a middle-aged dude with close-cropped hair who was already casting a suspicious gaze her way. Maybe she was just paranoid.

"Hey man," she called. "There a bus station nearby?"

He watched her insolently for a moment, appraising her, then he gestured east. "Transit center's a block over on 1st. Buses run out of there."

She nodded, took another long swallow. "Well, that's easy."

"Where you headed?"

It was her turn to appraise him. Maybe she was just distrustful by nature.

"South."

"There's a lot more to the north."

She let out a snicker. "Yeah, I guess that's the problem."

What happened next seemed to do so out of a nightmare—stuttering and shifting.

Tessa turned back to the window to try to get a glimpse of the bus station that was apparently a block east, and abruptly a familiar black Pontiac jerked to a stop in front of the store. Dank and Leo were glaring at her from the front seats.

She made a ragged choking sound in her throat and dropped her water bottle, which bounced and splashed. She felt her entire body blanch, as if all the blood had drained out of her. All of the confidence she had gained over the past few hours—gone in a blink.

Coughing, she staggered backward.

Impossible!

She was immobile for a split second as she watched the Pontiac's doors fly open like dark wings.

"*Back door?*" she managed, still coughing, but she was already running numbly toward the rear of the store, ricocheting off two displays and scattering snack food.

"Hey!" came the clerk's voice, loud.

Tessa crashed through a set of gray double doors into a storage area that smelled like wet cardboard. She darted her gaze about and followed her feet through the dimness. She slammed into a shelving unit and spun crazily, reoriented herself, and rushed past it. She found herself suddenly at an exterior door and punched the steel bar at its center to send it flying open upon a rear alley. She ran like hell to the south, her sneakers slapping pavement. The sound smacked back at her along the close concrete walls as her breath escaped her in quick gasps. When she reached the mouth of the alley and made the turn east, she heard the store's rear door slam open again behind her, and Leo's voice said something heavy and stupidly menacing, but she kept sprinting, letting his shouts thunder along the concrete walls and die out as her ears throbbed with the sound of her breath.

She slowed to a quick walk along the sidewalk, and only then did it register that he'd said, *"You can't hide, bitch!"*

A nightmare.

She was inside a nightmare!

She took what she thought would be an unexpected turn onto Gold and jogged east, checking behind her at every fourth or fifth step. Not seeing Dank or Leo, she took an abrupt left onto 3rd and slowed down, thinking. She needed a place to hide. A good place. Or she needed a ride. What she *really* needed was to get to the transit station and board a bus when they weren't looking, and get the fuck out of this town.

She continued down 3rd until she reached Silver, and turned east again toward the station. She didn't see Leo or Dank anywhere. Once she got to the station, there'd be enough people around to protect her. There was probably security that would discourage them. She quickened her pace.

Halfway down the block, she heard a screeching of tires somewhere behind her, and she jerked, turning around. There was nothing there but her paranoia shouting back at her. A white dude walking on the other side of the street gave her an expressionless glance, then another more curious look, then continued on his way, lost in his Beats headphones and filthy jeans and ragged tee.

Looming on the left was a gaudy apartment complex bordered by rainbow-colored fencing. She scanned the building for an opening. She found a glass door on the side of the building, tried it, locked. She skirted around the corner and the front entrance came at her like salvation. She swept into an empty lobby, went immediately to the edge of the window and peered out. No movement out there.

She backed away from the window, hiding. Falling into a couch against the wall, she waited for a solution to occur to her. She thought that if she could only wait a while, she could find a way to the transit station—only a block away. Fuck the bus, she'd get on a high-speed train, head to California or something. Florida. An entirely new direction. Anywhere but here.

Her thoughts stopped swirling, and she found herself back at the most basic question: How had they found her? *Again!* She would never, ever escape them, would always be in their sights, would never outsmart these two fucking goons who only wanted to drag her back, and why oh why had she stopped at that bar in Malvado? She should've kept on going, she should've rushed past Floyd and his stupid cock, and if she *had* done that, she'd be in friggin' *Baja* by now, in the warm surf, free and clear in the yellow bikini that was now lost to her, along with everything else in her life, but instead she was cornered in the middle of goddamn Albuquerque! *How in fucking hell had they found her?* It was preternatural, the way they'd—

It hit her like a blow to the chest.

Images of Floyd checking the Beetle flashed through her brain, his frustration when he'd found nothing, and then rifling through her shit, intent on finding whatever it was that Perkins had used to follow her. Because *it had to be something*, he'd insisted. But no, there was nothing. And she didn't have anything left, did she? Nothing!

Well, except for one thing.

The only thing left to her name.

"Oh no." The words leaked out of her.

She drew the necklace away from her skin, fingers quivering. She studied the Chicago pendant with mute, helpless horror, unable to move. She began to weep, quivering gasps overtaking her lungs, and she couldn't stop them. *It can't be.* She pictured her brother's face, but his features blurred behind her tears. *Why would—? When—?* She couldn't process anything. Everything was a jumble.

She felt her hand yanking the necklace over her head, snagging it briefly in her hair, and then she was throwing the necklace away from her in a feeble spasm. She distantly heard the sound of it tinkling against something metal, and then there was silence.

When Dank pushed through the door, she felt as if she had no energy left in her limbs. He was shouting at her with his tinny voice, but she couldn't focus on him, couldn't make sense of language. She let him lead her out, and she barely registered Leo standing against the Pontiac, which was idling at the curb. She felt herself shoved into the back seat, and then the rough movement of the vehicle as she stared at the grimy black floorboards. There was a brown nickel lying there, its face regarding her passively.

Dank was talking up front, but she wasn't hearing him. Her head felt stuffed with cotton.

It wasn't until minutes later that his voice got through. He was reaching into the back seat and clutching her thigh with the claw of his grip.

"Did you fuckin' hear me?"

She blinked.

"I'm serious, you fuckin' try anything like that again, and I will slaughter you and your brother myself."

The weathered vinyl of the back seat smelled like gym sock. She pushed herself up, felt Leo watching her closely but dumbly from the passenger seat. She felt dizzy as hell. Lost. Dank made a wide turn, and with the motion Tessa let her head fall against the window.

"She's good now," Leo said, as if from far away, as if from underwater. "She'll be good now."

Dank was laughing too. "I can't believe you didn't go to the police! Boy, you're a piece of work."

"Ha! We got her!"

Tessa tuned them out.

As they passed a certain intersection, she might have seen—had she glanced up—a black Camaro stopped at the light, waiting for a trio of teenagers to cross Route 66 from the corner 7-11 toward their after-school basketball practice. Had she seen the Camaro's driver drumming his fingers on his well-worn leather-wrapped steering wheel, hope might have blossomed inside her, fleetingly, only to be trampled into the red New Mexican dirt as the Camaro receded behind her.

But the Camaro went unnoticed.

SEVENTEEN
FLOYD TILLMAN WEATHERS

The burger tasted like a spicy wafer of shit.

It was slathered with green chile, leaking into a pile of twice-battered fries. Floyd thought he probably would've loved the meal under other circumstances. You know, if his life hadn't been turned completely over and flushed into a landfill, all in the space of a day and a half. Maybe it was inevitable that his tastebuds had gone to hell, along with everything else.

He'd spotted the greasy joint on his way back to I-25, had almost passed it until he realized somewhere in the center of his demoralization that he was fucking ravenous and needed to pee. And what was the hurry now, anyway? He needed time to gather his wits—Christ, man, he needed a moment to reevaluate every goddamn choice he'd made throughout his existence. Because he had *nothing* now. Nothing.

Well. He had *something*. And it would have to do. He would have to *make* it do.

He still had Perkins' phone.

The thing was sitting black and mute on the other side of the wobbly table, and he was staring at it between miserable bites of his burger. What had it given him so far? It had given him a lifeline—to both Tessa and the cash—that had led him to an Albuquerque apartment building lobby where he could practically smell her lingering scent. *That* was how close he'd come to her, he *knew* it. *Minutes*. But she'd been snatched away from him again. He'd waited in that lobby like a fucking idiot for a half hour before understanding the futility of his inaction. They were gone. Again. They'd been there, he was sure of it. All three of them. For whatever reason. But they were gone now, like smoke dissipating in the wake of a flash fire.

He'd taken the necklace, but he'd ground the microchip under his boot heel.

His mind kept struggling—perhaps pointlessly—to fashion a narrative out of the earlier movement of the blue dot on the screen as it had ricocheted through the city. Tried to make sense of the weird route Leonard McQuoid and Ron Dankworth had taken. But Floyd had nothing real to grab hold of. There was only the necklace, and it would no longer tell him anything. It was hanging uselessly around his neck, and it felt so heavy that he felt it might pull him down to the ground.

Had Tessa dumped the necklace herself? He doubted there was any way in hell she'd gotten away from the two assholes, considering their intentions and their artillery, but it was possible she'd let it drop inconspicuously while held captive. More likely, Dankworth or McQuoid had come to the belated realization that Floyd might be able to hack into the tracker app, and *they'd* been the ones to yank the necklace off Tessa and toss it into some meaningless *nowhere* to throw Floyd off the scent. They'd proven themselves to be wilier than Tessa had suggested.

In which case, all this speculation meant absolute dogshit because the end result was the same: He was back to square one.

He finished off the burger in one massive bite, chewing it like cud while he absently wiped his fingers on a greasy napkin.

The way he figured, he had two choices. He could chalk up the whole deal to a massive loss. Turn around and head immediately for the border, aligning himself closely with Tessa's original plan, actually, except that he had the experience—and frankly, the age and race and gender—to do it right. He'd disappear into Mexico and find a way to elude the repercussions he'd inevitably face from Little Rock. Change his identity, his appearance. Get lost in the world but carry that albatross on his back, like *always*, till the end of time or his own demise, which was undoubtedly closer on the horizon than he'd realize. He'd always be looking over his shoulder. But that was the coward's way out, wasn't it?

No, the only choice was to go forward.

Get the goddamn girl, get the goddamn money.

He *had* to go to Illinois, and yet there was *no way* he could go to Illinois. He was *supposed* to be in Malvado, waiting for Philip's call. The burner was in his pocket, quiet as a brick. But it wouldn't be quiet forever. It could go off *right now*, vibrating its urgency, and then Floyd would be fucked in real time. Pockets turned out, shrugging like a retard. The burner was like a timebomb against his left hip. Yeah, it had been silent for months, but fuck, man, it had the potential to overturn his existence in its own way during the space of this wretched lunch.

His was a tale of two phones.

He knew his only immediate recourse was to dive deeper into Perkins' personal information and conversations, and come up with a plan for Illinois. Which meant he was about to hop into the Camaro and head north.

He felt himself putting off the inevitable, but he knew he'd soon be immersed in Perkins' texts and email messages. He wanted to deny it, but it was gonna happen. He'd do it while seated in this very seat. He found himself wolfing down his fries and Coke, as if gearing himself up for it.

After a few minutes, Floyd became aware of voices coming from his left. He turned to find two young women at the next table, regarding him peripherally. He hadn't even seen them sit down. He was suddenly certain they'd been talking about him as they nibbled at their fries. The woman closest to him was a perky pretty blonde with a fashionable ponytail, light fresh makeup, big blue eyes, an annoying expression that said life was good. She was wearing white shorts and a sky-blue halter. The other woman was a fetchingly freckled redhead, same age, in gray yoga pants and a black tee shirt that read NIKE in gigantic letters. He watched the two of them coolly for long enough to make them shift in their seats uncomfortably.

"It's not gonna bite ya, y'know," the blonde said, nodding at Perkins' phone, and the redhead smirked.

Floyd watched them over the rim of his soda cup. Swallowed, said, "You can't be sure of that."

Emboldened, the blonde faced him more fully. "I'm Stephanie. She's Melanie."

"That's cute," he murmured.

"What?"

"You gals rhyme."

The women shared a delighted bout of giggles. Floyd wasn't feelin' it.

"I like your necklace," Stephanie said after a pregnant pause.

Floyd glanced down at Tessa's pendant against his shirt, nodded slowly. Actually, it was her brother's pendant. Terrell. A man he'd probably never know.

On a sigh, he said, "That's the flag of Chicago."

"Hmmm." Smiling, encouraging. "Sounds like there's a juicy story behind that."

He grunted. "Used to be."

Stephanie shared a look with Melanie. "Wow."

"Sorry," he said, "just got some . . . got some bad news."

He regretted the words as soon as they left his mouth. He didn't want to encourage *anything* right now, let alone an extended conversation with a couple of locals.

"Oh no!" Stephanie said, and there was the sound of a plastic chair scooting closer.

"No, no," he gestured, warding her off, "just something I gotta deal with."

"Now don't be that way. We're pretty good problem-solvers. Anything we can help with?"

Floyd slumped back in his chair, took a breath, wished he'd just gotten up and left without a word. The burger joint was mostly empty, between lunch and dinner. Employees were busy behind the counter restocking and shooting the shit, laughing, horsing around. The old-school pegboard menu over the counter was yellowed and cracking with age. The smell of grease permeated the entire place. Normally, this was the kind of joint he'd savor. And these were maybe the kind of young ladies he might typically have time for, but today . . . .

"Yeah?" he said.

"Sure, lay it on us."

He tried to take their measure, but his focus was off. He felt dulled by the long morning's events and the constant buzz of adrenaline. Suspicion flared somewhere deep but then trailed off into nothingness. Stephanie and Melanie were just two lonely women looking for some kind of wrong-headed excitement with the scruffy dude at the grease pit.

"I don't think so."

"Oh, come on," Stephanie insisted, "we won't bite, either. What's your name, anyway?"

Floyd was watching the redhead, Melanie, the prettier of the two, as she sat in her chair saying nothing. She was giving him the coy eye, keeping her lower lip moist.

"Joe," he said.

He didn't pick up any odd flickers in their gazes, as if they might've expected a different name. These girls were actually trying to pick him up. They probably had husbands at home, working jobs for them, but here they were tempting fate.

"Well, Joe, Melanie and I just came from this big get-together at the church, and it was all about fund-raising and how great we did with it. So, I'm tellin' you, we know what we're talking about. We know how to take care of stuff."

He watched her mouth as she talked, then turned to Melanie. "That right?"

Melanie only smiled, nodded.

"You don't talk?" he said.

She cleared her throat, and her cheeks flushed. "Oh, I talk."

"She's shy," Stephanie offered.

"Nothin' wrong with that," Floyd said.

That seemed to energize both women, and then the whole scene was *really* depressing him. For the next fifteen minutes, the women babbled on and on about their lives in Albuquerque while Floyd said essentially nothing. Stephanie had been homecoming queen in high school, five years ago, and Melanie had been a varsity cheerleader, still had her uniform in her closet, still brought it out sometimes. They'd been debating heading downtown and getting matching beach henna, even though they were stuck here, hundreds of miles away from any beaches for the fore-seeable future. See, they had pretty good jobs in the business district, and Melanie at least was getting matching employer contributions to her 401(k), and Stephanie had already accrued a bunch of vacation time, and they could both see a lot of opportunities for advancement up the corpo-rate ladder, and their dreams were opening up in front of them, and *blah blah blah!*, and by then Floyd was only nodding and grunting and thinking about Tessa Rae Jayne, the way she bucked in the saddle at the bottom of the world.

After a while, Stephanie was batting at his upper arm playfully, and then she was developing a little habit of covering his rough hand with her small one, as if in commiseration, but her fingers were warm and seemed to pull at him, and the expression on her face only increased the gravity.

"Listen, uh, ladies," Floyd said, "I would *love* to hang with you two, *believe* me I would, but I gotta go over to that Camaro there and get back on the road."

Stephanie let loose with a disappointed chuff, and Melanie spoke up with a heated whisper—"We'd make it worth your while." He watched her for a long moment, watched her faux-innocent smile, her dancing freckles, her sparkling perfect eyes.

Later, Floyd was sure he could've let that little scenario play out to its sticky end, and a part of him might've even felt a kind of satisfaction. But he couldn't deny the overriding understanding that his destiny lay elsewhere now. A couple days ago, this whole scene might've played differently. But what the hell was he thinking? If Tess had never set foot in his life, he'd still be planted in his little hovel of a motel room sucking on a toothpick, and he'd never even be in Albuquerque right now.

Fucking Albuquerque.

He left Stephanie and Melanie sitting at their table, shrugging at him as if he'd botched a once-in-a-lifetime opportunity—and just maybe he had. *Holy shit*, maybe he had. But all he could do was watch their faces, their moving mouths, behind the smeared glass.

He dropped into the Camaro's driver's seat and fired her up.

An hour later, Floyd was planted at a rest stop halfway to Amarillo, alongside I-40, going through Perkins' fucking phone, muttering to himself. There were suddenly too many possibilities, too many paths possibly taken. It was enough to make a man feel hopeless.

He had Tessa and packaged bundles of cash and Philip's clenched-jaw gaze and two eyebrow-wiggling Albuquerque women taking up space in his head, and his fingers were actually trembling as he tried to parse scads of coded messages in Perkins' texting app. The man had been engaging in a series of conversations right to the end—perhaps half a dozen—and in all of them, the recipients didn't have names but rather numbers. One of them was a series of asterisks that ended with 69, a strange combination of smart security and adolescent humor. The most recent text string's top message read:

THE OTHER TWO GOT HER COME BACK

Floyd scrolled down this efficient conversation, and it was clear Perkins had been texting with some kind of ringleader. The messages were mostly oblique, but he found a few zingers, descending chronologically.

D AND L WENT ANYWAY YOU RETARD WHERE ARE YOU

WHERE THE FUCK ARE YOU

H SAYS REMIND YOU WHAT HE SAID LAST NIGHT RE: BROTHER. SHE DOESNT KNOW

DONT LET HER CROSS IS THE MAIN THING

OBV WHERE SHES HEADED

Floyd remembered Tessa talking about a man named Harlan, but she hadn't shared any details beyond his tattoos and sullenness. She'd thrown out the name with a grimace, had made it clear he was the guy heading the show. For now, Floyd would assume Harlan was H, and this message had come from a middleman. The conversation petered out two days previous, suggesting to Floyd that Perkins had had the presence of mind to permanently delete messages along the way. He simply hadn't gotten to these most recent missives.

There were a brief couple of unanswered texts from Perkins, sent to the middleman.

FOUND HER

MALVADO TX

Another conversation took place two days earlier, between Perkins and a recipient known only as a series of Ks bookended by percent signs. Floyd decided to make the leap and speculate that this individual was either Dankworth or McQuoid. It was more than an educated guess. Whichever one had pressed the firearm to his skull—that was the one who'd written these texts—Floyd felt it in a tingling of the skin on the back of his hand as he scrolled through them, again backward through the past few days.

GOT HER. WHERE ARE YOU, YOU USELESS FUCK?

ARE YOU IN POSSESSION? TELL ME WHAT I'M READING.

ON OUR WAY.

H MOBILIZED US TO BACK YOU UP, YOU FAT FAGGOT.

I SWEAR IF I HAVE TO COME DOWN THERE, I WILL NOT BE HAPPY.

The guy used correct punctuation and big words like *mobilized* in his texts. Reading the messages, Floyd immediately flashed on the auditory memory of the dude with the gun. His gut told him this was Ronald Dankworth. Reasonably educated asshole. Floyd fixed the name in his head, heard the words of the texts coming out in that weird voice, heard him talking still, behind him, cowardly, out of his sight range, backing out of the motel room.

Floyd was able to piece together a scenario that made basic sense:

these two guys, Dankworth and McQuoid, batting cleanup for the bumbling and now-deceased Perkins, hauling Tessa back home at the behest of Harlan Eckhart, the ringleader, and an unnamed fifth man known to Floyd only as Mr. 69.

He grabbed Tessa's phone again and found the address she'd searched for in Forsyth. He copied that into Google and checked news items, quickly bringing up a breaking news story.

Woman Identified in House Fire

Two days after Evangeline Eastman of Hickory Point was presumed dead in a house fire in Forsyth, a sheriff's office in central Illinois confirmed that her remains had been unearthed in the debris. No arrests have been made in the arson-related incident, and no persons of interest have been identified.

In a statement Monday, the Macon County Sheriff's Office said the family of Eastman, 66, reported her as missing and suspected dead in the blaze that occurred in the early morning hours of July 19. Identification of the recovered remains occurred through DNA analysis last night.

The investigation of the house fire by Illinois authorities revealed earlier that the home in Forsyth had been a purported drug den, echoing statements from neighbors. Police uncovered the burned remnants of a methadone laboratory, drug synthetization paraphernalia and cultivation products, as well as the charred remains of a large quantity of methamphetamine, cocaine, marijuana and other illegal substances. Prior to these discoveries, the Macon County Sheriff's Office's Criminal Investigations Division had received multiple complaints over the past three years, but two separate multi-agency investigations during that time frame had found no incriminating evidence.

This article will be updated as new information becomes available.

Floyd powered off the phone, let it drop next to the other one in the passenger seat.

He sat there for a long moment staring up a low hill toward a brown edifice that contained a couple of expansive shitters and was surrounded by covered picnic tables. A couple families milled about in the shade. As he watched, a woman strode from the bathroom toward her vehicle. She had a pandemic mask on her face—one of the holdouts. Floyd supposed the things would simply be a part of life now. It was disheartening, and it brought back the mess the country had fallen into for no good reason other than anger and lies and stupidity, and it all made him want to turn right around and head for the border again.

But he looked away, and he twisted the Camaro's ignition, and he pulled out of the rest area, joining the steady flow of traffic heading east. He was bound for Decatur. And maybe to a village called Forsyth. He'd have to think about where to start.

Although he had no way of knowing it, he was only a ninety-three miles behind the Pontiac carrying Ronald Dankworth, Leonard McQuoid, and Tessa Rae Jayne.

EIGHTEEN
TESSA RAE JAYNE

The earthy heat-shimmering scenery diminished behind the Pontiac like a dream she'd been jarred from. She wanted to reach through the rear window, keep hold of it, extend herself out into the ether, but there was no escaping fate now.

She was headed back home, and she couldn't do a goddamn thing about it.

As Leo and Dank babbled away up front, sometimes shouting, sometimes laughing, Tessa was fixated on what lay ahead. To her surprise, she found her thoughts dwelling on her family. Maybe it was denial about her current predicament, maybe it was lingering fear about what she'd done in Forsyth, maybe it was the fact that her fucking hands were tied together with twine . . . but she was focusing on the familiar.

Home.

To her brother, of course, but also her mother. It wasn't fair what Tessa had done to her, she knew that. Leaving her to tend to Terrell all on her own, but obviously it went *waaaaay* beyond that. When she thought of her mother's face, she couldn't help the low burn she felt in her gut. The two of them had never been close, and whose fault was *that?* Tessa would admit she'd always been a daddy's girl, even when her daddy'd wanted little to do with her, and maybe it was only because of the look her mama gave her when Tessa always ran first into her daddy's stiff arms.

Tessa felt a hollow shame when she thought of home, where now Terrell was probably laid up in *his* bed, and her mama didn't know what the hell was going on.

She shouldn't have done that shit.

Wasn't it enough that she'd watched her father die in a hospital bed ten years ago? She'd observed the slackening of his face, the graying of his skin as the machines had begun to drone. She'd screamed at him not to go, not to leave her with Mommy, no, not with Mommy, and of course her mom had been right there behind her, her hand on Tessa's shoulder flinching away as if stung. All of nine years old, Tessa had let her emotions consume her, and she'd cried out something unforgivable. Something neither she nor her mother would ever forget. She'd tried! She'd begged her mother to forgive her, years later, but Kendra Jayne offered only the barest efforts to hear Tessa, the lines of her face betraying the wound that would never heal. The wound Tessa had inflicted.

She couldn't get past it.

Uncle Johnny had promised in those last moments before she'd fled that he'd look in on them, provide for them, but she felt the weight of the responsibility crashing back into her. She heard her mother's voice wailing.

Now, in the back of the car, she felt tears flowing down her cheeks, and somewhere deep she registered shock at her own thoughts.

"Ah, what's a'matter, kiddo?" came Leo's thick voice. "Can't handle the heat?"

Through blurred vision, Tessa glared at him. The man was pushing out his lower lip like a cartoon infant. She bent to wipe her eyes on her shoulders, kept watching him until he looked away. Leo had been un-characteristically jubilant since they'd gotten back on the interstate, as if he'd just loaded himself with Twinkies and Mountain Dew.

"She can't handle the heat," he told Dank.

"Will you shut up?" Dank said, his voice a barely contained shout. "Will you please just shut up? Between you and that girl, I'm gonna die from a cerebrovascular event right here in this seat."

"A what?"

"A *stroke*, man, I'm gonna have a *stroke*, and you'll see what happens then."

"What'll happen then?" Leo said, smiling, happy.

"My foot'll be like deadweight on the gas, this car'll get on up to a hundred, hundred-twenty, blasting down the road till my dead hands jerk the wheel and send all of us careening off road. Head-on collision with a bank of Texas dirt is what I'm talking about. They'll be mopping up your blood and brains for weeks."

"Sweet."

"Oh Jesus, just . . . just shut the fuck up."

Leo faced her again, still smiling goofily. "Didn't know we were *trackin'* you, didja?"

She didn't say anything.

"It was the necklace, ha! You figured that out, though. It was the necklace Harlan gave your brother. That's so fucking awesome. Your *brother* was the one he wanted to track, cuz he was being a fucking idiot all the time, not *you!*" His words dissolved into laughter.

"Shut up," Dank said.

Tessa turned her head back to the rear window and tuned out the chatter. She vaguely sensed Leo trying to further rile her up, but she suppressed his voice so that it began to sound like the adults in the old *Peanuts* cartoons she used to watch with Terrell. It was the way she dealt with Leo back home, whenever he got within ten feet of her at the bar. His fumbling drunken come-ons, his attempts at inappropriate jokes, whatever. She remembered one night at Wayne's when he'd cornered her by the bathrooms, and she'd seen the look in his eyes—the silver glint behind the fumbling foolishness—and she *knew* that given the opportunity he would hold her down and rape her. It was not even a possibility open to debate. It was *what would happen* given no restraint. Fortunately, that restraint came in the form of Wayne himself carrying supplies to the back, and Leo had backed off, laughing, shrugging, all a joke, *hahaha.*

She'd always considered Leo to be *that kind* of hulking retard, but even hulking retards could be dealt with, if you knew how. Problem was, now the retard was dangerous *and* armed—and had her tied up in the back of a car.

"Why are you so talkative all of a sudden, anyway?" came Dank's voice.

Tessa found it more difficult to tune Dank out than Leo. Resigned, she turned back to face front. She wanted to hear this.

"We got her *back*, Ronnie, that's why." Leo's eyes glinted sharply as he grinned at her. "Look at her, there she is."

"We were always gonna get her back."

"You don't know that! Back there on the side of the highway? We were *fucked*, man. Are you *kidding* me? And she could've easily gotten into a precinct somewhere, like you said!"

"Again, *please* shut up."

"Whatever, Ronnie, all I'm sayin' is it feels good. Feels good to be on our way back." Leo began drumming his sausage fingers on his thighs. "Mission accomplished, right?"

From the driver's seat, Dank only glared at his counterpart. As the interior fell into silence and Leo continued watching her from the passenger seat, Tessa let her head fall back against the black upholstery. Through half-lidded eyes, she gazed straight ahead at the Pontiac's dusty center console. The radio was turned on very low, glowing a soft green, and some kind of AM program was murmuring. There was a photo fastened with tape below an air vent, and it appeared to show Dank posing with a rifle like Lee fucking Oswald. To the left of it was a rinky-dink phone mount holding Dank's cell, which was powered off and smeared, probably with fecal matter. This image almost made her laugh, but she held it in check. Kept her face slack.

For the past few hours, Tessa had been steadily testing the give on her restraints. Her sweaty wrists moved together behind her waist, pulling, wrenching. She hadn't made a lot of progress. Whenever she tried to free one of her hands, vital bones seemed to be on the verge of crunching. And when she felt the inevitable frustration and wanted to cry out, she focused her mind on her front right pocket, where she could feel the weight of the screwdriver she still had from the trunk. Somehow, neither Dank nor Leo had noticed it.

"Fuck, man, I'm just looking forward to a coupla beers," Leo said, still staring straight back at her. "You gonna serve me up, once we get there? No spitting in the suds, now."

Tessa watched the monotonous scenery come at them, the struggling yellows and greens, the sparse trees, flatlands as far as the eye could see. It was like looking sideways at a map of Texas, that was how flat it was. The sun was approaching the horizon behind them.

"We're about nine hundred miles from Wayne's," Dank told Leo, "so better get comfortable."

Finally, Leo turned forward. "Maybe we can stop at a store somewhere, then. I could use a sammich."

By instinct, Tessa's eyes flicked to the gas gauge, saw that it was low. When her gaze came back up, she noticed Dank's steely eyes considering her in the rearview mirror. There was suspicion in those eyes, and hatred too. He was gearing up to something, fixing to ask her something. She could feel it. But it was another mile before he opened his mouth.

"So, where's Perkins?"

She locked her eyes on the mirror. "How the fuck should I know?" she said evenly.

It wasn't the first time Dank had asked her the question. In fact, it was the fifth. He'd been peppering their eastward journey with variations of it.

"Oh, I think you *do* know."

"Yeah?"

"Yeah, I think you have firsthand knowledge. I think you and that good ol' boy back there in Lordsburg took care of Perkins at the border." Dank watched her for a reaction, but she let her eyes go unfocused. "You burned rubber west with that boy after you hogtied Perkins in Malvado, is that it? Your new fella got some people watching Perkins across the border? Because I've had nothing but radio silence from him for two days."

Leo blinked, glanced from Dank to Tessa. "Yeah."

Tessa shrugged. "Look, I told you I saw his truck, but I didn't see the man." "Uh huh."

"He was parked outside a diner there, and when we saw it, we took off—okay? That's what happened. Believe it or don't."

Dank continued to glare at her in the rearview, and she gazed back defiantly despite her churning guts. She was sure he could read her, and that only compounded her misery because she knew Dank was nothing compared with Harlan—and that's who was at the end of this ride.

At some point, resigned and under the drone of the road, she managed to fall asleep.

Two hours after nightfall, they were deep into Oklahoma. They had topped off the gas on the Texas border, Leo warning her against anything fishy as Dank filled up the Pontiac at the pump farthest away from the cashier in the little convenience store. Tessa had felt Leo's eyes wandering all over her. He hadn't said a word, but his gaze had felt like some kind of gross tongue. Dank had returned from the sweaty-looking store with a sixer of Bud, and now Leo was four cans into it, staring straight out into the oncoming night. Tessa was crammed into the corner of the back seat behind Dank, feigning sleep now, working her wrists and fingers against the twine and imagining the feel of the screwdriver in her grip.

Up front, Leo slurred, "Gonna have to piss."

"Use the bottle."

"It's full."

Dank made a sound in his throat. "Then dump it out the window."

"C'mon, Ronnie, I don't want to piss in the bottle anymore, not with *her* in here."

"She's asleep."

"C'mon, man."

"Fucking hell, six hundred more miles of this."

There was just the noise of the road for long minutes. Tessa felt herself starting to nod off, and she pinched her own ass a few times, knowing that she had to stay sharp.

"So can you pull over somewhere?"

"Look, you reprobate, I'm not stopping again for about another three hours, so use the bottle or hold your piss till your bladder explodes into your guts, see if I care, just *do not* soil your pants in my fucking car."

"Jesus, Ronnie," came Leo's wounded voice.

It wasn't much longer before Leo was reluctantly opening his window and then reaching way out to let his stale piss fly. It sloshed out of a big green Mountain Dew bottle that had apparently been hidden near his feet. *Christ, just like Perkins.* Tessa had to assume it had been there for days, long before their gas station stop. And now there was the wet-drum sound of new piss jetting like a torrent into the plastic bottle. She smelled the sickly sweet diabetic urine and tried not to gag in her pretend-sleep. No further words were exchanged up front on the topic, and Leo twisted the cap shut on the bottle, stored his piss on the floorboards, and then cracked open a fourth beer, settling back into his seat.

Tessa watched the side of Leo's whiskered face, calculating. She figured she'd have exactly one shot with the screwdriver, if she could even get to that point. She had begun to manufacture a fantasy of Dank stopping at a rest stop to catch a few winks—giving her the opportunity to put the screwdriver into Leo's head, steal the pistol that was currently nestled against his thigh, and escape like an antelope into the night. But she was getting the depressing idea that Dank had no intention of stopping the Pontiac again any time soon, except for tightly monitored fueling stops that were packed with threats. And so far the threats had worked just fine.

"Eric ever get back to you?" Leo's voice sounded sleepy and heavy.

Through the slit in her vision, she watched Dank shift and turn to look at her as if to satisfy himself that she wasn't listening. Then he shifted back.

"He said no word from Ossie still," he said in a low voice that she could hardly pick up over the road noise. "The big man is ready at the house. He has a plan." There was suddenly a dark smirk in his tone. "It's a good one."

"Well, what is it?" Leo said, unmistakably drunk now.

"Later."

"Shit, man, you're not gonna tell me, are you?"

"Will you lower your voice please?"

Leo lowered his voice. "Why don't you ever clue me in on this shit?"

"Cuz you have a mouth like a goddamn fire hose."

"That's not true, man, I'm a fuckin' vault, and you know it. You treat me like I'm stupid or something."

A pause. "I wonder why that is."

"Man, that's just not nice, I'm reliable as the fuckin' wind!"

"Tell that to Huey, huh?"

"That was *two years ago*, Ronnie, how long are you gonna bring that up?"

"Well, as long as he's, uh, *not alive*, I guess."

Leo's head fell back, and he seemed at a loss for words for a moment. Then, "I didn't mean for that to happen, Ronnie. I mean, Huey was like my best friend, okay? He was funny. He was crazy." He laughed as he frowned. "I mean, we had some crazy times."

"Just because you didn't *mean* something, that doesn't mean it didn't *happen*. You're a fucking blabbermouth, just take responsibility for it and move on."

Leo shook his meaty head. "I didn't . . . I didn't do that to him. I'm not the one that fucked him up."

"Yeah, I know, whatever."

Out of nowhere, Tessa felt her breath quickening. The twine had abruptly loosened behind her, as if from all the sweat her skin was producing back there. She wriggled her wrist while trying to remain otherwise immobile. Her muscles were rigid beneath the appearance of unconsciousness.

She found her half-open gaze locked on the flesh of Leo's neck—the quick pulse there.

She pulled hard against the twine, her hand deforming under what felt like razor wire.

It was coming free. It was happening.

As she listened to the inane conversation up front, she weighed her options. The one thing she was sure of was that she had no intention of getting dragged all the way back to Decatur. What was she gonna do, just slump here in the fucking back seat and wait for Dank and Leo to toss her in front of Harlan for some kind of drug-lord reckoning? Who knew what Harlan or even Eric, that square-jawed, calculating mid-level hoodlum, would do to her once they had their hands on her? They probably wanted to draw and quarter her, or attach a cage full of rats to her belly, or set her bare ass atop a Judas cradle and split her whole body down the middle in screaming agony, like she'd seen once at a torture museum in Chicago.

She'd spent *days* now avoiding the thought of Harlan's rage—mostly because she'd been certain she'd never see him again. When she'd thought about his reaction to what she'd done to his house, she had laughed. Roaring south toward the border, it was safe to say she'd had a totally different attitude. *Now*, when she envisioned the man, she saw his crooked teeth as a mouth full of toothy blades, and he was no longer in the shadows surveying a dim bar, he was standing over her, glaring down at her, his hands busy with something that was about to do her great harm. She recoiled from these visions as if from heat, and then that heat was replaced by a seething adrenaline.

She had to get out of this fucking car.

Leo was fully drunk now. He was sipping at the final can of the six-pack. His eyes were moist and bleary; he kept wiping at them with his forearm as if shedding tears, then blinking exaggeratedly. Tessa took the opportunity to lean forward slightly and glance at Leo's lap. He still had Dank's pistol against his thigh. She tried to gauge what his response would be if she tried to grab it. She didn't think that kind of strategy was anywhere near intelligent.

She continued working at her wounded hands behind her, against the upholstery, not caring if she was bleeding profusely all over the seat. Her wrists were screaming at her.

"I guess we won't be stopping somewhere to sleep, then," Leo murmured at length

"Are you mental?" Dank poked the cigarette lighter, let it began heating. "This girl is as slippery as an eel, and now the tracker's gone, so fuck that."

When Leo lolled his gaze toward her, she was already back in the dark corner, eyes mostly closed.

"Yeah, but I think we took all fight out of her, Ronnie."

Dank angled his head toward Leo, just a little bit. "I see your brain is firing on all cylinders."

"What?" Leo said petulantly. "She's out like a light."

"That girl is wide awake, I can tell you that."

"Ronnie, I'm tellin' you—"

"And *I'm* telling you, you can't afford to be this stupid."

"See, that's what I'm *talkin'* about. You always—"

"Shut up! Just shut the fuck up! Jesus Christ, why did I let you swallow a goddamn gallon of beer? Did you really drink that whole six-pack? Look at this fucking sty." His voice had risen an octave. "Clean that shit up!"

Leo dismissed Dank with a drunken flap of his hand. "I'll take care of it at the next fill-up."

"No respect at all." Dank disengaged the lighter and brought it toward his mouth to light his cigarette.

"Just get us home, man."

"You need to be *watching her.* Okay? Otherwise, my God, what are you even *here* for?"

"I *am* watching her, *see?*"

Leo turned his big head and stared at her with peeled-open eyes, laughing, and Tessa began stabbing him in the face, the screwdriver pistoning like a motherfuckin' junkyard dog.

NINETEEN
FLOYD TILLMAN WEATHERS

The sun filled the Camaro's side mirror like a nuclear blast on the horizon behind him, an apocalyptic vision of both his past and his future—should he fail in this ridiculous panic-trek. The light seared into his eyes, sharpening his headache. His mind was pulsing with exhaustion, sending off sparks of hollow agony behind his sinuses, and the light brought a whole new aspect of torment. He reached out the window and shoved the mirror out of alignment, sighing raggedly with relief.

He'd had the radio on for a short time a while back, as he'd passed through Oklahoma City, but the music had grated on him. He'd tried several stations, from '50s nostalgia to modern rock to heavy-ass thrasher shit, but it all seemed incongruous, everything coming out of the old speakers harsh and discordant. He'd stabbed off the radio, remembering Tess horsing around with the radio in search of some kind of jaunty soundtrack to their suddenly shared life. Any other circumstances, he'd have laughed at the recent memory, but not now.

All was silent, just road noise. Occasionally he tossed back a mouthful of peanuts from a bag he'd grabbed at a gas station in El Reno, followed it up with caffeine-laced soda pop.

He'd entered Oklahoma a few hours earlier. It was humid here—far different from the aridity he'd come to know at the border—and the climate translated into a sea of rolling green, like entering an oasis from out of a desert. It was all bringing him back home; these roads could just as well be outside Little Rock. He remembered Oklahoma from his own lonely journey weeks earlier, diving southwest on the I-30, through Texarkana, and he recalled the gradual transition from subtropical verdancy to cracked aridity—and the way that literal descent had echoed throughout his goddamn soul. Now he was driving the other way, but he didn't feel any ascension.

Far from it.

His thoughts had been returning to Philip. Fuck, man, he was *always* thinking of Philip. The man had taken up permanent residence in his skull. But the call on the burner was overdue. Had been overdue a week ago. It was hard not to conclude that, if Philip had called him within the timeframe he'd *promised*, he never would have met Tessa Rae Jayne and never would have found himself on this pedal-to-the-metal up-country roadtrip just to recover his *status quo*. But, nope, the burner had remained silent, *still* remained silent. He glanced over at it in the passenger seat, and it was quiet as granite, yet he checked it compulsively for power and function. Nothing wrong with it.

Last he'd seen Philip in person had been *that night*, the eve of Floyd's departure, and the man had been chewing gum, probably nicotine gum. The muscles of his jaw had been so pronounced that Floyd had considered them a visible threat, as if Philip had the literal capability to chew him up and spit him out. Philip wasn't a physically imposing man. You saw the man on the street, you'd walk right by, maybe be tempted to flick him on the forehead, even. He was nondescript, prone to long silences. By all outward indications, a nerd. He wore prescription glasses and was always well-dressed, although his clothes were at least three decades past the trend line. He wore loafers.

And yet he was one of the more frightening people Floyd had ever come across.

Floyd couldn't precisely recall the first time he'd been aware of the man's existence. He'd just sort of materialized into Floyd's life, ghost-like. On the periphery. It was like Floyd had to have made a long series of wrong turns and ill-advised side routes to end up face-to-face with Philip Crouch. Jesus, his life was so full of fucking regrets.

The cooling road came at him like hypnosis. He let his arm hang out the window, catching the wind, trying to achieve a kind of zen state, trying to ease the palpitating anxiety of the drive.

Floyd supposed it all started with Duane. Man, Duane Swetson. Floyd had come up with Duane, all the way since grade school. Not like they were ever *friends* in elementary school, exactly, but they'd hung out here and there. Round about eighth grade, their paths in life had wildly diverged. Floyd had made an initial push into sports in early high school— had actually achieved some things. Coaches appreciated his initiative, that kind of shit. He glimpsed a future. Duane, on the other hand, had receded into the background, not a stoner or anything, more like drifting toward prison chic. Dyed his hair, got some tattoos of snakes and shit. He'd taken to associating with mysterious people farther and farther outside the school grounds until he flat-out didn't show up at school anymore. Floyd hardly noticed, they'd drifted apart so long ago.

But then Floyd had reconnected with Duane in Floyd's junior year after they ran into each other downtown—Floyd having inherited an old Honda Accord from his sister and Duane having somehow afforded a used six-gear eight-cylinder Ford Mustang GT that delivered an absurd 525 horsepower. Duane had insisted on blasting Floyd around Boyle Park in that monstrous gas hog (the thing got, like, three miles to the gallon) and on a few occasions out into no-man's land, taking the white behemoth up past a hundred, roaring along the empty county roads. He had a blinking speed radar on the dash and knew the geography of police traps, and he was so confident about it all that he could just jaw with Floyd while occasionally sipping from a tall can of Coors that he kept nestled at his crotch—at seventeen!

Even now, as Oklahoma yawned at him along I-44, his muscle memory recalled those rides through rural Arkansas, a world of possibility opening to him. Something like freedom.

The testosterone kick of Duane's Mustang had been fever-contagious. The animal roar of that growling eight-banger had touched something at Floyd's core, and he began to crave it for himself. He'd probably tooled around Little Rock with Duane a dozen times before deciding— against his father's wishes—to buy a fourth-generation '90s-era V8 Camaro that gave him 300 horsepower, plenty of power to fill the hole that Duane had dug out in his stomach. The purchase, from a highly dubious used lot on the outskirts of Little Rock, had nearly wiped out the savings he'd spent years accumulating, but the fuck-you to his dad had been the icing on the donut. And, yeah, Floyd had ended up clearing out the *rest* of the bank account thanks to badly needed repairs the dealer hadn't disclosed, but hey—youth, right?

The Camaro, which he was still driving today, had become a sound vehicle once the transmission was overhauled.

But fuckin' Duane, man. Right after he turned nineteen, Duane had eaten it one misty pre-morning along Kanis Road toward Ferndale, had rolled over a couple times. His precious Mustang had ended up flipped and ticking against some trees out there, Duane's pelvis crushed beneath the wheel. Floyd had read about it in the paper, had seen the photo of the twisted wreckage—and just knew it was him. He remembered locking eyes with Denise—his girl at the time—over the breakfast table, feeling like he was gonna ralph. Two months after that, Duane rolled out of Arkansas State Hospital without the use of anything below the waist.

Floyd took to visiting Duane at his suddenly wheelchair-accessible home and watching him hold back snotty sobs. They'd be watching cable in the basement while Duane's oddball folks were still at work, and Duane would go on about the cars he'd never drive, and the girls he'd never finger, let alone fuck, and what was the point of living? So *Floyd* had become *Duane's* driver, actually carrying the diminishing dude to the car and dropping him into the passenger seat and taking off to wherever. Over time, Floyd inherited Duane's radar device, learned what he'd learned about driving and the cops. The difference was that Floyd kept their wild rides *reasonable*—didn't stray *too* far over the limit, ixnayed the booze, kept everything *just* this side of illegal. And he'd been able to restore at least some of the verve to Duane's existence.

With the help of some previous connections, and thanks to a settlement that a savvy lawyer made with the Mustang's tire manufacturer, Duane bought out the failing MacArthur Pinball arcade on 10th. He hired some fellas to fix up the place and opened it like a retro beach joint. Maybe inevitably, thanks to Duane's sordid connections, the place became a center for local hoods with its big back room and its clanging façade.

Aaaaand *that's* where Philip came in. At least, eventually.

Floyd had drifted from Duane yet again, shying away from the dangerous business going down in that back room. It wasn't until he was twenty-three that Floyd realized life wasn't bringing him what he wanted from it. Stuck in a thankless job at a fucking cellphone shop at the Park Plaza mall, sensing the waves of disappointment radiating from the home on Tyler Street where he grew up. And so yet again he'd found himself drifting back to Duane, who was sporting very different kinds of wheels and getting fatter at the arcade . . . but for some reason the one person in his life that Floyd kept returning to. It was something he'd never really be able to reason out. Still couldn't.

Floyd took a sip of Coke from the bottle at his crotch, trying to remember when he'd *seen* Philip for the first time. The moment when Floyd's future had been sealed. The moment that led to right now, here in the Camaro, roaring northeast.

It was impossible, really, to nail the precise moment. Philip had just sorta . . . *been there*—hard gaze from across the room, checking out Floyd sometimes, more often just overseeing things. He was the money man (Duane called him the *ching-ching*), but you couldn't know that without already knowing. The man was good at fading into the background. Philip wasn't *always* there at the arcade, but you could count on it whenever something was brewing. He had a producer's keen eye for projects, and he liked to coordinate things once they got going. Randall with the glass eye was always there first, it seemed, when a job was brewing—his cock-eyed vision heralding controlled chaos. And then there was Joyner, who always wanted to be the driver, but no one trusted that pegleg, so he always had to make do with reconnaissance and complained like a bratty kid. Everyone would laugh. There was that other whiskery guy who was a competent driver, Floyd couldn't remember his name, but he got out after some close calls. No one ever saw him again. Maybe he was in prison now, fuck if he knew.

That was how Floyd got in. That was how it came to pass that Philip had actually spoken to him that first time, a private meeting in a corner booth. The gravel voice, the designer cigarettes on his breath. The man had asked about his friends and family, who do you hang with, who do you love (he'd actually said that, used those words), and Floyd had said: *No one.* Eliciting the smallest of smiles from the lips of Philip Crouch. *Me too.* But it wasn't like the man simply *believed* Floyd's word. Later, there'd been another meeting where Philip had asked him about his folks, and the man suddenly knew *everything about them*—their modest histories and their habits and, fuck, man, even their insecurities and their fears. And rather than scare Floyd away, that had thrilled him.

The early jobs were simple transport gigs for small-time shit, town to town, mostly to Conway—that was where the warehouses were, the epicenters of the property theft—and sometimes to Hot Springs or Rockport. On his own initiative, Floyd worked out a cover story involving a fictional night class he was taking, had even gone and printed some information about extension schools in the towns he was sent to, filled a backpack with textbooks he picked up at the Goodwill, scrawled fake notes in a couple dog-eared notebooks. It was pretty slick, and Philip had been wordlessly impressed with Floyd's initiative, and even as the man had praised him with his eyebrows, Floyd had felt a tug in his intestines.

But the cover had worked, and more than once. The Camaro was a cop magnet, no doubt. He recalled being pulled over one night for gliding through a stop, too confident, and the cop had let him go with a warning after hearing Floyd's tale, and all along there'd been about ten grand worth of stolen coins in the trunk. Couple other times, he'd been nabbed with speeding tickets, but those were easy for Philip to take care of.

Floyd found himself almost emotional under the weight of the memories—*what the fuck?* He shook himself out of it. Rolling toward the night, it was too easy to go deep, to let the memories wash over him and make him sick all over again.

Because every job he took came with that nauseated feeling, the humiliating certainty that—given two diverging paths in his life—he'd *taken the wrong path.* His dad, muttering over breakfast, always railed about Floyd's stupid pride, had even turned his back on his son that one morning because of it, and Floyd acknowledged that was true, but there was no way to admit it. Just no way. And his *stupid pride* was consuming him from within, all for what? Proving his old man wrong?

What was he—a child?

Despite the caffeine and the urgency of the drive, Floyd felt himself blink heavily, his thoughts shifting. His body was crying out for unconsciousness. He shifted in his seat, sat up straighter, shook his head like a dog. Pounded more Coca-Cola. Crunched some more peanuts.

In that moment, everything sharpened to a point that was focused on Philip's impassive face. The man who'd shared a private joke with him the first time he talked with him, and then later—the *last* time he talked to him—threatened everything he knew. The handshake before Floyd settled into the Camaro for the trip southwest, Philip's sandpaper hands cold and clenching like metal. The piercing, somehow silver eyes, communicating the enormity of Floyd's task—the biggest job he'd ever been assigned, possibly the largest job *Philip* had ever coordinated. The bank job, all its planning and strategy, all its players—it all came down to Floyd and what he was taking far away, out of state, nearly out of country, at least until things calmed down. And then the image of Philip in the rearview, standing in the middle of the street utterly still and yet somehow oversized, an optical illusion. Objects in the mirror are not necessarily less significant than they appear.

Floyd glanced over at the silent burner on the passenger seat and felt a roll of slow self-revulsion in his guts.

A mileage sign appeared to the right, and he saw that he was at the outskirts of a town called Bristow, Oklahoma. It was full dark, the ghosts of trees extending into the black distance. In the thrumming silence, he felt as if he were surging forward through water, surrounded by roiling green-black seas, in constant danger of foundering. He knew he'd set his mind off into the oily waters of memory to counter the desperation of the drive. Or more accurately, to avoid the question he was asking himself more pointedly every day: What had *happened* to him? If the answer to the questions of his life involved Philip Crouch and hiding at the border and ultimately blasting northeast on this interstate toward a salvation that he didn't deserve . . . then maybe he'd been asking all the wrong questions.

That thought left him clenching his jaw, his glazed eyes fixed upon the whisking road, the vehicles far ahead in the distance, the darkness overhanging everything. He supposed it said something about him that, all this time, he'd thought very little about his father, and he let his thoughts edge in that direction now—just wisps, flitting reminiscences, the hard military jaw, the crewcut atop the pockmarked face, the posture. The man who never spared the rod. The sky-high expectations communicated only through hard glances and withering disappointment. Or even Floyd's mother, never one to dote, never one to spare a smile, or when the smile did come, it was one of quiet regret, as if she were dismayed by her inability to be more for him—trying and yet failing to be the counterpoint to the man at her side.

After a while, Floyd became vaguely aware of a shimmer on the horizon, and it developed into a colorful jitter. At first the distant bray of lights seemed like a migraine coming on, but then it was very real—several police cruisers strobing their urgency into the night, surrounded by an EMT wagon and a fire truck that looked as if it had come off the assembly line in 1940.

Floyd came up to the throng of emergency vehicles with a strong sense of foreboding. Traffic slowed to a crawl through a single constricted lane, and as he drew even with the scene, he saw a black Pontiac upside down against the far rail, and a large body covered by a sheet.

A burst of dread rippled from his gut, emanating outward.

That was the car. He was sure of it.

TWENTY
TESSA RAE JAYNE

"Fuckin' buttfuck Oklahoma, that's where you fuckin' do this to me? How am I even here with you, you bitch whore, you piece-of-shit murderer, got half a mind to kill you right now, I mean FUCK Harlan, that fuckin' degenerate—"

Dank angrily hoisted the strap of the duffel bag full of money farther up his shoulder, then continued dragging her. His stream-of-consciousness cursing went on and on as they moved through the trees, Tessa flailing along behind him, his grip vice-tight on the delicate bones of her already ravaged wrist. She wouldn't cry out, though, she wouldn't do it. Leo's blood was still dark red on her forearm, she could see it under the intermittent moonlight, and she could *smell* it, metallic and strong, as if her nostrils were filled with it, as if she were drenched with it.

She could see the glow of a town ahead—another nothing town, probably, abandoned and graying red-brick buildings in red-state America, surrounded by cheap, lurid convenience marts and gas stations and fast-food places and pawn shops and bail-bond joints, story of the nation. On the interstate—after the car had come to its violent halt and Dank had yanked her out—she'd caught a glimpse of a gigantic Walmart sign at the edge of an offramp. How typical.

She was being dragged down a low hill toward a clutch of what appeared to be oaks, stunted by the eternal onslaught of road pollution.

"Hurry up, you stupid cunt!"

"You call me that again," she said, "and I'll kill you too."

He only yanked at her harder, but she heard a quaver in his voice. *"Jesus fucking Christ."*

When she glanced back toward the road, she could no longer see it, and she could hear no sound of traffic. There were no shouting voices, no sirens. She couldn't even be sure whether anyone had *stopped*, let alone was chasing her down this hill to take her back from this psychopath. She no longer had the slippery screwdriver in her grip—she had no idea at what point it had left her fingers—and she was only slowly understanding that she'd sustained several injuries. The pain was awakening in her from out of blunt, numbing shock. Her left wrist ached sharply, her skull throbbed along a straight line from the crown of her head down beyond her left ear, and her left thigh complained with a high whine of agony. She felt dampness down there and wondered if she'd pissed herself.

They reached level ground, and now Tessa saw a ramshackle fence, and she realized she was at the edge of a neighborhood. There were lights in yellow windows and dim shapes coming into focus—an abandoned trailer, some kind of kid's jungle gym, crooked and weathered, hulking TV antennas, a deflated American flag, a stack of bald tires.

"This way!" Dank spat.

He was brandishing his firearm boldly, carelessly, perilously. Tessa watched its barrel wobble like a divining rod as he dragged her forward. She saw that Dank was limping, and for the first time she began observing him for his own injuries. He'd been buckled in—and she had *not* been—when he'd reacted instinctively to Leo's frothing death by cranking the wheel and flipping the car. While Tessa had tumbled into the ceiling, banging from one side of the Pontiac to the other to the soundtrack of screeching metal, Dank had remained rooted in place, arms flailing as Leo's bulky and bloody deadweight lolled in place.

It would probably be much later when Tessa would fully acknowledge that she was lucky to be alive, let alone still in one piece, but in the moment she hadn't cared a single bit. She'd wanted Leo dead.

Mission accomplished.

Dank had blood on him—she could see that now as the lights from the homes ahead illuminated him—but she couldn't tell if it was his or Leo's. Leo had been like a blood sprinkler inside that car; she'd felt droplets pinprick her face as she'd stabbed him and as the car had begun to flip and spin. Then everything had been chaos until going abruptly still, the smell of gasoline fierce in her nostrils. She'd become aware of a sound flowing out of Dank's throat, some involuntary kind of scraping groan. And then he'd taken hold of the situation with a series of grunts and yanked her free of the glass and steel. Now the guttural grunt had returned to Dank's throat, and it sounded desperate, coming hard and fast with his uneven breathing.

Had anyone even seen the crash? Her mind felt scrambled.

Dank slashed his gun hand at her—*"Keep your mouth shut!"*—and took her through an open back yard into a low alley. They stalked between homes and out onto a darkened street, and now Tessa heard sirens in the distance behind her. The highway was already so far back there—as if far behind her in time, as if reality were skipping forward like a stone.

Dank paused at a sidewalk, glared glassily about, still nearly hyperventilating. Tessa stopped next to him, her wrists aching, that left one in particular.

There were voices coming from somewhere, and she tried to focus on them, understand them from out of her fog. They were coming from her right, children's voices. Four or five kids jostled together in a small, weedy front yard, some kind of makeshift ball game, totally oblivious to the two bloody strangers five houses down. Dank yanked her in the opposite direction toward a quieter cross street.

She didn't know what he was aiming for—didn't care. She was trying to control her own breathing and focus her thoughts, but every time she began to strategize, to think about how to overcome her next challenge, the synapses in her brain misfired and she found herself blinking in confusion. Maybe she was concussed.

Now that there was light, she could see that her throbbing left thigh was red with blood.

"I need to check my leg."

"*Fuck you, you need to check your leg.*" His voice was a dagger. "*Jesus fuck. Come on!*"

"I'm bleeding."

"*You think I give a flying shit?*"

"Well, I mean, you need to get me to Harlan, right?" She yelped as she turned her ankle on a crack in the sidewalk. "Like, alive? You need to bring me back alive. That's what your buddy Leo was saying. At least, that's what he was saying when he was alive."

Dank only muttered to himself, shook his head with lip-curling loathing, kept hauling her down the dim street.

Tessa felt as if clarity—moment by clanging moment—was slowly returning to her. She was unconsciously flexing her jaw to pop her ears, and that simple act seemed to be clearing her thoughts. As Dank pulled her forward at practically a jog, she breathed evenly and kept her eyes focused on permanent objects in the distance—a red Jeep, a peeling silver Festiva on blocks, a crooked For Sale sign planted in a yard. Doing so helped her begin to strategize how to get away from Dank, or, even better, murder the asshole just like she'd murdered his retarded buddy.

Because she had to face it: She was a killer now. No question about it. A few times over.

It was if what she'd done in Forsyth had broken some kind of dam inside her, and now she was a goddamn *serial killer!* Not that she'd killed Perkins in Malvado, but she'd been there in the room, and he was certainly dead *because* of her. She would probably be dealing with these things long into her future, but right now she had literal blood on her hands, and when she thought about what she'd just done—with full forethought, this time—to Leo McQuoid, she felt almost impossibly strong, like some kind of black-ass superheroine.

The sharp, seething pain at her thigh was becoming more of a problem with each step. She could hardly recall her torment inside the Pontiac as it had flipped—it was all just a blunt buffeting in her mind—but she wondered what had cut her. Maybe it had been the very screwdriver she'd used to both escape the Pontiac and eventually murder Leo. Didn't really matter. The wound was there, and it was bleeding, and regardless of its cause, she had to get it taken care of. As her world clarified inside her skull, and as Dank dragged her across a street, she took measure of herself and figured she also had several bruised ribs, a significant bump on her head, and a couple of numb fingers on her left hand.

"Where are you taking me?"

"Just shut up."

"Is the hospital this way?"

"What the—? Clam it, bitch."

"Aww, you're sweet," she managed through the pain.

Dank yanked her arm so violently that it nearly popped out of its socket. *"Get moving!"*

They entered a mobile home park and quickly skirted along a dark corridor littered with trash bags and faintly illuminated by kitchenette windows. A long cinderblock wall loomed to their right. She weighed the probable repercussions of screaming out for help: She was sure he'd lash out. He'd kill her, no doubt. Consequences be damned.

"At least let me tie something around my leg, huh?"

Dank was silent for a few moments while he continued to drag her down the lengthy passageway. Then, halfway through it, he came to an abrupt stop. He glared in all directions and then hauled her toward the cinderblock wall. He backed up against it to catch his breath, which came raggedly despite his stillness. He let his head drop to his chest.

"Do what you need to do," he said, close to gasping. "But if you try anything—I swear to fucking Christ I'll fill you with every round in this Magnum. Do you get that? I mean, do you fucking get that?"

But he wasn't even waiting for her answer. He was already bending to examine his legs, which both looked bloodied and traumatized. Her mind immediately went to ways to take advantage of his wounds, but the pistol overruled everything. She unbuttoned her blouse and removed it over a sore clavicle, revealing the sports bra—which she was suddenly glad she'd sprung for at the Albuquerque thrift store. She began tearing the blouse apart from the bottom, using her teeth, and she came up with several ragged lengths of white cloth. She wordlessly offered a couple of them to Dank.

He stared at her for a hard moment, then snatched the torn cloth from her. He backed away from her, watching her carefully, placed the gun at the small of his back, and began wrapping his legs. Tessa turned to her leg, finding a slash that ran from just above her knee to halfway up her thigh, leading directly toward her crotch. At its deepest, the slash was about half an inch deep and still weeping blood. She wrapped three lengths of cloth around the leg, knotting them tight.

When she straightened up again, her spine complained bitterly, and she winced.

"Yeah, I *hope* you're in pain," Dank said, staring at her.

"What, you think I was just gonna lay down and die?"

His eyes burbled over with tears, and he wiped savagely at them. *"We're talking about Leo! That was Leo! I've known Leo for—for five years! He was my—he was my best friend!"*

"He was a fucking kidnapper, just like you."

"What the fuck are you even *talking* about?" He glared at her with angry confusion. "You fucking *murdered* Harlan's *mother*. Do you even understand why we followed you? Do you get what you did? Or are you just like—like—like some kind of sociopath? *Jesus!*"

Tessa felt as if she'd been punched in the stomach, but she didn't let it show. She took in a careful breath, followed it with another. The woman in the house had been Harlan's mother. His *mother.* The words resonated inside her skull like a live wire. She wouldn't show it.

Dank was still talking, his strained voice riding an obvious terrain of pain and shock. "You're a fucking *child.* Your generation—" Disgusted shake of the head. "—just an amazing abdication of responsibility, it's like you're entitled to this fucking warped and . . . *naïve* . . . vision of the world, like you expect everything to go down like a fucking fairy tale. You have no idea what—"

"So where are we going?" Tessa interrupted him, wincing. "What's your plan now, asshole?"

He stared at her in disbelief for a long moment. "Jesus *Christ,* listen to you! You and your brother—scourge of my fucking existence."

"Don't talk about my brother, you prick."

"Oh my God."

"You ain't fit to shine Terrell's Air Jordans."

His whole body jerked with fury. *"You fucking bitch, you just have no idea—"*

It was working, this baiting, but her heart was trip-hammering against her sore ribs, and her breath was coming shallowly. She pretended disinterest, standing there slumped, but she was hyper-aware of Dank's body language. She was ready to fend him off however he finally reacted—and it was inevitable that he would.

"Oh for Christ's *sake,* man, *blah blah blah*—are we just gonna spend the night here, or what?"

There was a fraction of a moment when it appeared Dank might collect himself and understand what Tessa was doing to him, but then he was up and away from the wall, wrangling her arm cruelly so that she was facing him.

"You killed my partner, you fucking whore! I am so done with you." His voice warbled dangerously. *"I don't care if you drop dead right now. I don't care about Harlan, do you understand me? You can die right now, for all I care. You can—"*

With that, he brought the pistol up to her forehead, and she felt the cold hardness of the barrel against her skin, trembling and ferocious.

Tessa stared back into Dank's vicious gaze. She could see his mouth working, his nostrils flaring. She would not close her eyes. She would not flinch. She wouldn't give him the satisfaction. And yet she felt so close to death that her mind manufactured a white light behind Dank, a brilliant halo silhouetting him, and she watched the light flare and shiver, and a burst of awe enveloped her.

Then the pistol fell away, and Dank whirled.

"Hey!" came a deep male voice. "What's going on there? Whoa, whoa!"

The flashlight shook, angled away. The man had stopped, and now he had his hands up. He was large, decked out in sandals and beach shorts and a straining black tee shirt emblazoned with the Atari logo. Dude had long straggly hair framing a red face and small confused eyes.

"This isn't your business, asshole!" Dank said, but his voice quavered unmistakably.

"Absolutely, man. Take it easy."

"Get lost."

But now another man was jogging toward them, down from a porch across the street, and then another. Stocky white men, both wearing baseball caps, both of them holding bottles of beer in their hands. They were jovial types whose wary curiosity seemed to come reluctantly, as if their default allegiance was on the side of the white guy manhandling the colored girl. She felt their eyes on her, felt the scales tipped out of her favor. Tessa had known this feeling her whole life—the sideways glances, the bred-deep postures, behavior so ingrained in her life that she never expected anything else. Except now it felt dangerous.

"What is it, Curt?"

"Hold up, hold up!" Curt shouted.

Dank moved to escape down the alley, but his limp was more pronounced now, and he cried out in a hoarse voice.

The two newcomers came closer, still had their eyes all over Tessa, and then they were assessing the wider situation, half-drunkenly, sloppy uncertain smiles on their faces. They seemed to catch sight of the Magnum simultaneously.

"Hey!" said one of them, a thick man with a red mullet and a goatee. *"Gun!"*

"Stay back!" Dank warned.

And then everything went haywire.

The two men leaped past Curt in an almost primal surge, and Dank let loose with a high shriek, raising the Magnum, but not fast enough. The redhead clamped down on Dank's right arm with a fat fist. The sounds of the gunshots were like twin lightning strikes—quick, deafening—and there was a shocked pause, the tinkling of glass somewhere, stunned gazes flitting everywhere to determine whether anyone had been struck.

"Holy fuck!" yelled Curt.

And then Curt's buddies fell on top of Dank in a pile. A thick ropy forearm was immediately at his throat, and Dank emitted a strangled cry. Someone hammered the pistol away, and it went clattering across the asphalt out of Tessa's view. The duffel bag full of money flopped to the ground, and Tessa quickly nabbed it up, wrapping its strap around her neck, backing way.

Somewhere far off in her periphery she heard a squealing of tires, the gunning of a motor, hiccupping over bouncy terrain. She staggered farther away from the sweaty melee in front of her, unsure what to do.

Floyd's black Camaro made her decision for her, its headlights blooming the scene into full brilliant view. All eyes were on the Camaro as it lunged toward them. Tessa flattened herself against the cinderblock wall, pointed a long arm straight at Dank. The Camaro growled like a beast, and the three men lifted away from Dank, who watched deliriously from the ground. He went under the wheels of the Camaro with a horrible bone-crunching racket. The Camaro screeched its brakes, Dank's body scraping under the rear-right wheel. Tessa watched his head cave in and pink-purple brain matter splat out under pressure like an infected boil. She knew instantly that she could never, ever unsee that.

She caught a glimpse of the three men at the rear of the mobile home—watching the scene stunned, unmoving—and then the Camaro was reversing back to her. The passenger door was already flung open, and there was Floyd's beautiful face, like an impossible dream.

"Let's go," he said.

TWENTY-ONE
FLOYD TILLMAN WEATHERS

Floyd got to the interstate without any problems, keeping the Camaro at a steady thirty miles per hour when every instinct told him to floor it past the century mark. A block away from the onramp, two police cruisers blared past him in the direction he'd just come from. He watched the vehicles in his rearview mirror, praying they wouldn't flip a sudden U. They didn't. The flashing vehicles disappeared around a turn, and the howls of their sirens dwindled away.

Floyd eased onto the northeast onramp and merged into sparse traffic, a cold sweat trickling down the back of his neck. After a mile or two, he felt as if he could take at least a shallow breath. And he could ponder when Tess might realize that he'd taken the northbound route.

He glanced over at her. She was staring straight ahead at the road. She looked rattled and battered. Floyd knew she was beat up, possibly concussed. He'd seen her shock-stunned gaze in the blast of the Camaro's headlights behind the mobile homes, but he didn't know the extent of it yet. She had some makeshift bandages around her thigh that were spotted with blood. She was clenching and unclenching her left hand around the strap of his duffel bag.

God love her, she had his money.

"You all right?" he said.

She flinched a little. "Am I really in this car right now?"

"This ain't no dream, darlin'."

She touched the dash as if to ground herself in the moment. "I don't—"

"*Goddamn* it's good to see you," Floyd said.

Now she looked at him. "How in the *hell* did you find me?"

"Maybe I just recognize the sound of a Magnum."

Confusion squeezed her features together. "But—I mean—"

"Divine providence, honey."

He tried a smile. He figured he'd lay the gory details on her later. For now, he sensed the need to keep things light. He knew it wasn't easy to bounce back so quickly from what she'd just been through. Hell, he was having a little trouble with it himself. He wasn't gonna show that to her, though. What had just happened along the back streets of Bristow, Oklahoma, was something of a dark marvel, and he simultaneously gloried in it and replayed it with a sense of disbelief.

Tessa gazed at him blankly, seemed to give up on the train of thought, and went back to staring straight ahead.

"Seriously, are you all right?" he said. "All your parts workin'?"

"Gonna need to get some medicine, coupla Band-Aids, but I think I'm functional."

It took some coaxing to get her story out of her—her tale of the past sixteen hours or so—but finally she began to do so in fits and starts. She was still breathing uncertainly, and in between bursts of words, she drank from two water bottles sloppily, as if she'd been denied any nourishment for the entire day. She told him about being thrown naked into the Pontiac's dark trunk and finding a way to escape, about how she'd found clothes by posing as a hotel employee, about convincing a sweet and dorky sandwich-store kid to deliver her to downtown Albuquerque, about being tracked and abducted *again*, and about stabbing Leo McQuoid to death, causing Dankworth to inadvertently flip the Pontiac on I-44 and then drag her desperately into that backwater Oklahoma town.

Floyd felt a sudden and frank admiration for Tessa Rae Jayne.

"Christ, you are *somethin'*."

"Yeah, well."

She glanced over at him with an inscrutable smile, but he noticed a small tremble at her lips. His efforts to keep things lively and upbeat didn't seem to be working. Tessa had been through some shit, no doubt about it, probably a lot more than she was letting on, even. And, as if to punctuate that thought, she closed her eyes and bent down over her lap, and he could see her lips moving around careful breaths.

"Take it easy, now, darlin'."

She nodded quickly against her knees, and the movement caused a tear to leak from her eye and dribble onto her lower leg, making a shiny dark line toward the floorboards. Floyd caught the glint of it in the shifting glow from the yellow high-mast interstate lights.

"I saw—I saw his *brains*, Floyd, I saw his brains on the ground."

"Whose brains?"

"*Dank's.* He's the one who—"

"I know who he is."

Tessa's emotions took a left turn, and she snapped at him. *"How the fuck do you know who Dank is? I don't even know what's happening here."*

"Hey, I did my research, okay?"

"I think I'm going crazy."

"It's all good."

"But Dank . . . *Dank* . . . I saw his fucking *head* cave in—"

"Hey, hey—you're all right now."

"I killed Leo, man. I fucking killed him. I did that."

"Fuckin' A, you did."

She lifted her head and faced him. Tears had smeared her cheeks, and her eyes were brimming, glassy.

"What? I—I was never supposed to—I never wanted any of this! I'm not this person! Everyone's fucking dying! Everything's gone to shit, and it's all my fault! What am I supposed to do with all this? How am I supposed to get past this mountain of—of—of DEATH?"

He tried to counter her shouting with a reasonable tone. "Well, the way you deal with it is by admitting that these people are fucking evil, Tess, you said so yourself."

"I killed an innocent woman, Floyd! An innocent old woman!"

"An accident," he reminded her. "You said that was an accident."

"She'd be alive right now if not for me, and so would all the rest of them!" She sat back against her seat, mouth half-open, still appearing stunned. *"Harlan's mother."* The words came out in a soft squeak.

"Hmm?"

"The woman." She shook her head miserably. "The woman who died in the fire. Remember I told you about Harlan? The—the fucking *freak* at the top of all this? His mother is the one who died."

Floyd didn't know how to respond to that except to let silence drop heavily into the center of the Camaro.

"I'm doomed, all right?" she said. "It's like—it's like I never had a chance. You think he's just gonna let bygones be bygones? Harlan's gonna release the hounds of hell to find me."

"All right, all right."

"You disagree?"

"I'm not sayin' that." He took a moment to light a cigarette, used the pause to calm down the conversation. "I'm just saying . . . wisdom follows calm."

She frowned at him, eyes brimming. "Okay boomer."

He laughed. "We'll work it out. Okay?"

"But how—?"

"We'll work it out."

Floyd knew Tessa was gonna have to get through some of this shit by herself. That was normal and healthy. That's how life worked. She'd get through it. She was a tough chick. But he planned to provide the assist however he could. This new revelation did change things, though. Whoever this Harlan was—whatever strength he held over Tessa and her family back home—he loomed suddenly much larger in the story. What would Floyd be getting into in Illinois if he stepped in on Tessa's behalf? And did he have any goddamn business sticking his schnozz in the middle of it, given his *own* responsibilities back home?

He checked the time—7:34 p.m.—and thought about what to do. Tessa still hadn't asked him about the direction he was headed, but he knew it was probably a smart idea to get off the road for the night and rest up. He'd need gas again in the next hundred miles anyway, and it was likely time to grab new plates. About twenty minutes out of Bristow, he caught sight of a mileage sign that told him Tulsa was twenty-five miles away. He decided they'd stop there and figure out what to do next.

He found some music on the radio when they were in range of Tulsa, some good ol' rock-and-roll, and he let Tessa do her thing. She sobbed for a while, and then she almost angrily gave that up, and then she told him she was famished, and then she was leaning against him, holding on to his upper arm. He let her do it all, merely anchoring his rough hand against her thigh.

"I guess I should thank you," she whispered against his neck as they rolled toward the city lights.

"You're the one who did it, sweetheart," he whispered back. "You're the one who got away."

"Thank you for finding me. I don't how the fuck you did it. I'm gonna need you to tell me all about that. But thank you for finding me."

"Hey, baby," he said. "Any time."

As far as explaining how he'd done it—well, no time like the present. He withdrew Terrell's chipless necklace from beneath his shirt and pulled it over his head. He handed it to her, and her eyes opened up wider than he thought possible. He let loose with a little laugh, and it felt good. And then he explained how he'd gotten back on her trail—not without some pride.

Later, after rolling off the interstate into Tulsa, Floyd found a Pizza Hut, and they shared a cheese pie in an out-of-the-way booth, the duffel bag full of cash nestled between them, the Beretta at the small of Floyd's back. Given the adrenaline expenditures of an insane day, the fast-food pizza tasted delicious.

After that, he pulled into a motel called the Good Gracious Inn, about a mile off the interstate, away from the low-key bustle of downtown. It was a stately looking joint but was actually a Motel 6 in disguise. He parked out back, having wrangled a rear room with a view of the parking lot. After he and Tessa locked up the Camaro, he kept his right hand dangling at his side, primed to whisk out the Beretta at any provocation. The duffel bag hung from the strap around his neck, and his left arm guided Tessa toward the key-lock side door.

The room stank—a heady mixture of fragrance-disguised body odor and mildew. Floyd opened up the window and almost immediately heard shouting in the distance. Some kind of domestic squabble, or a drunken scene outside a local bar.

"Nice place," Tessa murmured from the bed.

She was slumped on the edge of it, gingerly examining her leg. He was aware of the other problem areas all over her body—the ribs, the bump on the head, thrashed wrists, what could be fractured fingers on her left hand—but the leg was the worst of them.

"Lemme take a look at that," Floyd said.

He carefully unwound Tessa's bloody blouse strips and revealed the wound. It wasn't horrible, but it wasn't fantastic, either. It wasn't particularly deep, but it was still weeping crimson. He instructed her to take a hot shower and clean the cut as best she could, and then to keep some pressure on it with towels. He'd go get some supplies at the Walgreens about a half-mile east on 51st Street. She registered his plan, and her eyes went wide.

"What is it?" he asked, and she closed her eyes and sighed.

"Look, man—" Her voice was sharp but tinged with fatigue. "You know I'm not the damsel-in-distress type. I'm not the kind of girl that'll start bawling when the boy leaves her alone. That ain't me." She sniffed, then winced as she rotated her arm in its shoulder socket. "But I'm not at my best right now. I mean, I'll admit it. It's been a goddamn day, okay? And, well, fuck it, man—I don't really want to be alone. That's it. Not after today."

Floyd sat down next to her on the edge of the bed. He let long moments go by as he rubbed her back and felt a surge of appreciation for the friggin' *fact* of her, here and now.

"I get it, girlie. I do. But I *gotta* go get this stuff, or you're gonna be in a world of hurt. That cut's gonna get infected, and you're not gonna be any use to me or anyone."

"Then I'm goin' with you."

He shook his head. "Not gonna happen."

She cocked her head and glared at him. Her left cheek was scraped up, and her eyes were red. Her hair was in rough shape, all frizzy dark tendrils defying gravity.

"Listen," he said, "this I know for sure: God is done fuckin' with us. I don't know if you believe in that kind of thing, but at least for the moment, he's had his time with us. We made it through a trial, and now we get to rest. I'm *sure* of it."

Despite the high drama of the day that was now ebbing toward an unexpectedly calm end, he felt almost none of the wariness he'd felt back at the Lordsburg motel. There was nowhere near the level of looking-over-the-shoulder paranoia he'd felt then. If there was one thing he was certain of, it was that they were safe from any pursuers. So at least there was that.

On top of everything, they'd goddamn well *earned* this reprieve, and he'd enjoy that reprieve come hell or high water.

"You're safer right here than anywhere. I'm gonna leave my Beretta here with you. You take it into the bathroom and lock yourself in if you want to. You're also gonna lock the room door behind me. Twice. You're gonna be absolutely secure here while you clean up. I promise."

And it worked. He got a reluctant okay from her, and he stashed the money up inside the closet behind an iron and extra pillows, and then he kissed her and left, listening to the door lock reluctantly behind him.

Behind the motel, under darkness, he took a screwdriver from his little kit in the glove box and quietly stole license plates off a Toyota sedan parked a few slots down. That done, he slid off to Walgreens and went straight for the medical supplies—bandages, disinfectant, antibiotic ointment, pain pills, superglue for closing the wound. Then he stocked up on water and food, found some cheap clothes for Tessa to replace the bloody garments. He got it all taken care of within twenty minutes.

Back in the motel parking lot, he found a spot on the other side of the property and slid into the space. He shut off the engine and sat there in the silence.

He was forgetting something.

He shut his eyes, concentrated. He was only four hours from Little Rock, messin' around with this crazy girl, all over again, except now he'd murdered a man—in no uncertain terms—to get back to her. To reunite with his cash. Now that he'd *done* all that, against all fucking odds, he felt a kind of adrenaline-giddiness inside his chest, a trembling and urgent sense of power, and he wasn't sure what to do with it. Dashing east on the 44 earlier, he'd dared to imagine this impossible scenario right here, and he'd envisioned himself pulling a 180 and hauling Tessa back west. Keep goin' with the notion of getting lost out there. Together.

But now . . . ?

Tessa's injuries spoke of unfinished business.

Hell, Floyd had his *own* unfinished business, and now he felt equipped to deal with it.

Upstairs, Tessa was freshly washed but still damaged when she opened the door to him. She wore one white towel around her midsection and another smaller one around her thigh, and that one was only a little bloodied. After locking the place up again, he guided her to the bed and bent to the task of stopping the bleeding. He applied the ointment carefully, then used the super glue to bind the wound at its deeper points. He affixed several bandages along the ragged cut, finishing with a wrap that kept everything tight. Then he spent some time on her fingers, immobilizing them with tongue depressors and wrapping them tightly with white tape. He felt her eyes on his work, on his face.

"You're good," she whispered.

"I've had some practice."

When he was done, she accepted six ibuprofen pills from him, washing them down with water.

Then she opened her other towel for him.

"Go easy on me, all right?"

He was very careful.

In moments, Floyd had lost himself in this amazing woman, his new hero. He even whispered those words into her ear as he filled her up, and although she resisted his whispers at first, telling him to shut his mouth, he kept at it, and after a while she seemed to savor his mumblings. And the more he voiced the words, the more certain he was of their truth: Tessa Rae Jayne was the most astonishing woman he'd ever met, and he had fallen for her as if from a cliff.

A half hour later, after using his mouth to bring her to an aching, on-the-edge-of-tearful orgasm, he held her for a long time in the darkened room. The air conditioning was rattling, and the room still stank, and this remarkable woman was still going to require a heap of healing, but Floyd felt a measure of control over his destiny that he hadn't felt in months, if not years.

They lay next to each other, murmuring into the night. Floyd recounted his pursuit, and the tricks he'd used to find her, and Tessa filled in the gaps. They even shared some quietly amazed laughter over everything they'd accomplished along the same route. *Not a bad team*, she whispered at his ear, nibbling it, and that jumpstarted him all over again. He wanted to devour her, and he felt as if the feeling was very mutual— and getting more mutual with each passing moment. They were merely a couple of lost souls finding purchase in each other, clicking together jigsaw-like, hungry for more and more.

And after *that*, fatigue attempted mightily to overwhelm them, but it wasn't time for sleep yet.

"Look, Tess," Floyd whispered as the clock ticked toward midnight, "I'm all in. Okay? I'm yours. I'm with you all the way. So let's finish this. Together. We're only seven hours from putting an end to all this shit and getting on with—well, with whatever it is that we figure we want to do. Let's go take care of everything. Fuckin' *everything*. Cuz we ain't gonna be able to move on until we do that. And then we'll take it from there."

She reared back so that she could look him in the eye. For the first time, she seemed to realize what he was really saying. What he was willing to do for her.

"I never asked you to do anything, okay?" she whispered, voice cracking. "You don't have to do this. I mean, it's not your problem."

"Darlin', the way I figure it, if it's your problem, it's mine too."

Tessa snuggled into him a little uncertainly. She was done talking. Time for her to think.

"Tell me more about this Harlan asshole," he suggested.

When Tessa found her voice again, she began to speak in hushed tones about the man who had destroyed her brother's life and was well on his way to destroying her own.

Meanwhile, Floyd's burner phone sat buzzing on the Camaro's passenger seat.

TWENTY-TWO
TESSA RAE JAYNE

Harlan Eckhart.

Harlan fucking Eckhart.

Maybe she'd been destined to face him again, all this time. No matter how far south she went, no matter where she ended up in the world, she would stand before him in judgment. Not because of the color of her skin, or on the basis of her genitals, but for the simple fact of what she'd done. What she'd done to *him*. Didn't mean she hated the inevitability any less.

Hurtling headlong toward the scene of her crime, Tessa was lulled by the low, rolling greenery of southwest Missouri. She gathered from the mileage posts that they were approaching Springfield.

They'd bolted out of Tulsa around nine after a belly-busting breakfast at a joint called Mom's Family Diner. Floyd had been quiet all morning, since hopping into the Camaro and starting her up. Something was bothering him, and she didn't blame him. She'd never asked him to involve himself in her ocean of excrement, but here he was, next to her, hauling ass directly into the maw of all her mistakes. He'd seen firsthand the repercussions of what she'd done in Forsyth, and yet what he was basically saying was that he wanted to enter Harlan's target zone, right alongside her. No wonder he was on edge. She could sense his mind churning.

Probably about *Harlan fucking Eckhart.*

Terrell used to laugh about the freak, back before he attached to him. She remembered that, oh yeah. Months after Terrell had dug himself in—first using, then sharing, then becoming part of the chain—he'd actually started to defend Harlan. *Aww, he ain't so bad once you get to know him. Dude's fuckin' sharp as a shiv, sis, got some killer ideas.*

Later, when she was working at Wayne's, there was the introduction—*Tess, this here's Mr. H, the magnificent bastard I was tellin' you 'bout*—and the genial laughter that she'd felt forced to participate in. The way Harlan's hand felt like a spider's hands, if spiders had hands. Bony, skeletal, enveloping. The eyebrows that looked real but must have been manufactured, pointing like an accusation. The shiny shaved head, tattoos etched at the rear, an assemblage of screaming skulls, exposed spinal columns snaking down his gangly neck. First impressions meant everything, right, so what was she supposed to make of the steel bars that adorned the backs of his knuckles like Wolverine adamantium? Looked painful and stupid-ass evil as fuck, the first thing he extended to you when you met him, as in *Watch it, girl, I will poison you the first chance I get.*

Harlan became a fixture at Wayne's after that. It had happened right beneath everyone's noses: The goddamn *Decatur mafia* invaded the neighborhood watering hole that Wayne himself had apparently built from the ground up ten years earlier. But of course, that insight about Harlan only came later. Terrell was the one who shoulda fucking well known better, that's what *she* thought, but by then it was too late: Harlan had made it a habit on Saturdays and a few weeknights to lord over his corner with his cronies—yeah, that included Perkins, Leo, Dank, and Eric, along with some other stragglers—and conduct business now and then. Wayne's mood soured a little more every day, but what was he supposed to do? Wayne was an older man—one of those groovy hippie types. Sara called him a *pacifist*. (Tessa had to Google that word later.) It wasn't like he was gonna yank a friggin' shotgun from under the bar and order the local mob out of his joint, and he wasn't even gonna involve the police—even though he had a couple of buddies among the men in blue. Wayne was savvy about the situation: Above all, he didn't want to invite retribution.

Harlan was a cancer that had begun to rot Wayne's from the inside out, growing and metastasizing over there in the dim corner. And at first, Tessa hadn't even cared! She was new to the job, trying to fit in with the seasoned staff—Jesus, looking back at her ownself, it was like peering down at a child. And that's exactly how Rhonda behind the bar and even Sara had spoken to her, sometimes rankling her. But she'd deserved all of it, the talking down and the gentle ribbing. It was time to grow the fuck up, and what she came to grasp was that she wasn't in school no more.

As Terrell literally diminished, Tessa matured. At least, that's what she *thought* she'd done at the time.

"You know, Wayne blames you," Rhonda told her once on a wave of smoky breath, fresh from a cigarette break.

Tessa had stopped stunned in her tracks. "For what?"

"For *that.*" Subtle gesture toward the corner, where the whole crew was in force, Harlan's spindly arms gesturing forcefully to a new group of sweaty-looking hangers-on.

"Wha—why *me?*"

"You think they'd be here if not for you bringin' your brother in here?"

Tessa recalled the way she'd initially flinched at the question. Common wisdom when Tessa started at Wayne's months earlier was that Rhonda was burned out, often surly. Apparently she got her kicks from acting that way. But Tessa had felt the truth of Rhonda's words like a slap, and that had really been the beginning of the end.

She'd told the whole story—and more—to Floyd the night before, murmuring into the night, and he'd absorbed it all with cold calculation. She told him about how not only Terrell but Sara, and Herb the delivery guy, and Sid the whiskey rep had fallen under Harlan's sway, and it wasn't like it even felt sinister at the time. There was laughter and there was the steadily growing business, as awareness grew. Tessa remembered the night Terrell yelled at her, insisting—even as his hands were shaking in pre-withdrawal!—that Wayne and Richard should be *thankful* for the crowds that Harlan was bringing to the joint. Hell, Harlan should be getting a *cut!*

And then there'd been the gradual but noticeable decline of the bar—once a modestly proud institution on Decatur's north side. The regulars started not showing up, and they were replaced by a whole new caliber of clientele that diminished the place with their crude shouting and their paraphernalia and their violent eyes. Wayne took to slumping over the bar on off nights, lamenting his future, pondering the sale of the place.

Misery led to quiet outrage when kids—*middle-schoolers* among them—started hanging out by the trash cans. And yet Wayne still didn't do anything. He'd rather have hoisted the white flag than put up any kind of fight, and that way of thinking had seemed to become fucking *contagious.* Harlan in the corner side-eyeing her from the shadows, side-eyeing *everyone*, getting away with *everything* as if that's what he'd done his whole sordid life, and there was absolutely no one calling him on it. Everyone was so goddamn *meek.*

Even Terrell! Her brother had fallen almost effortlessly under Harlan's sway—boggling her mind, because he'd always been so strong, so willful. He'd become a soldier in the ranks, even had his own territories in Wabash Crossing and Torrence Park toward the end, before he went too far. And when he *did* go too far, everything seemed to spiral out of his control. She didn't know until he'd spun out that he'd been sampling the merch. That's how naïve she was. She'd had that nightmare glimpse of his Ziploc goodie bags—the rainbow chaos of what he called his zanies and sobos and dollies and fizzies and kickers and roxies and hydros and dexies and vikes and vallies—and it was an image that would stay with her as she wiped the sweat from his brow and the vomit from his thick stubble in the days before she burned everything down.

Her little brother, her stud brother, the linebacker who used to have mischievous stars in his eyes—*diminished*. She couldn't even *look* at him like that.

Some miles later, as if he'd read her mind, Floyd turned the radio down and asked her a question.

"When's the last time you talked to your brother?"

She broke from her reverie as he pushed the Camaro toward St. Louis.

Tessa sat up straight, removing her bare feet from the dash. By instinct, she grabbed her phone, which Floyd had returned to her last night. In actuality, it was *Floyd* who'd used her phone the most in the past forty-eight hours, or whatever it was. On Uncle Johnny's advice, she hadn't had any conversations with *anyone* since she'd left. Ever since she'd taken off in the Beetle, she'd been extremely careful not to make any calls, send any texts, log on to social media. Even the couple of Google searches she'd done had given her the heebie-jeebies. She dropped the phone back into the cruddy drink holder.

"I've been incommunicado since I left," she said. "Fat lot of good *that* did. But anyway Terrell was still unconscious when I left."

"So you have no idea what you're going home to?"

"I mean, sorta. My uncle promised to keep an eye on things."

"Your *uncle?* Against the sorts of assholes you've described to me?"

"Johnny's plenty capable. And he knows some people. A lot of people, actually."

"What kind of people?"

"You know. Second amendment people."

"Ah. Wonderful."

"What?"

"In my experience, the folks who identify themselves as second amendment people are a little tweaked."

"Well, those are just my words. But I've met some of these guys. They're the good ones."

In St. Louis, Floyd gassed up the Camaro on 7th Street, and she went into the little convenience store and got cigarettes for him, Twinkies and Coke for her. Her wrapped-up thigh under her loose jeans was hot and itchy, and her other more superficial wounds on her face and wrists brought some glances, but she got through it. At least she was able to walk mostly without a limp. When she came back out, she found Floyd leaning against the rear of the Camaro in a fetching way, looking off toward downtown. He seemed to have perked up from the hours of tight-jawed concentration he'd subjected her to, thank Christ.

He asked her if she was hungry for something more substantial than Twinkies, and she admitted that she could eat, and that conjured a crooked smile from him.

"You know what's straight ahead?"

He nodded his chin north, and she turned, glimpsed the shining curve of the familiar St. Louis landmark against a blue sky dotted with wispy clouds.

"The arch?"

"Sure, but what else?"

She squinted. "Dude, how the fuck should I know?"

He gave her a look and a little frown, arms folded across his chest. "We're only two hours from Decatur. I figured little Tessa came down to St. Louis all the time."

"Nah, we never went anywhere. Never traveled."

"Your daddy never dragged you and your brother to a baseball game?"

"My *daddy* kicked when I was way young, thanks, and before that he never had much time for me. Hell, man, I never left Decatur till I went on a field trip in sixth grade, and that was to Chicago for museums and shit."

"What about later, you know, jettin' to the big city with your friends? Boyfriends?"

She shrugged. "Couple times to Chicago, some concerts. When we could afford it. Most times, we couldn't afford the gas. But family trips? What, you think I grew up in, like, some ideal suburban American family, church on Sundays in our best duds, prayers before bed, TV dinners, all smiles and hugs, day trips to the big city? Get the fuck outta here with that shit."

Floyd didn't respond. She felt his eyes on the side of her face, and she returned the gaze defiantly.

"What?" she said.

"Nothin', darlin', just—"

"What?"

He raised his hands in surrender. "Hey, I'm just learnin' more about you all the time."

"Uh huh."

"That's Busch Stadium over there. Back in the ol' days, we'd head up here to catch a Cardinals game. 'Bout a five-hour drive for us, so it didn't happen real often, but those were some good times. Hard to believe we're here right now." There was a wistful look in Floyd's eyes, but there was weariness, too, or an acknowledgment of what lay ahead. "My sister and I would beg my dad for popcorn or hot dogs, shit like that, but he'd always hold us off for a burger afterwards, this little old joint called Eat Rite 'round the corner. We'd sit in those stadium seats watching the game, hungry as hell, and he'd drink his plastic cups of Busch, and we'd wait through nine whole goddamn innings and then whine and complain through the crowds streaming out of the stadium, and then *finally* we'd make our way to Eat Rite, and *fuck* me if it wasn't the best burger I've ever had in my life. *Still is* the best burger I've ever had. Place has been around since before World War II."

"You're fixin' to take me to a burger joint, aren't you?"

It was a short drive to the little shack called Eat Rite, which sat like a deserted island on the corner of Chouteau Avenue and—Tessa had to do a double-take—Route 66. Floyd pulled into a big empty parking lot and circled the small building. He immediately began cursing. The Eat Rite diner was closed up, its windows plastered over with wood. Floyd came to a stop right next to it and stared at it. Traffic moved steadily through the intersection beyond the shack, indifferent.

He ended his cuss stream with a loud, declarative *"Fuck!"*

Tessa couldn't muster much of a response, except to touch his thigh sympathetically. She was in pain, and she couldn't seem to get past the numbness that invaded her after yesterday. Their northward trek had a depressing inescapability to it, as if Floyd were marching her down death row. Any food she had, or might have, would have the bitter echo of a last meal.

She expected Floyd to jolt roughly back into traffic, find another place to eat, so she was surprised to hear the Camaro's motor switch off. It was a couple minutes before he spoke again.

"Well, if this doesn't encapsulate *fucking everything* . . . ."

She watched him. "It's just a *dive*. A burger joint."

"It's not just a dive, Tess, this place was a friggin' institution. Sat right here for eighty years or more. *Eighty years!* I mean . . . I sat next to my dad in his old Lincoln chowing down on a greasy burger and fries *right here*, right here in this spot, when I was, like, *five*. Now look at this shit."

"It was the pandemic, man, *everything* closed. Everything *worth* a shit, anyway."

He was shaking his head. "Who'd a' thought the world would be taken down by a plague with a one percent mortality rate?

"Well, one percent is still, like, *millions of people.*"

"This planet was due for some population control."

"Dude."

"Ah, hell, I'm just sayin' . . . I don't know what the fuck I'm sayin'."

He was slumped over the wheel, staring out at the plywood-covered windows—kinda reminded her of Wayne slumped over his bar.

"We're both in a mountain of shit, aren't we?" he mumbled. "Just like the whole world. And over what? Everyone wants to do the *right thing*, whatever the fuck that is, but the right thing always bites you in the ass somehow, doesn't it? Everyone puts a mask on their face, and it saves a million lives, but hey look, the world is forever altered, and everything you loved before is gone. Or a big chunk of assholes *don't* put a mask on their face, cuz they're assholes and cuz *freedom*, but hey look, now grandma's dead and the hospitals are overrun. I'm just sick of this whole fuckin' world, and I'm talkin' about the world *now*, when everything's supposedly under control. It's like—it's like the assholes are reigning supreme, baby, taking up all the oxygen with their anger and hate, and the good people have to devote they're fucking *lives* just to getting on the playing field. And even if they get there, they realize they're playing the wrong game, and the real game is *stupid as fuck.*"

She watched the vehicles crossing in front of them to and fro in the shimmering heat, endlessly, inexorably.

"When's it gonna get better? I mean, I really want to know. Huh, Tess?"

She didn't answer him, merely rubbed at her own thigh, which was one long flaming itch. She knew she ought to clean up the wound soon, swap out the bandages. She stretched out on the vinyl seat, and her sore ribs complained like a series of deep cramps. She winced hard, grinding her teeth. The fingers of her right hand drifted unconsciously to the bump on her head—it felt like a hard apple, and it stung. At least the two fingers on her left hand were regaining some feeling. Instead of outright numb, they were starting to throb with pain. She wanted to flex the ache out of them, but Floyd's makeshift restraints prevented that.

He had stopped talking, and the only sound was road noise through the open windows and the hum in her ears that was there all the time now, the anticipatory thrum of the miles ahead, the road to Decatur, where her past and all the remaining villains of her life lay in wait, like a spider's web.

TWENTY-THREE
FLOYD TILLMAN WEATHERS

So here they were.

The afternoon was ebbing, and the Camaro was parked under the shade of a massive, lush sycamore. A sad, crooked mailbox sat next to the car, its empty maw yawning at them. They were on a side street off Columbus Drive in northern Decatur. They'd been here for an hour now, waiting. Waiting for anything to happen.

The neighborhood surrounding them was lived-in, comfortable, more than a little shlumpy, decidedly low-rent. The homes were small and crowded together, mostly unkempt in their little quarter-acreages, although a few of the structures were meticulously, almost militarily maintained. Floyd imagined that the neighborhood's population was a mixture of straight-backed retiree codgers in knee-high white socks with shiny lawnmowers alongside welfare trash and snowbillies.

Floyd's ass ached.

Time to get out of this fucking car, he thought. *Time to man up.*

And at that moment, the burner phone in his pocket vibrated.

Again.

And, again, he ignored it.

It was the sixth time the phone had rung, and it was the sixth time he hadn't answered it.

When he'd punched up the call log this morning in Tulsa, he'd found that the phone had buzzed three times in his car while he'd tended to Tessa at the motel, and then it had buzzed twice more *in his pocket* during the drive.

Even now, it was insane to him, the way he'd abdicated his own responsibility. How was it that a life could get completely shaken from its foundation—so thoroughly as to become profound?

Of course, the old poem flashed through his mind.

As a kid, halfway through Central High, Floyd had become obsessed with Bukowski, and there was a poem that had stuck at the rear of his brain and stayed there for a decade, all the way to Malvado. He'd even scrawled it on a napkin and pinned it to the wall above his creaky motel bed. It spoke of the contentment of waking up in seedy solitude in strange cities, and there'd just been something about its brief existential lucidity that had resonated like a snare drum. He'd known all along it was a life that was in store for him, somehow, even at the expense of everything else that mattered. Once the assignment from Philip had actually *put* him there, once he was *inhabiting* that separateness, he'd reveled in it, fucking *loved* it.

For about a week.

Wasn't long before he'd started venturing out of his depressing hovel and making connections where he could in that little shit town— George at the bar, Sal and the crew at the diner, Irene and Peter at the Texaco down the road, Eduardo and Camilla at the grocery, their kids, Esteban and Alejandro and the rest of them at the shoulda-been-condemned pool hall. Jesus, man, he'd managed to enmesh himself in the entire measly community, even as he'd postured himself as the quiet loner out there on the periphery. Was it any wonder he'd been drawn to Tessa like a neodymium magnet?

He'd been *primed* for this whole escapade, staring at that infuriatingly mute burner phone in his silent dusty border-town room but fuckin' *aching* for unlawful adventure.

Even if he were face to face with Philip Crouch at this very moment, Floyd wouldn't be able to answer why he hadn't responded to the calls on the burner. Tied up in it was a wanton disregard for his own moral code and an even more contemptible disdain for the well-being of his *parents*, for god's sake. How could he even begin to defend his actions? And yet the phone had remained there, deep in his pocket, throbbing against his thigh, untouched as he stared straight ahead at the road—and no, he wasn't on the fast track to Little Rock with Philip's cash but rather moving steadfastly in the wrong direction.

For the simple reason of seeing this through. For her. Was that all? Or was there more to it? Maybe he just found it difficult to admit to himself that he wanted to keep the cash. Use it to disappear. With her.

Next to Floyd, Tessa was still staring intently at a dirty white ranch-style home that was framed by fat maples and fronted by an assemblage of deep-green shrubs. A cracked-asphalt drive meandered around the left side toward a detached garage and a leaning shed. The place had been utterly quiet for the hour they'd been parked under this tree.

It was the house where Tessa had grown up.

"Okay, so I'm a little freaked out," she'd whispered a while ago.

Not long after he'd parked the Camaro, he'd volleyed a series of questions at her—*Does anything look different or not right? Are the shades in the windows usually drawn like that? Are any of these cars familiar?*—but they were more than fifty yards from the place, so some things were impossible to tell. The only thing Tess had pointed out was that two vehicles parked a few houses down were unfamiliar, but cars came and went on this street, especially on a warm afternoon like this one. Hell, *neighbors* came and went in a neighborhood like this.

Not much had happened out there. Floyd hadn't noticed a single hint of any surveillance, and he considered himself a pretty good judge of that kind of shit. There'd been a number of folks coming home from jobs, or from the grocery with a few plastic bags in their fists as they moped up their front walks. Not much outdoor activity that he could see, except for a man tinkering with something in his garage eight homes to the south and some foot traffic that didn't sound any bells. No movement at all in the vicinity of Tessa's place.

A whirlwind of emotions had crossed Tessa's beautiful features in the space of this hour. For a long while there was only her uneven breathing. But then something would pass between them. At one point, he'd reached over to take her hand and found her grasping fingers cold, despite the simmering heat outside.

The girl had steel ovaries, but—again—she could regress to little-girl anxiety, too.

Earlier, as the Camaro had rumbled toward Decatur, Floyd had noticed Tessa getting more and more squirmy. She'd clammed up not long after St. Louis, shortly after they'd spent some downtime consuming an ungodly pasta-and-mizithra concoction at a joint called the Old Spaghetti Factory in the shadow of the arch. After that, Tessa had been a bundle of nervous energy—tight-lipped and jumpy—as he'd cleaned and re-wrapped her thigh outside a CVS pharmacy that his phone had directed him to.

The primary reason for Tessa's mood since St. Louis? On her own phone, she'd been trying to reach her family, and she'd been having no luck at all. Initially reluctant, for some reason, to make *any calls*—as if in denial that they could be facing serious trouble—she'd relented and rang her Uncle Johnny. He seemed to be the voice of reason in her family, at least about things non-political. He was the guy Floyd wanted to talk with himself, see if he could determine a starting point in Decatur. But neither her Uncle Johnny nor her Aunt Georgia had answered her call. Next, she'd tried her mother, whom Tessa said was an unpredictable mess but *should* answer—but didn't. Finally, her brother Terrell, whose fate was completely up in the air, given that she'd left him unconscious in his lumpy childhood bed following his overdose. Again, no answer.

Yeah, so after that, that's when Tess had become *really* unsettled. The remaining miles to Decatur had been so quiet that Floyd was surprised he couldn't hear her heartbeat.

"I need to get in that house," Tessa murmured now. She was shrunk down in her seat, having shut off the radio in favor of silence. *"I need to fucking get in there, but I don't think I can do it."*

"Uh. No way you're going in there."

She gave him the stink-eye. "I think I can fucking well go into my own house if I want to."

"Well, this is the one time you can't."

"Fuck that, dude—you think I'm just gonna sit here? My family could be dead in there."

"I'm goin' in, okay? We already established that."

"They don't know you! I mean, my mom would probably have a heart attack if *I* suddenly showed up, let alone some strange white man *with a gun!*"

"I'll be careful."

Floyd had already told her what needed to be done. None of this was coming out of his ass. They'd pieced together a plan like some haphazard puzzle during sporadic moments while Floyd had sped northeast. They'd hashed it out between them. First thing they needed to do was shore up Tessa's family, make sure they were all whole and safe—and it made sense that Floyd would be the one to do that. It would defy logic for Tess to walk into that house. Floyd figured there was at *least* a fifty percent chance that it was being watched—maybe even *right now*—by the exact people who were after her.

The second part of the plan, to put it quite baldly, was to put an end to the remnants of Harlan's crew. Simple as that. They needed to weed out the rest of them, and they needed to fucking *end them*. Between them, Floyd and Tessa had already managed to dispatch fully *half* of the belligerent assholes, and they'd barely broken a sweat doing it.

It was big talk for a couple of ne'er-do-wells buzzing with adrenaline. Hot wind blowin' your hair, the road hurtling at you.

But—time to get real—Floyd had no strong concept of the operation here in Decatur, no detailed notion of what any of these people were like, beyond how Tessa had described them, the way they sauntered in and out of the bar where she'd waitressed. Hell, even Perkins. Floyd had gotten only a glimpse of Perkins before the pugnacious toad had croaked in his motel room. As for Dankworth and McQuoid, Floyd had registered only the murkiest of impressions, threatening though they'd been. The way Tessa described the whole entourage in Decatur, they were a ragtag group of loudmouthed yet barely competent tough guys prone to overdrinking.

Now that he and Tess were actually in Decatur and parked on this modest street facing her old house, the whole plan they had drawn out on figurative napkins seemed silly. And needlessly dangerous.

Plus, Floyd knew—despite what he'd done to Dankworth—it just wasn't in him to be a cold-blooded murderer. It wasn't like he was gonna outright snuff any of these bastards. Saving Tessa's life in the heat of the moment was *quite different* from smoking some bastard he'd never met.

He wondered if Tessa was pondering the same shit. Little over an hour earlier, as I-72 had begun its rise over the north edge of Decatur, the Camaro had passed a road sign for Forsyth, and Floyd had watched her register the signpost with a dismayed full-body twitch. The name of the town had tweaked his own memory of her tale, and he'd realized after a few seconds that Forsyth was where she'd burned down the meth house. It was the town mentioned in the article he'd read on her phone. Maybe at that point Tessa had dialed back her own expectations.

Especially about this dude Harlan—by her reckoning, the most dangerous man alive.

When it came right down to it, Floyd would consider this journey a success if he could simply defuse the Harlan situation. Find a way to neutralize the remaining members of this ludicrous gang. Best-case scenario: He and Tess, some of her friends and family, could join forces to point the Decatur police straight at Harlan, make it a goddamn community project. Lay out a version of the truth that excluded the drug-den blaze but focused on the would-be murderous gangster preying on her and her brother, rendering their lives a daily hell. Make the bastard so busy with criminal inquiry that Tessa and her family fell off his radar.

Floyd didn't feel the need to voice all that to Tessa, though.

"All right, here I go." He reached for the door.

"Fuck."

"You stay put, okay? I'm serious. I don't care if your brother suddenly comes out and starts doing cartwheels in the yard, you stay right here outta sight."

"Floyd?"

"Yeah?"

"Are we doin' the right thing? I mean, really? Or are we fixin' to make everything worse?"

A pause.

"You tell me," he replied.

She turned to face him, aghast. "What does *that* mean?"

"Listen, Tess, I'm here to help you fix this. That's what I'm here for. And somehow or other we're gonna put an end to it. I promise."

She nodded contemplatively. "All right then."

"You see anyone drive up and park out front, you send me a quick text, like we talked about, right?"

"Uh huh." Her right hand was already clutching her phone.

"You got the key?"

She handed it to him unceremoniously, having spiraled it off her key ring a half hour ago.

Floyd took it, then reached over and rummaged in the glove box, coming up with the little notebook he used to keep track of oil changes and shit. There was a ballpoint pen clipped to it, probably didn't work anymore, but that didn't matter. It was all for show.

"Floyd?"

"Yeah?"

"You better kiss me right now, and you better fuckin' mean it."

He leaned over to her and kissed her, and she grabbed his crotch with force, and after a while he came away feeling better about the general state of the world.

He caught his breath, scanned the street, waited for the fire in his loins to cool down, gave Tess a quick nod, then eased out of the Camaro.

Oh *Christ*, it felt good to stand up. His muscles and joints sang praises to the heavens.

He stretched for a moment, then walked with purpose to the sidewalk, crossed the street at an angle, strode in front of the house. He went straight up the drive, faux-relaxed, holding his notebook as if consulting it. He caught sight of the energy meter and went to it, pretended to write something while surveying the area.

He blew out a breath, glanced back toward Tessa. She was merely a vague shape from this distance, unmoving, but he felt her watching him.

Sensing no life inside the house, and no peeping eyes from next door, he pocketed the notebook and moved deeper onto the property, skirting the garage. There were a couple of dark, crusty hopper windows at the home's grade level, indicating a basement. Should've asked Tessa about that but didn't.

His mind was everywhere, too scattered. If he was gonna be any good to her, he had to focus. He found a section of garage siding that was out of view of everything, and he leaned against it and closed his eyes. He wanted a cigarette, almost reached for his breast pocket for one, but resisted.

He pushed away from the garage siding.

Up close, the home's disrepair was obvious: the peeling paint, the exposed timber, the water damage. As he moved around toward the rear, he glimpsed another low hopper window. This one was blocked with what looked like new cardboard, revealing the fresh black ink of an Amazon box. Someone had put that there recently. He stepped to the corner and peeked around into an open back yard empty of life—strangled plants, yellow lawn, remnants of a rusted metal clothesline like the weathered skeleton of some strange animal. There was a simple porch leading up to the back door, and beyond that a Weber grill that appeared to have cooked its most recent hot dogs before Tessa Rae Jayne existed.

Floyd listened for any movement at all inside the house, then made his move. He went for the screen door on the porch, pulled it open, knocked on the inner door. His heart felt like a drumroll. No movement inside. He glanced around, knocked again. Nothing.

He tried the knob. Locked.

He inserted Tess's key into the lock and twisted. The lock was stiff, needed some WD-40, but it finally gave, and he was inside the kitchen. There was a faint stink of cat piss, probably an untended litter box somewhere. He eased the door shut behind him.

"Hello?" he called, immediately swallowing off the end of the word.

No response. Jesus, if there was someone in this house, it was a friggin' ghost.

"Hello?" he called, louder.

Nothing.

He went to the fridge and opened it, checked it out. Pretty empty in there, and not very clean, but it held the basics—eggs, milk, bread, butter, that kind of shit. There were also a couple of pizza boxes from a joint called Fellini's, a half-empty two-liter of brown sugar soda, and three more of those unopened behind it. And a fresh sixer of Bud cans underneath all that. At least these were signs of life. He whispered the fridge shut.

Any other situation, he'd have figured the family to be out, but Tessa's inability to get anyone on the horn still unnerved him.

He moved to the hallway and immediately saw an open door. He brought his Beretta out from the small of his back, thumbed off the safety, and went to the door. He peered beyond it, saw darkened stairs leading down into an unfinished basement. Something drew his gaze down to his feet. Grittiness. He saw that the linoleum there was old and grimy—and also dirty with footprints. This area had seen some traffic.

He called down the stairs, "Anyone there?"

Silence.

He made his way into the front room, which lay quiet, undisturbed, pristine, lifeless. It looked like an old woman's front room—puffy floral furniture, a display cabinet holding an assortment of knick-knacks, a weathered antique coffee table. Dust particles drifted in the slanted yellow light coming through the open front window. Floyd could see the Camaro's left fender from here.

"Yo!" he called up the stairs to his right. "Anyone up there?"

His voice echoed back at him.

At the foot of the main stairwell, he took a second to send Tess a quick text.

NO ONE HERE

He pocketed the phone, glanced back in the direction of the basement, and went back that way. The house was so quiet that he could hear the hum of his own ears. He clicked on the light, illuminating the narrow descending corridor, and started down the wooden steps.

"I'm comin' down!" he announced to no one. He was sure the basement was empty.

A fresh ammonia stink reached his nostrils halfway down, and although his first thought was cats, his next was the more sinister conclusion. After all, he hadn't seen any evidence of felines. He got to the bottom of the stairs and faced a dark space full of portent. The air was humid and foul and close, like a locker room, and the other odor had intensified—ammonia alongside another strong chemical scent, like cleaning fluid. There was a second light switch, and he flicked it up, sweeping the barrel of the Beretta from right to left. There was no one here, but it *felt* like someone was here. Or had been here recently.

His gaze landed with a thud on the far side of the room. Against a concrete wall were several folding tables, and on top of them was an incomprehensible mishmash of soda bottles and jars and tubes. Sloppy connections had been mickey moused between these items with aluminum foil. The plastic and glass surfaces were fogged up and vaguely brown, like fresh lungs a few years into tobacco addiction. He glimpsed a small tin of paint thinner at one table's edge, and there was a propane tank underneath it all, along with a huge bag of rock salt.

Oh shit.

As Floyd came to a series of understandings, his personal phone buzzed in his pocket. Within moments, he heard heavy footsteps above him in the living room.

TWENTY-FOUR
TESSA RAE JAYNE

Tessa watched Floyd disappear around the rear corner of the house, off in the direction of the garage that contained the godawful wood-paneled Mercury station wagon—the lumbering vehicle her mom had dutifully driven to a menial early-hours stocking job at Sears for thirty-some years. It was the same car she'd driven Tessa to grade school in, and that thought brought a little twist of melancholy to Tessa's guts. If there were happy days in her childhood, she guessed they were around that time. Now the car was inoperable in there, gathering dust and grime. Her mom's doctor didn't let her drive anywhere anymore, and she was always grumbling about that.

There was no sign of Terrell's beat-up Mustang.

A silver bug-eyed WRX whisked past the parked Camaro, too fast, and Tessa stiffened, but the car kept on going, speeding out of view. Couple of teenagers.

God, she was a mess. She was sweaty and irritable and tired. Her head was still *killing* her, despite the dozen or so ibuprofen she'd scarfed since Tulsa, and she was still nursing her aching thigh and ribs and fingers. On top of all that, her nerves were jangling. Who knew what was going on in that house—or what was *about* to go down?

She'd had plenty of time during the final leg of this journey to imagine her family dead in a pile somewhere, cut into pieces, burned to crisps, strung up and swinging, whatever. Her skull was clattering with these images. She couldn't help it. No answer from *any of them?*

It was like goddamn karma, man—absolute silence from everyone she'd run away from three days ago—and she felt a self-loathing the likes of which she'd never before experienced. There was one part of her that wanted to rush into that house right now, see the lay of the land for herself, but then there was that other part of her that *still* wanted to twist the ignition of the Camaro and revert to her original plan: Tear back across the miles, cross that fucking border, and get lost in Mexico. Plop on a beach and make like she'd gotten away with everything. As if none of it—

none of it!—had happened.

As if Floyd Weathers had never happened.

She wiped moisture from her eyes, muttering to herself.

It was through those eyes that she watched a familiar gray primer-patched Dodge pickup come to a stop in front of her house. Tessa's breath stopped. Immediately, she knew it was Eric. Eric Broadstreet. The other one of Harlan's guys, the more observant and careful of the two. Terrell used to joke that he was Harlan's two-bit consigliore, like in that *Godfather* DVD her brother watched over and over in the front room, except Eric lived in the land of dollar stores. Didn't make him any less of an asshole, though.

Why the holy fuck is HE here?

His presence here validated her suspicions and raised the temperature on everything. On the drive up from Tulsa, Floyd had told her all about the messages he'd found on her phone, and she'd been able to fill in the gaps—namely, that the texts from the person he called Mr. 69 were most certainly Eric's. They just sounded like him: no nonsense, vaguely menacing, just get the fucking job done. She'd read through them as Floyd had whisked up the diagonal route through northeast Oklahoma, her heart going cold at the casually brutal way they'd all texted about her as they'd chased her through Texas and New Mexico.

Now, here was Mr. 69 himself, directly in her line of sight. She felt a mixture of fury and fear. Floyd had told her to text him if she saw someone pull up, but she could only sit there frozen, her hands numb in her lap. She felt as if any movement would betray her. She'd somehow draw Eric's attention, and he'd see who she was, and he'd unleash hell on her.

There was someone else in the truck with him, too, but she couldn't make out who it was. The two men were still in the cab, talking animatedly about something. Tessa felt herself inching down in her seat until she could barely see above the dash, but Eric didn't so much as glance her way. Floyd had left the keys in the ignition, so if worse came to worst, she could throw herself over into the driver's seat and tear out of here—but by then the damage would be done. Eric would know she was in town, and therefore *Harlan* would know, and then that would be the end of her, wouldn't it? Like Floyd had said, her advantage was that no one suspected she was within hundreds of miles of Decatur.

So she stayed quiet, and she stayed low.

Her phone beeped, startling her. She glanced down surreptitiously at the screen.

NO ONE HERE

The truck's door came open, and she took a breath, held it. Eric stepped down from the cab and walked around toward the front, and then she could see that the other man was that weird creep named Crowe. She didn't even know his first name, had only seen him maybe twice before at Wayne's. Both times, he'd acted jumpy, hopped up on product probably. Terrell had mentioned the guy a couple times early in his association with the crew; he'd said Crowe was a twitchy mother-fucker who nevertheless knew his shit, young but preternaturally gifted, like he'd been brought up in the culture. It was like Terrell was jealous of the guy.

Tessa stabbed her phone with tingling fingers, coming up with a nearly incomprehensible reply to Floyd:

THEY OUTSIDE!

From this distance, Crowe had the hunch in his spine that Tessa re-membered from the bar. Bad posture, always coughing into his hand, he was constantly staring down at his phone. Right now, Crowe was mostly eclipsed by Eric, who had the same kind of frame, the same thick neck, that Terrell used to have. Probably also played football back in school. Eric in his red tank top had a bold white-power tattoo prominent on his right shoulder, visible even from here.

The two men moved up the front walk like they owned the place. A plastic bag full of something bulky swung from Crowe's fist. They were laughing.

Tessa was itching to type out more to Floyd, to *call him*, but she felt incapacitated, as if literally paralyzed. Her hands wouldn't fucking move.

Eric drew a key from his pocket and unlocked the front door, letting it swing open. Tessa could only watch, powerless, as he disappeared into the shadows of the living room and Crowe followed him in. The door shut, and she heard the distant bang of it—it was real, undeniable. Those two ass-holes had sauntered into her mother's house as if they were squatting there.

What the hell was she supposed to do now? The world was suddenly a buzzing chunk of panic. Every impulse was telling her to bolt toward the house, but what good would she do? She'd run right into their web. She was practically crippled, and she was unarmed. Each second that passed had a hard weight to it.

Oh *Christ*, she *was* gonna go over there, wasn't she? Should she? Should she rush to her family's protection even when she had no fucking clue what was going on? Floyd could take care of himself, right? He'd proven that time and again in the three long-ass days she'd known him. He'd specifically told her to stay *right here*, no matter what, even if Jesus himself appeared before her and pulled her from the Camaro with his bloody mitts. Nope! *Don't do it!* She could jeopardize the entire gig if she went flailing in there.

She was gonna fucking do it. She *had* to fucking do it.

She pulled the keys from the ignition, including Floyd's scratched-up peace-symbol key ring. Then she took a flurry of breaths before opening her door. She got out, clicked the door shut, and locked the car, checked it. Crapload of money in the trunk, after all. She pocketed the keys and crossed the street to her left, and then walked diagonally toward the house, her whole body twanging like a high-tension wire. The entire way, she blurbled a streaming mantra from her lips: *Fuck fuck fuck fuck fuck.*

She got to the corner of the house, and nothing happened. No one started yelling at her.

She caught her breath, staring out at the familiar view of the neighborhood, varnished by memory—the Gutierrez family across the street to the left, where her childhood friend Helena had lived and where Tessa'd gotten her first taste of Mexican food; the Scarborough family next door to that house, where Jack had lived, her first tongue kiss; over the other way, the cheerful old Springers, the grandma and grandpa of the street, both of whom had died in that house; and the Robinsons, where the twins Kayla and Kiara had lived, her first black friends, even though they were a couple years older, the ones who showed her new ways to style her hair and taught her how to hold her head high. All of them gone, distant memories now, and no idea where any of them were now—but for just a moment she swirled into a nostalgic vortex that she desperately wanted to lose herself in, to re-do everything in her whole stupid life that led her to this point.

She squeezed behind a tangle of shrubs and went to the edge of the front window. Steeled herself. Craned her neck and peered in.

The living room was empty, but everything looked the same, in its place. She leaned over for a wider view, saw no one down the hallway toward the kitchen. She risked a look upstairs toward the bedrooms, but the stairs and the crooked photos along the wall faded into darkness. She pulled away from the window and listened. She couldn't hear anything at first, but then she barely discerned the two men's voices. She risked another look through the window and caught a glimpse of Eric's jacket. They were in the kitchen—at the fridge, it looked like. She plastered herself to the window again, continuing her *fuck* mantra.

Her phone beeped, and an electrical surge zapped through her. She hurriedly shut off the volume and stared at the screen. Floyd had texted back:

I'M OK. STAY PUT.

A few interminable moments went by, and the tone of the voices inside the house changed. She clenched her jaw and peered inside again. The two men were disappearing into the corridor that led to the basement, and then she clearly heard their foot stomps as they descended.

What the hell?

She bolted for the front porch, stepping lightly, and tried the door, hoping fervently that they hadn't locked it behind them. They hadn't. It opened in her sweaty grip, and she stepped inside. The smell of home struck her, years of cheap meals and her mother's occasional cigarettes and simply the presence of her family, but there was another scent there, something foreign tamping everything else down, something chemical. Crowe's voice was clear, coming up from the basement, a laugh in his tone. His words were nonsensical to her.

"… wouldn't even *say* anything to me, man, she just stuck it into the bag!"

"You're fuckin' kidding me," Eric responded, his voice rumbling a bass register.

"With all the chips and candy and shit."

"And you carried that out the store?"

"In front of, like, thirty people."

"Charmed life, man."

"What else could I do?"

"I don't know, maybe doing it *any other place at any other time?*"

Laughter, followed by the sounds of things scraping, clattering. They were busy down there.

Heart in her throat, Tessa launched herself up the stairs, stepping light as a cat, taking two at a time—wincing at the pain in her thigh. She got to the top, squinted into the humid shadows. All the doors were closed. She went straight to Terrell's room, where she'd left him three days earlier, only to find it dark and empty, obscenely hot, shades closed. In the relative darkness, the room felt so strongly of the brother she once knew—with its sports posters and football trophies, the old scuffed dresser, the scent of him—that she felt emotion fatten her throat. She shoved that shit down, and only in that moment did she realize that the room not only lacked her brother but also the bed itself. The mattress was gone. Just . . . *gone.* She frowned at the bare rectangular area in the center of the room.

She brought up her phone and typed out a message to Floyd:

WHERE ARE YOU?

Tessa returned to the hallway, listened for a moment to the voices still coming from the basement. She couldn't make out the words from here, but they had the same laughing tone.

She moved to the master bedroom door, took hold of the knob—and paused. A dark premonition opened like a black hole behind her eyes, and she yanked her hand back as if the metal had burned her. Instead of opening the door, she placed her ear against it and listened. The plywood was warm against her cheek, but it wasn't a good warm. Oh God, someone was beyond this door, and she knew she wasn't going to like what she found. She could barely discern a low throb coming from the room. She returned her hand to the knob—but at that moment her phone vibrated in her left hand, and she glanced down:

BASEMENT

Her eyes widened in the darkness. Floyd must be hiding down there. There were plenty of places to do that. Hell, she'd done so as a child with Terrell, escaping the glare of their father when he was still around. Floyd could take care of himself, right? At that thought, she heard Crowe's loud voice coming through the vents. Still seemed to be regular conversation, just pitched to the level of obnoxious, like at Wayne's after a few Coors. She replied to Floyd's text:

I'M UPSTAIRS. I KNOW THESE GUYS. WHAT CAN I DO?

She stood there sweating, her forehead against the warm door, waiting for a response, but the phone was a sweaty blank brick in her hand for long moments.

She steeled herself, opened her mother's bedroom door softly, and glanced in on near total darkness. Immediately a wall of stinking heat assaulted her—a vaguely sweet chemical scent overlaid by the unmistakable odors of body odor and shit. She went in, breathing through her mouth, and ran her hand along the wall, searching for the light switch. She found it and flicked it up.

Her phone finally buzzed in her hand, but she couldn't move. Couldn't process what she was looking at.

A chaos of brown flesh lay before her. She saw her mother first, sagging on her side, facing her. She was naked, her skin hanging loosely—mottled, sweat-sheened, tinged with gray—and her arms were twisted above her head, zip-tied to the wrought-iron headboard. Her face appeared to be melting into the filthy sheets, which were stained with sweat and vomit.

"Mama!" Tessa gasped, childlike, lurching toward her.

She stopped short when she heard a low moan, recognizing Terrell behind her, naked too, and also bound. They were back-to-back, and the mattress was stained with their collective filth. A stifled cry burst from Tessa's throat, and she couldn't breathe. She went to them, her searching hands impotent, wanting to cover them, but their bodies were infernos of fever, slowly writhing in what was either agony or elation. They were drugged. Deeply. Both of them had an IV line stuck rigidly in their forearm, and the crimson tubing snaked to saline bags that hung from wire hangers attached with gnarled duct tape to the headboard. Panic seized Tessa's chest. She didn't know what to do.

"Mama, it's me," she whispered urgently, finding her breath. *"Wake up, Mama. Terrell, wake the fuck up!"*

But they barely acknowledged her. Terrell's lips moved dryly on an incomprehensible sound, and her mother was gone gone gone. Their faces were gaunt and desert-parched, muscles clenched and grasping beneath flaccid skin.

Something moved to Tessa's right, and she flinched. Beyond her mother's bed was a second mattress, the one from Terrell's room, and it was on the floor, and it held the unclothed bodies of her Uncle Johnny and Aunt Georgia. They were similarly bound with zip-ties and drugged, their IV lines dangling from a makeshift rack against the wall, where her mother's antique dresser had been rudely shoved out of the way. The bodies of her aunt and uncle looked small and withered, both face down, and their mattress was also stained with urine and feces.

Tessa couldn't help it: Hard sobs exploded out of her. She clamped her free hand to her mouth, trying to hold her sound in, but it was if her entire body were collapsing inward with the strength of the emotion. She was helpless to it; it overtook her completely. She could hardly keep her eyes open for the tears streaming out of them. She let the sobs wrack her body until it felt as if she'd been wrung out, and then she could barely overcome her hyperventilation.

There were sheets twisted up on the floor, as if her family had flung them off in drugged desperation. Breathing raggedly, Tessa pocketed her phone and grabbed the sheets, untwisting them and then covering the bodies to preserve their modesty. She went to the big window and quietly opened it. Fresh air leaked in. Then she crossed the room and opened the smaller window next to the bathroom, and a cross breeze began flowing. She pushed her face against the screen and tried to take deep breaths. Her chest was hitching and cramping, and she couldn't stop swallowing for some reason, and she could barely get her limbs to function right.

Her phone buzzed again. She dug it out and saw the two texts from Floyd:

HANG TIGHT

I GOT THIS

She shoved the phone back into her pocket, turned back to study the slack faces of her family. They were all alive, but she didn't know how long that would remain true if she didn't do something. Like, *now*. She scanned the dresser surfaces to her right, registered the collection of hypodermics there—a torn-open pack of them, and three used ones just lying there. Next to that, a bag of cotton balls and a couple of stained spoons, rubber tie-offs, two red Bic lighters. A dozen or so unused zip-ties. And a splayed-open Ziploc containing smaller baggies of brownish dope, exactly like the monstrous shit that had sent Terrell into his spiral, the fentanyl-laced heroin that had turned him into a gasping, psychotic stranger.

It was at that moment when Tessa's shock turned to fury.

TWENTY-FIVE
FLOYD TILLMAN WEATHERS

As the clamor continued above him, Floyd drew the phone from his pocket and read the new text.

THEY OUTSIDE!

He paused, reversed course, stepped backward toward the makeshift meth lab.

Well, shit. Thanks for the warning, Tess.

After wearing out his ass in the Camaro for an hour, he'd gotten inside the house, into the fucking basement, and *this* is the moment someone enters the place?

He pocketed the phone, checked the Beretta, steadied himself.

There were voices now, loud and casual, moving across the main floor above him. Sounded like men. At least two of them. By all indications, *not* Tessa's family.

He glanced over at the little science lab, the collection of illicit equipment. There was a box filled with discarded Sudafed packages. The whole setup was making terrible sense—and Floyd knew it didn't bode well for Tessa. He felt like he should've seen something like this coming: a giant *fuck you* to Tessa and her brother, hell, her whole goddamn *life*.

Payback. Monstrous and evil.

He scoped out the rest of the basement, saw how the bare hanging lightbulbs threw a section of it into severe shadow. That was where he'd have to go.

Soon enough, clomping footfalls were echoing down the stairwell's unfinished walls, and Floyd had already moved into the dark corner, situating himself behind an ancient, nearly rusted-out washer-and-dryer pair. He felt his left leg disturb probably a decade's worth of spiderwebbing.

"He's due back after six," came a deep voice that was flattened into a midwestern pancake.

"Said he'd grab some Chi-Town Dawgs on the way back." This younger voice was a loud clang compared to the other man. "The one on State Street is right around the corner from Keller."

"Yeah, we'll see. He's usually got his mind on other things."

"I'm fuckin' *hungry*, man. Need some goddamn meat in me."

"That's what she said."

"Haw haw."

"So you're okay with eating pig lips and assholes?"

"Top of the food pyramid!"

"You're fine with that kind of shit in your stomach?"

"It's all just shit in the end."

"Hey, it's your body."

So there were only two of them, unless there were more upstairs still. Floyd doubted it. These two sounded like a unit. He held his breath, waited, and then the two men were at the tables in Floyd's line of sight. The first one, the louder one, had a gangly aspect to him, skinny and a bit hunched over, with a greasy tangle of hair so black it appeared dyed. Bad skin, looked like bad teeth. It was no stretch to imagine that he often sampled the wares. Dude was the jumpy type. The other one, coming in to view now, was obviously the one in charge. He commanded the room with his broad shoulders and thick neck and military crewcut. A straining red tank top contained a body that Floyd could tell had once been chiseled but was fading from lack of focus. There was a disgusting white-pride tattoo on the man's shoulder that managed to resemble both a gunsight and a swastika.

The two of them had started tinkering with the plastic and metal equipment on the tables as if to move things into position. Jesus Christ, they were about to cook a batch. With the clatter as cover, Floyd took a moment to withdraw his phone and text Tessa, instructing her to stay the fuck in the Camaro.

"Where you headed tomorrow?" the big dude with the tattoo said, all casual, his voice echoing against the basement's concrete walls.

"I got Wabash and the east side."

"Get the fire going. You covering MacArthur?"

"Wasn't planning on it, should I?"

"Used to be Terrell's turf, although he fuckin' sucked at it. Never took to it. You should take a shot at it, I mean why not? Score points with H."

Their conversation went on inanely as they moved industriously about the confined area, moving things around by some unspoken strategy. Another text vibrated in from Tessa, and he checked it. She'd asked him where he was, so he responded.

"Here's the iodine."

"Okay. The red?"

"Yeah, right there. I'll get the lye."

"No hurry. I think we're all set, otherwise." He started gesturing at the table with a thick finger, enumerating things. "Got the salt, every-thing powdered down nice and strained . . . batteries broken down. You got the plastic, right?"

"Yeah, right there. My sister goes to MacArthur. Freshman."

"I know. You ready to do this thing?"

"Fuckin' A."

"You sure about upstairs?"

"Out for at least a few hours."

"Still want you to check on 'em every hour or so."

"On it, boss."

"Told you not to fuckin' call me *boss*."

High-pitched nervous laughter.

Just as Floyd was preparing himself to extricate himself from the shadows, another text buzzed his pocket. He took out the phone and stared at Tessa's message:

I'M UPSTAIRS. I KNOW THESE GUYS. WHAT CAN I DO?

Floyd felt a wave of irritation. Of *course* she was in the house.

The men were affixing masks to their faces. Now was the time. He tapped out a quick response and shoved the phone back into his jeans. He double-checked his weapon's safety, stepped gingerly away from the washer/dryer, and walked straight and true across the room. Neither man saw him until he was upon them and speaking.

"Hey! Assholes!"

The assholes jerked almost comically, ripping the masks from their faces. White Power reached halfway down to the weapon at his waist but stopped when he saw the Beretta pointed at his chest, then merely stared at Floyd with contempt. Chicago Dog grunted out a screech and, also see-ing the gun, gagged for a moment, bug-eyed.

"Step away from there," Floyd said. *"Right now."*

White Power stepped away from the chemicals and contraptions, reared his thick head back, sneered. Next to him, Chicago Dog had his eyes blistered wide and was darting his gaze from his buddy to Floyd and back again. He was suddenly animated by nervous tics.

"Who the *fuck* are you?" White Power said.

"You can call me Mr. Beretta," Floyd said, raising the pistol rock-steady toward the man's forehead. "Now back up against that wall."

The two men did as instructed.

"I'm gonna guess you're . . . Eric?" Floyd said, nodding at White Power.

The big man emitted a little grunt, but the subtle flinch at the mention of his name told Floyd he'd gotten his identity right.

"You have no idea what you're doing," Eric said.

"Maybe." He turned to the little guy, showing him the Beretta's business end. "Now, *you* . . . *you* look totally out of your depth."

Floyd watched the kid's face go red, and he lost eye contact, and then he realized Chicago Dog was in the process of pissing his pants. A quick glance south revealed a broadening stain down the left thigh.

"Aren't you guys housebroken?"

"Hey, *fuck* you, man!" Chicago Dog spat, all defiance despite his accident. His face was still deep red, though, betraying his mortification.

"So what do we got goin' on here? Cookin' up a little white-trash meth, are we?"

"*What'd you just say?*" Eric said.

"Someone burns down your crackhouse in Forsyth, so you take the opportunity to move in to this basement, set up this pathetic rinky-dink outfit? Gotta get a fresh start somewhere, I guess, but *here?*" He gestured with the Beretta at the close, dank confines of the unfinished basement. "I mean, cookin' a batch on cheap folding tables, by bare lightbulb?"

Eric had something calculating going on behind his eyes. He was trying to figure out who Floyd was. The man was smart, certainly smarter than Chicago Dog, but Floyd got the feeling he wasn't as smart as he *thought* he was. Eric had the look of someone who would slip up if provoked, and that's why Floyd was provoking him.

"This is, like . . . *amateur* hour, fellas."

"What do you want?" Eric was glaring it him, teeth clenched.

"Well, since you asked so nice . . . I want Harlan." Floyd offered a pleasant smile. "And you say he's due back after six?"

Eric gave Chicago Dog a withering stare.

"All right," Floyd said, "phones out, put 'em right there on the table. Weapons, too. C'mon, double-quick time."

Chicago Dog was only too willing to do as he was told, digging out his device and slapping it onto the closest folding table, next to what Floyd assumed was a bag of powdered Sudafed. Eric moved a little more slowly, apparently hoping for Floyd to slip up and provide an opening that he could take advantage of. But Floyd wasn't gonna slip up.

"Do it," he told Eric.

Then Eric's phone came out and joined Chicago Dog's on the table. It was a late-model iPhone that looked as if it had been dragged through a gutter somewhere. Then, oh-so-slowly, Eric reached for the pistol attached to his belt—looked like a Glock 19, the same pistol favored by a few of the guys back home in Arkansas—and unclipped the little holster with his thumb.

"Careful now," Floyd intoned.

Eric placed the Glock gingerly on the table.

"You boys heard from Perkins yet?"

"Man, really, who the fuck *are* you?" Eric said.

"How about any word from Dankworth or McQuoid?"

"What's going on here?" Chicago Dog put in, squinting.

"I mean, all three of them just disappeared off the face of the earth, right?"

"Christ, you're not a fuckin' cop, are you?" Eric asked. "No way."

"Am I to understand that pretty much your entire operation has been taken down . . . by a girl?"

Eric cocked his head a little. "Wait a minute. You're *with* her, aren't you? You're with that cunt."

"I don't think she'd appreciate that kind of language."

"Holy *shit!*" Chicago Dog cried. "He *is* with her! What'd you do with them?"

A creeping smile was taking hold of Eric's face, and Floyd wanted to slap it off. The thug looked like any number of sociopathic assholes that Floyd had come up with in Little Rock. The world was full of them. It was almost human nature now, this low abrasiveness, this petulant narcissism. For five years, people like this had been emerging from their hidey-holes, emboldened by politicians and cable TV wingnuts.

"I'm just up to date on current events," Floyd said.

Eric was nodding. "So what now, smart guy? You've snuck up on us, for damn sure, but you don't have a fucking clue what to do next, do you? You don't have a single idea about what you've gotten yourself into."

"*Yeah!*" Chicago Dog brayed, encouraging his partner.

Eric raised his hands defensively as Floyd moved the pistol back in his direction.

"I think your best option is to turn the fuck around and get out of this house, okay?" Eric said. "Unless you want your life to become a living hell. Because that's what's coming for you if you keep up with the stupid."

Eric swallowed the word *stupid* as he and Chicago Dog both reacted to something behind Floyd. For a split second, he was *certain* Harlan was back there, and that he—Floyd Tillman Weathers—had run out of his so-far-remarkable luck. He was sure the main boss had returned early from Chicago, to his brand-new meth lab, only to find his two remaining goons held at gunpoint by an unlikely guest, and now it was time to take care of the situation—disarm Floyd and bury him in the fucking ground. Right in the back yard under cover of night.

But it was Tessa herself, approaching quietly, her haunted eyes locked on the two men at the wall. She appeared to have been crying—and crying hard. Her lip was trembling. She was carrying four or five plastic zip-ties between her clenched fingers, loose-looped and ready to bind.

"*Jesus fuck,*" Eric breathed, and for the first time there was fear in his eyes. Then he looked down and away, almost as if ashamed.

"*It's her! Eric, that's the bitch that—*"

Eric unleashed a ragged fury that filled the basement like something tangible. "*Shut your fucking mouth!*"

"*But that's her, that's Terrell's—*"

"*I swear to fucking Christ, if you don't shut—*"

"All right, that's enough," Floyd intoned, jostling the Beretta to remind Eric and Chicago Dog of its existence. "Settle down, or someone's gonna get kneecapped, I promise you."

Tessa came to his side and considered the two men.

"Look who I found," Floyd said.

"Yeah, I know these miserable motherfuckers—and they know me."

She'd shoved a few of the loose-looped zip-ties onto her still-raw wrists and was preparing one of them. "They also know what they've done to my family upstairs."

"You're not putting that fucking thing on me," Eric said, restless, watching the plastic strips.

"My mother. My brother. My aunt and uncle. All four of 'em, tied up and drugged."

"I'm serious, get that shit away from me."

Floyd touched the Beretta's muzzle gently to Eric's left eyebrow. "Hey. Listen to me. I don't know you. I don't know either of you. Hell, I don't even know *her*, really. I'm a stranger here. Nothing ties me to this place, nothing at all. All I need is one more reason to put a round in your fucking head. One more. I will have no regrets. And I will drive away, knowing that I've done some good in the world. So go ahead. Try me."

"Oh Jesus," Chicago Dog whined.

Floyd pulled the weapon back. "Now let this gal do what she needs to do."

"Turn around," Tessa said, her voice like a rake over gravel, "both of you rotten pieces of shit."

Chicago Dog turned around so fast that he nearly tripped and fell. Eric stayed put for a long moment—his hard dark eyes flitting from Floyd to Tessa—but then he turned to face the wall, shaking his massive head.

"Hands behind your backs."

"Unbelievable," Eric muttered, complying.

"Couldn't agree more," Tessa whispered.

"Goes without saying you're making the biggest mistake of—"

"Yeah, yeah, shut your mouth," Floyd warned. "We're gonna do this real quiet-like."

She secured zip-ties around the wrists of first Eric and then Chicago Dog, yanking both tight and eliciting teeth-grinding winces.

Floyd watched Tessa out of the corner of his eye. She was rattled, yeah, but she was strong as hell, too. She'd found something awful upstairs, and a big part of him had wanted to be her protector, had wanted to shield her from the inevitability of what she'd discovered—but she'd gone ahead and charged in anyway. It was something he'd think about later, the way this woman had evolved in his estimation, the way she managed to become ever more complex.

Well, at least her family wasn't *dead* up there. For now.

"Take that gun there," Floyd told her, and she obliged. "Careful now, that's a quick trigger. Good."

Eric appeared humiliated with impotent rage.

Floyd helped Tessa guide the men up two flights of stairs. The second level of the home was sweaty and hot. When they got to the small master bedroom, it was a little cooler thanks to opened windows, and that's when Floyd observed the fate of Tessa's family for himself. Covered loosely by wrinkled gray bedsheets, their grasping arms poked out from underneath almost unnaturally, as if reaching for something impossible. She had cut the ties from their wrists, but he could see the evidence of their bindings: curled-back fingers, cruel indentations, blood on the wrists. Their faces were uniformly trapped in a prison of euphoria, their mouths moving as if desperately thirsty. The makeshift IVs and the drug paraphernalia cluttered on the dresser next to the open window told Floyd everything he needed to know.

"*You motherfuckers,*" he growled at the two men, who stood still, facing what they'd wrought.

"Hey, man," said Chicago Dog, nervous and babbling, "they're on good stuff, okay? It's not like gravel or brown skag or—"

"*Shut the fuck up,*" Eric seethed.

"What is it?" Floyd asked. "What'd you put in them?"

"I put it together," Chicago Dog went on. "It's not new, okay? I've used it a few times, it's safe. Don't worry. It's a little meth and Special K mixed with, like, ten micrograms of fentanyl to keep 'em in it longer, y'know, keep 'em deep. They'll be in the sky for hours. I mixed that shit myself, it's safe, I mean they're okay is what I'm saying."

"You're a real hero, huh?" Floyd said.

"They're not gonna *die* or anything."

Tessa was already at the dresser, and Floyd could see what she had in mind. He considered cutting Chicago Dog temporarily loose so that he could move Tessa's family to other rooms, but the kid didn't deserve to lay another finger on these people.

"Sit down over there," Floyd gestured. "Against that wall."

"Do I need to do anything to make sure they wake up fine?" Tessa asked Chicago Dog.

The guy was suddenly all chatty.

"They're gonna feel like dogshit coming out of it, I won't lie, it'll be like a fuckin' richter-scale hangover, but that won't be till morning probably. You could ease 'em out of it with something else I could cook up, some methadone maybe, but, well—" He shrugged. "—they haven't been on it that long, it's not like they're *addicts* or anything."

"Great."

Tessa was glancing at all the shit. She was going to administer Chicago Dog's potent heroin-ketamine-fentanyl combination into the assholes' veins.

"All right, let's see how it works on you two, then."

"Look, I'm sorry, okay?" Chicago Dog said, shaking a little, watching the prepared syringe. Floyd couldn't tell if it was nervousness or fear or something else. "I never wanted to do that to them. That wasn't my call."

"You could've stopped it, though, huh?" Floyd said. "Maybe think of it that way."

"Man, don't put that in me. Please? They're all right, they're all right. We never meant them any harm—"

"Will you shut the fuck up?" Eric intoned.

"It was just about getting you back, he just wanted to get you back here."

"Well, here I am," Tessa said.

Floyd stood sentry at the window, watching for any new movement, while Tessa prepared for the next step. Eric had sat stone-faced while Chicago Dog spoke to Tessa almost eagerly, instructing her, as if part of him was dreading what was about the happen, but another part was looking forward to the blast of drugs that would tweak him toward xanadu. He watched her carefully, reminding her to take care—*Haven't you ever done this before?* With fingers that shook only minutely, Tessa prepared the payload in the bowl of the scorched spoon, filtered the drugs through cotton, dissolved the concoction into a measure of distilled water, and then the first needle was ready for Eric's arm. She tapped the syringe, staring relentlessly at the big man, and the whole time, Eric merely shook his meaty head, observing the proceedings with a mixture of incredulity and unease.

The first injection went smoothly once Tessa found a vein. Eric's face relaxed into troubled bliss, and then he was out, his features completely slack. Newly pliable, he was a cinch after that to tie up more intricately so that he couldn't move at all.

"I'm sorry," Chicago Dog said, calmer now that Eric was gone. "I'm really sorry, Tessa. I really like Terrell, I always have. I mean, I've, like, looked up to him. We were gonna team up in the neighborhood down there, that's what Harlan said."

"I think you're lying, but that doesn't matter," she said.

"No, really! I mean it."

"Tell me the truth now. My family's gonna be okay?"

Chicago Dog was shaking, but his eyes appeared to contain truth. "They'll be fine."

"You better hope so."

"Don't kill me, okay?" Chicago Dog said. "Seriously, okay, don't kill me. Please?"

"I ain't gonna kill you, white boy." The look on her face was one of angry resignation.

He guided her through his own injection, and soon he was out, too.

When that was done, Tessa melted into Floyd's arms.

"Help me take care of them?" she whispered.

"They'll be okay," he whispered back. "It won't be easy. They'll be a little traumatized, but you'll help 'em out of it."

Tessa nodded.

"It's my fault, isn't it?"

"It absolutely is *not* your fault."

"Why did I *leave* them?" The tears began to flow, and she shook in his embrace. "Why did I ever *do* that?"

"You had your reasons."

"Yeah, but—"

"Don't get too comfy. Still one more asshole to take care of. And apparently he's on his way here."

TWENTY-SIX
TESSA RAE JAYNE

It was getting on toward full dark. The summer night had fallen.

Her family lay peacefully in front of her. She watched them from a folding chair at the feet of the two lumpy beds, a lump in her throat. She desperately wanted to move them away from this fucking crime scene, to do *something* more for them, *anything*. Preferably take them to the hospital, find them professional care, or at least move them somewhere inside the house less stained by this awful thing that had been done to them. Dress them, embrace each one of them in turn, over and over, and guide them to health again. But of course she could do very little of that. Not yet.

She had cleaned up their messes as thoroughly as possible, had preserved their modesty with washcloths and clean sheets, and when her mother had begun shivering half an hour ago, she'd narrowed the gap of the open front window to just a few inches and found her favorite quilt to cover her up. At that moment, her mother had opened her crusty, bleary eyes and recognized her, and her expression had shown deep confusion and qualified relief. *"I'm here, Mama,"* Tessa had whispered, but then her mother was out again. At one point, Tessa had glanced up to find her brother Terrell propped up on his elbows, staring at her as if she were something out of a dream, a sort of uncomprehending awe on his face, and then he, too, had fallen back to the mattress.

Tessa wasn't gonna just *blindly* trust what Crowe had said about her family, but so far things looked hopeful. She'd taken all four of them off those awful duct-taped saline drips, had thrown all that shit in the garbage and bandaged their arms, and then she'd managed to get a little bottled water into their mouths, all four of them. Terrell looked the most miserable of all of them, recovered from his near-death a week ago but still in the black clutches.

"I shouldn't have left you," she whispered to him.

She'd also prepared and administered second doses of fent-k-meth to Crowe and Eric when they'd begun to wake up too much, and now they were thick as syrup over there in the corner again, their jaws sagging and drooling, their labored breaths loud and sour. *Fuck them.*

Floyd was downstairs watching the street now. Last she'd checked on him, he was watching through the barely parted front curtains, three phones laid out next to him on the worn couch. Several texts had come in on the assholes' phones—coded just like they were on Perkins' phone, the way Floyd had showed her—and in the most recent text Harlan had sent Eric this:

EVERYTHING UNDERWAY? IF WE'RE GOING TO STICK TO THE SCHEDULE, IT'S GOTTA BE DONE TONIGHT.

Floyd said he couldn't get past the lock screen to answer him, so all he could do was wait. After a while, this text came in:

ALL GOOD?

And then nothing. That was about an hour ago—when the wariness set in.

Seemed like for the past couple days—during the long hours of driving, and over quick meals at fast-food joints along the interstate—Floyd had consistently asked her questions about Harlan's crew. He'd gathered whatever details he could from her about what she'd seen at Wayne's and what she'd gathered through her brother's interactions with them. Frankly, her interactions with those people had been peripheral, dealing with them as they made clumsy, obnoxious moves on her, and the truth was, she didn't know a lot about what they were *really* up to. Even with the shit they pulled on Terrell, she saw only the effects on her brother at home: his evolution into a sarcastic know-it-all asshole, his short tenure as the man on high, the man with the shades and the cash, the help with the Beetle—and then the gradual descent, the paranoia, the babbling anxiety. The threatening calls and the beatings, the hiding in his room and the nervous, sleepless nights. The overdose.

She hadn't been able to tell Floyd a whole lot about the other side of her brother's equation. Like, what that crew murmured about at Wayne's, under the soft lights and under the thudding music. But she *could* tell him about who she saw most often there, who orbited Harlan most often at his booth—at least, when he was there. And although there were others who occasionally entered that atmosphere (she remembered a contingent of business-suit yuppies who'd converged on the joint in May, and later a menacing trio in sunglasses who looked like the fucking Men in

Black), she and Floyd had managed to overcome every single one of Harlan's main squad. Yeah, there were others who came and went, but those were all the usual guys.

She was sort of astonished by that. She wasn't even sure now that it was real—that between them, she and Floyd had actually taken down all five of the miscreants they'd come across over the course of their wild road trip. And that three of them were quite dead.

Floyd was quiet, as if in silent acknowledgment that he'd learned everything he needed to know, and now was just a waiting game. She sat on the middle step of the stairwell, gazing down at him, wondering how on god's green earth she'd been fortunate enough to land in his lap. She'd had her issues with her mother over the years—deep and rooted—but sitting there looking at him, she wondered what her mom would think of this ropy white man, and what she'd say to him upon meeting him. What she'd say to *her* afterward. At the thought, Floyd glanced up at her, surprised to find her sitting there.

"What are you doin' over there?" he asked her.

"Watchin' you."

"He should've been here a couple hours ago. That's what they expected."

"Yeah."

"He knows something's up."

"Or he doesn't."

"Fucker could be gathering an army."

"Or not."

He gave her an uneasy smile. "Since when are you the optimist?"

"Since I found *you*, baby." She framed her face between two wrought-iron bars. "And since *you* found *me*. Everything's, like, inevitable. Don't you feel that? It's like everything's happening for a reason. It's like it was meant to be."

He was shaking his head. "You can't get complacent, Tess. That's the worst thing you could do. This ain't over yet. Not by a long shot."

She let long seconds go by, gazing down on him. The house was silent, and so was the street, for the most part. The action was elsewhere. It was an old bedroom community, and even the lower elements were quiet about what they were up to.

"You got room on that couch?"

"Of course, come on over here."

She wordlessly descended the stairs and placed her phone next to his small collection. As she nestled herself against him, Floyd kept an eye focused on the gap in the curtains. She took in the musk of him and found comfort in him. Upstairs, it was way too easy to fall into despair, but next to Floyd she felt as if everything would work out. Even despite his words just now, despite his insistence that forces were probably still aligned against them, she felt invulnerable and warm, even freshly invigorated by the permanence of him. The quiet house, the danger they'd already bypassed—it lit a low flame in her.

Time stretched out.

Almost subconsciously she began caressing him. He was slow to respond, and at one point he whispered with dry amazement, *"Little lady, you're gonna be the death of me,"* but it wasn't long before she had drawn him out and moistened him and then slipped out of her jeans and mounted him, she couldn't control the need, and *she* was the one watching the street as she moved languorously, embedded, the moonlit neighborhood alive with portent.

And indeed it was twenty minutes later, around ten, Tessa still astride him, when a familiar dark-blue Acura slid in front of the house, behind Eric's truck. The Acura's motor rumbled to a stop, and its lights went dark. As it sat there, Tessa clambered off of Floyd, and he buttoned up, craning his neck to look through the window. She pulled her jeans back on.

"Listen to me, Tess," he whispered. "If this is who we think it is, remember that he thinks you're alone. That you've done all this by yourself. That's our advantage, okay?"

"I want to kill him," she said on a low growl, enervated by the heat of their coupling.

Floyd already had his pistol in his hand, and he was checking its magazine, making it deadly. "I know you do, darlin', and that's why I'm holding this and you're not."

"What's *that* supposed to mean?"

"I mean the killin's gotta stop. You get that, right?" His eye was affixed to the gap at the window. "We have to finish this the right way."

"The right way is them dead."

"Look, it may *be* that this man ends up dead like the others. Hell, even those creeps upstairs might end up dead. But that depends on what *they* do. It's not gonna depend on what *I* do. Or what *we* do. Do you understand?"

She wasn't sure that she did. He didn't know what it was like to find what she'd found upstairs. To go through everything she had.

"So what do we do now?" she said.

They were both looking through the curtain now. Floyd didn't have an answer for her, and she knew he was waiting for the next opportunity to make the decision for him. That was his way.

And the opportunity did come.

Her phone began to vibrate on couch, and it was an unfamiliar local number that appeared on the screen, but she knew exactly who it was. Floyd did too. He nodded at her. *Answer it.*

She swallowed, pressed the screen with her thumb, brought the phone to her ear.

"Yeah?"

"Do you know who this is?"

She looked straight at Floyd. "Yes."

"Looks like we're at an impasse, huh?"

"I guess so?"

There was a dry chuckle. "I have no idea how you've done it, but here you are. I gotta hand it to you, girl. You're in there, aren't you? You're in that house."

She paused, burning inside. "What house?"

The chuckle became a hearty laugh.

She waited.

"I don't expect you to tell me what you've done with my guys," he said after an uncomfortable amount of time, "but I'm intrigued."

"You sicced 'em after me, right? Maybe they're just not too smart."

"Maybe we underestimated you."

"Or that."

"Or you had some help somewhere along the way."

She tried not to let any kind of pause give herself away. "I guess it's possible."

"'Course, we know all about your boy in Texas . . . ."

Tessa didn't respond, only stared at Floyd. Her heartbeat was throbbing in her ears, and she was afraid Harlan could hear it thumping over the phone. She pulled it gently away from her earlobe.

"... and that he's sitting right next to you," he said. "Doing a lot more than *that* to you just a minute ago, am I right? Well, hell, he's probably listening to me jabber on right now."

She kept quiet, watched Floyd close his eyes and flex his jaw.

There was no movement outside. The Acura's windows were tinted black, but she was sure no one had gotten out of the car. Earlier, Floyd had barricaded the rear of the house, so there was no getting in that way. She felt as secure as she was gonna be—and yet the sight of that darkened car on the darkened street sent a shiver down her spine.

"I want to talk," he said.

"Go ahead."

"No, I want to talk face to face. I think we can put this whole situation behind us. I mean, I think that would be easier than you think. We need to talk about my mother, and we need to talk about *your* mother. We need to talk about your brother, and we need to talk about the past couple days. You see? All of that."

"What if I don't want to? What if I just want to, like, move on? Call things square?"

"Because that's not how this is going to work, girl. There are some things that can't be gotten past. For example, suppose I go back to Lieutenant William Carver at the Decatur police department and tell them that I suddenly remember some pertinent shit about a certain young woman's involvement in the fire that killed my mom? Cuz that asshole has *really* been on my case."

Tessa's mind was like a mass of buzzing wires, but none of those wires seemed to be in control of her mouth. She couldn't speak.

"Look," Harlan said, "I'm going to go ahead and come to that door, and I'd like you to invite me inside. I'm unarmed. I know it's easy to *say* something like that, and you have no way of knowing whether I'm on the level, but it's true. I'm leaving my weapon in the car. I have a greasy bag of hot dogs here, quite the gourmet item straight from Chicago earlier today. It was for one of those boys in there with you, but I'm willing to offer it to you. And I have something else for you." He paused. "But I need to give it to you in person. So do you promise to be nice and let me in?"

She swallowed hard. Floyd was staring back at her, considering. He'd heard the entire call, she knew. They both glanced down at Floyd's Beretta, and after that shared glance, he nodded.

"Yes," she said softly into the phone.

"All right, then. Now, in case it's not already clear to you, I'm watching you. And not from the car. Before I come in, I'd like to remind you that I will be *unarmed*, and I would like your friend to extend me the same courtesy. Can you ask him to put his weapon in a place where he cannot reach it? And by that, I mean, place it outside the door, on the front porch."

"How do we know you're gonna—"

"Put the fucking gun on the porch."

The line clicked dead.

Tessa let the phone drop to the couch, not wanting it in her hand anymore. Floyd had perched himself on the edge of the couch, his Beretta hanging loosely from his grip. When she glanced up at his face, he was surreptitiously monitoring the room. She knew he was trying to figure out how Harlan was watching them. A camera? She doubted it, although his capability with GPS tracking had proved surprising. Her instinct was telling her something different, though. She felt as if someone was watching her at this moment, and not by digital means. It made her feel sick.

"Okay," Floyd whispered. "I'm with you. I want to kill him."

"What do we do?"

He removed the magazine from the pistol, cleared the chamber, and a round went spinning onto the floor, rolled under the couch.

"We do what the man says."

TWENTY-SEVEN
FLOYD TILLMAN WEATHERS

Harlan Eckhart walked straight through the front door like he owned the joint, chest puffed out, a look of strange pleasure on his face.

"So *dark* in here, what the fuck?" He flipped the light switch near the door, and a hanging yellow dome light above them lit the room.

Floyd stepped backward, motioning for Tess to do the same behind him.

"There she is!" Harlan said fake-joyfully. "The woman of the hour!"

Floyd took the measure of the man as he stepped across the living room's past-its-prime beige carpet, a greasy brown bag swinging from his left hand. He was a taller man than he'd envisioned, and his voice was a deeper, heartier baritone than he'd imagined, but everything else Tessa had laid out was right on—the vivid sleeves of tattoos, the piercings on the ears and face, the shaved and inked skull, the angular brow, the bony but powerful frame. He appeared to be unarmed, as advertised, but looks could be deceiving.

Harlan extended his hand toward Floyd as he got closer, but Floyd remained reared back on high alert.

"*Careful*—" Floyd said.

"Hey, I just wanted to meet the man with the plan." His hand was still hanging in mid-air. "I come in peace."

Floyd stood motionless, letting the man's gangly arm float.

"Seriously, man, go ahead and make this easy on yourself."

After a beat, Floyd accepted the handshake in a stare-down.

"I'm Harlan. You probably already knew that."

"Floyd." Gritting his teeth.

To have come this far only to lose his advantage to this freakish reprobate was a low blow. Last Floyd had seen of the Acura outside, there still wasn't a goddamn hint of movement behind any of the tinted glass. Could be one person in there, could be three or even four. Could be *another* vehicle—or six or seven—strategically parked in other areas around the block. He didn't *think* so, based on the high-level overview of the crew that Tessa had given him, but it was something he had to consider.

"So I'm thinkin' we should take care of the elephant in the room, huh?" Harlan said, glancing from Floyd to Tessa, who stood behind Floyd chewing on her thumbnail. "I don't know if she told you, but this young lady over here straight-up murdered my mother a few days ago. Burned her right up. Burned her alive like a witch from yore."

"*I didn't know she*—" Tessa started, urgently.

"*Hey!*" Harlan interrupted, staring hard at her. "Let me finish."

His dark-eyed gaze wandered over to Floyd, as if to commiserate. *Chicks, man.*

"What I was going to say is . . . *thank you.*"

He waited in the center of the open room, waited for a reaction— and that reaction was stunned silence on Tessa's part. Floyd watched the man's face closely. He could already see the excess bluster, the misplaced confidence, and a man's face was always the clearest indication of that kind of thing—the subtle tremble of the lip, the slight jitter of the eye, the unconscious tic in the tiny muscles of the cheek. That kind of shit happened mostly in the young ones, and Harlan was very young consid- ering the apparent amount of power he wielded in Decatur. Floyd judged him to be in his mid-twenties, couple years younger than himself. His self-confidence had gotten him far, clearly, but there were cracks.

"All right?" Harlan went on after his dramatic moment. "*Thank you.* That woman was one evil bitch, you know what I'm saying? You did me a fucking *favor*, ending *that* sad excuse for a life. Yeah, and we can talk all you want about how that cunt literally brought me into this world, but she never did me any favors after that."

"Well, that's one way to talk about your mom," Floyd said evenly.

"Anybody want a hot dog?" Harlan said. "These are, like, gourmet, and they're just gonna go to waste."

Neither Floyd nor Tess answered him.

"Well, all right, then." He set the cold bag on the scuffed coffee table, then stood straight, hands on narrow hips, and stared at Tess. "Might as well get down to it, huh? Why don't we have a seat, talk this out?"

"I think we'd rather stand," Floyd said

"I'm gonna have to insist." Harlan offered a wide smile, exhibiting bright healthy teeth that told Floyd he stayed above the dirty fray of the business he was in. Those choppers spoke also, again, of his youth, and not only that but also good middle-class upbringing. Kid probably went straight from suburbia to the street, and not long ago, all things considered. "You really don't want this conversation to go south. Now sit the fuck down."

When Floyd glanced over at Tess, she had a deadened look in her eyes. He nodded at her. She backed up a few steps and eased onto the edge of an old lounger. Floyd took a seat on the corner of the loveseat next to her.

"There," said Harlan magnanimously, taking his own seat on the couch that fronted the big window. "See, we can be civilized."

A low moan drifted down from upstairs, male, and Harlan flicked his attention in that direction. An inscrutable smile found his lips, could have communicated anything. But Floyd was certain the bastard knew about Tessa's family, what had been done to them. Or the smile might have communicated an understanding that his own boys were up there, too. The man seemed to know a lot.

"What do you want?" Tessa said, breaking the silence.

"Oh, well, that's easy," Harlan said, cheerful. "Compensation."

"Compensation," Floyd echoed.

"Right, fair compensation, primarily for the product lost in the blaze. I'd estimate that to be . . . oh . . . a rough value of a hundred-eighty thousand in the home at the time. We had an operation underway, not unlike the one in this basement at the moment, as a matter of fact—but at a larger scale, of course. Not to mention the equipment that was lost. So, let's say, two hundred thirty grand total, and that includes some existing merchandise, other assorted valuables. There's also the property value itself—but I'll be honest with you: The insurance payout is already underway, thanks to a very understanding agent. So I can forgive that. I'm a reasonable man. I grew up in that house, and let me tell you, it was a *shitty* house. And as far as a new base of operations, I think the setup downstairs is at least a good, fair start." He sat back into the couch, removed a pack of cigarettes from his shirt pocket. "Mind if I light up?"

Instead of answering the question, Floyd decided to test him.

"The way I see it, you're far from holding the upper hand here. This little lady and I just spent the weekend tearing through your whole crew like tissue paper."

Harlan finished lighting his cigarette, inhaled expansively. "You think I'm here alone here tonight?"

"No, I do not," Floyd said. "In fact, I *know* you're not alone. But the past couple days have given me a lot of insight into the quality of your . . . organization."

A twitch at the corner of his mouth was Harlan's only reaction to that.

"You've surprised me, I have to admit," Harlan said, smoke leaking out of his mouth like an oily fog. "I can only imagine what Tessa's fate might've been if not for your involvement along the way."

Floyd pondered that while he felt Tessa stewing to his left under the weight of the misogyny. The way he saw it, Tessa would probably be safe and sound on some Mexican beach right now if not for him. His presence in her life had paved the way toward a string of insane obstacles that she'd otherwise have avoided. All she'd had to do to sidestep all that was keep going down Route 67 and cross that easy border. Yeah, she'd have unknowingly doomed her family here in this newly minted crack shack, but she'd have been as free and clear as was possible in this world. To Floyd's mind, he hadn't helped Tessa as much as he'd *complicated* her life.

"Fuck, man," Harlan went on, "maybe after this is all done with, you come work for me. Good people can be tough to come by up here."

Floyd couldn't help but murmur a laugh. "Right."

"I think we're getting beyond the point, though," Harlan said, relaxing into the couch, hanging his illustrated arms over the ragged cushions on either side of him. "And the point is, whatever sequence of events that have taken place over the past few days, whatever has happened to the men I sent after Tessa, my goal has been accomplished. Here she sits." Harlan Eckhart eyed her with intense clarity, focused and relentless. "Surely she understood that compensation would be necessary."

"You tried to kill me," Tessa said quietly. "You wanted me dead."

"*And I still do,*" Harlan said, hard. His eyes flickered, glanced away as if he regretted the words. "Let me rephrase that." He brought his arms back down and scooted forward to the edge of the couch like a lean, hungry animal poised for attack. "No one ever in my life has inflicted as much damage on me as you have. Perhaps you can empathize with my initial instinct to end your *fucking life.*"

The man's eyes were filled with power—Floyd had to give him that.

It was a little unnerving, and unexpected, being on the receiving end of a gaze that cut like his. Hearing the man speak, too. Harlan was educated beyond what Floyd had figured him to be—well spoken, measured, precise. It was clear to him why he'd ascended in Decatur.

"But, like I said, I'm nothing if not a reasonable man." He gave his cigarette a long drag, pulling the exhaled smoke into his studded nostrils. "On reflection, you've provided a service. You ever see that *Wizard of Oz* flick on TV? The way the house fell on that fuckin' witch?" He chuckled on the edge of a phlegmy cough. "Yeah, that kind of thing. You did that for me, Tessa, I'll be honest. My mother's death frees up so much for me. You have no idea."

"Glad to hear it," Tess breathed icily, though Floyd detected an undertone of anxiety.

"You've also shown me some strength. You got gumption, baby. It would be a shame to just wipe you off the planet, you know?—especially after the apparent trials of your own journey. I have to respect that, don't I? I have to respect everything you did—everything you both did—to make your way to that chair, sitting before me now."

Tessa shrugged. "So we can call it all even, then."

"A sense of humor, too!" Harlan wasn't smiling. "How about that? No, I'll be receiving that compensation one way or another. My associates outside will ensure that." He gestured toward the small window behind Tessa's head. "You haven't been stupid enough to try anything in here, and for that I commend you. Because if you *had* . . . well, *that* wouldn't end beneficially for any of us."

Floyd wondered if the man was bluffing about the threat from outside. What—camouflaged assassins with rifles at all the windows? High-level operatives in waiting vehicles ready to invade the home SWAT-style? More likely, a couple of burnouts itching for a fix and waiting for instructions from the freak at the top.

"But what I'm really getting at is this: You might *think* you have the upper hand in this little threesome, as my new friend Floyd suggested near the beginning of this friendly conversation—but you most certainly do not."

There was a long moment of silence while Harlan finished off his cigarette and ground it down into the worn wood of the coffee table.

"Now, I'm sure somehow, between you, you can come up with the two hundred thirty thousand I spoke of earlier. You've shown yourselves to be resourceful."

Floyd felt Tessa's gaze on the side of his face.

"I don't have any money," she said.

"That's neither here nor there," Harlan said. "I never expected you to pull out your purse and count out your bills. But I do expect you to find it. Somehow. Your methodology doesn't matter to me. Say . . . within a week? With the assistance of your new man here?"

Floyd supposed it was perfectly natural for his thoughts to go to Philip's duffle bag full of cash, which was right now stored high in Tessa's childhood closet, but Floyd would squeeze himself into one of the gal's most frilly dresses and dance a fucking jig for this over-confident male-factor before he handed any of *that* over. This Harlan Eckhart was beginning to test his patience. But before he could weigh in on the matter, Tessa had begun speaking again.

"Are we even gonna talk about how this all started?" There was a waver in her voice, on a knife's edge between despondency and fury. "Are we even gonna talk about how we got here?"

"Oh, you want to talk some more about the arson you committed? Or my mother's murder?"

"No, I'd rather go back further—as in, what you did to my brother." Now the anger took precedence, visible in the set of her jaw, the flash of her clear dark eyes. "You nearly killed Terrell. And even if you didn't finish the job, you destroyed his damn *life*. And did you forget what you've done to my family upstairs? You're trying to do the same thing to them that you did to Terrell! Are you being serious right now? You're a fucking *monster*. I don't owe you *anything!*"

Harlan let the resonance of Tessa's voice dwindle away along the walls of the quiet house. The man was still perched at the edge of the couch, his gangly limbs looking particularly spider-like in his pose. He was rubbing the fingers of his hands together, and the piercings between his knuckles and his wrists moved like pincers.

"Are you finished?" he said.

"No."

"Then, please, go ahead."

When Floyd glanced over at Tessa, he found her glaring at Harlan, arms crossed. The pose encompassed her mixture of hip-cocked defiance and naïvete that he'd come to half-adore but that he also knew might just as easily take her down. That attitude had gotten her remarkably far up to this point, but he wasn't sure it was the best play at the moment.

While Tessa remained boilingly silent for a few beats, Floyd continued to gauge the situation—and it wasn't getting any more promising. He was sure he could overpower this overconfident mashman; Floyd had probably fifty advantageous pounds on the lanky bastard. But Floyd could only guess at the extent of Harlan's backup outside. And a minute ago, as Harlan had jutted forward on the couch, Floyd had caught sight of the distinctive skeletal grip of a Ghoststrike blade sheathed at the man's ankle—and Harlan wasn't hiding it. He'd meant for Floyd to see it.

"So you *are* done?" Harlan said. "Then let me tell you something, okay? This may not be convenient for you to hear right now, but your brother was the worst runner we've ever had. I'm talking legendarily incompetent, all right?"

"Fuck you, Harlan."

"Terrell took ineptitude to a whole new level. I mean, even Crowe—you met Crowe, right, he's here somewhere—Crowe has taken other neighborhoods and basically transformed them within a week from disasters to pretty good revenues, and Crowe is kind of a retard himself. The difference is, he isn't misusing his own product, Tessa. That's, like, *basic*. Your brother fucked up his own shit—monumentally."

Tessa was biting her lower lip, and her big eyes had gone glassy.

"See," Harlan said, watching her, "you know this shit is true! You *know* it. *Jesus*, I mean, how do you even *feel* about that?" He glanced over at Floyd, shaking his head again as if conspiratorially, then turned back to Tess. "Are you capable of self-awareness? Look at everything you've done in the name of someone who's really just a *colossal fuckup!* Do you actually think I've *wronged* him? The truth is quite the opposite, honey."

"Don't you call me 'honey'," Tessa growled.

"Then what *should* I call you? 'Dumbass'? All I'm definitely sure of is that you're Terrell's sister. You come from the same stock."

"That's enough," Floyd put in.

"*No, it's not!*" Harlan erupted. "If goddamn *Terrell Jayne* is at the heart of this fucking stupid murderous *debacle*, then that *really* pisses me off.

Because—" He began counting out with his bony fingers. "—I've lost my mother, my childhood home, a fat chunk of my fucking business, and—and—what?—*five* of my crew because this gal was upset her brother was a moron who got himself over-tweaked on the dope he was supposed to sell? I gave that fucking kid all the opportunity in the world to make a killing in this business, but he flushed it down the devil's crapper. He was *reckless*, Tessa, he was fucking reckless—*he's* the one who didn't follow the rules. Everything that's happened to Terrell has happened because of *Terrell himse*—"

It took Floyd a long moment to determine exactly what happened next.

At first, he was only aware of the concussive report that bludgeoned the room—a sharp crack with a thunderous, reverberating undertone. Then, there was the crimson spray that appeared instantaneously across the couch in a misting, almost decorative fan. Only when Harlan crumpled forward onto the floor did Floyd realize what had happened. When the man's skull hit the carpet, it was only half there, and what was inside of it tumbled out in purple-gray lumps.

Floyd looked up to the top of the stairs to see the barrel of a long rifle poking between the bannister slats, and a dark, determined face beyond it.

TWENTY-EIGHT
TESSA RAE JAYNE

One of Tessa's earliest memories of her daddy was hunting with him in the natural areas up around Bloomington—those cold, foggy autumn mornings, rising with him before dawn, knowing he'd rather have taken an eldest son but making do with her when Terrell was still in his crib screaming his fool head off. Out in the clear wide open, he'd never let her actually *hold* any of his rifles (especially his precious Henry Golden Boy), but he'd allowed her to touch them, and she'd felt that rush of powerful potential in the wood and the slick metal, but then—on their third trip—after she'd kneeled down in the dirt next to the first ruined deer, witnessing its final snorting, struggling breaths, she'd never wanted to go with him again. Not ever again. Where at first she'd longed for the time alone with him, just her and her daddy, the next time she'd screamed and cried to be left at home. He could go with his drunk greasy hovering buddies, for all she cared. Her mama let her clutch at her skirts while they both gave him stern looks, making him laugh and give up and go out on his own with his cooler full of cheap beer.

He'd be dead a couple years after that, never having had an opportunity to drag Terrell, the hoped-for son, out into the countryside to slaughter an animal. He'd also left behind his small collection of hunting rifles. His modestly grieving widow—wanting nothing to do with the things and not having the slightest idea *what* to do with them—stored them away in a corner of her bedroom closet, behind old shoe boxes and photo albums.

The rifle Terrell used to murder Harlan Eckhart was a Montana 1999, the last rifle their father had ever purchased, about a year before his death. Even after all this time, Tessa recognized the scope, the walnut stock, the bolt action. She could even hear—as the noise of the report clamored away—her daddy's voice echoing through the years, *Lookit that beauty*, and never saying anything as remotely complimentary about his daughter.

"*Terrell!*" Tessa shouted, but suddenly Floyd was right in front of her, holding on to her, moving her toward the corner.

"Hold up," he said. "Wait."

On the landing, her brother had already fallen onto his back, drained, the rifle clattering between railing posts and then falling away from him and coming to rest on the worn carpet up there. She wanted to go to him, she didn't care about anything else, but Floyd's arms were hard and strong, and now he was manhandling her into the corner away from the windows.

"*Stay there!*" He was glaring straight into her eyes. "*Okay?*"

She nodded.

Floyd took a defensive, breath-held pose, waiting for something to happen at the windows, at the front door, at the back of the house—she could see it in the quick movements of his head, the scan of his eyes. *Something was about to happen.* But only silence descended. No movement, no flickering shadows. No kicked-in doors, no shattered glass. He edged over to the closest window, peered out. Then he leaped forward to the entry, crouched low, opened the door. Even Tessa from her angle could see the unloaded pistol still there on the old concrete. He reached out in an abrupt motion and snatched it up, sliding in a full magazine that had been in his front pocket. He stayed there at the door, ready and waiting—but nothing continued to happen.

"We should be dead right now," he breathed.

"What do you mean?" she whispered back from the corner.

"Harlan wasn't alone."

"Are you sure?"

"Yes."

"Well, who . . . where are they? Where'd they go?"

"That's the question."

Tessa watched Floyd at the door as the room hummed with anticipation. He didn't move for a long time, and she found her eyes moving inevitably to Harlan on the floor. The flung-out arms, folded unnaturally around and underneath him. It seemed like the body was still deflating into death. She could see what was left of his head, and as incomprehensibly *final* as the image was—the tattooed skull was only meat now, torn apart, brutal—it reminded her of all the other death she'd seen in the past few days. A heavy weight of wretchedness tugged at her, physically, and she felt herself sliding down the wall. This was the price of what she'd done, and a distant part of her was asking her whether it was worth it. She knew she'd never be able to answer that question, not in this life. No, the only answer would be the animal irrevocability of this shattered mess of bone and gore, like the dying deer at her feet when she was five years old.

Her ears were ringing.

Floyd was still at the door, and Terrell was still on the landing, moving slightly, making little sounds under the hopefully diminishing sway of the fentmeth.

"His car's still there," Floyd said. "No movement."

Tessa realized she was crying, and that it was because of *everything*. Who knew what the next minutes or hours would bring? Despite the fact that she was still alive, after *all this*, maybe those minutes or hours would bring the end of her. At that moment, she didn't care. All she really wanted was to go upstairs and tend to her brother, tend to the rest of her family, and apologize to them for the rest of her life, however long it lasted.

But the next few minutes and hours *didn't* bring the end of her. She wasn't sure how much time passed, but at one point she glanced up to find the front door closed and Floyd gone. She didn't hear anything at all for long moments, until he was directly in front of her, urging her back to her feet. She staggered up, bracing herself on his forearms. Over his shoulder, she saw the closed and locked front door, the blank, quiet finality of it.

"There's no one out there." His breath was hot on her cheek. "No one. It's like . . . it's like they just ran off."

"How's that possible? I mean, come on."

"There's no one out there. Car's empty. Nothing."

She shook her head against him.

"I don't like it," he said. "We should get the fuck out of here."

"I can't, Floyd. Not anymore. I can't do that."

"They could come back."

"They're not coming back."

"Why do you say that?"

"It's over. It's over. I mean, there's . . . there's just . . . no one left. Maybe a coupla flunkies, but . . . I mean . . . that's really it."

"How sure are you of that?"

"Pretty positive, dude." A burst of laughter escaped her, and she pulled it back in. "It's possible we've trashed, like, the entire Decatur drug scene."

"If that was the entire Decatur drug scene, then I'm the mayor of Little Rock."

"Well, no one's coming back here." She gestured to the corpse in the living room. "Not after that."

"Well, fuck, maybe it *was* only him in the car." She could see Floyd's mind working, watched his Adam's apple bob as he swallowed, searched for words. "Maybe *he* was the one creeping around the house, peeping into the windows before he came around and knocked. Maybe he *was* the only one left."

"That's what I'm tellin' you."

She faced him, watched him considering it, and then she couldn't help but embrace him, hard.

"Yeah, but I still don't think so," he said into her ear.

"*We're okay,*" she whispered.

"Yeah," he said, surprise in his voice. "Yeah, we seem to be. That's what scares me."

"I need to go upstairs."

"Go ahead. Be careful. Keep that rifle nearby. You know how to use it?"

"Fuck you, 'do I know how to use it'." She gave him a dirty look through smeary eyes, but it felt all wrong. She immediately softened. "Yeah, I know how to use it."

He seemed reluctant to let go of her as she went for the stairs. When she got to them, she took them two at a time. In her peripheral vision, Floyd was already heading for the kitchen, but she didn't care because here was Terrell on the ground at the top of the stairs, and he was staring up at her, giving her that crooked smile. He had a bedsheet wrapped loosely around him like an afterthought. The fired rifle had left a haze of smoke that was half metallic, half sulfur, and it was an odor that brought her father instantly to mind. Those early mornings.

She dropped to Terrell, shoved her arms around him.

"Hey sis," Terrell murmured, his voice dry and drug-slurred.

The tears exploded from her then, and it took her some time to form her own words.

"I'm sorry, T, I'm so sorry."

It took him a moment to register her words, as if his brain were on a three- or four-second delay. He blinked his eyes in an exaggerated way and smiled his toothy smile.

"Shit, Tess . . . it ain't nothin' . . . I'm jus' glad you copacetic, you know?"

Tessa actually felt a laugh bubble up from deep inside, and the bullshit from the past half a year melted away and it was only her little brother lying there in front of her, as if she'd just got done tickling him, his helpless laughter filling the house until their mother yelled up from the kitchen, and then their quiet stifled giggles and settling next to each other to catch their breath and stare at the yellowed popcorn ceiling while their mom continued to curse under her breath.

What did it say about her that she'd left Terrell when he'd *most needed her?* Just because he'd become kind of a dick under the sway of this ridiculous crew didn't mean she should've *abandoned* him. Her brother had pissed her off more than just about anybody in her life—yeah, she'd say that to his silly face—but who was she to just up and leave? Jesus, he was *unconscious* when she left. And, yeah, she'd had her moments with their mother—*lots of them*—but that didn't mean Tessa had to burn this house down, too. She'd never say that the years she'd grown up here were *wonderful*, but they were the best she could've hoped for, weren't they? They were all she had.

"I'm so sorry," she kept saying into his chest.

When she came up for air, she saw Floyd downstairs watching her. He had a bewildered look on his face, and his Beretta was hanging at his side.

"You all right?" he asked her.

"Yeah," she said, nodding through tears.

"Everything okay up there?"

"Uh huh."

"At this point, I'm just waiting for sirens. Neighbors callin' in about the rifle shot. Who knows?"

"In this neighborhood? Not likely."

"It can't be this easy."

"You call that easy?"

Floyd moved to the light switch and flicked off the hanging light. The house plunged into darkness. She caught flickers of movement as Floyd returned to the front curtain and peered out. He stayed rock-steady for moments that seemed to stretch out like taffy.

She could smell Terrell's sour breath, and she glanced down on him. The whites of his eyes were yellow in the warm gloom.

"Who's that?" he croaked, a distant suspicion in his weak voice.

"A friend," she whispered back.

His eyes remained on hers. Suspicious. "A white friend."

"You're gonna have to trust me," she said.

Everything felt unsettled, as if they were in the eye of a hurricane, or waiting for an aftershock following a massive earthquake. As much as she wanted to believe that everything was over, she knew it wasn't. There was a gaping queasiness inside her, accentuated by the tsunami of guilt that was still breaking against her.

"So, you . . . you really did it?" Terrell whispered.

"Did what?"

"The house." He blinked at her, barely able to stay awake. "You really burn down that house?"

"You bet your ass I did."

"Ah, shit, Tess."

"I know."

"I told them there was no fucking way you'd do that." He started laughing in a slow, drawly way, and his eyes rolled back. "Just no fucking way."

"You shot him," she whispered, as much to change the subject as anything else. "You killed Harlan."

A grimace took hold of his lip, a bit of a snarl. "The earth is better for it."

"You loved that guy. I mean, you used to adore that guy."

He shook his head slowly. "Not no more."

"Let's get you back in that room. You got some healing to do."

Terrell offered precious little help getting himself back to the mattress. He'd gained some weight since his prime. A lot of that linebacker muscle had turned to fat. He'd definitely lost some of that high school definition thanks to the daily illicit highs, and the loss of the morning workouts with his bow-legged buddy Yeltsin, and Peter with the puffy birthmark, and the rest of that loud crew. Not to mention months ago when Jada dumped him. The two of them had been together since just before ninth grade, met at the Hickory Point mall back when that joint was still kinda cool, and Tessa had made fun of the two of them when she should've been the awesome younger sister. Why hadn't she been that? About *all* of this? Why hadn't she talked to him more, like, really talked to him? They might've avoided all this shit. Their shared history, such as it was, whirled in her brain as she half-carried him, and even though she was the healthier one at this particular moment, she felt much less significant—small and stupid. Like in her smallness and stupidity, she'd failed him utterly, only to have him come to her ultimate rescue.

She strained under the weight of his heavy arm as he limped, and finally he half-fell next to their mother on the bed. She helped him get untangled from the sheet and covered both of them properly, and once they were decent, she watched their faces with tears drying on her cheeks. Terrell fell instantly back to almost desperate sleep, lightly snoring.

There was a clamor downstairs, and it sent adrenaline through her like biting on tinfoil. She hurried back to the landing, where the rifle still lay against the painted wood of the scuffed railing. She took it up, the whole unwieldy length of it, still breathing in the rotten-eggs smell of its discharge. In the darkness, she caught a shadowed glimpse of Floyd over Harlan's body, checking the pockets. She could just make out the flat-black glint of the Beretta on the coffee table.

She realized she was still bracing for a death that wouldn't come, for accomplices that weren't showing up to finish the job. It simply wasn't happening.

She carried the rifle back to her mom's bedroom, leaned it against the dresser. All six people in front of her were out again, not even stirring. She stood there with her arms crossed. If what Crowe had said was true, the rest of her family would probably start stirring in the next couple hours but not regain full consciousness until morning or even later. She suspected even Terrell would be out for another long while as his body worked through the rest of the shit. It was a miracle that he'd had a moment of clarity so that he could be the hero. Regardless, she would be here for when they woke up for good, would help guide them out. She would be sure of it.

The two assholes in the corner were blotto and would continue to be that way for the long term. She and Floyd would figure out what to do with them, but at the moment she was incapable of thinking about it. It was difficult to fathom that this scene right here might herald the end of this whole embarrassing escapade. That, against all reason, she'd conquered so many, so thoroughly. Was she actually on the verge of getting away with all of it? It felt dangerous to even contemplate that. And if it did turn out that she'd won, then she'd have done it not by escaping to some far-off fantasyland but by turning right back around and taking the fight to these pitiful motherfuckers.

As she watched the blotto boys, she gradually felt a different gaze on her. She searched the dimness and found her Uncle Johnny staring at her through cloudy eyes. He'd lifted his head just slightly from the damp pillow, and those eyes were locked on her. He didn't seem to recognize her. His expression was one of doped-up confusion—to be expected, she guessed.

"Hi," she said softly into the warm air of the room. Her heart was pounding.

His expression didn't change.

"It's me," she said. "It's Tessa. I'm back."

As the words left her mouth, she experienced a distant kind of shame. She felt the emotion register on her face.

That's when Uncle Johnny recognized her for who she was. He blinked, and a slow resignation took hold of him, and he pulled back into himself, his head slowly falling back to the pillow.

"I didn't mean to come back," she said, so low that she was certain he couldn't hear her. "But I had to."

The old man was still gazing at her, and she couldn't read his expression. It was too dark. She saw only small glint in his open eye.

"I know what you're gonna say," she said. "I know where you think I should be, and I'm sorry."

Uncle Johnny turned his face slightly into the pillow, but his gaze remained on her, and now she could interpret him. Everything he'd told her days ago, the urgency, the pleading, the preparations—all of it, dead on his tongue. The anguish in that dark, gaunt face.

"I'm sorry, Uncle Johnny." A tear dripped down her cheek, startling her. "But you're alive. You're alive, Uncle Johnny! I saved you. If I was in

Mexico right now, you'd—you'd—well, I mean, *all of you* would be—"

But goddammit, he was still watching her with that swiveling brown eye, and she couldn't bear the sadness in his gaze anymore. She knew what he would say to her right now if his mouth were working, and she even knew the tone he would use. It wasn't so much the admonishment that would characterize his gaspy old-man voice but the drawling melancholy at the simple sight of her. The insistence that he hadn't been able to get through to her after all . . . that despite all the crazy evidence to the contrary, Tessa Rae Jayne was gonna get what was coming to her.

She had a lot to do to prove him wrong.

TWENTY-NINE
FLOYD TILLMAN WEATHERS

As the night deepened, Floyd became contemplative.

Maybe it was exhaustion, the long hours on the road, and now the constant high alert at the window. He found himself sinking further into the lumpy couch, increasingly but reluctantly at ease. Because, by all appearances, it seemed like he and Tess were gonna come out on top of this thing.

Couple hours earlier—specifically, when gangly, whipsmart Harlan Eckart had crossed that threshold—Floyd wouldn't have been so certain. The Decatur crew had proven until that point to be a bumbling ragtag assemblage of blowhards and morons, but Harlan himself, yeah, he'd been cut from different fabric. Even now, with the man dead at his feet, Floyd couldn't deny a certain admiration for the guy. If not for Terrell finding the gumption to rouse himself from his drug slumber and arm himself with his dad's old rifle . . . well, it wasn't beyond probability that Floyd and Tess would be unconscious on a mattress upstairs—or worse. Far worse.

Floyd had decided not to tell Tess about the evidence he'd found outside—at least, not yet. There were footprints in the soil near the small window looking in on the living room, and they were fresh, etched in the stark shadows created by his phone's flashlight. The prints also appeared to be disturbed in such a way that suggested quick flight, as if whoever'd been there had fled when Harlan had been shot. If Floyd had to guess, this peeper, Harlan's backup, had probably been an unwilling partner, in it for the chemical payoff. Not one of the team's best, more like a fifth-string guy. And once the confrontation went south, he was *outta here*. No way a shot of meth was worth *dying for*.

The other possibility was that the peeper had gone off to get backup somewhere, but as time wore on, that seemed increasingly unlikely. There was simply no one left.

And that was really the jumping-off point for Floyd's contemplative slide deeper into the couch.

If there was one thing the past few years had taught him, it was that the good guys finished last these days. Not that he'd automatically figured his ownself as one of the *good* guys, but Floyd had consciously distanced himself from what he thought of as the Age of the Asshole. It was one of the big reasons he'd lunged for Philip's assignment at the bottom edge of the country. The villains had taken hold of the world.

It was in that light that the past few days were something of a fucking miracle. The events that had gotten them here, to this point, had required more than their combined skills and movements, for whatever those were worth. They'd necessitated *good goddamn fortune.* Repeatedly. Somehow, everything had gone their way. In the Age of the Asshole, that was simply improbable. Floyd had never considered himself a religious man, but the word that came to mind was *blessed.*

He didn't shine to the word, but he'd take it.

More and more, he was convinced that Tessa Rae Jayne was the one that made all the difference. Floyd had been with his share of women over the years, but Tess was an altogether different entity. She shined bright, man, and that brightness radiated beyond her immediate effect on him— an effect that was prodigious in itself. It was as if she exuded a buoyancy that counteracted the Age of the Asshole, as if she was the cure. All the other women in his life, he hadn't felt one way or another about their departure, but this one? He didn't want to leave her behind.

He could barely hear Tess upstairs, murmuring to her family. She was caring for them, soothing them. She'd get them past the pharmaceutical horror in which they were imprisoned, Floyd had no doubt. And she'd get him past his own demons.

Not that he'd ever let his guard down.

Close to midnight, she was still upstairs tending to her family. Floyd felt himself drifting off, so he jerked himself to full consciousness and pushed off the couch. He checked the front yard—no activity—then moved to the front door, testing the lock for the umpteenth time. Then he moved the makeshift obstructions away from the rear door and checked the back yard. Nothing.

Was he going to leave Tess here, after all? She needed to be here, it seemed. She was feeling it, he knew. She was thinking she'd made a mistake, leaving in the first place. He couldn't blame her. He understood the value of fixing a mistake. Righting a wrong. But he had a place to be, a day's drive from here. He had some catching up to do back in Little Rock. Part of him had already entertained the notion that Tessa might spring from this interlude straight back into his lap, that she'd jump into shotgun just like before and accompany him to his own past, wait for him to finish his transaction there, and then ride into an uncertain but eager future in his Camaro. Stranger things had happened.

He decided to check out the basement.

He clomped down the stairs, yanked on the chained lightbulb. Yellow light filled the basement with sickly shadows. He tinkered with the illicit equipment on the folding tables for a while, trying to make sense of the mess, then he spent some time rifling through the Rubbermaid storage bins beneath the tables, came up empty. He had a sense that there was more to find here, though, so he kept looking.

He moved methodically across the basement, unearthing lots of old boxes of family shit but nothing of out of the ordinary. It wasn't until he reached the laundry area that his senses perked up. There was an old hand-fashioned shelving unit next to them, against the southernmost concrete wall, and it was filled with ancient tools and rusted, crusty cleaning products. The unit wasn't flush to the wall. He used his phone to shine a brighter light on the ground, immediately saw the twin scrapes. Something had been eased in behind the thing. He dragged the wooden unit away from the wall, revealing a hint of gleaming polished leather. His phone's flashlight put the briefcase under full, unsteady illumination, and Floyd's heart rate quickened.

He almost didn't want to touch it.

But he did. It was a surprisingly beautiful case, its dark leather rich and supple, and it wasn't even locked. A quick count told him it contained just short of seventy thousand dollars, all denominations and conditions of bills, very rough and tumble. The drug capital of a small-time outfit. A newly *defunct* small-time outfit, Floyd corrected himself, smirking in the grungy gloom.

He stood up with the fastened case, felt a little woozy. *Jesus, he was so fucking tired.* But when would it even be feasible to sleep? He wanted to get the hell out of Decatur by dawn, with or without Tess, and he didn't see himself settling in for even a nap before then. The briefcase full of cash would be a nice parting gesture, something to help her and her family get back up to speed.

He got to the main floor, stared for a long time at Harlan's corpse.

His mind had already begun conjuring a plan for the bodies of Harlan and his crew, but now it went into overdrive. It was easy enough to claim self-defense in this particular shooting death, but what about the wider scope? Thinking back to the beginning of this whole thing, Floyd doubted that Tessa's Beetle would ever be found, but Perkins' truck definitely would be—maybe already *had* been. His mind flashed on grizzled, blunt-chinned Deputy Whitcomb, wandering the deserted streets of Malvado all by his lonesome in his late-model black-and-white, marking and then investigating the abandoned Volkswagen. And then there was Tessa's outright murder of McQuoid—still self-defense but tougher to explain away—and his own mowing-down of Dankworth. Tessa's prints were gonna be all over that Pontiac, for one thing, and she could be identified by those beer-swilling yokels in Bristow. It was more than probable that a multi-state Tessa-hunt was brewing at this very moment. He figured the Camaro was safe, thanks in part to the stolen plates, so the Pontiac was gonna be the sticking point. They'd have to swing it such that Tessa was the victim, kidnapped by this unscrupulous Decatur crew, having been targeted—while on vacation—for an incident of arson-murder that she'd had no part in, and even when she returned to town on her own recognizance, she'd found that they'd victimized her entire extended family, turned her home into a meth lab, and intended to murder her slowly upstairs.

He'd need to talk to Tess about coordinating their story, ironing out the details.

In the aftermath of Harlan's murder, his mind had naturally moved in the direction of disposing of *that* body, or posing his crew so that it looked like the bad result of infighting, but now he thought the better idea was to leave everything as it lay. Wipe the joint of any trace of himself, just in case, then skip town as Tessa made the call to the law at dawn.

Floyd made his way upstairs to the quiet top floor. He went first to Tessa's old room and stuffed the briefcase up into the closet next to the duffel bag. Then he lingered a moment in the quiet warmth, imagining a young life lived in here, the homework and the toys, the clothes and the hairdos, the wins and the losses, the secret crushes and the books and the music, a life he'd only recently connected with but which had made a clanging impact. Look at what he'd done for this gal, but more importantly look at what she'd done for him.

He moved out to the hallway and paused at the doorway of the master bedroom, glancing in. Everything seemed calm and peaceful. His ears were ringing from exhaustion, but he detected something rhythmic and flowing. It was low-and-slow blues music coming from a clock radio on the other side of the bed, a black man's deep voice, soothing and steady. He couldn't identify it, wasn't his style, but man did it fit right with the atmosphere of the room—sultry and somehow a little dangerous but overall getting closer to fine.

Tessa was lying between her brother and mother but closer to her mother, her chocolate arm thrown over the woman's white-sheeted waist, and she was fast asleep. She had turned on a soft lamp above the clock radio, and by its light Floyd could see that everyone was out, the whole family breathing evenly. Over in the corner, the two assholes had twin slack faces, gone, high as the motherfucking space station. They were gonna be the toughest part of the equation. He and Tess would have to think of a way to explain their reluctant immersion into their fentmeth fog.

He was going to have to wake her up, as much as he wanted to let her drift.

Or did he need to?

His gaze lingered on Tessa's beautiful clever face. The features were only slightly troubled—just the vaguest hint of a furrow at her brow, a crease on the right side of her full mouth. Floyd felt that if he left her at this moment, she'd only descend further into slumber, safe in the arms of those she loved. He knew she had some big-time healing to do here, and suddenly he felt that he'd be an interloper if he were to involve himself in her immediate fate any further. She had a big ol' malodorous shitload of stuff to deal with in this house, but maybe she was in as good a place as any to begin that task—on her own. Start fresh, perhaps error-correct a little. Do a deep-dive, right some wrongs. With the strength of these recovering people behind her, she'd find a way toward a new destiny.

But, dammit, he friggin' *dug* this gal. After the whirlwind of the past few days, he found it impossible to think of embarking on the *next* day, or even the next *few* days, the next *untold number* of weeks, without her flirty, pervy, hard-as-iced-titty self by his side. You could go through a whole miserable lifetime seeking a partner-in-crime like Tessa Rae Jayne, or you could stumble on one by sheer dumbfuck chance in a nowhere town at the edge of a battered nation, and apparently his destiny was the latter. Who was he to just walk away? Holy shitballs, who was he to do *that?*

Floyd made a deal with himself.

If—as he stood here in the shadowed doorway for the next five minutes—Tessa woke to find him watching her, he would stay with her. He would stay close and help guide her along the path that lay before her. He'd remain off to the side, away from inquisitive eyes, but he'd wait for her to join him south, where they'd settle up with Philip and then ride into the sunset, baby. No one alive knew about the money in the case, and they could keep it that way, using the cash as a stake into who-the-fuck-knows. Maybe end up, as destined, in Mexico. On the beach.

But if she *didn't* wake up . . . well, then that was a sign, too.

He settled his shoulder into the doorjamb, crossed his arms, and went completely quiet. Counted his breaths. Listened to the house around him, the slow-heartbeat groove of the blues coming from the clock radio. A minute went by, then two. He felt himself smiling, *actually smiling,* as he waited for her to stir, and after a while everything became dreamlike, and he wasn't sure *how* much time had gone by when he stirred from a half-doze and found her directly in front of him, nuzzling into his chest.

"Is it over?" she whispered. "Or is it just beginning?"

And just like that, he knew he would be sticking around for a while.

"You readin' my mind now?"

She threw a glance over her shoulder. "They're all taken care of, probably all the way till morning."

"We're gonna have some explaining to do."

"To who?"

"Cops."

She went quiet for a few seconds, then, "Yeah . . . figured."

"They'll be here sooner rather than later."

"I know."

"What do you want to do?"

"What time is it?"

"Little after one."

She was leaning more heavily against him now. "I just want to lay down with you. I'm so fuckin' tired. I want to lay down with you in my room before . . . you know, before whatever happens next. Can we do that? I know we need to talk about everything, hash it all out . . . tie everything up in a bow . . . but, right now, can we just . . . ?"

He led her to her bedroom, and he placed his pistol on the night-stand, and Tess leaned the rifle against the wall and closed the door. There were no words for a while. They took off their shoes and climbed onto the small bed, and he held her close. They were road-weary and smelled of stress and the long hot miles with the windows rolled down. But here they were together, and as their eyes relaxed, they murmured into the wee hours about what a fuckin' dream it was that they'd made it to this moment mostly whole and unharmed.

At one point, after a long silence, Floyd assumed Tessa was fast asleep against him, but here came her soft, whispering voice again.

"Thank you."

"For what?"

He felt her smile against the underside of his arm.

"You're not gonna make me spell it all out, are ya?"

"Aw, hell, darlin', you're worth it."

"Haven't had many people tell me that in my life."

"I mean it, baby," he murmured, his voice almost gone. "It's all you, Tess."

Floyd was beginning to drift, and he was feeling about the best he'd ever felt in his miserable life. There was something about a rough-and-tumble trek like the one he'd recently endured, by turns with and without this young lady, that filled a man's chest with a weird kind of hope.

"What are we doin' next?" Tessa whispered. "I mean, after all this?"

"I don't know," he whispered back, into her hair. "Feel like meetin' my folks?"

When he pulled back, he saw a small smile developing on her lips. "Little soon, don't you think?" she said. "You haven't even met my mama yet."

"We'll get the formalities out of the way in the morning," he said. "Along with everything else."

"You're serious?"

He shrugged. "I know you gotta figure some things out here, Tess.

You gotta make everything right. That's cool. I'll help you. But the way I see it, we were rudely interrupted on our way to doin' somethin'. Somethin' that would've been pretty cool. Somethin' that mattered. I gotta take care of my own shit back home, but as soon as I do, I wouldn't mind gettin' back on that road, y'know? With *you*, I mean. If you're up for it."

She twisted on the bed to face him.

"Fuck yeah, I'm up for it."

She took his face in her hands and kissed his mouth.

THIRTY
TESSA RAE JAYNE

"Fuck yeah, I'm up for it."

She took his rough, gorgeous face into her palms and kissed him.

It was like it was meant to be. Like, destiny, you know? As long as she could hold him, she'd never be in danger. He was the answer, Floyd Tillman Weathers, the impossible boy she'd found in the unlikeliest place in the world.

Tessa was exhausted beyond comprehension, but she melted into him, and the deep night became like a dream, half in and half out of her consciousness. She pulled at his shirt, and it fluttered away, and she plucked at the button fly of his old jeans, and her own stale clothes came off like afterthoughts, and then she and Floyd were flesh to flesh again, as if seamlessly resuming that night in New Mexico, seemed like *sooooo* long ago, when their futures had intertwined.

She climbed into his lap and felt him slide into her, fill her up, and she knew that she wanted this feeling to last forever—this feeling right here, right now. She wanted it to expand until it consumed her utterly. She'd never been so sure of anything in her ridiculous life. Yeah, even what she'd done to the house in Forsyth, and even her hell-for-leather escapade to the border. Even what she'd done to Leo in that Pontiac. None of that meant anything anymore.

A moment ago, Floyd had whispered something so corny that it was beautiful. *Feel like meetin' my folks?* She might have burst out laughing if she weren't so fucking exhausted. But her body wouldn't let her do much more than mumble and glide atop him now, her breasts mashed against his hairy burly chest, her nipples describing infinity symbols of pleasure.

Truth was, she *did* want to meet his fuckin' folks, and everything that came with that. Her whole life, the few times she'd ever had a fleeting notion about Little Rock, it was less than nothing, and now it was like the endpoint of a poignant journey—or even the beginning.

Just minutes ago, after tending to her family, she'd gone to the window and peeked through the curtains, down at the street, ostensibly watching for furtive movement, dangerous activity, and then—still seeing none of that, and knowing it wasn't gonna come—she'd rested her elbows on the sill and gazed out at the sloppy row of houses, reminding herself again of the people who'd once lived in them, the fixtures of her youth, romanticized in her mind and yet . . . gone. Youth had a way of layering nostalgia over fuckin' *anything*. Truth was, the street had been a shitty place to grow up, and yeah maybe as a feisty teen she'd blamed her mother for that, but, man, you had to do the best with what you got, and this was what she'd got. This run-down joint in a neighborhood where all the homes looked defeated, in this cast-aside section of this white-bread town, and maybe that was it, she thought now, coiled in Floyd's strong ivory arms, maybe it was because of this man, for the first time, really, she felt like she'd escaped her skin. Like a moth or something. And not just the pigment, but the persona she'd built up, the youth she'd felt trapped in, all of that.

She knew her friends—hell, even her brother—would've laughed in her face, counterpointing these musings by telling her she'd been blindsided by the simple fact of a good fuck. Because certainly Floyd was *that*. She'd had exactly six cocks in her young life, all of them dark—none of them in this bed, by the way—and none had been as impressive as Floyd Tillman Weathers' junk. He had competition in size and girth, sure, but everything came down to how a man wielded it. Came down to how Floyd used his whole body, really. He was in tune with muscles that most men didn't even know they had, and one of those muscles was in his mouth.

But it was more than that. *Yeah yeah yeah*, shit like that was easy to contemplate while she was rocking her hips against him and enjoying the everlovin' *fuck* out of it, but it really was more than the sex.

Floyd was the greatest detour of her life.

All those years in Decatur, she'd lived in a fantasy of her own making. She'd devised an idealized version of herself to better deal with the realities of a miserable life. All the way up through school, unmotivated by her surroundings, assholes everywhere, and, yeah, always glanced past by the fact of her blackness. Automatically passed over, every time. That shit wore a girl down. Wore a community down. And after a while, wasn't it natural that she wanted no *part* of that community? And yet at the same time she grasped how firmly trapped she was inside it. Surrounded by subliterates and malcontents and smackheads, like *everywhere*, and what was she supposed to do? Just deal with it? It was like being trapped under ice, and in her case, in that last year, the ice was a layer of *actual meth*. Her brother had borne the brunt of her anger when that reared its head in her life, and he'd probably deserved it, but she couldn't hang on to that. She *wouldn't*.

Because as she'd become an adult it seemed like the *entire fucking world* had gone sideways with hate and division and stupidity. It wasn't just Decatur, it was *everywhere*.

It was enough for you to go a little crazy and try to burn the world down.

Or, at least, that little part of your world that encapsulated the worst of everything.

And then . . . Floyd.

He was like a slap in the face. *Don't just run away, girl! Do it right! Take ownership of that shit!*

That's the way it had turned out, anyway.

Was it naïve of her to come to this understanding—that for the first time in her young life, she'd felt free? On the road, on the run with this man, she'd felt like she'd grown up, okay? Like she was part of a larger world. Not only that, but a meaningful part. A world where she could make real decisions, and they mattered. A world where she could take charge and make a difference in her destiny.

Gawd, it felt powerful. It felt wonderful.

Floyd eased her off his lap and maneuvered her on the bed, entered her from behind, and it was like he was splitting her open. Her eyes fluttered, and she eased her head to the sheets. The room swam with their combined road-traveled musk, sweet and steamy.

Yeah, she wanted this—and she felt like she *should* have this. Silly to say, but she *deserved* this.

Hell yeah she'd meet Floyd's parents, and they'd fucking *love* her. Because that's the kind of thing that happened in a just world.

There were still masks littering the ground out there in the world, and there were motherfuckin' racists everywhere, some still braying their monstrous crap but a lot of them retreating back under their rocks, and the world was on the long rebound from its nadir to its zenith, she felt that shit in her soul, it was something like feeling invincible. Her thoughts flashed out in front of her, in tune with Floyd's thick rhythm—

—a blues-jangly trip down to Little Rock, bare feet on the dash, thrum of the engine in her tummy, scenery whippin' past while she sang along to the tunes, probably a couple bouts of road head and maybe he'd finger her some, and then they'd roll like champs into his home town, dinner with his folks around a dainty table, cloth napkins and treasured fragile china, something like game hens or pork roast on the menu, and later helping Floyd's mother with the dishes cuz that's the way Tessa was, that's the way her mama had taught her, laughin' with the kindly white woman at the sink, and then gin rummy after that in the front room over coffee, cigar smoke on the breath of the men, and she even imagined the hard look on the father's face, years of stern work behind him (although she had no concept of either of his parents' histories, didn't matter), an early bed-time and she and Floyd would fuck in HIS childhood bed, just like they'd done in hers, she luxuriated in the synchronicity of that, and they'd fall asleep to the deep quiet of the neighborhood, and he'd do whatever he had to do with the money-crammed duffel bag, and he'd get paid his share, and then they'd get the hell out of there, just hit the road, man, no destination in mind except maybe their orig-inal one—west—and they'd wind their way along interstates and rural routes and see a reborn country in tune with her own newfound freedom, like really livin' life, LIVING IT, hittin' the Colorado slopes and the Utah cliffs and the Vegas slots, and they'd dance at a Hollywood rave and rut like animals on the sand of the California beaches, that beautiful ivory prick thrustin' and glidin' into her like myth, and then out of the blue Floyd would say somethin' like "I've heard Florida is weird," and off they'd go across the country, you know, just to check it out, and—who knew?—maybe they'd end up livin' down there for a few years before they'd move on to the next thing, but the bottom line was that they were puttin' all this bullshit behind them forever—

She was on her back staring up into his metallic green eyes, and she was kissing him eagerly because this beautiful man had a way of arcing his body such that his cock crushed relentlessly against her spot, and now she felt that whole area fattening with a giddy weight, and then the sensations were pulsing north, throughout her, and she was coming, and she felt his lips smiling into her gasps, and their teeth clicked lightly to-gether, and her body was like a live wire sparking, and her arms were pulling him closer, as close as possible, and she angled her hips up to meet him, pulling at him, urging his own release, but he only kept smiling, doing that slow soaring thang, and she was loving every delicious movement, and when he came, his body clenched hard around her, and he even laughed a little, and she laughed with him, and it felt like the fruition of the past three days.

It was only an hour later—after they'd disentangled and dressed, after she'd checked on her family and he'd checked all the doors and windows downstairs—that she managed to quit with the goofy smile.

They decided to try to get a little shut-eye before dawn. It was almost impossible to keep her eyes open, and she knew it must be the same for him. Jesus, the things she'd put him through.

They spooned together in her little twin bed, and she felt his warm breath on the back of her neck.

"You did it, Tess," he whispered again, just when she thought he might be drifting.

"*We* did it," she corrected him.

There didn't seem to be a dividing line between consciousness and dream. But the conversation went on, somewhere deep, and damn if that goofy smile didn't come back, and it was all mixed up with flashes of the road coming endlessly at her, and she wasn't sure whether she was seeing her immediate past or her immediate future. Inside her dream, she felt herself letting it go, because it didn't matter, and she also felt sleep coming hard to her now, as if her body craved it more than anything else in the world, and somehow it was the greatest sleep she'd ever known.

I think I really do love this guy, was her final thought.

THIRTY-ONE
DESTINY

After the well-dressed man fires two suppressed rounds into the two skulls—one into the boy's, one into the girl's—he walks silently out of the bedroom, down the grungy hall, and checks the slowly writhing bodies in the master bedroom. The flat clacking reports of his old Smith & Wesson M&P had been loud enough to stir the four dark-skinned folks from their drugged slumber—just barely—but the two white boys are still out.

He'd purchased the blocky Silencerco Osprey suppressor at the back metal door of Red Target Guns & Ammo in east Little Rock a month earlier, after hours. (Five crisp c-notes, no questions asked.) The proprietor there, a grizzly old-timer by the name of Jeremy Rickles, had called the Osprey the quietest suppression device he'd ever tested on his private range. The thing extends like a silly rectangular brick off the pistol's business end, but it's effective enough.

One at a time, he takes care of the brown folks on the mattresses. The only one betraying any degree of consciousness is the young man, who stirs from his sweaty languorous high long enough to study him with one blank upturned eye—a mix of dull confusion and resignation—before receiving a round straight through the other eye. Then he finishes off the tied-up Caucasian fellows. Fucking junkies, all of them. He has zero desire to know what the fuck has gone down here.

The well-dressed man is sporting blue Stapleton Forensics nitrile gloves, a disposable nylon hairnet, and an entire set of dark high-thread-count clothes and comfortable shoes that he purchased for this sole purpose. His mind has been strategizing these precise movements for three hours.

Given the traffic and movement through the house over his time surveilling it, he has anticipated most of the things he's found, but there have still been still surprises—like the two drugged-up white boys tied up in the master bedroom. He doesn't really care who incapacitated them and pumped them full of illicit pharma, or why they ended up this way—none of that matters to him. He'll leave that to the law.

Back in the girl's room, on a child's nightstand next to Floyd, he'd discovered a pretty, sheathed Ghoststrike blade, and he uses that blade now to dispatch the white boys, deep cuts straight into their carotid arteries—quick gurgle and bleed-out, little fuss, one at a time. And he keeps the boys tied up. No need to pose them or anything—they're fine as is. He wipes the blade on the bedclothes, calmly returns to the small bedroom, and places the weapon back on the nightstand next to Floyd.

He takes a moment on the edge of the small bed, eyes barely closed, to focus on his own heartbeat. Still under sixty—but *just*. Not bad.

It takes him all of three minutes to find the duffel bag up high in the girl's closet, and he's surprised to discover a nice leather case next to it containing an additional wad of messy cash. He'll count that later, but it appears to be at least fifty or sixty grand. A respectable bonus. Call it interest. He places both the duffel and the leather case just outside the door in the hall on threadbare carpet that probably hasn't been vacuumed in a decade. Disgusting.

He finds Floyd's jeans draped over a small desk chair next to the closet. He draws the burner phone from the pants' left front pocket, picturing the micro GPS chip within, and he also takes the personal phone from the right pocket. He walks back to the hallway and places both phones securely in the duffel with the cash. The tracker was one of the finest precautions he'd ever taken, turns out, and thanks to Craig Michaelson downtown, this one was rather ingenious—powered by the USB charger in an undiscoverable way inside the burner phone's chassis, professionally soldered.

Philip Crouch checks his watch.

It's 2:13 a.m.

He wants to be on the road back to Little Rock by 2:30, which will get him there for a late breakfast. Takeout bagel from the café around the corner from the shop, medium roast poured straight into his tumbler to keep it hot for hours. He can taste it already. He'll need the coffee after this night. Intravenous would work. He wants to be sharp for the lunch meeting with Deakins and Boothroyd. They're going to hand over the tapes for that next thing down in Pine Bluff.

First things first: Take care of the corpse in the living room.

That had been the only moment of the evening to give him real pause—the rifle crack, the flash coming from the front room. Not long after the tattooed fellow had sent his two companions around either side of the home with their short-range weapons, the well-dressed man had slipped out of his Porsche and eased across the street, applying a rear naked chokehold to the first of the rangy smackheads, who was poised at a small window staring in, and then the same on the other, whom he found waiting nervously on the back porch. Both of them stank of body odor, which disgusted him (*I mean, have some self-respect!*), but both had succumbed quickly to suffocation, like submissive animals. He'd carried the bodies into the pitch black behind the garage. Piled there, both the bodies smelled like they'd pissed themselves. He didn't know if that was their regular meth-head ammonia stench or if they'd released their toxic fluids post-mortem. Really could've been either.

After only minutes of silence, the rifle had discharged at the front of the home, and he'd had no choice but to wait out the aftermath in the midst of the piss stench, among the wolf spiders and the ryegrass weeds. The night could have gone any number of directions from that point—curious neighbors, called-in cops—and he'd felt only adequately prepared. But there'd been zero neighborhood response. Not surprising, he supposed, in a place that was probably accustomed to the rattle of gunfire, but he'd stayed put, waited out the inevitable.

In the wake of that single rifle shot, Philip hadn't been surprised at all to see Floyd taking a quick circuit around the house, flitting through the darkness, using his phone's flashlight to check out the area. The kid had strong instincts, always had—at least, where it mattered. That was obvious from the early days, when Swetson had pointed him out at that ridiculous arcade. Floyd was young, wiry, obedient but clever, willing and able to improvise, and he was extraordinarily patient—a product of his upbringing, perhaps. A rare thing these days, patience. Made Floyd ideal for squatting at the border.

Or so he'd thought.

He should never have underestimated the lure of border pussy. He'd learned that lesson one other time: That was Maurice Bender, the man with the acoustic guitar. Maurice could sweet-talk and serenade with the best of them, but all indications back home were that he'd achieved a mastery over his genitals and his hormones, always left the ladies craving more, and yet two weeks after arriving at the border just above Tijuana he'd been cock-smacked by a crazy-blond UCSD sophomore and started spraying cash everywhere. The GPS tracker had lit up with a chaos of streaks crisscrossing lower San Diego—lamplight district bars, mostly. At least Maurice hadn't high-tailed it a thousand miles away for his split-tail, for god's sake.

Maurice is now five feet deep in clay soil just south of Lower Otay Lake east of Chula Vista, California.

Downstairs, the similarly dead body of one Harlan Eckhart—ID'd thanks to a wallet already excavated by Floyd from the man's pocket and placed on the coffee table—is crumpled unnaturally across the dingy carpet. There's a sizeable stew of congealed blood and brains next to the broken head.

Philip has to carefully withdraw Harlan's right hand from underneath the man's midsection before unfastening the suppressor from the untraceable Smith & Wesson and securing the weapon in Mr. Eckhart's fist. Next, he goes to the kitchen and unlocks the back door, stepping out onto the darkened porch. He listens for a long moment, hears nothing pertinent, then moves in pitch-darkness to the garage to retrieve the first of the bodies there. He arranges the first young man so that he's sprawled face-first across the kitchen floor. Fortunately, there's still some blood left in the body that drips out onto the linoleum. Then he carries the second corpse inside and up the stairs to the landing, which is doubtless where the rifle shot originated, according to his reasonably educated blood-spatter analysis.

He measures his heart rate when he reaches the top of the stairs. The exertion up the stairwell got him above ninety beats per minute, so he closes his eyes and meditates in the darkness. He inherited a bad ticker from an old man who never grew old. His father had kicked off the mortal coil while seated on a stool behind the register of an all-night drugstore. He'd been in the midst of balancing his drawer, alone on a Saturday evening, and his plastic-nametagged body hadn't even been discovered until the store was due to open again Tuesday morning. The humiliation of that conclusion. It was an indignity he has promised himself to avoid at all costs. He sees his cardiologist four times per year.

He breathes evenly now, lets his eyes drift open again, goes back to work. It takes a mere seventy-five seconds to arrange the spent rifle in the corpse's grip.

In the utterly silent, darkened home, he finds himself drawn back to the girl's room, where Floyd still has his arms wrapped around the young lady, just as he'd found him. Before he'd delivered the suppressed rounds, he'd examined their peaceful faces in the near darkness for long minutes. He'd watched them sleep. Now he watches them again. It's a goddamn shame they'd had to get greedy.

He wonders now whether the past few days have been worth it for the young couple. He wonders if those expressions of calm contentment have justified the price. By his measure, the young couple had started roaring west toward California for some kind of ill-considered adventure with his cash—but they had changed their minds a hundred miles into it and headed back east in the direction of Little Rock . . . only to fade north toward the gal's childhood home.

Why come here? he wondered. *Why detour all the way to Decatur, Illinois?*

He'd never have the opportunity to flat-out ask Floyd *now*, of course, and that was unfortunate. Because he was genuinely curious. If Floyd had continued along his wild route west and become increasingly rebellious, he probably would've eventually ditched the burner with the chip and disappeared into the ether, making him *much* harder to track down—though not impossible. Instead, he'd barreled northeast to this shit town just hours from Little Rock, all the way here only to end up sleeping soundly above not only a makeshift meth lab but an extensive crime scene.

He considers the woman—her smooth body only partially covered by the thin sheet, her milk-chocolate face, her wild kinky hair like a nest under Floyd's chin. He removes the sheet fully and runs his hand lightly along her still-warm skin. He cups her left breast for a long moment, then enjoys the youthful pliancy of her ass.

He has no doubt that *she's* the answer to any question he might have in this situation. Look at her. The embodiment of the multiculturalism burning America to the ground. Beautiful and yet sinister. Seductive and yet monstrous. Hell, there's attitude flowing from her even now, with her arched eyebrows and the crooked line of her sultry, half-smirking mouth. She's got that self-righteous angle to her features so common with the upcoming generation, the kids today, every one of them wanting to be part of a new social fabric, some awful oatmeal utopia in which everyone is linked arm-in-arm in the name of social justice.

Jesus.

Floyd had simply gotten dragged around by his willie. The man was weak in that aspect, no question, and then, in the end, subsumed by misplaced idealism.

It's a generational scourge. To Philip Crouch, it's nothing more than naïveté.

If there's one thing the past few years have taught him, it's that America is not a place for weak idealists. Few years back, it seemed like everyone in Arkansas was yapping about making the country great again, but that was all talk. Worse than talk. *Nonsense.* When you really looked at it—when you really examined it closely—you could see past the idiotic slogan and the con men braying it. No one really wanted that. To go back to, what, the goddamn fifties—the age of backward conformity and bland culture and black-and-white repression? Good luck.

No, the real message was individualism. That core concept may have been lost on a legion of ridiculous mouth-breathers, but that didn't make it any less true. In the grip of a world that was going flat . . . in a worldwide community that was culturally homogenizing . . . amidst the stress of a global pandemic that anonymized everyone—cramming them under the weight of conformity, forcing them into a sense of weepy-eyed community—the only answer was to find strength in the self. Because that's where the only real moral worth could be found.

Self-reliance.

Liberty—a heinously misused word by the politicians and the egregiously stupid, but it's a potent concept for Philip Crouch.

In short, fuck everyone else.

In this crumbling world, you have to be ruthless in your pursuit of what is rightfully yours—as a human being, as a *spiritual being.* You can't depend on anyone. Times past, he would have sent a crew out for a task such as this, but not anymore. Hell, sending Floyd to the border in the first place had been a fool's errand, against all his instincts. And that's the crux of it, really: instinct.

You have to go with your gut, and you have to trust yourself.

Only yourself.

Philip is still gazing at the young woman, whose body has sagged into the mattress, same as Floyd's. She's lit only by a child's nightlight plugged into the wall opposite the bed. He removes his gloved hands from her ass and rears back to study them both. There's surprisingly little gore revealed near their heads, only the dime-sized entry wounds on the left temples and a hint of black blood on the shadowed pillows. He can almost imagine the two of them sleeping and dreaming. It's probably a play of the light that makes them seem as if they're smiling. And the longer his gaze lingers on the young woman's face, the more convinced he is that her slitted eyes are watching him. Mocking him.

The well-dressed man stands and leaves the room. He gathers the money from the hallway and descends the stairs. At the back door, he forces himself to pause and consider every movement he's made inside and outside of this house, to relitigate the strategy. He finds no flaws. He lets himself out onto the back porch and strides to the side of the garage, where he switches out of his crime-scene garb in favor of the clothing he'd placed here before entering. He balls up everything into a plastic bag and stuffs that into the duffel with the money.

At the front of the property, he faces a quiet, deserted neighborhood. He waits that out, too, observing every minute detail, then calmly makes his way across the street toward his Porsche.

He's alone in the world.

The drive back to Little Rock is interminable. He tries to listen to his book on tape, and then he tries to find something to listen to on the AM dial, and then he turns it all off with a grumble and listens to the purring motor and the buffeting wind. He curses himself for dwelling on Floyd and the young woman, their inscrutable half-smiles in the darkness of a child's room.

It's still full dark as he passes through St. Louis. The Gateway Arch glows against a sleeping city. It's a landmark that underlines his thoughts as the Porsche whispers south—the pioneer spirit of its making, the rugged, shining stainless-steel strength of it. At this hour, the roads are ethereally empty, dotted with monstrous, roaring big rigs and not much else, even as he skirts east of downtown along I-55. He feels more alone than he's ever been in his life.

It's not until he's past Farmington and approaching Fredericktown that he becomes aware of a red-orange glow taking hold of the eastern horizon, and he feels the grit in his eyes. He both craves the sensation and loathes it. He's halfway home.

The well-dressed man spares only half-thoughts about what awaits him in Little Rock. The ascetic, metallic house on the outskirts of the city with the five-car garage and the ultra-high-end security and the clean windows. The tricked-out gym in the basement, the well-stocked bar, the high-def monitors everywhere. The audiophile sound system, the single-lane indoor pool, his tools and his toys.

The silence.

It's all he needs.

At the dawn of the new day, the Porsche slices down the middle of the country. He coaxes more power out of the flat-6, and then some more, knowing that he's untouchable with his dashboard radar tech, and—if not that—the people he knows in high places. He finds himself skimming a flat stretch past a hundred-ten, a hundred-twenty. Even at those speeds, even with all that rumbling power thundering beneath his ass, he can't outrace the impenetrable smiles on the faces of the boy and the girl.

Acknowledgments

Constant gratitude to my family and friends, but particularly to Kirk Whitham for his cover art, design, and layout.

Big thanks to Gary Phillips, Sally Sanders, Mike Parish, and—of course—Barb Bovberg for their sharp observations during the early reading phase. And finally, cheers to the authors who took precious time from their own writing schedules to read this book and provide gracious cover blurbs: Eric Beetner, Wallace Stroby, and Jim Thomsen.

About the Author

Jason Bovberg is the author of *Loser Baby*, the *Blood* trilogy—*Blood Red*, *Draw Blood*, and *Blood Dawn*—and *The Naked Dame*. His forthcoming books include *A Small Poisonous Act*, a suburban crime novel, and *Little Miss Nobody*, a mystery novel based on a true crime. He is editor/publisher of Dark Highway Press, which published the controversial, erotic fairy tale *Santa Steps Out* and the weird western anthology *Skull Full of Spurs*. He lives in Fort Collins, Colorado, with his wife Barb, his daughters Harper and Sophie, and his canines Rocky and Rango. You can find him online at www.jasonbovberg.com.

Made in the USA
Columbia, SC
16 August 2022

65054344R00157